Felix Unbound

by

Cathy Gunn

Published by New Generation Publishing in 2023

Copyright © Cathy Gunn 2023

The author asserts the moral right under the Copyright, Designs and Patents Act 1988 to be identified as the author of this work.

All Rights reserved. No part of this publication may be reproduced, stored in a retrieval system or transmitted, in any form or by any means without the prior consent of the author, nor be otherwise circulated in any form of binding or cover other than that which it is published and without a similar condition being imposed on the subsequent purchaser.

ISBN: 978-1-80369-829-8

www.newgeneration-publishing.com

New Generation Publishing

'What Readers Love About this Novel'

The best fantasy fiction book for adults that I have ever read. (Bookread2day, on Amazon, and on GoodReads)

I highly recommend this book. Give it a try, you may find Felix as alluring as I did. (reviewer JM McQueen on GoodReads)

A little bit of magic, a lot of imagination and some Egyptian history all wrapped up in a fantastic story about relationships and families. (Natalie – reading_with_wine)

A captivating read which will delight the heart as the irresistible charm of Felix unfolds in a most entertaining, and intriguingly mysterious manner. A lovely mix of fantasy, reality and character study, tied into a reflection on myth with a modern day connotation! (blue.wolf-reviews.com)

A perfect amalgamation of magical realism, adult fiction and fantasy. Must read. (Anasua Basu, on GoodReads)

Felix Unbound plays in my mind probably more than any other of the dozens of books I've read over the last 2 years. (reader Jan Burgess)

An original story that is truly delightful, clever and funny. What a fun movie this would make. (audiobook listener Melany, on GoodReads)

A sort of steam punk fable. (Facebook comment from reader Damien McC)

If you love cats and a sprinkling of magic in your books, then this unique story is definitely for you. (author Denise Brown, review on GoodReads)

Very entertaining and twisty. 5* (Sue Wall, review on Twitter)

Good storytelling and character development, a well-crafted plot. (Anarella on GoodReads)

Highly entertaining but a story that is also haunting with a twist in the tale. (JB on Amazon)

Such an exciting and unique read! (review by Cosmic Latte, on GoodReads)

Chapter 1

'Well I'm already there now so tonight's definitely off. I'll call you as soon as I get back from Cairo,' Anthony snapped, and hung up. Tiffany exploded with rage.

How dare he stand her up? She slammed her mobile phone down onto the sofa, but it skittered across the taut fabric and shot into the shrine nestled in the old fireplace, toppling the joss sticks and tumbling flowers before smacking into four bronze Egyptian statuettes. Osiris, Isis, and Nephthys crashed together into a triangular but delicate balance, while Seth – that old trickster – clattered dramatically right out of the grate, knocking over the cat figurine on the hearth. The duo fell sideways, narrow eyes accusing.

'Now look what you've made me do!' Tiffany shouted. All desire to see Anthony had popped like the soap bubbles sometimes playfully batted by her tabby cat. She hated the man tonight, and glared at the mute phone now resting in the wreckage. It flickered in a panicky blue burst and went blank. The sleek tabby, woken by the commotion from his snooze beside a bowl of geological crystals on the coffee table, sat up bristling. Tiffany reached out a hand to soothe him, cupping his chin, and bent to rub her forehead gently against his.

'Oh Felix, dearest moggy, why can't some men be more like you?' she muttered, but the cat was not appeased, and jumped down. He stalked to the open ground floor window. When things got noisy at home, a neighbour's cluttered study was worth a sly visit, but as he dropped down onto the garden path the air outside seemed as charged Tiffany's mood, and distant thunder grumbled. He hesitated on the warm flagstones. Inside, Tiffany knew she should rescue the tumbled figurines, but her head was throbbing and now her throat hurt. 'Shu!' she sneezed, ignoring the chaos. 'And now the blasted cat's taken off as well. Ptah,' she finished, crossly, as if appealing to that life-giving Egyptian god about whom her great-grandfather Freddie once wrote his pamphlets. She had loved playing with these sounds as a small child. 'I can't be getting a cold now – it's almost summer.' She stalked over to a small sideboard tucked into the alcove next to the fireplace to find her bottle of whisky and poured a shot into a tumbler, hoping the Elastoplast-y taste and kick of the peaty malt would numb her sore throat. It made her gasp – *'hehh'*, another ancient incantation – and she poured a second shot to savour more slowly. Thunder muttered again, louder and closer, and the gauzy curtain at the window fluttered anxiously. Tiffany turned away, deciding that a deep bath might help to soak her ills away, with a generous libation of perfumed oils.

As she left the room, bearing her consoling glass, a gust of wind rattled down the chimney, costing Isis her fragile balance in the fireplace. The figurine slipped forwards, her bronze headdress striking the abandoned mobile phone's screen with a sharp *'nt'* sound. Its blue-green flash lit up the mocking features of Seth, just as a sudden crack of lightning outside breached the early evening sky and a violent burst of rain clattered on the garden flagstones, as if crying the name of its ancient goddess Tefnet, *'tf-nt, tf-nt!'* In the same moment a loud yowl exploded outside, and an expanding ball of fur hurtled through the open window into the protection of the apartment, tumbling heavily onto the floor perilously close to the fallen figurines. The thud made Seth rock again, while more thunder growled and the rain cackled harshly.

Upstairs, Tiffany heard only the water filling the bathtub. She sat on its edge, alternately sipping whisky to dispel her throaty feverishness and pouring swirls of iridescent oils from an array of glass bottles, one after another, onto the steadily clouding water. Then she leant across to turn on the radio on the windowsill and prepared to descend into the waters, unaware of the outraged creature racing silently up the stairs beyond the closed door. Badly ruffled and tingling with static, it sped past the bathroom and turned the landing corner to flee further upstairs. Gaining the open door of Tiffany's room, it leapt straight onto the large bed and huddled into the soft duvet. All the air seemed humming with electricity. Then the whole room crackled with vivid white and green light, and thunder crashed directly overhead. No respite, then. The creature pressed deeper into the comfort of the duvet, waiting for the next shock.

Tiffany also heard and felt that explosion of the sky as she lay in the cloudy water, steam rising above her. She sat up in alarm, wondering if a bath was really the best place to be with so much electricity raging directly above the building. Then her radio, which had buzzed abruptly with the lightning, resumed its quiet chatter on the windowsill above her.

'Some say myths seem to be ancient stories, but they can actually happen again at any time – it's like a game that asks "what if?", and moves in and out of time,' a warm, mezzo and vaguely familiar voice said, and then softly repeated the phrase: 'Myth moves in and out of time.' It sounded like a mantra. Tiffany relaxed back into the silky water to listen, as the speaker warmed to her theme.

'I'll demonstrate. Look how mythical thinking and science interact. They both reach us through our imagination and by following their imaginations – exploring their curiosity, if you like – scientists have already brought some things from the world of myth into our reality. For example, space travel and visiting the moon, both once only possible in ancient myths. You see my point?' The voice was brisk now, commanding.

Yes, Tiffany thought, although I wish I could just imagine myself up to the moon – so much easier. Or Anthony to hell.

'So myths can transform us,' the speaker warned, 'and many modern physicists agree that the border between science and myth is porous. Things can cross; and in my view a myth that makes us live more fully today, is still valid,' she concluded, her voice rising on 'valid' and challenging the interviewer, who chimed in.

'I'd like to explore that idea further with you, Iris—' he began; but Tiffany's own imagination had already drifted too far away, lulled by the perfumed water, and conjuring visions from the radio's faint chatter while outside the thunder receded. Through the dissipating steam images of a young man with hazel eyes and a sly, inviting smile drifted behind her closed lids. Trying to remember which old tale he might have sprung from, she returned to wakeful reality with a start as the radio crackled faintly again. More lightning out there somewhere, she thought.

'That's why ancient Egyptians used animals to communicate with the gods,' the mezzo voice was now saying. 'They saw that animals always sense first whatever's happening in nature, so they believed the animals must know the secret language of the gods, which made them like an interface between humans and the divine. Cats, for example, being beautiful and self-indulgent creatures, were dedicated to the goddess of love and beauty and self-indulgence, Bastet.'

The programme was out of time now. As Tiffany stretched her limbs and prepared to climb out of her bathtub, the presenter wrapped up with the detail that next week the Egypt-based opera, *Akhnaten* would be explored. Surely that's what that old rogue Ozzy's doing the stage sets for quite soon, Tiffany thought, as the busy radio pipped the time signal for seven in the evening and a news report began about stricken boats of refugees at risk of capsizing in the Mediterranean Sea. She turned it off. Stepping out of the clinging water, and wrapping a fresh towel securely around her, she still felt oddly exhausted and went rather slowly up the stairs to the bedroom – where she stopped, in the doorway, in shock.

On her bed, naked and lying stomach-down, his elbows bent and his face propped in his hands, sprawled a muscular, lightly tanned young man. Soft strawberry-blond hairs on his back and limbs made his body look almost stroke-able. He turned his head towards her, and the expression in his tawny-green eyes – somewhere between smug, mischievous, inviting, and questioning – seemed weirdly familiar.

'There you are,' he said.

'What the hell are you doing in here?' she snapped. Her anger at this intrusion fused with alarm. In the electric moment Tiffany did not know whether to turn tail and flee, or to hit him over the head with the nearest suitable object, but nothing solid enough was within reach. All she could see was him, and although his presence was alarming, his pose was utterly relaxed. So she stood there tensing for flight and waited, almost aggressively, for an answer. He rolled on to his side, revealing a lightly furred chest, and well (but not excessively) endowed genitals, and smiled cheerfully before replying.

'Apparently you invited me! Downstairs.' He paused, but she could only stare, uncomprehending. 'You don't remember?' Now he sounded slightly hurt. He was not physically aroused, which made her feel a fraction safer. She noted the toned and downy body, the well-muscled legs and arms. Some sort of athlete?

'No, I do not. Nonsense.' She almost growled the reply.

'Look.'

I *am* looking, she thought.

In one quick movement he was off the bed and standing in front of her.

What?

Cupping her face in his hands, he held her gaze with those tawny eyes, then gently rubbed her forehead with his. Now she could not turn and run; her shocked mind was quite unable to command her body.

'Like this, barely half an hour ago. Remember now?' he said, and then he actually purred.

'Felix?' She was nonplussed. 'Don't be ridiculous! Cats don't turn into people. You must have been listening outside – and broken in somehow...' She wanted to tell him to leave immediately, but astonishment constricted her throat and for a moment she could say nothing more. He released her, to reassure her that no menace was meant, and shrugged.

'No, no, the garden window was still open,' he said. 'I *was* spying when you were rolling all over the floor in here with the dreadful Anthony, though!' Appalled, Tiffany suddenly could step back from him, and hastily did. *A peeping tom!* Embarrassment and fury gave her a new voice.

'Well you must either leave right now or – or turn back into a cat!' she spoke harshly as she tried to gain control of the situation. Far away, faint thunder still rumbled and echoed, and the air was heavy, as if the storm might roll back around and return.

'I don't think I can go back,' said the invader, glancing briefly over his shoulder towards the bedroom window, whose panes had rattled softly as if echoing the thunder. 'I'm not sure I know how to, yet. You're being very ungracious, considering it was your idea, and you're not the only one who's just had a huge shock. Anyway, as you've noticed, I've no human clothes. I can't just walk out of your home like this.' He indicated his nakedness with a sweep of his hand from head to thigh. 'Where would I go? No, I'd definitely like to stay on for the time being. It's been a pretty good home so far, apart from having to put up with the dreadful Anthony taking over most of the bed, including my corner.'

Tiffany thought that she might faint, but fought it. Everything in the room but the naked intruder seemed out of focus. The bath oils on her skin felt cloying, their perfume overwhelming. Fever, or the aromatic whisky, or both, must be catching up with her. The young man studied her stunned expression and wondered if his nicely muscled, slightly downy forelimbs could still catch her fast enough if she did fall.

'Don't worry,' he said. 'I'm not a stalker, or no more so than most cats, of course. Rather a good one, in that context. I'm genuinely just a "pussycat", as you and your girlfriends do like to say about some men, you know.' He folded his arms across his chest, and waited. Tiffany breathed out shakily but her alarm was ebbing, like the thunder, somewhere into the near distance. In its place a weird curiosity tapped lightly like the rain on the window pane, and whispering through the leaves of the garden. He seemed quite peaceable. How could he know all this? She considered. Not by peering through windows. Her bedroom was too high up and its white voile blind was almost permanently drawn, with floor-length gossamer drapes pulled across it every night. Parkour, perhaps? She blinked, trying to clear her thoughts, but all she could picture was how frequently her tabby cat found a space on the large bed regardless of any other occupant. Anthony had kicked him off more than once, to Tiffany's (and the cat's) indignation. As she hesitated, words from the radio programme came whispering seductively again in her mind: "Transformation myths... are valid".

'Are you really expecting me to believe that you are Felix? My lazy moggy?' she asked. 'Made man, and—' Recalling that she had never got round to having the cat neutered, she paused. Was it relevant? This man was certainly all there.

'Exactly,' he replied calmly, still trying to soothe her. 'Your idea. I merely took it up, although I dispute the lazy bit.' Thunder growled again. 'OK, you could say it rather forcibly took hold of me. I was nearly electrocuted out there you know, which was your fault. If you hadn't thrown that silly tantrum over the ghastly Anthony, I would never have been outside when lightning struck. I raced to the safety of our room in a fearsome state.' Our room! Tiffany shivered a little.

'I was definitely not myself, half-stunned, totally confused,' he continued, watching her reactions. 'Couldn't tell if I were beast or man, as I think your saying goes? Anyway, I fled up here and collapsed on the bed with your words ringing in my mind at the height of that awful storm, and woke up as you see me now. Rather splendid, don't you think?' He grinned. 'It's not the first time I've made myself comfortable here, but I might need a bit more space now.' He glanced past her at his reflection in the cheval mirror. 'You've always been perfectly willing to share the bed, and to give me a cuddle in the morning so far, Tiffany dearest.'

He knows my name, she thought, and Anthony's. Not just a random intruder then. As she continued to stare wordlessly at him, he spoke again.

'In fact, no-one has been a more constant or affectionate companion than me. Frankly I think you owe me a bit more respect for my devotion, and for my willingness at least to pretend to tolerate your latest appalling boyfriend.' He stopped, partly to assess the effects of his words, but mostly to rest after so much conversation. Hoping he hadn't gone too far and has finished on the right sort of note, he casually brushed his left cheek with the back of his right hand and then rubbed just under his left ear, while he studied her expression. She looked less alarmed, but still confused. He cleared his throat, and tried again.

'But right now I think we could just settle for a spot of supper. I take it that all cat food can be dispensed with? I've always preferred the look and aroma of what you prepare for yourself, as you may have noticed.'

Tiffany was too astounded to reply but a tactic was taking shape in her reeling imagination. Unsure, like a feline's cornered prey, of which way to turn before a pounce came, she took the best gambit that seemed available. Moving this weird intruder from the bedroom to the ground floor, and its escape routes, somehow felt logical in this fog of confusion.

'You might at least put something on first,' was what she said. He was delighted, and immediately asked if he could wear her white Egyptian cotton robe, whose cool lines and elegant folds had always appealed to him. As the robe was currently out of sight, inside her wardrobe, the request somehow seemed to support his tale of metamorphosis (and associated voyeurism). Tiffany stepped backwards cautiously to the wardrobe, felt for its handle, keeping her eyes on him at all times as she pulled its door open enough to reach for the folded robe on a shelf inside. Then she silently moved towards him, opening the garment and holding it out like a gift whose bounty in return was her own physical safety.

Opening his arms in acceptance, he let her slide one sleeve over his right forearm and then turned so that she could sweep the garment behind him to manoeuvre his left arm into the other sleeve. The fine material felt cool on his skin, and made the golden and russet hairs on his limbs and body tingle and fluff up. As she drew the garment across his torso to tie the belt, the folds of material eased into a flattering fall that also hid a dropped thread in the fine fabric. She stepped back and studied him. They looked at each other silently. The process of wrapping him in the robe seemed to have transited them into a fragile co-conspiracy. He considered. Should he rub his cheek affectionately against hers now? Not yet. He waited.

Are his eyes greeny-gold, or mostly hazel? Tiffany was wondering, intrigued against her better judgement. The more she stared into them, the harder it was to tell. He studied her eyes too. One was a deep blue, the other dark brown, and their depth of colour meant that not everyone realised this at first. He had always thought they seemed quite magical, and splendid. During this pause, her temporary tolerance of the situation seemed to settle more convincingly on her, much as the cotton robe did on him. Tiffany risked turning away slightly to gather up a finely-embroidered lilac kaftan (a gift from Anthony) from a chair by the door, and left the room. Glancing back, she caught the Felix or not-Felix person now studying himself curiously in the full-length cheval mirror, and clearly liking what he saw.

Chapter 2

Felix stopped admiring his current reflection after a few seconds, and followed Tiffany to the bathroom landing, one hand lightly caressing the banister for reassurance as he descended. He waited by the door for her to re-emerge in the lilac kaftan, and sporting a towel-turban over her dark auburn hair still damp from her bath. It drew attention to a faintly regal quality in her face, and flattered her high cheek bones. He found this reassuring.

She barely glanced at Felix but led the way silently downstairs and into the kitchen where he perched more than sat on a wooden barstool, and watched intently as she wordlessly investigated cupboards and the fridge for something they might both want to eat. Tiffany also took the precaution of opening the door onto the gleaming garden, where the air was now fresh and beautiful. If she needed to make a run for it, she could probably scale the side wall onto the street (forgetting that perhaps he could too, and faster). The sun had returned for a lingering hour, bringing a glow of warmth and long, soft shadows to this lovely evening poised between spring and summer.

Tiffany put a scratch supper of pastrami, cheeses and salad on to the table, and was careful to sit in the chair nearest to the open garden door, through which the light danced. She studied the lithe tawny-eyed young man, dressed in her loosely-tied fine white cotton robe, who said that for now he preferred to eat with his hands, tried salad leaves with a frown, asked to drink milk, and water – using both hands at first to lift each glass – and refused any fruit. He seemed completely at ease in her kitchen. There was even something pleasingly conspiratorial about this largely silent supper.

Now what? she wondered. I can't really go on suspending disbelief and playing 'what if' – although if he is right about what happened that makes him *my* experiment and, though strange, not exactly a stranger.

Considering this angle, she looked at him more curiously. He carefully put down his glass and wordlessly offered her the fruit bowl. A fresh breeze pushed the garden door wide open; and a thrill of empowerment laced with pure, wild, irresponsible mischief raced through her.

Oh yes I can.

Beyond the garden something silently shifting within the warp and weft of the fabric of space-time paused for a nano-second, leaving a tiny lacuna in the weave much like the almost invisible dropped thread in the robe Felix now wore. Tiffany was smiling back at Felix: a dancing, expanding what-fun-if-it's-true-and-we-launch-you-on-an-unsuspecting-world smile. She took a warm, fresh fig from the proffered bowl, parted and bit into it deeply, looking directly at him, her dark eyes full of mischief and challenge.

Felix was delighted. As she set down the remains of the fig, he stood up and held out his hands to her.

'Come,' he said, pulling her easily to her feet. He bent and kissed her. It was a long kiss that she accepted, melting into each moment, enjoying the sweet dizziness that flowed through her.

Am I mad? Does it matter? they both thought.

Now Felix had no reservations about turning Tiffany gently by the shoulders towards the kitchen door, and she led him through the hall to the living room, where they tumbled together onto the sofa. It seemed he had not wasted his claimed access to neighbouring window ledges and bedroom chairs and had taken particular note, she realised, of her own predilections. It was an astonishing night.

Waking as dawn edged nervously round the curtains, Tiffany wondered sleepily why she was downstairs on the sofa, half-covered by the colourful throw that usually lay across its back but now flowed across her to the floor – and what had triggered such sensuous dreams. She glanced across the room, and sat up sharply. Stretched on the floor between the sofa and the coffee table with its bowl of crystals, the rest of the bright cloth caressing his torso, was the very man. Beyond him, by the hearth, lay her figurine of Seth, and tumbled in the grate, her other statuettes. Her silk lilac kaftan sprawled untidily over the arm of the sofa.

What had she done?

Impossible, she thought, in the clear morning light. Cats do not turn into people – which only makes this worse. Carefully gathering up her discarded garment, Tiffany edged off the sofa as quietly as she could and got out of the room, pulling the door almost shut without risking the final 'click' of closure. In the kitchen, behind another softly-closed door, she felt shaky.

I should leave. Get help, to get rid of him. She put on the robe, tugging its sash closely around her. The garden door had been open all night. I must find the cat, she thought, and then I'll know. She stepped carefully outside, and looked around. All was still in the early morning light. A blackbird flew up in alarm as she went swiftly across the tiny square of dewy grass to the end wall, where she paused, and whispered, 'Puss, puss! Felix – moggy – are you there?'

But no cat came. She called 'breakfast!' softly, and quietly chirruped her usual call, but there was no answering 'prrr', no rustling in the bushes, no sudden eruption of galloping tawny fur and stripes from within one of the thickly-leaved shrubs by the wall. Then suddenly, from behind her, a male voice said, 'Here I am. What are you doing? Didn't you see me on the carpet? I've moved on from early birds chasing their silly worms and, whatever you think, I still wouldn't slope off completely without a goodbye. I've tidied up in the sitting room for you, by the way,' he added casually.

'Have you?' She turned slowly in his direction. There he stood, with the throw from the sofa draped casually across one shoulder; a tall, tawny, handsome man in the kitchen doorway, between her and any easy escape to the world beyond her front door. He smiled reassuringly.

'Breakfast, did you say? I'll have bacon, and some milk. What shall we do today?'

What indeed, wondered Tiffany, watching as he stepped back into the room.

'I'm supposed to be going to Emma's party tonight.' She said it brusquely, as a brush-off, keeping her voice as steady as she could as she cautiously re-entered the kitchen.

'Oh, good. I quite like studying Emma. I'll come too.' He sat down at the table.

Tiffany eyed him warily. This plan was not what she had intended.

'I'm not sure that would be a good idea,' she said, still playing along for safety. 'What happens if you turn back into a cat halfway through? Assuming that you are my missing mog; and you'd need some proper clothes.'

'I think I'm going to be like this for some time,' said Felix, ignoring the disrespectful mog-word and rubbing the faint stubble on his upper lip. He glanced towards the garden again. Until he was confident that the previous evening's stormy weather pattern had passed, he was in no hurry to stroll into it yet. All seemed calm, however, and sunshine was starting to brighten the grass. 'There are so many places to go and things to do in this form,' he said, 'and, party or not, I'll need some clothes of my own. I can't wear many of yours. You'll have to get them for me though, at first, until I'm sorted out.' He stretched his legs out under the table.

'Sorted out?' queried Tiffany, now carefully filling the kettle (she could pour hot water on him if necessary). Perhaps he was planning to return to cat-hood after all. Don't be daft, focus, try to act normally if possible, she decided. She put some thin slices of bacon under the grill, as he answered.

'Did you think I'd just be a cosseted playboy? Despite loving comfort, cats are very independent. You should know that! Before, if I wasn't ready to come home, I'd find my own food, and I had a really luxurious coat. I'll just have to adjust my methods a little now.' He stretched his arms above his head, contentedly, and yawned. 'Unless I am to go marauding for them, I just need a few accessories to get started – clothes, and perhaps some cash – until I generate my own. Generous though you are, dear Tiff, you probably won't need to provide more than that for me.'

Tired by this speech, he leaned back in his seat and waited for her reaction. The bacon, already spitting a little under the grill, smelled delicious.

Too right, thought Tiffany, there's no way you are sponging off me forever, cat-man or chancer. Cash indeed. It was time to be firm. To strengthen her resolve, she took a packet from the cupboard by the fridge, and spooned ground coffee into a one-person cafetière for herself. Finest arabica, Felix noted with approval. He had always liked the aroma. He nodded, and watched her make the coffee. As its fragrance filled the room, he resumed talking.

'I just need you to help me out a little, while I explore my options. I'd still like to stay here at first.'

'Really,' she said, still keeping her voice steady, while thinking – what cheek, but he's not angling to stay for long. That's good, isn't it? Aloud she added, 'We certainly have things to discuss; and if you are Felix, my former moggy, you won't get very far without any human ID, a local bank account – all the things most people need to get started.'

There was a silence. Tiffany added milk to her coffee, took a deep drink, and then poured more of the milk into a heavy earthenware mug for Felix. She knew he disliked being called a moggy, and thought it might sting him into admitting that he was some other kind of some miscreant – a cat-burglar perhaps, or an illegal immigrant – and did have identity papers from somewhere to fall back on. Felix considered her words, and shrugged.

'My record card at the vet's?'

Tiffany stared.

'Unhelpful. Idiot – and I mean you, not the vet. So how would you actually plan to earn anything? Bank-rolling a cat is one thing but financing some itinerant chancer's career launch is just not on the cards, however much you plead.' She dumped the heavy mug of milk on the table in front of him. Deal with that, pussycat, she thought. He paused, and then with both hands lifted it confidently and drank neatly from it. Tiffany would have been better reassured if he had asked for a bowl instead, or tried to drink without lifting it at all. He put the mug down carefully, licked his lips to be sure there was no lingering milk there, and then looked challengingly back at her before replying.

'I'm an exceptionally fast learner, and very observant wouldn't you say? Balanced, controlled and reliable most of the time, though the build-up of electricity before a storm, or a whiff of cat mint, may make me excitable. I hardly need to remind you about the recent effects of lightning.' Tiffany took another deep drink of her coffee, watching him silently over the rim. He rubbed his nose and returned to the topic of his upkeep.

'I could earn my living, you know. I've been watching the neighbours, and how people do things, all my lives. Life,' he amended. 'I reckon I could redecorate your walls, and brighten the place up no end. You can pay me in clothes, food, and some cash for the work and then recommend me as a handyman to your friends. How about that?' He experimented with raising an eyebrow, resisting a temptation to twitch his stubbled upper lip.

How about it indeed, thought Tiffany. Painting and decorating? I'll believe it when I see it, and what else might you decide to do for them I wonder?

'Have you considered a career as a gigolo?' she asked acidly, and flipped the sizzling bacon over with a fork, to grill the other side. 'You may be better qualified and it's probably better paid.'

Felix beamed. 'I take that as a significant compliment after last night.' Once again he looked and sounded as if he were purring. (That'll have to stop, Tiffany thought.) 'Perhaps it's something I should consider. I'm sure both jobs could be happily combined but first, as I'm still devoted to you just now, we could just explore our developing relationship a bit further?' He gazed at her with wide eyes, tilting his head inquiringly.

'Your bacon's cooked,' she said crisply, snapping the grill's control tap to 'off'. 'You'll have to learn to cook, you realise,' she added. Felix eyed the gas hob warily.

'Tricky. Not too keen on naked flames, though a real fire in winter is irresistible if there's a fireguard. Could you get an electric hob instead? I'd prefer to learn on one of those.' He had watched a man a few houses away cope with one, and felt safer with that idea.

'Absolutely not. My overdraft limit won't cope if you expect new clothes, pots of paint, cash wages – and a new stove as well. It's cheaper to keep a real cat.'

'But not as much fun!' Felix slid off the kitchen chair and moved towards her. He draped his left arm across her shoulders. 'Think of it, Tiffers! All those lovely evenings that we can have now, and you can show me off to your friends, take me to parties – and all the time the two of us will be sharing a private joke about my real nature. We'll have a wonderful time.' He whispered in her ear, brushing his cheek against hers. 'Don't fight a god-sent opportunity to explore life's surprising side.'

Or I could just kick you out, she responded silently, again turning over in her mind how and whether to extricate herself from this hypnotic invader. She could just ring the police, but how would she explain letting him stay here all last night instead of seeking help straight away? Felix could claim, perhaps too-accurately, that he's an old friend, been fed, and made welcome. I might not succeed in getting him turfed out – if I do want him out, she thought. She turned her face away from his embrace and raised her coffee mug again, inhaling the curling aromatic steam as if it could give her renewed courage of conviction.

'It's going to be a ball,' Felix persisted. He could feel faint tingles from the resurgence of her lingering doubt – well, he thought, who could blame her? It was hard enough for him to believe this luck, if luck it was. But he couldn't let her lose the plot now.

He went over to the cupboard by the stove, opened it and took out a plate with his left hand. Turning, he stretched a little gingerly with his right hand to pull the grill pan further out of the oven, paused to check that the bacon had stopped spitting, and then swiftly hooked the rashers by hand onto the plate. Licking a trace of bacon grease off his index finger and thumb, he leant back against the cupboard with a triumphant smile at her.

'Perfectly done,' he declared, teasing her, and put the plate down carefully on the table.

The bacon, or the performance? she wondered. He picked up a rasher in his fingers and bit off a large piece, crunching it happily while he waited for her reaction to his new skills.

'Very good', she said, 'but you'd better learn to eat with your mouth shut, for starters.'

Felix, unperturbed, continued to crunch his bacon noisily.

'So, what about that party tonight?' he persisted, mouth still half-full. 'You could pop out today and get me a set of clothes, and then we could hit town together for something more in my style, before I stride into the world large as life and twice as natural, as people like to say. I never fully appreciated that expression before.' Playing with words is fun, he thought, grateful again for past evenings on sofas in front of a diversity of television programmes, and the frequent mutter of the radio in a variety of neighbourhood kitchens most mornings. He finished crunching the bacon and concentrated on licking his fingers again, very carefully, absorbed in the task.

'Oh lord,' said Tiffany, amused again now, watching him. 'Perhaps we could.' Her own picaresque sense of adventure and love of the unexplained were returning as the caffeine kicked in. Felix could certainly mix it up at the party. Her cousin Emma's charming gatherings rarely yielded major surprises. What harm would it do to play along for a while? He's *my* experiment, she reminded herself again, and it might be fun. She raised her eyebrows at him in renewed complicity, ignored another faint twitch of apprehension, and focused instead on silent appreciation of her coffee before it cooled too fast.

Chapter 3

Felix does looks good in that olive linen shirt and the chinos I chose, Tiffany decided. They had spent the rest of the morning leafing through her stack of glossy magazines to gauge his taste, before she measured him lingeringly and then left him to snooze on the sofa while she slipped out to shop. Initially Tiffany was a little put out by his blunt refusal to try the boxer shorts, or wear the deck shoes chosen so cleverly to avoid the bother of socks; but perhaps his insistence on going barefoot (and 'commando') into the warm, early summer night would add to his mystique at the party. They agreed that their aim this evening was for everyone to be so mesmerised by his looks and charm, that they would overlook any stray, too-feline, gaffes.

'People love talking about themselves,' she advised Felix now, as she admired his turnout and her own good taste. 'You can't go wrong if you always turn the subject to them. Remember that, officially, you've never met any of them before. And don't drink any alcohol, we don't know what could happen. It might make you ill,' she added, as a disincentive to mischievous experimentation on his part.

We're experimenting enough already, she thought. Who knows what he might say or do after a drink?

'Stick to the plan,' she reminded him again quietly as they pushed open Emma's welcoming front door, left unlocked for her guests. The uncertainty sent an anticipatory shiver of excitement through her body now they were actually doing this crazy thing. She felt as if she had taken something that intensified her perceptions and experiences.

Too late to back out now.

Someone just inside the doorway said that Emma was in the back garden, and Tiffany led Felix towards his social debut.

As he leant in to brush Emma's cheek with his own (as instructed), after Tiffany's quick introduction – 'this is Felix, my new lodger, I hope you don't mind me bringing him along' – Emma felt a delicious tingle spread down her neck and shoulders. Tonight, he noticed, she was in her cultured bo-ho look – a gauzy sea-green mid-calf dress, laced at the front of the bodice, with an asymmetric hem revealing faintly tanned bare legs, neat ankles and her slender feet in delicate, retro-hippy, barely-there, strappy sandals. She wore her blonde hair up messily, letting its trailing strands artfully kiss her shoulders. Emma looked at Felix in surprise.

'Not at all,' she managed to say. 'Welcome!' She regained her poise as hostess. 'So what would you like to drink? There's prosecco on the go just now, and plenty of wine, or some soft drinks of course.'

'Water's my drink of choice,' Felix replied earnestly, to Tiffany's approval as they stood with Emma just outside the open French window. Beyond them in the steadily darkening evening, the narrow city garden was lit by a scatter of flaming torches planted in a handful of carefully-positioned terracotta pots. Guests holding glasses and chatting together, drifted in and out of the flickering circles of light and shadow, occasionally risking immolation. Felix had not ventured as far as Emma's place before. In a blink, he noted the back wall, where a white rosebush against the warm red brick offered its own faint gleam. To his alarm, Tiffany was already weaving past the fiery torches towards it, leaving him to manage the rest of this encounter himself. She glanced back and raised a hand in temporary farewell. Felix continued his rapid assessment of this new terrain. Over to his left, a well-established tall camellia by the side wall yielded flirtatious glimpses of flushed blooms as a light breeze lifted its glossy leaves and revealed a generous retreat on the soft ground beneath the dark stem and branches. No need to brave the torches to reach that. Its proximity relaxed him.

'Alcohol clouds your senses,' he quietly explained to Emma during this quick scan. She widened her almost lapis-blue eyes. Tell me something I don't know, she thought. Does this gorgeous 'new lodger' of Tiffany's really not drink? He felt her scepticism.

'Chilled water keeps me alert, ready to pounce on any opportunities around the corner,' he added mischievously, enjoying the camellia's dance and already forgetting Tiffany's instruction not to volunteer much about himself. His crooked smile, revealing slightly pointy incisors, made Emma's breath come faster.

She put a subduing hand to her throat, as she answered: 'Goodness. You *are* a purist! I'm not sure I could cope without a glass of wine after work.'

'Clarity, not purity!' he replied softly. She had to lean in to hear him properly, and felt that odd shiver ripple through her neat form again. 'Clarity of purpose, design, and execution,' he elaborated. She looked startled to him – like a cornered kitten – so he too bent forward, to stare more deeply into her eyes, and elaborated: 'And patient observation. Watch, learn, and then act!' But this sounded a bit too predatory and, suddenly grasping the wisdom of Tiffany's advice, he straightened up and added, with his sweetest smile, 'It's a technique that I use to tune in fully to how others are responding. I mean, feeling.' (Stop talking about yourself, Felix, Tiffany's voice seems to command in his head, ask about *her*).

'Oh,' Emma replied with a degree of relief. 'I suppose it would. I think I've read about that watch-thing somewhere – what's it called again?' She stared at him. 'You're not that guy who invented it, are you?'

'Er – I call it W-L-A,' he ad libbed. 'Watch. Learn. Act. But that's enough about me.' He hastily shifted the focus. 'What about you? And your party! It's kind of you to let me gatecrash…'

'Oh, Tiffany is family, as well as a good friend – any visitor of hers is welcome. The more the merrier.' Emma was burbling, she knew, but was back in hostess mode. She wished she could think of something more interesting to say to this slightly weird but alluring man. (He must be some sort of lifestyle guide; or perhaps a business guru?) 'W-L-A. I'm sure I've read about it,' she continued. 'Odd that she's never mentioned knowing you...'

'Emma! Let's have some decent music,' a voice commanded loudly from inside.

'I'd better go and see what's wanted,' she said, without conviction. 'Let me introduce you to someone interesting.' She looked around for a male guest, if possible – no point in handing him straight on to a potentially predatory woman yet, unless absolutely unavoidable – and laid her hand on the arm of a tall, older man just stepping through the French window into the garden, a glass of prosecco in each hand.

'Have you met Ozzy yet? Uncle Ozzy, this is Tiffany's – and now my – new spiritual adviser!' she half-teased. 'W-L-A and all that, I'm sure you know all about it. Will you look after him, while I sort out my more demanding guests? Ozzy knows everything there is to know around this town.' She smiled brightly, already slightly regretting her choice of minder, and went indoors to face the music-seekers.

Ozzy – ageless in spirit, yet could be taken for pushing sixty, sinewy, tanned, and in his soft linen suit as elegant as Felix though considerably more lined about the eyes – examined the young man curiously. Felix, enjoying his secrets but more mindful now of Tiffany's advice, seized the conversational advantage before Ozzy could ask him about this WLA thing that was taking on a life of its own.

'Ozzy? Is that a variant of Oswald?' he risked. He had sometimes wondered. The older man replied drily.

'No. Some people may think it's an affectionate diminutive, but they soon realise their mistake. Here, have one of these. It was for Emma but we've lost her to her duties.' Ozzy extended a glass to Felix's left hand, leaving him little option but to take it, and then shook right hands. Felix accepted the ritual carefully. It had always seemed odd to him. Ozzy continued: 'A few people think I'm a bit of a cad of course, apart from the ever-forgiving Emma.'

'A cad?' Felix, thinking he had perhaps misheard, was briefly startled. 'Are you?'

'Only when necessary.' Ozzy seemed amused. 'And yourself?'

Perhaps Ozzy only had Emma's welfare in mind, but Felix had not expected the topic of conversation to swing back to himself so rapidly.

'I think of myself as focused,' he responded cautiously, and to buy time raised the glass in his hand and took a large sip of the fizzy liquid. Immediately he was ambushed by bubbles bursting around and in his mouth. They made his nose and lips twitch.

'Bit too sweet, I agree,' Ozzy observed. Felix swallowed uncomfortably, now feeling anything but sweet himself, but smiled back just enough through tautened lips to show the tips of his very white, slightly pointy teeth, while trying to think of another way to bring the focus of attention back onto Ozzy. Where is Tiffany when I need her? The bubbles tingled oddly in his throat and stomach; and the hair on his torso and arms rose slightly.

'Being focused would be part of your spiritual advice system, perhaps?' Ozzy inquired. His continued direct gaze and dark, almost obsidian eyes, were unsettling. 'Hardly novel, but perhaps good advice for Emma. She doesn't really seem to have found her true persona yet. And how exactly do you apply this WLA theory of yours, out in the real world?'

Felix bristled. The man was rude. He could feel downy hairs on his back tensing now, and replied stiffly:

'It's entirely practical. It stands for watch, learn, act,' He extemporised further, under Ozzy's penetrating stare. 'I'm exploring new fields to apply it to.' He took a defiant second swig of the prosecco, and again forced himself not to sneeze. 'What opportunities would you recommend I explore up here?' His toes were tingling now. Felix resisted a growing desire to drop onto all fours and hiss.

'That would still depend on what successful applications you can claim so far. I design rather clever stage sets.' Ozzy was usually recognised and often feted in creative circles, but as this slightly odd young man was clearly newly arrived he patiently elaborated, opening his hands wide as he explained: 'For plays, operas, comedies, tragedies. The bigger and bolder the production, the better for my reputation. To keep the ideas fresh, I too am constantly on the watch.'

'On the watch?' echoed Felix, eyeing those long-fingered hands and keeping as still as he could.

'Well, for example, sometimes I team up with one or two of the obscurer, more experimental theatrical companies, *pro bono* if necessary – that means for free – in order to explore possible new applications of my arts. And I collect curiosities. It's always important to know what's lurking, or just brewing up, out there.'

Now Felix's eyes gleamed wickedly. He couldn't resist a little sideswipe at Ozzy's ego.

'I'm doing a spot of painting and decorating for free myself,' he said, deadpan, casually waving his glass and almost spilling some of its contents. 'Staying with my old friend Tiffany and planning to tart her place up a bit in exchange for my bed and board, while I plot the next phase of my own life.' Emboldened now by the popping bubbles, he pounced. 'Let me know if you need a temporary "gofer" or apprentice, with the experimental design stuff! I'm quick, and observant. W-L-A at work, you see,' he added, silently thanking Emma for this useful mantra. He took another large drink of prosecco, ready for its fizz this time.

Ozzy, frowning slightly, decided to ignore the newcomer's misplaced reference to painting and decorating.

'It's the quality, more than the speed of the outcome, of your application that counts, young man,' he replied. 'What's your own track record?'

Felix blinked. What indeed. He was growing twitchy again under this questioning, and had to concentrate hard to keep still. Where the hell was Tiffany?

'I'd advise "hurry slowly" and all that,' Ozzy continued into the silence, still watching Felix closely. 'Personally, I distrust people who learn too much too fast. Cast them off, and see if they can really swim yet. For centuries it was expected that apprentices would serve at least seven years learning the mysteries of their master's craft,' he added severely.

Swim? Felix grimaced, which made his eyes grow narrow and his expression seem more thoughtful. He said gruffly: 'Well, your seven years do seem rather long from my current perspective. WLA is – is a bit faster. I'd be grateful for seven weeks, to get up to scratch. I'm sure Tiffany will recommend me. I do like to take my time watching things, but once I decide to go for something, I seize the opportunity, and pounce – I mean, act.' He managed to sound more civil than he felt and, although his whole body radiated challenge, his words were clearly freighted with truth. Ozzy clapped him on the shoulder, as if he had just passed some sort of test.

'Bravo!'

Felix started back, and instinctively wanted to cuff him with a quick paw – but the prosecco had slowed the link between thought and action, and he just rocked a little on his feet for a moment, while he heard Ozzy say: 'Then come and see me in action, if you're genuinely interested. I'm working on set designs for a new production of *Akhnaten*. Are you at all familiar with that opera? No? It's set in a brief but turbulent period of ancient Egyptian history that saw a foolhardy attempt to discard and deny the old, deeply embedded, mystic world – tragically, of course – and ends revealing the disastrous aftermath of those events still happening, contiguously with modern time. In ghostly parallel, if you like.' Since Felix looked as though he was wrestling with all this information, Ozzy added, 'You might want to look it up. Come at four. I'll give you a glimpse of what I do, and we'll see if your W-L-A theory has any resonance with the creation of my spectacular illusions.' He handed Felix a neat business card. 'My address.'

So instead of lashing out, and wary of Ozzy's interest in history and illusion, Felix silently opened his free hand for the card, and considered it as it lay on his palm. Despite his mistakes so far, it did seem that things were still working in his favour. Naturally.

'Thank you,' he finally said, finding the words coming a little thickly. 'I'll be there.' Ozzy nodded and walked off, deeper into the garden. Felix eyed the card again, and then eased it gingerly into the back pocket of his chinos. His fingers felt less tactile, blunted. Tiffany would have to help him to find the place, and explain this opera. Of course he knew the old story Ozzy was talking about, if not in this particular form. Where was she, anyway? He scanned the garden. Still near the back wall and now Ozzy, as well as the flaring torches, was between them. Felix had had enough conversation for the moment. He moved carefully, softly, towards the side wall of the garden, concentrating on going unnoticed now. By the lovely old camellia he bent, set down his glass with its tiny remainder of prosecco, and crouched as if inspecting a particularly frothy, low-hanging bloom. Another quiet glance up the garden and, confident that in that moment he was unseen, he slipped swiftly into the generous space beneath its sheltering branches, where he sat on his haunches and silently rested, watching through the dark, glossy leaves as the partygoers gyrated in the paved garden. It had been more difficult to keep on top of things than he had expected but nevertheless, so far, so good, he thought, and relaxed on the soft earth, waiting contentedly now for the troublesome bubbles to wear off and his sure-footedness to resume, before making his escape from the party.

Chapter 4

Ozzy frowned a little as he strolled down the garden, pondering what curiosity Tiffany had dug up this time, and stopped to greet a redheaded young woman who had been watching him talk to Felix. He smiled at Jenna, and kissed her cheek.

'You look as cool and lovely as ever,' he complimented her. 'I've just met Tiffany's latest handsome waif and stray. You'd better be on your guard. He seems to be very much on the make. Trust Tiffany – irresponsible minx – to conjure up a fellow like that, without warning.' He stopped, aware that Tiffany herself had broken away from the dancers, and was approaching.

'Tiff, my dear! How particularly enchanting you are tonight. I assume this has something to do with the striking young man who claims to be your latest house guest, and has I think just asked me for a job? He says you will vouch for him. Anthony not in town?' Tiffany's blush was only faintly visible in the flare of the nearest garden torch.

'He insisted on going on this trip to Cairo, despite the difficulties—'

'Ah well, Anthony would be anxious just now about his big construction project there. I must ask him about it. Perhaps his architectural practice should sponsor the opera production I'm working on – an old Egyptian subject, so it could be a nice little link for him. Give him my regards next time you speak. I've told your new protégé that he can come and see me at work in my lair tomorrow, by the way. Four pm sharp at the house. Can I get either of you a fresh drink?' Ozzy had spotted a table set up as a small bar, beside the white rose bush against the back wall. He took their requests and empty glasses, and strolled towards it.

'Oh dear,' Tiffany – who had downed at least two glasses of prosecco already – confided unwisely to Jenna who, as ever, looked stunning tonight, in an almost transparent slither of chiffon which grazed her maddeningly perfect body in just the right ways. 'Ozzy might be in for a shock, if he takes Felix too far under his wing.'

Tiffany paused, wondering suddenly what creature Ozzy would have metamorphosed from, if any. A heron? A hawk? A showy yet intimidating ostrich? Definitely something powerful, with an unexpected kick.

He could be unsettling, with his dry way of speaking in riddles that somehow implied that he was all-seeing, and trapped people into confirming things they had not meant to reveal. We'll have to be careful around him, she decided.

'Ozzy, shockable? Never,' Jenna responded automatically as she scanned the small shrubbery towards whose shadows Felix had just slouched, somewhere near the camellia – but now he had gone, and she had missed where. 'Though I can see why anyone might be interested in that guy,' she said, returning her gaze to Tiffany. 'So *you* brought him to the party. I suppose he's your "walker" while Anthony's away. Why is it that the best-looking men are always more interested in themselves, or in each other?'

'Walker? If by that you mean gay, Jenna, I think you'd be mistaken where Felix is concerned. Although...' Tiffany recalled that her cat was happy to be stroked by any gender, but would take against certain individuals, such as Anthony. She briefly pondered the other implication that Felix and Anthony were both self-obsessed – but I know that already, she recalled. 'Definitely tactile,' she admitted in reply to Jenna, as a blast of music left the rest of her answer unheard, but not unheeded, in the night air.

'Ah,' Jenna said lightly, adding softly, 'and how might you know this, Tiff?' Although her words were also lost beneath a surge in the music, her quizzical expression was understood.

'We're old friends,' Tiffany said hastily, just as Ozzy returned with the filled glasses and mimed an invitation to retreat closer to the back garden bar. Tiffany, with no desire to risk further questions about Felix until she knew what he had claimed so far, shook her head just as Jenna nodded yes.

'Let's get together for a proper gossip on Monday night, Tiffany?' Jenna suggested more loudly, above the music. 'Usual winebar, seven o'clock – or a coffee break, if your evenings are all taken up just now?' Tiffany laughed at that, reached out to accept her refreshed glass, made a 'call me' gesture to Jenna, mouthed 'thanks' to Ozzy and went to seek Felix who, she suspected, would soon be driven out by the surging volume of the music. She moved lightly and swiftly across the small garden, smiling quickly to acquaintances with whom she would normally have dawdled. No sign of him, and the shadowy shrubbery where, if Jenna's gaze was worth following, he might have been, seemed empty. She paused by a billowy camellia, where an almost-empty flute glass had been left on the ground, and softly called his name; but there was only the rustle of the dark leaves when the breeze lifted them lightly. She did not want to be seen searching under bushes for him.

Then she glimpsed the side wall behind the camellia. Of course. She slipped out through the flat without making her farewells and found him, looking restless, lurking outside Emma's front door.

'There you are. I didn't spot you sloping off.'

'Scrambled over the wall behind the bushes,' he confirmed. 'Let's go home, I'm exhausted now. How was I?' He decided not to mention his mistakes, the unsettling prosecco, the catnap under the sheltering camellia.

'Alright, I think,' she answered. They began to walk slowly down the road together. He linked arms with her. It steadied him, and seemed a friendly gesture. 'Emma seemed totally smitten,' Tiffany continued. 'Jenna's intrigued, and she didn't even get to talk to you; and Ozzy has never offered help to anyone so suddenly before. I think you'd better be careful there. Ozzy's sharp, and if anyone were to rumble your secret, however improbable, it'd be him. He probably plans to collect and study you, rather than the other way round.' Felix nodded.

'I will tread warily. Jenna looked tasty tonight, didn't she? I've always thought she's sensational.'

'Tread carefully there too, Felix – and don't start to tomcat your way through all my friends!'

'I'll always adore you, Tiffany,' he almost purred, leaning into her a bit more. 'But I can't deny all of my old nature. I can sleep alone on the sofa, if you want.'

'So soon,' she teased him, 'and what about Ozzy's invitation? Will he really help you?'

Felix curled his lip and answered: 'A maestro who likes to show off his skills to a willing acolyte. I'm not sure he likes me, but he's curious to see what the cat brought in. You in this instance being the cat, Tiff, or so he thinks, but I'm "in" there for now; and he'll help to transform my career as a brilliant artist – although he doesn't know that yet – in return for some simple flattery.' Felix grinned at the prospect. 'I'll sit at his feet, or his table, and observe all that he does. Watch, learn, act! I am still a hunter, you know, never the prey. W-L-A, W-L-A,' he chorused loudly.

'Don't yowl in my ear,' Tiffany reprimanded, mystified. 'Even ambitious house cats can be dispatched by a fierce creature protecting its territory, so watch your back, and don't stalk him too heartlessly.' Felix stopped walking. House cat? Older, darker memories coursed through him. He let go and looked at her unblinkingly.

'My heart is forever yours. The rest of me is anybody's that I choose,' he said grandly, and as she started to laugh, corrected himself. 'I choose you first, here, of course; but I've always been admired and fussed over by all sorts of people – and a little flattery in return opens many doors. You never objected before to anyone else fondling me, or slipping me the odd titbit, even complete strangers; and you got that splendid cousin of yours, Thomas, to cat-sit for weeks. So what's the difference now? You even saw me sit on Anthony's lap once.'

'Ha. Better not try it now. He would have apoplexy. But why did you do that? You obviously loathe him, from what you said yesterday.' Both Tiffany and Felix revealed pointy teeth happily at the memory of Anthony's suppressed fury, and resumed walking.

'To put cat hairs all over his just-brushed dinner jacket of course, just before you two went out to some fancy event for one of his clients. He was livid but couldn't say a word, in case you sprung to my defence and held things up with an argument. It was a huge success. The effort of controlling his annoyance almost gave him a heart attack.' Felix almost skipped with amusement at the memory.

'Cruel beast, very cruel,' but still Tiffany smiled.

'That's part of my nature. Like toying with a too-sleek rat. I'm not afraid of Ozzy's all-seeing gaze either.' Felix's eyes narrowed. 'I might have some fun teasing Anthony again, when he gets back. What do you think – will Mr Wonderful Architect like your new live-in painter and decorator?'

Tiffany had only thought of Anthony twice in the nearly thirty hours since Felix's curious metamorphosis.

'Not if you try to sit on his lap now,' she said, side-stepping the issue. 'Anyway, I'm not speaking to him at the moment, as you well know.' She lifted her chin in remembered annoyance and stalked along the pavement.

'Only because he's a thousand miles or more away,' Felix pointed out, pacing beside her again. 'If he had sworn to rush back really quickly, you'd have forgiven him for staying to salvage his project in a volatile hotspot when he was meant to be having a cosy evening with you. He'd have swept in with some glittery little present, and persuaded you to say sorry to *him* for any misunderstandings. You did eat out of his hand, sometimes, Tiff – you should know better.'

I do know better, she thought, it's all just another game – I'm more like you than you imagine. She glanced sideways at Felix.

'And whose hand did you eat out of back then?' she retorted, but gently, and linked arms with him again to make it easier for him to keep up. His gait still seemed a little unsteady. Failing to read her thoughts, and unaware that it was the fading tail-end of the prosecco that made him unsubtle, Felix continued with the blinkered zeal of the convert who had himself only just given up taking real titbits from other hands.

'That other fellow, Thomas, now he was OK. He liked me. You could have paid more attention to him.'

'Thomas?' Tiffany was hugely amused. 'He's my cousin, practically a brother. He really was just being my lodger for a while, as you should know. No fireworks there.' Felix, despite being no lover of fireworks, persisted.

'A fine fellow, who couldn't care less about cat hairs, and fed me on time. Reliable, and quite interested in your welfare too.' Tiffany rolled her eyes at this.

'Yes, in a *brotherly* sort of way,' she repeated. 'Why are you prattling on like some maudlin drunk, anyway? You didn't have a drink, did you?' She recalled the almost-empty glass flute, and frowns. 'You only like him so much because he's called Thomas. Stick to your own talents for seduction, and let others find their own paths.'

'I do have many talents,' Felix purred, 'and I am going to enjoy redeploying them all. As I told kitten-ish Emma tonight: watch, learn, act. As for Anthony, with his jaunts and his business tax dodges, I don't trust him an inch. At least with me, you know what you've got.'

'No, I don't. And what tax dodges? What would you know about such things anyway? You're just a transmogrified moggy at best, and at worst some sort of weirdo stalker who really should be shown the door instead of being paraded at parties,' she pointed out crisply.

'And you think I'm the one who's off their head?' he protested. Definitely best not to confess to the prosecco.

'Ha! You're so right about having the sofa to yourself now to sleep on,' Tiffany retorted. Did she mean it, she wondered, but he was already seizing the moment.

'Give me a room of my own,' he said, 'that boxy spare room Thomas used, the one you shove your suitcases into again now. I'll make it into a cosy retreat, and only venture out to paint the flat, or when otherwise needed.'

She considered.

'OK, the room could be yours. I've already told several people tonight that you're my new lodger. As for needing you, I'm not going to share you vicariously with every Tom, Dick and Harriet that you seduce even if – and maybe especially if – they're all my friends.'

'You were the one who decided it would be fun to risk launching me amongst them,' said Felix, nuzzling her ear. 'But I hear you, O mistress.' He attempted a mock bow, which, with their arms still linked, almost made them lose their balance and trip.

'Steady,' she warned.

'And tomorrow, I'll begin to transform your home into a painted paradise. Where shall we buy the paints? I spent hours watching the man several gardens down redecorating last summer while you were away. I had a bit of trouble with how long it took the window-sills to dry but we reached an understanding, and yes, he fed me titbits to distract me from checking the paintwork. So I sat and watched, and studied his photographs and wonderful pictures in travel books that were moved off the shelves as he painted the room. Happy days. They could be useful now – but I do have one problem.'

'Only one?' They were nearly at her flat now. He ignored the jibe.

'I'm fine with pictures, but when Ozzy gave me his card, I realised I've little idea yet what it says. I'm also supposed to know about this opera thing that he's designing the set for.' He frowned, old memories stirring again, and then turned to her with his most appealing look. 'I still need your help, Tiff. Will you help me to brush up the art of reading, in exchange for the full benefit of my own skills? As I keep telling you, I learn very fast. Lightning fast,' he risked saying.

'Alright.' Tiffany was almost touched by his need. 'If you're such a fast learner, we can tackle some reading skills in the morning, fit in a quick local geography lesson and if there's any time left, study the colour cards I picked up earlier today. Perhaps I'll get some paints while you're at Ozzy's.' She considered. It was a lovely night. 'And maybe for all of that, one last refresher course in your dark arts before you try to spread your favours amongst all my friends? In case you need the practice.'

'Practice? I am a consummate artist in all that I do.' The prosecco was all forgotten; he had found his inner balance again now. He stopped under the streetlamp, kissed her, swept her up in his arms. He was surprisingly strong. Tiffany was enchanted again.

'What *have* you been watching on the TV? A screening of "Breakfast at Tiffany's"?' she asked. 'We'd better start your literacy programme with some romantic novels. Something tells me that you'll lap them up.'

Felix grinned, and carried her swiftly into the darkness.

Chapter 5

Emma ignored the scarlet 'missed call' message on her mobile's screen. 'Dad', it admonished her. She was enjoying the ritual of slowly restoring order and calm to her small domain on the day after the party. Now she felt unsettled again. Let him wait a bit longer, she decided. The Sunday afternoon sunshine and fresh air outside suddenly appealed. She stuffed the phone into her jeans' back pocket, extracted her bank card and a couple of notes from her purse, put on her pale blue espadrilles, and left the building. Not far away, in the bustle of a regular Sunday street market, she could lose herself in the crowd, potter and daydream, and be fortified for the conversation ahead.

It felt quite warm outside. The first tastes of summer, she thought, making her way along the pavements to the couple of streets closed off every Sunday for market traders to set up their stalls. She dallied, inspecting second-hand jewellery and silver-plated cutlery, scrimshaw, silk scarves, collections of old magazines, and the bric-à-brac on show. Something about a small bronze statuette of a cat caught her eye but she strolled on, away from the busier streets at the heart of the little market, into a pretty square. When the phone in her back pocket buzzed quietly again, she ignored it.

Passing a small café, a flutter of movement and colour did catch her attention. She paused. Through the café window, she glimpsed bright paintings on its plain brick walls. 'Sea Changes' – a small exhibition of watercolours – advertised a neat poster, pinned to the cross-bars of the open door. As she looked, the pictures seemed to ripple. Emma stared again, and then understood that the glass in their frames was reflecting the people moving in the café. Transposed into the paintings, the customers seemed to act within them, but distortedly, doubly-refracted through the plate glass window. She stood transfixed, barely noticing a small troupe of pigeons that strutted close to her, pecking at crumbs on the pavement.

The ebb and flow of life, she thought, watching the layered images inside the café waver and flex. Through the open door filtered another disorienting mix of a little world 'muzak' and fresh coffee. The place had a scrubbed and pleasingly threadbare look, and the smell of the coffee was very good. She could see what must be a homemade carrot cake behind the counter, and a rack of newspapers for customers to leaf through. Now she was doubly, trebly, tempted. She entered, scattering the pigeons behind her. Disregarding her usual preference for mint tea, or forays into apple and blackcurrant infusions, Emma ordered a large mug of full-on, frothed and aromatic caffeine.

I've earned it, with all that clearing up, she thought, and maybe some cake too. After paying she picked a folded newspaper at random from the rack and carried it, with her tray of purchases, to a small round Formica table near the entrance, where she could either look out of the window at the passing world, or turn inwards to observe the paintings where reflections of her fellow customers still busied themselves, obliquely and unawares. 'Migrant crisis worsens. Hundreds drown in Med', a two-deck headline on the newspaper lurched at her as she unfolded it. She laid it face down on the table, and looked around the café instead to gauge the exhibition. Perhaps because of the headline, the first picture that she registered on the far wall was dominated by a young man in the foreground climbing from a slippery rubber orange Zodiac onto a crowded fishing smack. The painting's bright sunshine mercilessly revealed how old and unseaworthy the boat was, but dozens of people filled its tilted decks while ominous slate grey clouds, sidling into the background, bode ill. A movement caught her eye as a hand suddenly waved in the foreground to hail the boat – or perhaps to call the young man back – and Emma realised that it belonged to one of her fellow customers in the café, his action reflected in the painting's glass as he reached out for a teaspoon from the stout mug of cutlery set on his table.

The man, elderly, frail-looking, in a baggy tweed jacket and cord trousers, sat at a table towards the back of the café with a slightly younger woman in faded jeans and a neat navy V-necked T-shirt. She had his nose and chin, Emma noticed, as she considered them through the steam of her unaccustomed coffee, breathing in its promise. She was just looking round for more reflections in other pictures, when a clear voice from the doorway startled her.

'There you are.'

Tiffany's new lodger stood before her, looking louche and handsome. He was still barefoot.

'Oh!' Emma felt dizzy for a moment. 'Hello. What are you doing here?'

'I might ask you the same,' he said, puzzling her. 'I'd have looked for you somewhere a bit more New Age – with hand-woven rugs on the walls perhaps, and cushions with little glass squares sewn into them. One of the quirky cafés near the market? Actually, I saw you turn into the square and followed you. Thought I'd just say thank you again for allowing a newcomer to join your gathering last night.' He leaned against the door jamb and smiled his disconcerting, pointy-toothed grin.

'Oh. Did you enjoy it, er—?' She was trying to recall his name – had Tiffany even said it? – and a little thrill ran through her at the thought of this lithe and unconventional being tracking her through the warm streets. 'You disappeared quite early,' she finished. He cocked his head and briefly considered before responding.

'It was interesting,' he decided, 'and now I'm just on my way to meet up with your rather unusual uncle. He's going to give me some career tips.' Emma was startled to hear this. Regretting too that their encounter in the café was clearly destined to be brief, she spoke a little tartly.

'Better watch your back, then – Ozzy is very astute. His sudden patronage generally comes with strings attached.' Felix eyed her with respect.

'Thanks for the timely warning. I'll tread carefully.' Still leaning against the doorframe, smiling down at her, he added, 'And it's Felix, by the way.'

'Hello Felix.' She would have offered him her hand, but he was slightly too far away. 'You won't be able to outmanoeuvre Ozzy,' she resumed, but then stopped, guilty at this outbreak of family disloyalty. Why am I blurting out all this? she wondered, as Felix looked curiously at her.

'OK, but I daresay you could charm the old boy for me, if you put your mind to it?' he said. He was probably only teasing, but Emma felt ruffled by his assumption, even though the same thought had struck her.

'Why would I want to do that?' Once again her tone sounded sharper than she would have liked. He shrugged.

'Because I'm a revelation, and I'm sure you could practise a little guile to further a friend's aims,' he suggested. 'Look how charmingly you handed Ozzy to me at your party last night. The perfect hostess, but,' he paused for a moment, 'perhaps it was all a bit too artless.' He considered her astonished stare, before adding: 'Maybe a bit more of today's edginess would be more fun, or even a tantalising hint of naked ambition, if you can carry that off. WLA, you know,' he concluded to give authority to this tease. Felix folded his arms and watched her reaction. Emma felt a flash of anger, far from her usual comfort zone.

Is this Felix still drunk? she thought. 'Handed' Ozzy to you – the other way round, surely – and you're not my friend. Not yet, maybe not ever, she wanted to say.

'You have no idea,' she retorted, aloud, and then suddenly suspicious asked: 'What has Tiffany been saying to you about me?'

Felix smiled that pointy-toothed grin again. 'Nothing much. I just see through people, whereas she often lazily stops at the surface, too busy with her own mystery. But if you must know, she finds you a charming if inconsequential cousin, whereas I would call you... disarming – a much more interesting quality, potentially.' He rocked forward slightly onto his toes for a second as he said this, as if about to move towards her, but then remained by the door.

Definitely still tipsy, Emma decided, yet he was intoxicating too. She was flattered by his last remark (although Tiffany was a cow). Felix's presumption and proximity were unsettling. The whole café suddenly felt as shifting and confusing as the reflecting pictures on its walls. Emma was unsure that she could keep her balance at the little table, and this time had no quick answer ready.

'Sadly, I can't stop to discuss you more just now,' Felix said after this moment's pause, and indicated the clock on the back wall. His glance also took in the tea-drinking pair sitting just beneath it. He seemed to study them fleetingly before glancing at Emma as if inviting her opinion and then, receiving none, turned to go. Her moment to suggest that he join her for a steadying coffee first, or to offer to walk a little of the route to Ozzy's with him, had swirled and eddied away.

'Good luck,' she managed to say to his departing back, hearing the phrase as if spoken by someone else in the room.

'You too.' A wave, but no backwards look, and he was gone. Irritatingly disappointed, Emma closed her eyes. The shape of Felix's departing silhouette lingered behind her lids. 'Charming, if inconsequential,' he had quoted from Tiffany. Is that really how other people regard her? She felt a little sick and, turning away, opened her eyes to find herself looking straight at the damn tea-drinkers again. What had caught Felix's attention over there? she wondered. Was it them – or maybe something in the painting above them? The duo sat, sipping tea and speaking quietly. She frowned, and tried to hear their words.

'Did you put enough sugar in, Dad?' the woman was asking. She has a handsome face, Emma realised. She would probably still look quite glamorous if she ever dressed up. The old man nodded.

'Yes, yes, two sugars, in both cups – I'm not senile yet.'

The woman smiled gently.

'It just needs a bit more of a stir, then.' She had a quiet poise. Emma sensed the teaspoon making circular ripples in the cup, as if stirring her own imagination. Is this a daughter visiting her father for the day? (Can they afford nowhere better?) Or does she care for him, at home, and finds a welcome change of scene for them both in the café? Has she given up an independent life because her ailing father needs help? A chill passed through Emma as she watched them, despite the sunshine outside. Her own father lived alone now. He had done so ever since her electrifying mother declared she now had 'things to do' that she wanted to get on with, on her own, while she still had some vigour left – and then had swept, with her bags and suitcases, out of the family home.

Emma was the only still-unmarried one of their belated brood and now, in this pair in the café she saw a disquieting image of what her own future could hold, and the fear that she had been repressing all afternoon since seeing her father's missed call on her phone flowed back. Roads untraveled and routes abandoned seemed to form in the steam unravelling from the woman's teacup. Emma looked down at her own dwindling coffee, and a small wave of self-pity hit her.

I must get my act together, she realised, instead of drifting along with other people's expectations like flotsam or, worse, like jetsam – thrown back into the sea. Even Tiffany's 'latest' weirdo Felix didn't really have time to find out more about me, did he? She bit her lip, forgetting that Felix had claimed to have followed her there. 'Inconsequential.' Her cousin's alleged description bit deeply. Until this moment Emma had assumed that, by taking life as it came, at any moment she could choose to catch a tempting tide and beach up somewhere new and exciting – but here, in this little café with its confusing reflections, she saw that it had always been Tiffany who actually had adventures.

Emma suddenly and profoundly feared becoming marooned without ever having embarked: probably stuck in her father's house, reeled back to that desert island when he would eventually have a fall, or a heart murmur, to play the part of a leftover dutiful daughter. A bigger dread, of how tricky refusing that call could be, immediately followed. Her older siblings, being married with young children, had bagged a neat excuse for side-stepping the task of caring for an ageing parent when a single, unencumbered daughter (without a stellar career) existed who could be landed with the role, also handily saving the rest of them from having to divvy-up for fulltime professional care. Her crafty sister even engineered a move to Australia with her new husband not long after their very expensive wedding.

Emma had usually played the peacemaker of their volatile family, taking responsibility upon herself to sooth prickly feelings, see everybody's point of view, and even disingenuously apologise for troubles not of her making: 'I'm sorry you're upset about what Dad said, about what Mother did, about what Janet says – she only got dragged into it – or about Jon coming home so late and a tiny bit drunk. But if you look at this way... I'm sure it will all be alright tomorrow... in the morning... by the evening... by the time you get back...'

Yet the family had still fractured. Janet and Jon bounded off into their own lives and marriages without any backwards glance. Then Mother had bustled her leftover younger daughter into a nice little job in town and a suitable flat, declared herself now surplus to requirements and taken off to live a new life of her own, leaving Dad to his own devices. Oddly, he had barely seemed to notice after the initial flurry of packing and suitcases. Perhaps he was relieved. Iris could be demanding and exhausting company.

So instead, Emma now distracted another mix of disparate people from their ups and downs, and gave little parties, at which she was resourceful, calming and charming, and yet apparently 'of no consequence'– thanks for that Tiffany, she thought bitterly – while they all sweep on with their lives. It did not occur to her in the café that Tiffany may not have actually said this about her to a newcomer like Felix. She just felt in her bones that it would be typical of Tiffany's casual attitude to say something of the sort, and suddenly envied her that freedom.

I've been wasting my time on enabling others and then being left behind, she realised, like being Ariadne stuck on bloody Naxos in one of Ozzy's wretched operas. Time to act for myself. She sipped what remained of her coffee, concentrating. 'Disarming' was what Felix himself had called her, and indicated this was better. 'Much more interesting, potentially,' he had said. She looked around the café again for inspiration, and caught her own reflection in a small beach scene not far from the disturbing migrant embarkation painting.

Within its frame, a lone gouache-painted girl dressed in turquoise and green turned away to look out to sea, where Emma saw her own reflected face rising from the waves beyond the pebbled shore, like some curious sea nymph staring back into the café.

'So which are you,' Emma imagined the reflection asking her, 'a rising force of nature like me, or just a washed-up reflection in someone else's story?'

Emma held her own stony gaze, silently replying to herself: A force of nature, but I've been dormant, and must wake up and seize the tide, or lose the moment. Maybe that's what Felix meant. He wasn't looking at that couple at all, but at the man getting onto the boat. I've got to get away too. Go abroad, like Janet, and Mother, or launch a brilliant career, and be really busy, or marry someone quickly first, who can afford to keep Dad in a decent nursing home, she thought cynically – someone ambitious, already on their way up. It may be a bit retro, but it's worked for millennia.

An idea was forming – one that would put Tiffany in her place too – and tugging at the edges of her imagination. Why not? Insight and fear made her ruthless. Emma absorbed the new sensation, savouring it. It permeated her mind and body more than the caffeine. It would help her to move forward, she decided. Details will have to be plotted, but an inner tide has definitely turned, and she will not just ride it but steer it, towards a place of her own selection. I am disarming, and will make my own waves, she determined. There will be Consequences (she pictured a capital C), ones of my choosing and of my making. What did Felix call that technique, again? W-L-A. Watch. Learn. Act. Of course, I get it now; and Tiffany – better watch your back, coz.

Emma stood up, breathed deeply, relaxed her shoulders and readied herself to leave the scene. Something was needed to crystallise the moment, to mark the shoreline left behind; so her polite but emphatic 'Goodbye' to the inattentive girl behind the café counter was deliberately loud enough to encompass the pair still quietly drinking tea. They looked up, surprised, and then nodded at her. Emma smiled back – a big confident smile now – and stepped out purposefully into the sunny square. She turned left, determined not to retrace any earlier steps, and headed for the main thoroughfare. The phone in her back pocket was no longer a carrier of lurking reproaches, but a slingshot loaded with shining pebbles that couldn't miss their mark. The sun shone, a brisk breeze caressed her; and she strode forth, a released huntress, unstoppable.

Arriving home armed with her new determination, Emma made herself a fresh coffee, and then pressed the button on her mobile phone that automatically dialled her father's number. He took so long to pick up the call that she was about to hang up, almost with relief, though surprised that the answering service had not cut in.

'Hello,' said his gruff voice.

'It's Emma. You called.'

'Yes I did. I wondered when you might be popping down? I'm planning my diary and want to check what spaces to keep clear for you.'

She paused before replying. This could be positive. He is obviously busy; or faking it, she thought.

'Let me see. What weekend might suit you?' She reached across the table for her slim diary. She still liked to keep a paper one, as well as her electronic calendar.

'Three weeks from now. I've got nothing fixed then,' he stated.

'Good,' she said, untruthfully, as she leafed through the pages. 'I've nothing much planned then either, so that would be fine. Are you OK? Anything you'd like me to bring?'

'Just yourself. There's something I want to discuss with you.' She did not much like the sound of that. But if it could wait three weeks it was also clearly not a crisis, yet.

'What is it?' she probed.

'Wait and find out – but it concerns the house. You may like to know what I have in mind, as it also concerns you, to some extent. See you that Saturday, then. You'll get here before lunch.' It was a command, not a question.

'Yes, of course,' she replied, her mind spinning fast. 'About twelve as usual?'

'Make it eleven-thirty. Time for coffee and a chat first. You well?' he finally asked.

'Perfectly.' She chatted for a minute about her party before they said goodbye and hung up. Well, he sounds fine – firing on all cylinders, she thought. But what does having plans for the house mean? Is he going to remodel it? Has he discovered something is wrong with him and that he needs to arrange to live downstairs all the time? What else might he want to discuss that concerns me? She forced back the old panic that was trying to rise up again. The new Emma did not panic. She considered ringing her siblings later on, to see if they had any inklings, and decided against it.

I've got three weeks in which to come up with a life plan for myself, she thought, and I'm not speaking to anyone in the family until I've worked it out, nor negotiating with them afterwards. Felix is definitely not the only one with a future to plan. I'm moving on now, as fast as I can.

In his lair, her father chuckled as he set the phone down.

'That's put the wind up her,' he said aloud. 'Time my youngest daughter got a grip and stopped drifting along.' He had got into the habit of talking to the air since Iris had left. The doorbell interrupted, and he made his way briskly to the front door and pulled it wide open. 'Here you are! Come on in. I've just fixed it all up; Emma's coming down in three weeks' time and we'll give her the surprise of her life. Trust me, she'll be thrilled. Over the moon with relief, I should think.' He roared with laughter.

'Shouldn't you tell her sooner?' asked his visitor.

'Not a bit of it. Let her scuttle around, reorganising her life for the better first. She will do, after the fright I've just given her, if I know my daughter, which is a lot better than she thinks,' he added, thoroughly enjoying his prank.

Chapter 6

When Felix at last reached Ozzy's studio, he paused to consider the lay of the land. The smart street bordering an expansive and tempting park had proved long, and the soles of his feet were beginning to regret his rejection of the deck shoes when he finally recognised the shape of the number on a fanlight above a front door, just as Tiffany had described. The short and rather muddy gravel path to the door looked neglected, partially masked by gloomy laurel bushes, and for a moment he wondered if he had made a mistake.

He surveyed the large but unkempt house, set back from the street. One of the broad steps up to the front door was cracked, and the building's stucco and paintwork were peeling. This was unexpected. He approached the steps cautiously, and studied the front door more closely before going further. A brass knocker in the form of the head of a hawk holding a large ring in its powerful curving beak had something so fierce in the shine of its eyes that Felix felt unwilling to use it. Above it he noticed the tiny bubble of a glass spyhole. The house number on the fanlight above the door definitely matched the one Tiffany had highlighted on Ozzy's business card. Felix considered the meaning of the dilapidated house, the drive, the bushes, the forbidding door knocker. Then he bounded up the steps and rapped twice, fast, before releasing the brass ring just as quickly.

'Felix!' said Ozzy, immediately opening the door wide as if he had been waiting just inside, watching through the security spyhole. 'You found it. Congratulations. Don't let appearances put you off, my boy. A set designer needs theatrical surroundings. Come and explore my domain.' Felix stepped carefully into the hallway, senses alert. He noted the once-expensive thick flock wallpaper, now painted over in pale sage. It too was peeling in places, and there was a yellowing patch high in one corner where damp, or rain, or perhaps an overflowing bath had left its mark. Ozzy followed his upward gaze.

'Yes, it's in outwardly poor shape, but the work space I have here is magnificent, albeit faded. It's Crown property, you know, and for reasons never clearly explained but perhaps because of its condition, available at a peppercorn rent for use as a studio. I even have the odd party here, to celebrate the end of a particularly satisfying project. The garden is a splendid wilderness, full of roses and overgrown old statuary. It constantly inspires me, so I mostly let nature take its course out there, with only minor interventions. Come in properly.' He led the way through the hallway, ignoring some steps down into what Felix assumed was a semi-basement area, and passed through a set of tall, open double doors into a large room overlooking the wild garden below it. Here the ageing wallpaper was intact: pale horizontal stripes of cream and café-au-lait, under a high ceiling with elaborate white cornicing.

Light poured in through the tall windows, scattering tiny rainbows across the broad wooden floorboards. Intrigued, Felix looked around for their source and found it in bands of sunshine dancing off the prismatic crystals of an elaborate, if elderly, chandelier suspended from a large ceiling rose. In the midst of this fluctuating splendour stood a vast glass table with sheets of drawings and designs in progress carefully laid out on its surface. Two large armchairs crouched by the windows, draped with throws in warm white tones beneath which glimpses of light blue upholstery peeked out at ankle level. Each chair also had two startlingly azure cushions tossed into its depths. Pushed back a little from the table, but centrally placed, was a large, burnished dining chair. A metal throne, thought Felix. Really?

'No cushion?' he asked, nodding in its direction. 'Very focused.'

'Indeed. You understand the different forms of concentration, I see,' Ozzy remarked. 'One seat for dreaming up ideas,' he indicated an armchair, 'one for a change of viewpoint,' he gestured at the second armchair, 'or indeed for clients, and one,' now he pointed at the metal seat, 'for executing designs.'

'You make that sound quite sinister,' Felix said.

'I suppose it is.' Ozzy walked across and sat in his imposing chair. 'Here I take ideas and give some of them temporary life.' He opened his hands as if letting the others trickle through his fingers. 'I spin briefly tangible illusions out of the dreams and fantasies of playwrights and librettists – and directors and others – and sometimes out of their nightmares too, if they'll share them with me. Often more revealing.' He smiled thinly.

'Do you ever use your own nightmares?' Felix asked cautiously, and wondered if Ozzy had many.

'Only if they throw some light on the production concerned. My designs may sometimes seem indulgent, but it's all strictly controlled. My sets must resonate with the story that the production is unfolding. They hold visual clues to its progress. If a beguiling idea doesn't fit, or fails to tell the audience something about the characters' state of mind, for example, it has to go.' He leaned forward, put his elbows on the glass table, and pressed his fingers together, watching Felix.

'I shall be quite safe, then,' Felix said levelly, and unblinking. 'I've always had a finely-tuned appreciation of mood, poise, and control.' He sat down, uninvited, in one of the armchairs. 'This place is a wonderful combination of the restrained and the strange, by the way. I'm keen to learn whatever you can teach me about your craft for a season.' He meant it, and Ozzy seemed to relax a little.

'So you said,' he responded, and rose from his magisterial seat. 'First, let me introduce you to the garden, as it's also an essential part of my working environment – the uncontrolled wilderness, pressing in upon the gently decaying building. This glass table that I work at inside is about establishing limits, boundaries, controls. It's where my imagination crystallises things into the possible, if you like.' He led Felix towards the bay windows, and opened a narrow secret door tucked into the side of the room. Covered with the same paper as the walls, it was almost invisible when shut. Opened, it revealed a few steps directly down to the garden. 'I hope you like unfettered rambling roses and long grass,' Ozzy said, turning to look at his guest.

'An ideal hunting ground,' Felix said carelessly, in anticipation.

'Ah,' Ozzy looked sharply at him. 'Is that so?' Felix changed his approach.

'Tell me about the sets for that Egyptian production you're working on,' he suggested, following Ozzy down the few steps into the garden.

'In good time, after appreciating the roses,' said Ozzy. 'They like a sheltered garden. The production itself is for next summer, but naturally these things are planned well ahead. I'll take you through how the opera uses the story of *Akhenaten* – are you quite sure you don't know it? – and explain how the atmosphere will be created visually to complement the music and voices. We can listen to parts of it, and then I hope you'll grasp that what I do is not about decorating walls. It's about reconstructing myth, and truth, and the permeability of time – while keeping control of, and within, the elements concerned.' He stressed the word 'control' and looked rather piercingly at Felix who felt rebuked, and a prickling sense of unease. Recalling Emma's warning in the café, and Tiffany's observation that Ozzy's thoughtful silences made others blurt out useful additional information that they had intended to keep private, he gave himself time to think. Ozzy's technique was one Felix used at times himself, even if limited in the recent past to staring meaningfully at a food cupboard.

'I should very much like to learn how to do all of that here,' he replied carefully, before catching a whiff of mint in the afternoon air. He saw a large clump of it, growing tall and green and inviting, next to one of the showy pink and gold tea roses. Something rustled in the long grass. A garden of delights indeed. 'Keeping within the elements' be damned, he thought, breathing the scented air. I've seen what the elements can do. Going beyond them could be even better.

'So be it,' responded Ozzy, almost as if reading his mind.

Chapter 7

'I must say, Tiff, that fellow you brought to Emma's on Saturday was gorgeous. Where did you find him?' Jenna leant back in her chair, soaking up the early evening sun, savouring the cool white wine in her glass. They sat at one of the wine bar's tables in the little front courtyard created out of its semi-basement area, catching up on life since the party.

'He's my new decorator. He's brightening the flat up a bit for me,' Tiffany said lightly.

'I'm sure he is, and brightening it quite a lot, I presume, if you're bringing him on your arm to parties after working hours. Does he 'do' for anyone else, or is he contracted to you all summer? I thought you said he was your new lodger?' Jenna turned her chair slightly to stretch her slim, lightly tanned bare legs into a patch of sunlight.

Tiffany nodded.

'He's both,' she said evenly, 'paying rent "in kind" by doing the decorating work, for now. He'll be in the market for more work soon, of course, and he's doing a surprisingly good job at my place so far,' she invented. 'The materials aren't exactly cheap, but worth it.' I hope, she added silently to herself. Felix's claimed decorating skills were still to be proven to her, while his taste in paint was already expensive. In the end they had gone together to choose some from a fashionable interior design store conveniently near the easiest way to Ozzy's place so that Felix – primed with her quick sketch on the back of Ozzy's card of the rest of the route, as well as her verbal directions – could continue onwards in time for their afternoon encounter. Felix had said he still preferred to walk, as usual, and the distance was no problem for him, but Tiffany suspected that he was also not yet ready to tackle public transport. In the shop's paint section, Felix had grown very animated about how many different colours and shades were available, wanting dozens of small sample pots of the costliest brand, as well as the large tin of the pale, not-quite-buttery 'Stone' colour that Tiffany firmly insisted upon as the backdrop for her calm sitting room. Felix's preparations on his return from Ozzy's that evening had looked thorough, however, and remarkably the first experimental coat of 'Stone' had gone smoothly on to one wall by supper time.

'So far, so good,' she had admitted, inspecting his progress, after emerging dishevelled and dusty from her own task of inspecting the things variously dumped in the coveted box-room since Thomas's tenure. She had cleared the broad divan bed, rescued a few items, consigned others to a bin bag and the rest to a couple of strong carrier bags to drop at the local charity bric-à-brac shop. Satisfied, Felix helped her to carry out the rubbish and to shove the charity bags into the hallway pending onward transfer. He wanted to get a first coat on the remainder of the sitting room after supper, and then to shut himself away in the emptied box-room, forbidding Tiffany to investigate in there until invited to do so, whenever that might be. On the subject of his meeting with Ozzy, he had been equally contained, saying in answer to her inquiry over supper about how it had gone: 'He's strange man, hard to fathom, but it was a useful afternoon. I think he will help me, and very soon. Where are all those little pots of paints? I'll need to get started with them tonight, on something exciting to show Ozzy and others as soon as possible. Then we can take some wonderful photographs for my portfolio, and invite people round to see the work *in situ*, at a little party or something.'

Tiffany had stared, thinking '*in situ*' indeed – my cat is talking Latin! And organising my social life around his ambitions, just like blasted Anthony.

Jenna's voice commanded her back to the present moment in the wine bar.

'Great!' she was replying. 'If he's good, my place could do with a lick of paint soon, and maybe he could take it on. So where did you find him, anyway? Recommended by anyone we know – Anthony perhaps?' she probed.

'Hardly.' Tiffany instantly regretted this crisp response. Anthony was still one of Jenna's PR clients after all. 'I mean, he's not one of Anthony's work contacts.' She hesitated, and then pressed on with her story. 'He's from my home village,' she said, carefully but truthfully. 'He sort of turned up, and asked for some decorating work. I wasn't too sure at first, but then I thought – why not?'

'Why not indeed. As I said, he's gorgeous.'

'Hmm.' Tiffany stalled, feeling that she and Felix still needed to agree more details of their cover story for his sudden arrival. She selected her next words even more mindfully, to feed back to Felix later: 'So he's not a complete stranger, although his sudden appearance in – I mean at – the flat, and the request for some decorating work did take me by surprise. It would have been inhospitable just to have shown him the door, though, and my flat could do with a bit of a makeover, so I thought I'd take him up on it and see how things go.'

'Evidently rather well.' Jenna poured some more wine into Tiffany's glass, and a little less into her own. 'So how long have you known him, then? You're still being a bit mysterious, you know.' From the controlled serenity of her own carefully structured and ordered life, Jenna enjoyed her friend's more picaresque adventures.

'Ah.' Tiffany took another deep drink of her wine, thinking fast. Probably still best to stick with something close to reality. Partial truths should be safer and easier to remember than too many fictions. 'Felix – did I say at the party that his name's Felix? His family lived on a farm near my parents' place, so I practically grew up with his tribe charging around underfoot.' She beamed innocently – she hoped – at Jenna.

'So a country lad, seeking his fortune in the big city?' Jenna seemed to accept this account of Felix's pedigree.

'How very Dick Whittington – but no cat rolled in, to secure his fortunes?'

Tiffany choked slightly on her wine.

'Sorry, went down the wrong way,' she spluttered. 'No cat as such,' she croaked after a moment to recover. 'Anthony hates cats, I've realised,' she added, falling back on another recently-confirmed truth, 'and my own moggy seems to have taken off somewhere in protest.' That should cover any questions about where the animal's got to, if and when anyone notices his absence, she thought; and paused for tragic effect. Perhaps Jenna will think the coughing fit had started as a sob.

'Oh Tiffany, I am sorry to hear that,' Jenna said, putting down her wine glass for a moment. 'But it may not be Anthony's fault. Perhaps the smell of paint has put your cat's nose out of joint. You know how they are about upheavals. He'll probably swagger back when it's all finished, and he's got tired of being winsome to the neighbours. Try not to worry. Anyway, it's very decent of you to take this Felix character in. How long is he staying on site?'

'I'm not quite sure yet,' Tiffany answered. 'For the time being he's taken over the box-room, like my cousin Thomas did for a bit last year?' Jenna had not met Thomas then, but Tiffany felt the detail still backed up her story nicely. 'I suppose it depends how well the work goes, and on his getting more of it, as there's only so much redecorating my own flat can take. I'm just helping Felix to find his feet in a new environment, really.' She warmed to her theme. 'He's already been for a professional chat with Ozzy, thanks to Emma introducing them the other night. Maybe he can help to paint stage sets. I'll alert Felix, shall I, if you really need some decorating done, or have any bright ideas about who else might?' This is shameless of me, she thought, Jenna has no idea how wild this all is.

Jenna considered for a moment, a small frown slightly creasing the centre of her forehead only for a second. Tall and slender, with neatly bobbed russet hair, already slightly tanned even this early in the summer – and never over-burnished – she always seemed immaculate although, in a less health-conscious age, a cigarette might never have been far from those slim fingers and well-manicured nails, Tiffany found herself thinking, perhaps even in a cigarette holder. She could certainly carry one off. Jenna took another sip of her wine, mulling the idea over, and decided.

'OK. I don't see why Emma and Ozzy should have all the fun of helping out the new boy in town. I'd be happy to get my claws into re-homing fabulous Felix for you, and have my place redecorated this summer – assuming his work's up to scratch. What do you think he would charge?' Tiffany wished that Jenna would use a different vocabulary. It made her feel uneasy and, despite the sunshine, she suppressed a shiver.

'I imagine that depends on whether board and lodging is thrown in,' she replied cautiously. 'I'm only paying for materials, with all the painting being done in lieu of rent, meals and so forth.' Jenna looked amused by 'so forth' but did not comment. Tiffany suggested, 'Why don't you pop round tomorrow evening? If you like what there is to see of his work you can put the idea to him yourself.'

'Alright. You're on.' Jenna raised her glass to salute the plan, and took another pensive sip. Maybe Tiffany really does want to help this Felix launch a new career, she thought, although clearly she has not yet consulted the absent Anthony – and I think I can see why. 'Shall we eat something before this wine goes to our heads? I could handle a salad,' she suggested, changing the subject for now.

'Lovely,' Tiffany agreed, pleased with the trail she had laid.

Re-running this conversation in her head later on, as she reached home feeling mellow and enjoying the still-warm evening air, Tiffany unlocked the main door and paused, registering different layers of smells filtering through the pale communal hallway. She detected paint of a mildly-headache-giving household variety, overlaid by something faintly fishy with a curiously vinegary finish.

'Here we go,' she murmured, moving through the short entrance hall and opening the door to her own flat. She went in as calmly as she could. 'Felix? How's it going?'

He sauntered out of the kitchen licking his fingers. His new khaki shorts, bought by Tiffany at the same time as the chinos and rejected deck shoes, and his bare torso were spattered with paints of many colours. He beamed indulgently her.

'Tiffers! Where have you been? You're almost getting nocturnal habits again. I bought fish and chips for our supper with the cash you left. Not bad, these chips that you people eat, though I prefer the fish of course. I'm still deciding about the batter, and the vinegar. Come and see what progress I've made! The living room's finished but as you know what it's going to look like, you don't need to see that first.' He gestured instead towards the stairs and led the way up to the bathroom. 'I've tried out some of my other ideas in here.' Tiffany peered a little nervously round the door. The multi-coloured paint splats on his body had alarmed her.

She stared in silent astonishment. On the walls around the bath was a startling, half-finished, mural. Bold cats – ginger, tabby, tortoiseshell – leapt, stalked, and snoozed in a landscape of tall reeds and vibrant flowers that turned the bathtub into a pool, or perhaps a quiet backwater of a river. A small, bright blue bird flew in alarm across the corner of one wall.

'It's amazing!' she said eventually, turning to Felix who had been observing her reaction closely. 'How did you do so much in only one day? I thought you were just going to repaint each wall in a different colour for me.'

'Don't you like it?' Felix asked sharply. 'I put my soul into it for you, Tiff.'

'Oh I do, I love it,' she replied hastily. 'It's just not what I expected. And you're right, it's wonderful in here.

The sitting room did need something paler, quieter, but this is remarkable. I had no idea you would be able to do anything like this.' She stared again at the lush world bursting into the small room.

'Well, I have spent at least one lifetime studying the subject matter, though there's a lot more work to do before it's finished,' he said huffily, hunching his shoulders. Her response seemed insufficient praise for his labour, and skill.

'Oh Felix, don't sulk, it's fantastic. I'm absolutely bowled over by it,' she soothed him. These murals put a whole new slant on what he could do on one of Ozzy's projects, she realised. She smiled at him. 'And I'd also love one of those chips, and we must talk urgently about tomorrow. Jenna has apparently taken a shine to you, and may want to hire your talents provided they are – in her unfortunate words – 'up to scratch', which on this evidence tonight they clearly are, though she might want something a little tamer. She's coming round to inspect progress tomorrow evening. How's the box-room, by the way?'

'Give me a chance. And it's still out of bounds to you.' He still spoke gruffly, but felt mollified. 'So you were out chasing up more work for me already – how delightful. Thank you.' His wicked grin returned. 'I'm sure I can come up with whatever Jenna wants. She's quite a cool cat herself you know.' Tiffany thought his slang sounded a bit forced, and dated; but she also experienced a twinge of jealousy. Don't be so silly, she reminded herself, he's still just a bloody great tomcat after all, allegedly. I can't believe I'm still accepting all this. Maybe encouraging Jenna to take him on for a bit will be enough of a break from him to think of a sensible way out of all this nonsense. She'll be alright. Jenna never gets emotionally entangled.

Aloud she said, 'If you say so, Felix – but I'd better fill you in a bit more on the cover story I've had to develop for you so far. We'll need to synchronise stories, and find you a surname. At least "Felix" works just as well for a man as a cat. In fact, isn't it cat in Latin?'

Felix shook his head, and began to lead the way downstairs to the kitchen, where the chips were waiting. 'Actually in Latin it's felis,' he said, rather pleased with his knowledge.

'Really? How do you suddenly know all this Latin?' she wondered.

'I think I picked it up from your neighbour a dozen gardens down, during my earlier study of basic decorating techniques there.'

'Well la-di-da,' said Tiffany. 'What a tramp you are.'

'You'd like him,' Felix admonished her, while busily investigating the fish and chip parcels again. 'He travels a lot, and has picture books on everything that you can think of, flora and fauna and history – and art books. I found the photos and drawings of cats living elsewhere in the world particularly interesting. When I stared hard at the pictures for a long time, he started telling me aloud about them.' Felix paused and waved a chip as if it were a baton, with a beat between each item on the list as he chanted to her. 'For example: *Felis Chaus*, a rather monochrome, gingerish, swamp or marsh cat. *Felis Sylvester Lybica*, the more attractively marked cat that the Egyptians treasured, and even worshipped, said to be the ancestor of all so-called house cats. You may have spotted one on your bathroom wall just now.' Another beat of the baton. 'I can be... Felix Sylvester. With a "y".' He half-bowed, and handed her the chip.

'Sylvester? That was my maternal great-grandmother's surname,' Tiffany said, considering the chip before biting it. 'Silvester with an "i" – Kitty Silvester. She made her husband double-barrel it with his name when they married. He was just plain Freddie Jones up to then, but he ended as *Sir* Frederick Silvester-Jones, to you!' She brightened, realising that in using this surname Felix could also deflect any awkward questions from Ozzy. Felix appeared delighted too.

'Kitty Silvester, well-remembered,' he said sleekly, making Tiffany wonder if he was congratulating her, or himself. 'Perfect. So now you and I are simply distant cousins on the Sylvester side of the family. Which one of us is the poor relation?'

'Obviously you,' Tiffany retorted. 'Emma's a distant cousin too, on my mother's side, but through the Jones bit. Will she be puzzled that she's never heard of your part of the family?' She sat down at the table, to work the story out more clearly as she snacked on the fish and chips. Felix rubbed his nose, and began to make some suggestions.

'Let's say... that I'd been doing some research inspired by all those TV programmes about finding your ancestors. Imagine your surprise and delight when I turned up here and explained that we seem to be related.'

Tiffany ate another chip thoughtfully.

'That could work. I've just told Jenna that your family lived near mine, and I grew up with lots of you underfoot in the village.'

'Perfect, and so deliciously true.' Felix sat down too. 'So, we were slightly acquainted when young, through village life, and now my researches have unearthed that your maternal great-grandmother Kitty's Silvester-with-an-i lot were distantly connected to my male Sylvester-with-a-y line, who were still living in the village, and back to which your mother's genes seemed to have been inexorably drawn.' Tiffany pulled open a drawer concealed under the kitchen table and got out a notepad and pen.

'Let me just start to map this out,' she said. 'It'll be less confusing if I draw it.'

'I think you will find it all makes me one of the grand old Sylvesters,' Felix said nonchalantly. 'No money, but an interesting pedigree, which is no doubt why you've made me so welcome. You and Emma can claim any grander Joneses if you like.' He picked up a piece of the battered fish in his fingers, and ate it noisily. Tiffany laughed at him.

'With those table-manners, it'll be a case of your lot trying to keep up with us Joneses – except of course that *my* surname, thanks to my father, is neither Silvester nor Jones. But it is true that Emma comes in via the Jones side,' she was working out a story steadily now, 'and that my parents moved to the village when I was a few months old. My mother always said that her family supposedly had some connection with it in the distant past.' She made a few more notes. 'My parents are still away at the moment, thank goodness, so I can say that you came to surprise me here with your news, instead of dropping in on them – cadged a place to stay, and begged for some decorating work, having evidently fallen on hard times and clearly not being above exploiting any family connections, no matter how tenuous,' she teased. 'This story could work, you know.'

Felix, admiring the speed with which she had jotted down names and notes and begun roughing out a family tree, thought so too.

'*Our* story, Tiff,' he affirmed, 'and now I really am just another cousin who, as Thomas did, is lodging temporarily with the lovely and hospitable – and dare I say curious Tiffany – while reinventing myself in the big bad city.'

'Let's not get too fancy. Just the basics will do for now,' she warned, setting down her pencil. 'My parents are in Australia for several more weeks, conveniently, so no-one,' she chiefly meant Ozzy, 'may bother to check with them till they're back. I'll pave the way with them at some point anyway, just in case. Remember that Thomas is a lawyer. He might start asking you for more details about the family history, or even doing his own research, if you make it sound too interesting.'

'He's not that pernickety about everything,' Felix answered, 'and probably too busy, given the hours he worked when he stayed here. If I show him a family tree – I can use your sketch to draw a really good one – he'll be quite happy for the time being. I'll leave scope for some things to have been "intelligent guesses" if that seems safer. What did your great-grandfather do, again? Remind me, before anyone asks me.'

'He was a minor Egyptologist, always fossicking about in the desert. I thought you knew that.' Felix looked startled. Another memory rustled like dry sand blowing across stone, as Tiffany carried on talking. 'My mother says all my statuettes were his or Kitty's originally,' she said. 'He was pretty old but still alive when I was born you know. Apparently he loved it when I was a toddler and couldn't say my name properly. He thought it sounded as if I was calling myself 'Tefnet' instead of Tiffany. Egyptian goddess of rain, to you,' she added, as Felix was now looking hard at her. 'Married to Shu, god of air and clouds, and generated a whole dynasty of deities. Old Sir Freddie taught me all the sounds that he – or someone – had worked out that were used to summon the gods and he'd let me play with his little statues of some of them as if they were dolls. I do vaguely remember him, along with the old photos and family stories, but Kitty had died quite young, long before. She was taken ill during one of their excavations I think. Malaria, or an outbreak of flu or something.' Felix listened intently as Tiffany reminisced. She smiled at him. 'He left the figurines to me in his will, apparently. My mother says they can't be really ancient things, or he'd have given them to a museum along with other bequests – not to a toddler. She reckons they're only twentieth century copies, made as souvenirs or even forgeries to tempt gullible rich visitors in the midst of Egypt-mania back then – but I always liked to imagine them as thousands of years old.' She gazed dreamily towards the garden, remembering childhood games.

'I expect he was keen on cats too,' Felix said rather briskly, dragging her back to safer territory than fakes and forgery, 'seeing as he married a Kitty.' Tiffany cuffed him lightly on the side of his head.

'Silly beast,' she said. 'Pass me another chip.'

Chapter 8

Jenna arrived at Tiffany's flat promptly at seven, after work, on Tuesday evening. Immaculate in a pale olive raw-silk suit that complimented her light tan, the cut of which she knew particularly flattered her elegant legs, she strolled into the living room. After placing a sleek briefcase (how does she always manage to travel so neatly? Tiffany briefly wondered) on an armchair, she looked approvingly round the room.

'I can smell the paint, but that'll fade. I do like this colour, Tiff, so calm and understated. How clever of you to have it in here. But where's the artisan?'

'Artist,' said Felix from the corridor. He leaned into the room. 'The artist is putting the finishing touches to the bathroom, and to his own tasteful corner. Come and see.' He led the way upstairs to the landing without offering a hand to shake. Jenna followed him to the door, and stared.

'Heavens, how exotic,' she said after a moment. 'I suppose you've seen some of Ozzy's early sketches for parts of his *Akenahten* set, though you've obviously introduced the multitude of cats yourself. Unusual – but original – for a bathroom.'

'I have seen some of his preliminary sketches,' Felix conceded, 'but his designs are more stripped down and stylised. I've already investigated a good many similar landscapes myself. Cats have been my,' he paused, 'my *leitmotif* for some time, but a change has set in and this mural is probably my affectionate farewell to feline life.'

'Good,' Jenna replied. 'Adorable creatures, but not really what I have in mind for my place. Tiffany's told you I'm interested in employing your talents? If we can come to an understanding, I wondered if you'd do some redecorating – murals even, now that I see that you can do them – in my flat. It could do with a thorough revamp.'

'Vamps, re-vamps, both always worth a second thought.' Wearing his laziest smile, Felix made the silly pun into a gentle tease. 'Come down into my little box-room bedroom next, and I'll show you what else I can do.'

Good lord, thought Tiffany – hackles rising – lighten up on the double-entendres, Felix. Unlike you, Jenna's no alley cat.

'I'd love to.' Jenna responded politely, pretending not to register Felix's skin-tingling proximity and dubious remarks. 'You lead, I'll follow. Coming, Tiff?'

Tiffany rolled her eyes and said, 'Of course.'

Tiffany had partially misjudged Felix. The tiny box-room really was a revelation. When he switched on the light in the windowless room it was transformed, and magnified into a complete world. Down one wall a hazy, reddened evening sun slid sideways towards the horizon, behind darkening trees. From the skirting board below, flowers and grasses grew tall, glimmering in the twilit foreground, and small nocturnal creatures slipped indistinctly between their stems and shadows. On the right of the descending sun, a midnight blue sky graduated upwards, almost to black, pinpricked with pale stars, and a sickle moon rode in front of a gauzy suggestion of the distant Milky Way that too soon dimmed and faded into the dark. Almost immediately the night softened into greys, and the pinks and blues of the dawn flowed across the turn of the wall, where a strong new yellow sun, edged by an aura of cloud, blazed magnificently. Below it, the foreground was still sketchy, with tall grasses still only suggested, and there seemed to be the glimmer of water.

'It's not finished,' Felix broke the impressed silence. 'You can't see the river properly yet, and there'll be geese in the reeds. I'll take the picture further round to the next wall, but probably leave the end wall fairly indistinct and cloudy so that the bedhead doesn't hide anything important. I'll be sleeping in the clouds, with the evening and night, dawn and day, spread out around me. What do you think?'

'It's fabulous,' said Tiffany.

'Spectacular,' confirmed Jenna. 'Wonderful. Tiffany didn't let on that you were this good, Felix.'

He beamed.

'She prefers me to stage my own surprises.' On this occasion he and Tiffany thought in unison and, catching each other's expression, smiled conspiratorially again.

'But why does it start with the sunset?' Jenna wanted to know. 'Most people would begin with the daybreak and move round to the night, wouldn't they?'

'I am not most people,' Felix stated honestly, 'and the space is being used as a bedroom, a place to settle at night-time, and rise with the dawn. Plus it's tiny with no windows – like a chamber in an Egyptian tomb – so it cries out to become a magical doorway to a world beyond. Besides, I like the dusk and the night. They're probably my favourite times, full of possibilities. Smells are more intense, and colours too, just before the sun leaves, have you noticed? A brief glow in the gloaming, and then the power and passion and mystery of night. Day has its charms too, and warmth – glorious and restorative – but my most creative and satisfying experiences begin with dusk. I painted most of this through two nights, for instance.'

Jenna was captivated.

'Then I'm glad I came round in the evening, not in the glare of noon,' she said. Almost as impressed by Felix's effect on Jenna as she was by the mural, Tiffany judged this a good moment to intervene.

'Talking of dusk, what about a sundowner?' she suggested. 'I can offer suitably retro pink gin, or chilled white wine or, if you need something stronger, perhaps a mint julep?'

'Er – that would be lovely. A mint julep, why not? Not too strong, though.' Jenna, recalled to her poised city life, recovered her balance of mind.

'Chilled water for me,' Felix decided, recollecting his first experience of alcohol with a slight shiver, 'though you could pop a bit of mint into that for me. I brought some back from Ozzy's wild garden – he has plenty – and there are lots of bottles of still water in the fridge.' Tiffany went to fix the drinks and to investigate what else might have found its way into her fridge.

'Still water, how appropriate,' Jenna said to this astonishingly talented and attractive man. 'Runs deep, they say.'

'None deeper. Emma already introduces me as her new spiritual adviser.'

'That's Emma, always finding a new guru and then searching for a happy medium,' she observed.

'Mediums?' He took her literally for a moment. 'Not my favourites.' A memory flickered, an unfortunate moment of brushing against someone's leg under a table, having dropped in to investigate what proved to be a neighbour's experiment with a séance. Recalling the reflex kick, the shrieks, his yowl and the general hullabaloo raised both a smile and the downy hair on his back.

'You don't believe in psychics? Tiffany may be disappointed,' Jenna admonished him. He shrugged.

'Not in a ghostly afterlife way. I'm more interested in reinventing myself several times on the ongoing journey through life. Maybe a mystical number of times to get it perfect. I've heard of the seven ages of man, but why be so stingy?' He looked piercingly at her.

'Perhaps you'd prefer nine lives, three times three, like a cat?' Jenna suggested, and Felix felt she had tuned in to his thoughts rather satisfactorily. 'Although I think most of us would need even more than nine attempts to get anywhere near perfection,' she added, without specifying whether those needing the additional practice-runs included herself, Felix noticed. He smiled down at her. Jenna was quite tall, but he had the advantage – indeed, almost all the advantages, he believed.

'Shall we follow Tiffany? I can hear the rattle of ice. The mint is calling,' he said. At the kitchen door, he indicated that Jenna should go through first. Glasses collected, the trio exchanged the scent of aromatic paint indoors, which threatened to taint their drinks, for the freshness of Tiffany's real garden, where they sat round a pretty table in the last slanting rays of the evening sunshine.

'So, Felix,' said Jenna, 'when do you think you will finish painting here? If we can fix a date, I'll get organised – pack away some bits and pieces and generally de-clutter the rooms ahead of you getting to work on them.'

'De-clutter?' Tiffany protested. 'Jenna, your place has the least clutter of any home I've seen.'

'Well, I want change. I like order, but not stasis,' Jenna replied, and sipped her drink.

'I can promise you change,' Felix said earnestly, leaning across the table towards her. 'Exactly what degree of change depends on what I find there.' Tiffany shot him a warning look and he shifted to safer ground. 'Tiffany, for instance, wanted less active walls in the more public areas of the flat, though I still might scatter the odd bird watching from a lintel, or tempting butterfly skittering across a surface, here and there, as conversation pieces. So I could be finished here by the weekend.' He set down his water glass.

That quickly! Tiffany swallowed. Is this good or bad? she wondered, and said, a little sarcastically, 'Felix is a remarkably fast worker as well as a skilful one.'

'Great. Come over on Saturday – for lunch – and have a look,' Jenna suggested. A moment passed before she added: 'You too, Tiff!' Tiffany declined, with a little shake of her head.

'I've seen your flat a thousand times, Jenna, and Saturday's usually my morning for doing as little as possible, gathering my strength. Felix prefers to work alone with his clients, anyway, don't you?' He smiled sweetly back, the pointy teeth glinting. She could almost see the ghost of whiskers twitching with anticipation.

'Tiffers, you know my ways so well,' he answered. 'Saturday, then Jenna, at one?' He nodded towards the now slowly descending sun. 'When the full glare of noon will be easing a little, though of course, I will need – eventually – to see the flat in all its times and moods of day and night, to be able to complete my ideas for it.'

'Fine. Good. I'm sure that won't be difficult to arrange,' murmured Jenna, feeling slightly dizzy now, possibly due to the mint julep, and wondered if he would expect to paint all night at her place, too – in which case, suggesting that he stay there for the duration of the project could be a necessary evil, as well as a temptation difficult to resist. She'd decide after Saturday. 'Heavens, these mint juleps are strong, Tiffany, what measure do you put in them?'

'It's a recipe I got from a surprisingly lively Boston matron, the mother of an American friend, some years ago. Good, aren't they? Very mellowing.'

'Yes. You don't drink cocktails at all, Felix? Always still water?' Jenna was sure she had seen him with a champagne flute at Emma's party.

'I prefer water, though the mint appeals.' He contemplated her glass, and the leaves in his own. 'Some types of mint do have an effect on me. It livens me up when I need it.'

'Mint does that?' she queried. 'I always thought mint was more soothing and *digestif* than enlivening. I must try it more often. What about in cooking?' She considered. 'Cold pea and mint soup, perfect for lunch on a summer day. I'll make some for Saturday, and then perhaps you'll be on sparklingly creative form all afternoon.' Jenna knew that her forays into cuisine generally turned out well. She was a precise and orderly cook when necessary, though preferred to invite people to try out newly-established restaurants said to be worth sampling, particularly if either or both parties were her clients and the foray doubled as research, or support. Friends enjoyed feeling that their opinions were part of the launch process; and she enjoyed avoiding the disorder that lingered after dinner parties at home.

'Sounds delightful,' Felix accepted. 'I'll take mine with a dash of cream stirred in.'

'Alright. Well Tiffany, Felix, I should go home and sleep off the effects of this heady concoction. I've some seriously important clients to see tomorrow morning. Until Saturday, Felix.' Jenna rose, and Felix stood up too. As she shook his hand, he leant in to brush her cheek with his. An electric surge ran through her. The stock farewell phrase "time to make my escape", faded on her lips unsaid but lingered in her mind. Out in the street, after collecting her neat briefcase and saying her farewells to Tiffany at the door, the evening suddenly seemed to have turned cooler and she shivered slightly as she walked away.

Briefly alone in the garden, Felix sat down again. He picked up Jenna's almost-empty mint julep glass and sniffed the contents. He was in a safe place, so he tried it, wrinkling his nose at what remained of the ice-diluted bourbon but, liking the taste of the mint, drained the final drops. A warm and slightly fuzzy sensation percolated through his body. He set the glass down and stretched, pleased with how things are going.

'Publicity?' Tiffany queried, returning to the garden. 'Isn't that a bit soon?'

'Nonsense. I told you, I'm building a portfolio, and what's the point of a portfolio if you don't show it to the world?' His words sounded a little muffled. He must be very tired after all that high-speed painting, she supposed, seeing nothing significant in Jenna's empty glass.

'Mmm. Well, if you need a good photographer, don't look at me,' she said. 'It's not one of my skills.'

'Don't worry. Jenna will have someone in mind.' He yawned.

'Of course she will. Another trusting soul to work your enchantments on?' Still standing, she finished her own mint julep with a flourish. Felix shrugged.

'Actually I might suggest she gets you to approach him for me, given that you can be perfectly enchanting yourself, when you want to be. You don't need any lessons from me except perhaps to be more discerning.' He was burbling a little; the mint julep had made him indiscreet again. 'Anthony, for example, is blind to your real charm and can't see beyond the surface, lovely though that is, because what he really seeks is a wife or mistress with ruthless ambitions to promote his own work. Pass him on to someone who knows how to run him, and look for a better man, who'll love you for yourself.' Felix had surprised even himself with this diversion, and rubbed his chin as a distraction. Tiffany was more amused than annoyed.

'That's not going to be you, then, Felix, on either count. Besides, you're a fine one to recommend "being yourself".' She sat down for a moment.

'Aren't they wonderful, my changed circumstances?' he said gleefully. 'I'm having such fun. And of course not me, you goose – why don't you invite Thomas round to dinner? Tell him you want his honest opinion of your new lodger, and his talents. Thomas could be quite useful to me.' Felix was plotting aloud again. 'I might tap him for advice about some things. Copyright for instance.' Tiffany stared at him.

'Copyright? Publicity, and now advice on copyright? What leaps and bounds you are making, Felix.' She was almost shocked. 'Just what are you planning? Don't you dare rip off Ozzy's designs – he'll have your guts for violin strings.' Felix recalled the curving beak of the hawk on Ozzy's doorknocker and felt the hairs on his back rise slightly, as Tiffany carried on: 'He won't take kindly to you playing games on his very lucrative patch. Anyway, as I told you before, I've no designs on Thomas, even if you do, and no idea if he knows anything at all about copyright. I've never asked him much about the legal work he does. He may not even be a very good solicitor, for all I know.'

'No, you wouldn't know,' Felix answered cruelly, the effects of mint julep, though fading, still loosening his tongue. 'You have paid far too little attention to your easy-going former lodger, whereas I – left alone in the flat with him on many evenings when you were out being led astray by Anthony's shallow charms, and the weather was too foul for me to seek my own distractions – *I* had plenty of opportunity to observe him. He does know about copyright, and about "intellectual property" law. I heard him discussing them on the phone several times.' He crossed his arms with a 'so-there' look on his face.

'Did you understand a word?' Tiffany retorted.

'Of course I did. I'm a highly intelligent and expert listener. Yes, Thomas is ideal. Frankly, I think I know him rather better, after his three month stay here, than you do after a lifetime of being related.' Again he looked challengingly at her.

'I was mostly away travelling,' she protested, 'and, if you remember, he was actually supposed to be house-and-cat-minding, so I'm glad to hear he was so conscientious.' Perhaps Felix had a point though, she thought, and ought to fish around discreetly for some sage advice. She relented. 'I suppose I could give him a call, to say that I have a new-found cousin for him to meet – and then we'll see if he'll take the bait. But don't try to skin him for too much free advice, as you still haven't a penny to pay for it, if you consulted him for real. It'll look bad.' She started to gather the empty mint julep jug and glasses back onto the small round tray, matte black and pierced with cut-out stars, which she favoured for these things.

'And, as you implied, he may not know the answers anyway,' Felix grumbled back. He was starting to get a headache, and sipped some of his chilled water. 'I'll just pick his brains a bit and decide about any professional consultations later. Given what I'll charge Jenna for transforming her habitat, I shall soon be a creature of independent means.' He folded his arms defiantly across his chest again.

'Her habitat, Felix, yes; but not her whole life. Do go a bit carefully. Please don't forget who you really are.' She meant that sidling up to Ozzy was already a risk for them, and courting Thomas might pose one, and their unfolding scheme needed Jenna most at the moment; but Felix heard only the rebuke. He bristled.

'You mean, know my place, and keep it?' He had narrowed his eyes again, and his body was tensed.

'Don't get so ruffled, you're turning out to be far more fun than many of the "real" people I know,' she said, getting up to take the tray indoors. 'I just don't see why Jenna should get tripped up by the speed of your progress. Besides, we'll need her fully on board.' Felix pounced on Tiffany's hint of concern for someone else.

'O Tiffany, so you *can* be a loyal friend!' he swiped. 'Though sometimes to the wrong people – I was thinking of Anthony!' he added quickly, seeing a flash of annoyance now in her eyes, and before she pointed out that technically it was Felix who lay in the "wrong person" category. 'Don't worry about Jenna; she's perfectly safe, I promise you. Worry about me. I'm still the one who may get badly caught out, although I am making astonishingly good progress, so far, don't you think?' He gave her the full benefit of his wide inquiring eyes, and her sense of fun bubbled up again.

'You are moving at the speed of light as usual, Felix, and maybe soon I'll be glad to lurk in the background and admire your starry ascent. Just don't leave too much fallout behind for me to have to sweep up. I do love the art,' she conceded, 'and the new food-shopping skills – with the cash that I loaned you! I investigated the fridge, and put the fish pie in the oven when I went to make the juleps. It should be ready by now.' He brightened. Supper time. Good. He picked a sprig of mint out of his water glass, and started to chew on it.

'Tiff, I love you,' he declared. 'Always have.'

'Cupboard love?' She walked away, heading indoors. 'It's a working supper. If we are still doing this thing, you have that family tree to draw. I'll ink in the names.' Felix's literacy was better than he had claimed but she wanted to be sure that nothing else unlikely was sneaked in to the record uninvited.

'I like this sort of story-telling almost as much as painting,' Felix said happily, pacing after her as the dusk, settling in behind them, heralded his most creative hours. The small dose of dilute bourbon had ebbed away – useful to know how fast it peaks and fades in his system, he thought – and the freshly-chewed sprig of mint was sharpening his imagination. He felt vividly alert, and licked his lips. Beautiful night was drawing in.

Chapter 9

Thomas accepted Tiffany's dinner invitation happily enough. He had enjoyed his long stay in her flat and, though he had seen little of her during it, was fond of his distant cousin and amused by her adventures.

'Good. Come a bit early, at about seven,' she added, preparing to end the phone call, 'for a drink and a chat before the rest of the crowd arrive? I've an interesting family update to share with you, and my latest lodger, a mural artist and decorator, might like to pick your brain too.' She squeezed her eyes shut as she said this bit, hoping it did not sound too pushy.

'Ah.' Thomas had idly wondered what had prompted the invitation. 'I'm to sing for my supper, then? No promises, but maybe I can point him – I assume it's a him? – in the right direction for professional guidance, if that helps?'

'Perfect. Bless you, Thomas. Until Saturday evening, then. Bye.' She smiled as she set her mobile back on the kitchen table.

Minx, thought Thomas, amused. I wonder what she's up to this time.

Felix's assessment of him was almost correct – Thomas was indeed observant, and practical – but regarding Tiffany, however entertained by her picaresque progress and interested in a cousinly way in her welfare, should it ever seem in any real danger, his interest stopped exactly there. Not only was she 'family', albeit at a few removes, but Thomas knew he had a history of his own, and had no desire to put at risk their long and rather charming friendship by making a move on his vagabond and self-indulgent cousin. He had long recognised that Tiffany could be an enchantress, and that he was probably no match for her kaleidoscope of wiles. He chose to remain safely out of contention throughout his tenure as her lodger and cat-and-house sitter – particularly while still licking his wounds after his unlooked-for divorce – even though technically he was a free agent then, and would soon move into a new place of his own.

Tiffany's casual taking advantage of his temporary need for a roof over his head, to sublet him a room and ask him to feed her cat during her travels, had suited them both. No fuss, no obligations on either side. Thomas had focused on his work, glad of the time and privacy to regroup his thoughts, and had grown to like the cat too.

So he arrived at the flat again on Saturday roughly on time, a few moments after seven, with a strictly family offering of scented creamy phlox and roses, whose perfumes swept the developing summer into the small flat.

'Oh, Thomas, what lovely flowers, and how wonderful they smell.' Tiffany buried her face in the frothy mass of petals. 'Come in, come in and inspect the place – it's changed a little since your stay.' As they entered the quiet sitting room, a tall stranger in a cream linen shirt, fawn chinos, and sockless tanned feet in brown leather deck shoes uncurled himself from the sofa, stood up, and extended a hand.

'I'm Felix. Good to see you.'

'Thomas,' the guest replied. 'How do you do?'

Thomas glanced quizzically at Tiffany as he shook Felix's hand; but she only smiled at him across her flowers, and said, 'Excuse me for a second? I'll just put these in water and bring in some drinks. I'll leave you two to make friends.' Thomas smiled politely at this, but reserved judgement on whether he wished to be counted as an instant friend.

'So, Felix, how do you know Tiffany? I'm a cousin, by the way,' he said. The stranger beamed.

'I know. And so, it transpires, am I! Very distant, of course.'

Thomas was surprised.

'Really?' He looked more intently at this Felix, not seeing any obvious family resemblance – but how many distant cousins do resemble each other? he reflected.

Still, there was something vaguely familiar about the man's manner. Thomas was already mentally scanning old family photographs but nothing leapt out from them yet. Felix did not let this silent scrutiny last beyond a few seconds, but forged determinedly ahead with the next part of the tale that he and Tiffany had so enjoyably concocted for tonight's purposes.

'Yes, it would seem so,' he replied, concentrating on a silken delivery of his account, 'although I grew up barely a mile from Tiffany's childhood home without any idea of the family link. It was only when a recent change of circumstances sparked my curiosity, that I discovered the connection – and then of course I felt impelled to reintroduce myself as more than a passing acquaintance. I met Emma the other night too,' he pressed on before Thomas might begin to interrogate him properly, 'when Tiffany took me to her party. But it wasn't really the place to spring a family surprise, so she's still in the dark. You weren't there?' Now he paused, watching for Thomas's reaction so far.

'Out of town,' Thomas responded non-committally before adding 'I should think Emma will be intrigued to be told that you're possibly a mystery relative. Is she coming to dinner tonight too?' He looked round for a seat and chose the armchair near the window.

'Oh yes.' Felix ignored the doubt conveyed by Thomas's use of 'possibly' and, feeling he had dealt plausibly with Emma's unawareness of his ancestral claims, let his narrative bound to its immediate goal. Too focused to sit down yet, he remained standing. 'Actually before the others arrive – and as Tiffany may have mentioned – I'd like to run something by you, Thomas, if I may. She's very generously putting me up for a bit, and of course I don't want to be seen as her latest waif and stray. In return for her hospitality, I've done a spot of redecorating for her – the changes that you'll be shown in a moment – and if she approves I'm hoping to photograph the work for my portfolio. I'm trying something new, in murals, and as I'm curious about what else I can do with the designs, I probably ought to clarify their ownership intellectually, if that's not too sudden a question to land on you?' Now he sat down, on the sofa again, and looked hopefully across at Thomas.

'So you're both the family update, and the artistic lodger?' Thomas responded warily, avoiding being ambushed into replying for the moment. To him, serving up a newcomer and then parading him and his work for inspection like a fresh entertainment was just vintage Tiffany – Anthony was another case in point – but Thomas was also considering, uncomfortably, if he too had been seen as 'the latest waif and stray' during his own stay here, when Tiffany came back into the room carrying her loaded drinks tray.

'Real martinis,' she said brightly, 'although probably not quite as good as I remember yours being, Thomas. I thought you might need one, after hearing Felix's news. Isn't it amazing? Virtually raised in the same village but no idea we were probably related!' Thomas relaxed a little.

'I haven't heard the detail yet.' He accepted the nearest martini glass from the proffered tray, and looked towards Felix again.

'Water for me. I like to keep my spirits clear, in a different sense.' Felix chose a full tumbler, still frosted with the condensation that had formed after the early crackle of just-drenched ice cubes, and Tiffany set the depleted tray down on the coffee table before settling on the sofa too, and selecting her own glass.

'A teetotal artist? Are you quite sure about being related to our lot?' Thomas delivered this like a joke, and took a trial sip of his own martini. Felix ignored Tiffany's 'I told you so' glance. He had anticipated this kind of question and prepared a useful reply.

'I believe some of our ancestors-in-common on the Sylvester side were well-known teetotallers in their day, perhaps thanks to one of them having famously married one,' he replied casually, and then paused briefly for maximum impact. 'It must be through those genes.'

'Silvester?' queried Thomas. 'So you found your connection somewhere on Great-granny Kitty's side of the family?' Kitty had been notorious for not touching alcohol, while being less of a stickler about almost everything else if family myth were true. He leaned back more comfortably in the armchair in case a long story was about to follow.

'Exactly. My Sylvesters, with a "y", seem to connect with Tiffany's Silvesters with an "i" a few generations back – both spellings were used in the past, and only diverged relatively recently.'

More literate thanks to Tiffany's help, and his own extraordinary ability to learn at near light-speed, Felix was still rather taken with this detail. He got up from the sofa and began to pad about the room, glass in hand, as he delivered his own careful concoction. 'My lot stayed in and around the same area, on farms mostly, but Tiff's moved further afield and were finally subsumed by the Joneses, after the marriage to Freddie Jones of her – and your – branch's last surviving Silvester heir who, as you rightly surmise, was Tiffany's great-grandmother Kitty.' Thomas nodded slightly. He was of course familiar with this marriage, and Felix took his wordless response as the prompt to introduce the next supporting ingredient. 'Perhaps it was a requirement that they graft Kitty's surname onto Freddie's, if she wanted to inherit any remaining Silvester assets.'

Very good, thought Tiffany, but stop there. She had warned Felix to go slowly with his delivery of the story. Thomas might be tempted to check some details later, and Sir Freddie was still of mild interest to Egyptology scholars. Someone might want to dispute any suggestion that he bagged a minor heiress to secure funds for his costly hobby and gain a grander-sounding surname to bolster his standing.

She intervened, saying chattily, 'I've no idea if it was Kitty herself, or her money, that led Freddie to keep the Silvester name within the mix, although Mum did once tell me that she and Dad explored the village when they were first house-hunting because she'd been told that her 'Granny Kitty' had mentioned a connection with the area – but Mum didn't know any more than that.'

Now to blend in more elements that Thomas will recognise, she thought, and leaned forward conspiratorially from her seat on the sofa. 'As you know, Thomas, there were only daughters for three generations in my direct family until my brother came along. Since none of them bothered to tag 'Silvester' onto a husband's name, I don't suppose there was any financial incentive – or none left – to do that.' She looked expectantly at him.

'Well, I should think any money Kitty brought with her all went on Sir Freddie's Egyptian expeditions, and anything left could have been consumed by now,' Thomas answered, accepting this part of the story for the moment but still eyeing Felix a little doubtfully. Felix had stopped by the small sideboard when Tiffany had taken up the thread, and now stood, leaning his weight comfortably against it, with his ankles crossed, listening.

'No funny little conditions unearthed at your end then, Felix, about anything remaining of Kitty's fortune having to revert back to another branch if the surname were unfortunately dropped by subsequent generations?' Thomas asked him. He knew the likely worth of Tiffany's parents' rather attractive if ramshackle house in what had steadily become, thanks to improved roads and faster rail links, a rather fashionable village for weekend cottages and was now popular with family-minded daily commuters. Thomas had asked the question lightly enough, but Felix sensed the possible trap. He had virtually set it up, after all – at Tiffany's earlier suggestion – as a useful double-bluff, and was ready.

'None that I know of,' he said, delighted, 'and of course what's spent, is spent. Tiffany and I have already been vying for the role of 'poor relation'. We'll just have to create a new Sylvester-with-a-y fortune here in the big city, perhaps through my artistic talents.'

Thomas seemed to relax. 'Good for you. I'm curious to know more. So what does your mother say about it?' He turned to Tiffany.

'Oh, they're still away at the moment,' she said airily, 'so I thought I'd surprise her with the news when they get back.' This was going really well so far, she felt. It was on discovering that her parents' trip would shortly include a familial visit to Emma's rather managing older sister Janet and husband that Tiffany had decided to refrain from mentioning Felix's existence to them yet. ('We don't need Janet butting in,' she had explained to Felix himself, 'and as Emma hardly contacts her, Janet won't hear it from her yet either.')

'I've started drawing up a family tree to show them,' Felix took up the tale again, 'and I'm hoping Tiffany can help me with more of her branch of the family's up to date details for it. I'll arrange a copy of it for you too, if you like.'

'Thank you,' said Thomas. 'I'd certainly like to see it. So what is it that you paint, Felix? You mentioned murals?' He couldn't remember evidence of artistic ability in the family, but Felix must have some non-Sylvester genes too, he supposed.

'Ah,' said Felix. 'Follow me.' He stopped leaning against the sideboard, set down his glass, and headed for the corridor and stairs.

'Very impressive,' Thomas commented at last, after silently studying the bathroom, and then was taken to inspect the transformed box-room. 'Congratulations. Quite a transformation.' Pausing in the corridor to examine a small butterfly skimming up the wall, he noticed the painted jay perched above the lintel of the sitting room door – a streak of almost turquoise feathers glinting brightly amongst its brown ones – as they all returned to their drinks. 'I feel very inadequate as a lodger now, or one of Tiffany's waifs and strays,' he observed dryly. 'I'm afraid my own contribution here was very unimaginative.'

'Ah, but you no doubt paid rent, whereas I'm a starving artist, and so must pay in kind,' Felix said pleasantly, without contradicting him. 'Now, thanks to Tiffany giving me a free hand with her walls, I've already won a new commission to paint a series of murals for one of her friends; and have more or less apprenticed myself for a season to a rather famous set designer into whose orbit she's brought me - known as Ozzy – have you met him too?' Felix was not quite sure.

'I have,' Thomas confirmed sparely. He had known Ozzy a little, through the wider family, for many years.

'So you see, I owe my new cousin a good deal,' Felix resumed, 'and if things go well, I might need some professional advice on various matters – whereas you're not in her debt at all.' Perfectly done, Felix congratulated himself, retrieving his glass from the sideboard for a sip of water, but would Thomas swallow the bait?

'Perhaps not,' Thomas said – startling Felix for a second before he realised this was still in reply to his spoken words, and not his thoughts. 'I might be able to provide some basic advice, or, and perhaps better, could refer you to other suitable sources if needed,' Thomas offered, as he sat down – on the sofa this time, next to Tiffany. 'By the way, when you said "we" would have to rebuild the Sylvester fortunes did you mean that Tiffany is involved in the next stage of your business plans?'

Felix had not prepared a reply for this, so drew on what he already thought.

'Well, that's up to her,' he said, glancing across at her. 'I'm keen to have as much promotion as possible, and introductions to potential clients, and I may well need help with the admin side of things. Artists are notoriously bad at that sort of paperwork, aren't they? I gather that Tiffany is a very good PA, and favours creative projects with a set duration so that she can wrap things up and then head off on her next lot of travels, between contracts.' He felt that this remark was a quiet masterstroke. Thomas could hardly fail to recognise the pattern Felix described. It was on her way home from her last trip that she had first captivated Anthony, seated next to her on the flight back. Tiffany travelled enough to get a cheap upgrade to business class sometimes – a useful ruse to network a little *en route* home, where she would soon be job-hunting again – and it had not taken her long into casual conversation with her new on-board neighbour to uncover that Anthony was a PR client of her friend Jenna's. Things had developed between them rather rapidly from there.

Thomas also knew that, although running someone else's business diary, contacts and basic admin came easily to Tiffany, even temporary jobs were getting harder to find these days. He supposed she might view a project with this Felix fellow as a useful stop-gap. Not that it was up to Thomas what Tiffany threw herself into, he reminded himself; but she had roped him in to meet – and perhaps help – this artist.

'Well, it all sounds very "you", Tiffany. Keep me in the picture,' he said supportively to his cousin, who was certainly looking rather pleased with herself.

'I will,' she said.

'Funny that we never met as teenagers, in the village pub,' Thomas suddenly commented to Felix.

'We must have rubbed shoulders in there at some point,' Felix busked in reply, 'although I daresay we might both have looked a bit different at the time.' Tiffany gave him another warning look, just as the doorbell rang.

'Felix, why don't you get the door,' she instructed firmly. 'I need to check the cooking again.' Keen to steer him away from unrehearsed elaborations that might dent the success so far of their cover story, she ushered him briskly ahead of her into the hallway.

Thomas interpreted this bustle as a reassuring glimpse of Tiffany already in client-management mode. Briefly alone in the sitting room, he decided to quit the sofa for the better observation point of the armchair by the window.

Felix opened the front door of the building with a flourish.

'You're early,' he greeted Jenna, who looked glorious in the early evening light that burnished her russet hair. 'I've barely started consulting my new legal friend.'

'Couldn't stay away for a moment more,' she said calmly, strolling across the threshold. 'Surely you don't need legal advice to paint my murals, do you?'

'I have grander plans too, but the details can wait. The introduction alone – a re-introduction really – is good enough for now. So in you come.' He brushed her cheek with his, and followed her into the flat. 'Tiff is in the kitchen doing something essential to our supper, the good Thomas is drinking martinis in the sitting room and I have just been appointed doorman, although maybe I can mix you a drink as well.'

'Lovely, but since you don't drink, I'm not sure of those results,' she said, smiling, savouring the frisson from his greeting that still flowed through her as she walked along the corridor towards the sitting room.

'You're right,' he said. As they entered, Thomas rose to his feet. 'Thomas here, though, mixes a mean martini according to Tiffany,' Felix advised her. 'You remember Thomas? He lived here too for a while.'

'Hello,' said Jenna. 'No, we never met – I'm not sure why. I'm Jenna.' As they shook hands, Tiffany's return interrupted Thomas's appreciation of Jenna's cool loveliness.

'You never met because I was away most of the time that Thomas was here, so you had no excuse to come round and disturb my unsuspecting cousin.' Tiffany explained. 'Jenna, darling, welcome. What would you like to drink?'

'Felix mentioned martinis. That would be lovely.' The bell rang again.

'I'll make this batch,' Thomas volunteered, setting off for the kitchen to practise his own seductive arts as Tiffany went to open the door herself this time. Left together in the living room, Felix and Jenna smiled at each other.

'Have you told her yet?' Jenna asked, settling onto the sofa.

'Not yet, but Tiffany won't be at all surprised. She may even be relieved to get rid of me so promptly.' Felix sat next to her.

'I can't think why,' she teased. 'I suppose she needs to turf you out before Anthony returns. I don't imagine he'll be too pleased to find a hypnotically handsome artist installed in her home the moment his back was turned.'

Felix grinned.

'Not due back for a while, though is he? Or do you know more?' He felt a twitch in the hairs above his upper lip, as if tuning in to something in her voice or manner.

'Doesn't she know? He's coming back early after all,' Jenna replied. 'Perhaps he wants it to be a surprise. Some of his partners here are getting a bit nervous about the Egyptian project in the current climate, and he's on his way back to give them a pep talk – reporting from the front line, so to speak.'

'Right,' murmured Felix 'and how come you know far more about what he's up to, than she does? Anything going on that I should know about?' Jenna laughed and patted him reassuringly on the knee. He was not sure that he liked it. I'm not a house-pet, Jenna, he wanted to say, but thought the better of it.

'No, though Anthony's very smooth when he wants to be,' she was saying, 'and of course I'm not above flattering him a little. I schmooze all my clients, in conversation, before getting down to the difficult tasks. Didn't you know that he's one of my PR clients?' she asked, registering and misreading Felix's discomfort. 'But yes, clever you, I'm not convinced either that he's the right man for our Tiffany – and that is as far as any ulterior motives of mine go! It's part of my job to keep up to date with his business activities, and he phoned me at work yesterday from Cairo to brief me in confidence about how things are looking there just now. He didn't mention Tiffany, and I assumed she would know his plans. Happy now? Or are you perhaps just a teeny bit jealous of him?' she teased. Felix leaned back into the sofa.

'Jealous of Tiffany, about to be blessed by his early return, or of his calling you? Of course not,' he said a little sharply. Having kept his good humour throughout the task of capturing Thomas's goodwill, he could not resist the relief of a little sideswipe at someone now, but instantly regretted it. Jenna suddenly seemed to close up like a lotus blossom at dusk as the coolness of night air descends.

'Of both, naturally,' she said coolly, her pose on the sofa suddenly becoming more formal, as she reverted from coquettishness to her customary *sang-froid*. 'Oh, that does look wonderful,' she added, turning a full and encouraging smile on Thomas, who was entering the room with the replenished drinks tray, loaded with a silvery cocktail shaker frosted with condensation and five luminous, already full, martini glasses. He came over to the sofa so that she could take one from the tray, before he set it down on the low coffee table.

'Thank you,' she continued, taking an exploratory sip and glancing gratefully at Thomas over the rim of the glass, while ignoring Felix. 'Perfect.' She too could toy with her prey.

Tiffany, returning with Emma in tow, failed to notice the sudden tension on the sofa, and happily quipped: 'Perfect timing, too – Emma, have a just-shaken martini. Now all we need is Ozzy, who's always last. He likes to sweep in once everyone else has arrived,' she explained – to Thomas for no evident reason – 'and manages it so well, that I suspect him of lurking behind hedges and in doorways until he's confident that all his fellow guests are inside, and well into their first drink, ready for his appearance.'

Felix found this description of Ozzy unsettling, partly because it had so often been his own *modus operandi*. He looked questioningly at Tiffany, but she was busy selecting a martini for Emma from the tray, unaware of how the soft golden hairs on Felix's skin had begun to prickle with unease.

'Well, I'm afraid I'm already on my second one,' Thomas was saying. He kissed Emma carefully on the cheek. 'Hello, coz. Looking very good.' Emma smiled charmingly back. She liked her ruggedly handsome, six-foot-something distant cousin – so obviously a rower or rugger player in his student days, and still a weekend sportsman. When Thomas's marriage had folded she had wondered whether to kindle a great romance with him, and had indeed led him on a little before deciding that he was too predictable and reliable, too solidly nice, too understated in manner, and so had withdrawn her attentions.

Thomas had seemed slightly baffled, both by her flirting with him and then by her cooling off, but she assumed from his greeting tonight that there were no hard feelings. It had never got beyond a handful of candlelit suppers out and about, after all; which she had initiated under the merry guise of good practice for him to get him back into circulation. Now she hoped that he had always believed this myth, and that her flirtatious manner then was simply in the spirit of cousinly support, in the early days of his unplanned return to bachelorhood. She certainly was not going to refer to it now; and tonight she was again sure that holding back had been the right decision on her part. (He's certainly not what I am after now – not enough naked ambition for the new me.) Nevertheless, she accepted his greeting with an alluring politeness. Felix after all was watching and it was satisfying to remind him, too, of her own charm, by directing it at another.

'We won't tell Ozzy about the second drink,' Jenna said to Thomas. 'The stage is set for him, and we'll have to amuse ourselves until he arrives. So, Thomas, tell us, why did Tiffany – and apparently you, Emma, sly puss – keep you under wraps to themselves, hidden away in a box-room for months, whereas Felix, who has only just arrived, is already allowed to try to sweep the rest of us off our feet?'

Jenna was mocking Felix, still getting her quiet revenge, but of course he was flattered. Thomas smiled back at Jenna a little ruefully. It might have been nice to have met her sooner, with less obvious competition around. With the sofa occupied by her and Felix, Thomas had remained standing, leaving the armchair for Emma. Tiffany was leaning against the little sideboard now, studying her guests.

'I was weighed down with work,' Thomas answered, leaving out his chief reason for preferring a period of retreat. 'We lawyers can be a rather dull bunch sometimes.' (Exactly, thought Emma, as she accepted the available armchair). 'Tiffany wasn't here to drag me out to play, and when she did come back from her travels to reclaim her home, it was with Anthony newly in tow, so she was rather preoccupied with her own affairs,' he added.

Tiffany stuck her tongue out at him. Emma, slightly put out that her cousinly socialising was left out of this account, decided that remonstrating might touch a painful nerve for Thomas after all. She crossed her neat ankles, and studied her drink for a moment instead.

'Oh, yes, we hardly saw you for a while, Tiffany, after your return,' agreed Jenna, glancing at her and still ignoring Felix, despite his proximity. 'We were all "out of sight and out of mind" then.' She sipped her drink again. 'Nothing dull about these martinis you've mixed, though, Thomas. Do you do everything this well?'

Astonished, Emma looked at Thomas to gauge what new quality she has missed that might make the usually impregnable Jenna flirt with him so openly, as Jenna smoothly continued: 'If Ozzy doesn't get his act together soon, all of us will be on our second or third of these before he joins in.'

She really was looking very lovely, Emma noticed, and Thomas seemed temporarily speechless. Clearly he, too, was not sure why Jenna was suddenly flirting with him. Poor Thomas, Emma thought, he's still a bit slow on the uptake.

Felix, however, confidently believed himself to be the true target of Jenna's manner with Thomas, and felt very smug. Thomas registered this air, and was suddenly amused. So that's how it is. They probably deserve each other, he thought. He had learnt to read signals faster and better since his marriage's collapse, and his near-lapse into a romantic tenderness towards Emma. He had worried for a little while afterwards whether he had hurt Emma's feelings when, though briefly tempted, he had failed to respond positively enough – after which she had withdrawn – but then his perspective had shifted. I knew I was on the rebound, he thought again now, and thank goodness she had the sense to back out before anything got awkward. He took another drink of his second martini and felt on good form.

As if cued by Jenna's remark, the doorbell rang for a third and final time, breaking the momentary silence through which everyone's thoughts had flowed.

'The ego has landed,' murmured Emma, to everyone's surprise and amusement. As her uncle made his entrance, heralded by a smiling Tiffany, ripples of laughter were still dancing in everyone's eyes and expressions.

'Greetings, my dears, how happy everyone looks. I hope it's because you're glad to see me at last,' Ozzy inquired.

'We are,' said Felix quickly. 'Thomas has been plying these people liberally with the contents of Tiffany's cocktail cupboard, and we need you to distract them from his machinations.'

'As your very own *deus ex machina*? Very much *ex machina*, in fact, as my wretched chariot is playing up and I had to come by cab, although if the thunderclouds gathering are anything to go by a boat might be in order

for the return trip. Either of which happily means, and although Felix here will disapprove, I can accept a strong libation from that cocktail shaker and judge for myself how skilful Thomas's machinations really are. Thank you.'
Ozzy took the glass that Thomas promptly held out to him, and briefly inhaled its atmosphere. He sipped, then paused, eyes closed for a second. 'Divine,' he intoned magisterially.

Ozzy's opening performance thus completed, and his blessing apparently given, Tiffany spoke: 'Bravo. Food should be ready in about fifteen minutes and now that we're all here, why don't we go into the garden before it deluges, as it's so pretty at the moment, and on the way those of you who haven't yet seen Felix's murals can pause to admire his work.'

'Excellent,' Ozzy responded. 'I've been looking forward to satisfying my curiosity about those.' He led the way out of the room. 'Where do we begin? Is this bold jay out here above the door your work? Very lifelike. Is there more like this?'

'Let me show you,' Felix said.

'By the way, Tiffany,' asked Thomas as they followed, 'where's that splendid cat of yours? Has he made himself scarce tonight?'

'Yes indeed,' called Ozzy from the hallway. 'What has become of the handsome beast?' Felix turned to grin at Tiffany. She stared insouciantly back. Thanks to Jenna's recent comments at the wine bar, she had an answer primed.

'The smell of paint seems to have gone to his head. Or do I mean, got up his nose? Anyway, he's being a bit unreliable at the moment.'

'Catty,' whispered Felix, as she slipped passed him on her way to the garden.

'I love you too,' she hissed back. It was an exchange that Thomas missed, contemplating Jenna's slender back as she went gracefully ahead of him, but Emma did overhear it and, though puzzled, was determined not to be outshone. She drew herself up and concentrated on moving confidently through the hall, only partially taking in the skill of the mural that Felix was now opening the box-room door to show to a thoughtful Ozzy. Emma intended to use the evening to try out her own new cocktail: a blend combining a more sophisticated version of her outward charm, with a pure inner ruthlessness. She felt that Felix, and probably Ozzy too, would appreciate it, and while neither man was her ultimate target – he was yet to be confirmed – they were both excellent to rehearse upon. Felix might drop more of his sly hints on the best measures to perfect the mix, and Ozzy would no doubt have his own peculiar brand of avuncular advice to offer on presentation and effective delivery. Variously inspired, each of the guests now passed into the garden before the gathering rain could break. Two courting pigeons stopped billing and cooing on the lawn, and flew off.

'Ancient Egyptians used to keep some pigeons as pets,' Ozzy observed, watching their flight, 'but mostly to eat them.'

'Really?' Emma said, 'as pets?' Ozzy nodded.

'There are tomb paintings of circular pigeon houses, and people with tamed birds.'

'Fascinating. I never pictured the pharaohs as pigeon-fanciers,' Thomas remarked.

The evening sunshine, reaching them between opposing banks of portentous dark blue-grey cloud, intensified all the colours of the garden. Before there could be any more talk of pigeons – or pharaohs – Tiffany turned to her flock of guests, clustered on the small lawn, and announced: 'I'm so glad you could all be here this evening. Please raise your glasses. Felix and I have exciting news to share with you.'

They all looked astonished, each one for a different reason.

Chapter 10

Tiffany's announcement that she and Felix had news startled everyone else in the garden. Jenna froze; what was this? Felix had given no hint of any engagement to Tiffany. Emma, after the exchange she had just overheard in the corridor, was agog. Even Ozzy looked intrigued. Of the guests, only Thomas had an idea of what was coming. Trust Tiffany to mislead for maximum dramatic effect. Little minx, he thought, amused again.

'Felix is much more to me than a childhood acquaintance,' Tiffany declaimed. Jenna's eyes widened as she heard that. 'And I have to confess that we have been keeping something quite amazing from most of you.' As Tiffany paused for effect, Emma was almost dizzy with suspense.

'He is in fact – one of us! Well, one of most of us here tonight. May I present my recently rediscovered, long-lost cousin Felix Sylvester – muralist, up-and-coming socialite and adventurer.' Tiffany ushered him forwards a little. Felix made his mock bow and stepped back again. Jenna breathed out with a quiet relief which, mixed with annoyance at Tiffany's tricksy way of delivering this information, also left her no scope for doubting its veracity. Emma just gaped at Felix, Ozzy chuckled, and Thomas applauded.

'Bravo, Tiffany. Won't you tell us a bit more?' he prompted. On this cue, she and Felix plunged into the explanations that they had earlier rehearsed on Thomas. The excitement and speculation about Sylvesters and Silvesters, old Sir Freddie and Kitty, whether a mystery inheritance was first secured and then spent, and how much it might have been, carried them indoors and continued over supper. How many excavations was it, that Freddie – or Kitty – apparently funded? Thomas speculated. What was it that they discovered, and where is it now? Emma inquired. How big was his team – did Kitty really go on all the digs too? Jenna asked.

'I believe so,' said Ozzy without offering any detail, while Tiffany silently wondered again where it was that the pair first met. The conversation took them through two simple courses until, by pudding and coffee, the subject finally turned to Felix's own interest in exploring Egyptian themes in his new murals. Ozzy looked across the kitchen table at him.

'So what are your plans ahead?' He had not yet crystallised his own ideas about helping Felix.

Felix seized the opportunity.

'I'm keen to develop my mural techniques in a range of subjects, including any opportunities that you're generous enough to share after our exploratory chat the other day, Ozzy. Jenna here, as you know, has already bravely invited me to revitalise her flat next, and so I'll take up my brushes and set to work there from tomorrow morning. As you can see, I've finished my work here.' He waited for a reaction. It was Tiffany's turn to feel a little surprised. Starting the work at Jenna's tomorrow? That's really fast footwork, she thought, but smiled her assent as if already fully in the picture, giving nothing away, or so she believed. Ozzy, watching her closely, smiled too.

'Clearly not a fellow to let the grass grow under your feet,' he remarked. 'I wish you joy, Jenna, and what, dear Tiffany, do you think of his prospects? I assume your chief role will be enabling some sort of business plan? I know your talents.'

She kept her tone bright.

'I think more murals are a splendid idea. You've seen some of the marvels he's done here, and Jenna's place has so much more wall space to work on. With photographs of the artworks here, and whatever he does there, he should have the makings of a useful portfolio to show to a few handpicked potential clients.' She looked directly at Ozzy.

'The makings, as you say. Two examples are not really enough.' Ozzy made a decision. 'Well, if I can nudge you towards some potential customers for murals, let me know when you've finished at Jenna's, and I'll consider what introductions might be conjured up for you.' Felix inclined his head cautiously. Although the success and excitement of the evening's talk and planning now began to make him feel a little skittish, Ozzy's choice of words once again troubled him a little.

'That's most kind of you,' he accepted graciously. 'All introductions gratefully received, Maestro,' he continued, 'and I'll be sure to hone my skills a little more before you lend your name too much to my cause.'

Ozzy set down his coffee cup.

'Well it probably won't be in my name, of course,' he said calmly, 'but blood is thicker than water, I suppose, so when you are fully up to scratch I might put in a good word for you as a talented distant cousin, or nephew at several removes, or whatever it is that you are.'

Felix was about to correct Ozzy genealogically, given that the set designer was a Jones, but not a Silvester link, but then stopped himself. If there is some other twist in the family history that Ozzy knows, 'Felix Sylvester' surely would not have overlooked it in his supposedly assiduous recent researches.

'Handsome of you, Ozzy,' he said instead. 'Nepotism, splendid. I hardly know what to say.'

Say nothing, Tiffany thought. Struck by a similar concern and uneasy about that 'up to scratch' phrase again, she kicked him sharply under the table. Don't bring in anything more than we've already invented, the blow said.

'Very extended family, surely, Ozzy, and only via Sir Freddie's marriage,' Emma had already interrupted, puzzled and quickly asserting precedent over any rival claims to Ozzy's avuncular goodwill. 'You're my uncle by blood, but only related to Tiffany very distantly, and that's still all through the Jones side, isn't it, not the Silvesters?'

'Correct, Emma. Tiffany's great-grandfather Sir Freddie Jones and my grandfather were brothers,' Ozzy replied. 'As for my connection with you, I do indeed believe myself to be your uncle, and also your second cousin once-removed, all on the Jones side.'

She looked at him more intently.

'Believe? I never thought there was any doubt.' She pushed aside the small bunch of grapes on her plate, losing her appetite for them.

'Ah.' He put his fingertips together. 'Tiffany is not the only one with surprises to spring upon us. I may be your mother's older half-brother, or I may be only her step-brother.' Emma stared hard at him, feeling a quiet chill spread through her.

'What exactly are you saying, Ozzy?'

He had everyone's attention now, and let it deepen into intrigued silence for a few more seconds before clearing his throat, and beginning to explain.

'Did you not know, Emma, that your grandmother Natalia and my father Jeb, who were first cousins, had each been married to someone else before their own love match?' Emma shook her head. 'So your mother, Iris, has never mentioned that she was actually formally adopted by my father Jeb, after he married Nattie?' Emma shook her head again, worried. Who might that really make me? she was wondering. Not Emma Jones Brown at all? Ozzy leant forward towards her.

'Your grandmother Nattie was always very close to her somewhat older cousin Jeb Jones from girlhood, and was even a bridesmaid at his first wedding to my waif-like mother April, just before the start of World War Two. Sadly April became increasingly agoraphobic after my arrival for some reason, and apparently Jeb took to chaperoning lively cousin Nattie around town instead, no doubt as a bit of light relief during his brief leaves from the front. Then Nattie suddenly got engaged to a broodingly handsome young NCO by the name of Tod, and married him almost overnight before he too went back to the front. To the desert war, I believe.' Emma's head began to spin as Ozzy spoke on. Without realising it, she began to shred the small piece of bread roll that still lay beside her plate.

'Your mother Iris was apparently the fruit of that whirlwind marriage, a honeymoon child, born a good month prematurely; so perhaps in hastily marrying her, Tod was just doing the decent thing by his young love,' Ozzy suggested.

Emma, nonplussed, felt furious with Ozzy for suddenly coming up with all this in front of Tiffany and her friends. He just can't bear not to be the main focus of attention, she thought coldly.

'I have never heard anything about this Tod person before,' she said, brushing the breadcrumbs from her lap, as if dismissing his revelation with them. 'I always understood that Grandpa Jeb was my mother's father.' Thomas, beside her, put a consoling or perhaps cautioning, hand on her arm but Emma barely registered. It was not pity she wanted, but validation of who she really was.

'Hear me out,' Ozzy answered her. 'It was some acid remarks by my late mother's aunt that drew my own attention, as a young man, to that very likelihood. April died when I was still tiny,' he added. 'I have very hazy memories of her, if memories they are.'

'I'm sorry,' Thomas interrupted, feeling little sympathy for the young Ozzy given how cavalierly the older one was using this material, 'but I'm starting to get confused about who's who in this story.'

'My very point, but probably not in the way that you mean it,' Ozzy answered. 'Consider this: Nattie marries Tod in haste one leave, before he returns to the front, and produces Iris eight months later. Tod, against the odds perhaps, survives. Oh, and my ailing mother expires shortly before Iris is born, making Jeb a widower by the time Tod comes home.'

'This is a cynical story,' says Thomas, suspecting what would come next.

'Quite so. According to my great aunt, there is then a huge row and Tod sues Nattie for divorce, claiming the child Iris is not even his. Jeb, a widower with a small child – me – either gallantly rescues his cousin Nattie and her babe from the scandal, or simply confirms it by marrying her himself and later formally adopting my new step-sister Iris. So perhaps Tod was right, and Iris really is my half-sister.'

'So why tell us all this now?' asked Jenna, unmoved, not being a family member affected by these permutations. 'What's the point?' Thomas privately agreed with her.

'My point is that there can be all sorts of versions of family history,' Ozzy said. 'We simply have to choose which one to believe, to suit ourselves.' He looked sideways at Emma. Felix and Tiffany sat very still, and silent.

'And what does my mother believe?' Emma demanded. Ozzy chuckled drily, always an unsettling sound.

'Iris doesn't give a damn either way.' That sounds like Mother, Emma thought, and then suddenly felt liberated, free to be whomever she likes – Jeb's grandchild, or the mysterious and absent Tod's. Since no-one seemed to know much about Tod, his bloodline might have allowed her limitless possibilities. She wanted no details about him yet, in case those pinned her down too much, and too soon, but Thomas broke in again.

'What became of the unlucky Tod?' he asked, now feeling very much on his side.

'Stormed off back to the desert, I believe,' Ozzy said, 'saying there was nothing for him here.'

That will do nicely for now, Emma decided, but since embracing Tod's genes to assist her reinvention of herself might also mean losing Ozzy's largesse as an uncle by blood, it seemed politic to inquire no further tonight – and she was not pleased when Jenna suddenly suggested: 'Well, Ozzy, you and Iris could do a DNA test nowadays, if she ever wants to know which one was her father. That would clarify whether or not you and Iris are half-siblings.'

Emma frowned and was relieved to hear her uncle – or step-uncle – reply: 'As it doesn't make a great difference to us either way now, I doubt if there's any need to go to the trouble and cost.' Felix opened his mouth to agree with Ozzy, but then stopped, in case his voice sparked the idea in someone else of DNA testing the supposed Sylvester/Silvester link too. He therefore continued to sit quietly and ponder why Ozzy did not want his own genes tested. Although Felix also kept this puzzle to himself, Ozzy had noted the tiny false start.

'Emotional cost, or financial?' Jenna persisted, almost forensically. Finding Ozzy's show-stealing performance rather tiresome, she could not resist providing a dose of practical reality, but now Ozzy himself decided to close the subject.

'I'd say that any emotional cost is long spent, rather like Kitty's possible inheritance, if it ever existed – and probably best left that way,' he answered, still watching Felix, who began to feign interest in passing the jug of water around the table. Aha, Felix was thinking, so perhaps there are things to do with Kitty that Ozzy prefers to gloss over, and all this Tod stuff is just his way of creating a diversion. Yet he sensed that Ozzy never did anything without purpose.

Jenna accepted Felix's offer to refill her glass with water. She had felt increasingly alienated by this suddenly confessional evening. Neither a relation – she fervently hoped – nor fond of melodramatic stories (the news of Felix's imminent move to her place had been placed skilfully and easily, she felt), it was time to slip off home, with or without him tonight. Felix could follow later or, indeed, tomorrow. Just as she was about to thank Tiffany and start her polite 'goodbyes' there was a muffled bang, like a front door slamming in the communal hallway, and then the unmistakable sound of the flat's own door being unlocked. They all looked up towards the corridor as someone tall strode into the flat, dropped a fat holdall on the floor, and called out loudly: 'Tiff! Are you here?'

Anthony had just walked in.

Damn, Jenna thought, I shall have to stay a few more minutes now. I forgot to warn Tiffany during supper that he could be on his way back tonight. As Anthony strode into the kitchen, almost everyone at the table turned to look at Tiffany, who seemed just as astonished. Felix glanced across to Jenna, who shrugged slightly, another tiny movement observed by Ozzy.

Tiffany rose reluctantly to her feet, answering: 'Anthony – you're already back? You might have called me. We're having a supper party—'

'So I see,' he replied, brandishing a duty-free bottle of brandy. 'While the cat's away the mice will play, eh?' On the heels of Ozzy's story, the phrase caused a faintly conspiratorial frisson, and some suppressed smiles, around the table. Anthony planted a perfunctory kiss on Tiffany's cheek. 'What's so funny? Mind if I join you? It's been a lousy journey. I'd kill for a drink, Tiff. May I?' He helped himself to a glass from the cupboard and opened the brandy bottle. 'This should do the trick. Good evening, Jenna, Emma, Ozzy, Thomas – almost a family gathering I see – and…?' He looked expectantly at Felix, waiting for an introduction but, receiving only an unenthusiastic stare, turned instead to Tiffany with a questioning and not altogether friendly look.

He had intended to surprise her, and even to apologise for standing her up last week at such short notice due to the urgent need to check on his Egyptian project, given the troubles now besetting the entire region. She had sounded genuinely worried on the phone about his being there, but here she was happily entertaining people, including a puzzling new face. Or perhaps the family have rallied round to cheer her up? The stranger must be something to do with Jenna. Anthony knew that he should have phoned Tiff back, to reassure her, and say that he was on his way. It could be a bit awkward if Jenna admitted just now that she already knew of his imminent return. Professional distance is all very well, he thought, but it would have been helpful if his own PR adviser had mentioned earlier that she knew there was a supper party planned here for this evening, and was herself coming with a guest.

'This,' Tiffany responded coolly and not entirely helpfully to his query, 'is Felix, from my childhood village. He's been painting the walls for me all week, and now he is about to tackle Jenna's.' She sat down without suggesting that Anthony do so too, and behind closed lips she curled her tongue back against her upper palate as she often did when withholding the whole truth. Felix continued to stare unblinkingly at Anthony, who mentally shifted the silent stranger from a social connection to a trade contact. Perhaps the fellow was feeling a bit out of place in Tiffany's city coterie. He certainly seemed struck dumb.

'A trusted family decorator?' Anthony surmised, setting the brandy bottle on the table near Tiffany. 'Excellent. Called upon to help to even up the numbers at the supper table, I see. Good for you. Pleasure to meet you, er, Felix. Well, now I'm here too.' He had not meant to sound condescending or graceless, and looked around awkwardly for a seat. 'Maybe we can chat professionally sometime,' he added. It never hurt to know an efficient decorator, for smaller projects, and a degree of civility was sensible if nothing else.

Felix bared his teeth in what Anthony assumed was a self-effacing smile of thanks. Tiffany rolled her eyes, poured a stiff brandy into her empty wine glass from his bottle since Anthony had plonked it so close to her, and decided that really the only way to cope now was to sit back and just enjoy whatever happened next.

Chapter 11

'Felix is far more than a decorator,' Emma said to Anthony, sliding to one side of her chair to let him squeeze onto the other edge, since Tiffany showed no sign of either making space herself, nor finding a chair for him at the supper table. Anthony registered something different tonight about Emma. What was it? Greater definition, somehow. Blonder, possibly? He had not noticed before, in their admittedly brief acquaintance, just how bright blue her eyes are. He hesitated, but as Tiffany, despite already drinking a glass of his brandy, still made no move to offer him a seat with her, he perched almost gratefully beside Emma.

'Felix paints murals,' Emma explained. Anthony is looking rather gorgeous this evening, she thought, in a grimly handsome, travel-weary way, back from a political hotspot and perhaps with the knowledge of some new commission or other in those steel-grey eyes. She smiled, and gave him the full benefit of her own confident new persona. 'You'll be able to give him a few tips, Anthony – haven't you just been in Egypt? Felix apparently plans an ancient Egyptian theme for Jenna's flat, and Ozzy is in the midst of designs for an opera that's set in that period, so your return tonight from the country itself seems rather well-timed. How is your project there?'

'Ah.' At least someone was showing an interest in his work. He set down his glass. 'It's still happening, Emma, thank you for asking. I'm sure Ozzy has already done his homework very thoroughly and can tell Felix far more about the deep history side of things than I can. Modern Egyptians are a bit ambivalent about the ancient, pagan past. It's a mixed blessing, though it does bring tourist dollars. Less so at the moment, of course.' The discomfort Anthony had felt, was subsiding. He settled more comfortably on the available half of her chair. 'But I won't drone on about all that tonight. So how are you, Emma? Looking good, I see. Nice dress,' he added. Perhaps its almost peacock-blue colour was what had brought out the startling blueness of her eyes tonight. The dress looked rather well cut, too, he noticed. Emma was evidently pleased with the compliment.

'Coffee, Anthony?' Tiffany interrupted this exchange. 'Or there's some pudding left if you're hungry?' Her tone was still cool, disinterested. He looked towards her again to reply. Her dark hair with its auburn glints had been neatly bobbed again since he last saw her, he realised, and her pale, rather ivory skin seemed to glow with reflected light. Like the moon, he unexpectedly found himself thinking, and being just as cold and distant to him this evening.

'No; no coffee thanks,' he said. 'Might have another brandy in a minute. It's been a "dry" trip – and with clients who don't indulge also flying back on the same plane, I felt obliged to stay off the miniatures as well. You look rather wan, Tiffany. Has it been a difficult week?' He ought to be more solicitous, he supposed.

'You could say that,' she replied unhelpfully, and took another sip of brandy. How on earth am I going to get rid of him this evening? she wondered. Diplomatic flu? He already thinks I'm pale, so that might work. She breathed in quietly and closed her eyes for a moment, then spluttered a little, faking a controlled sneeze. 'Sorry! I hope I'm not coming down with something catching.' She glanced at Felix for help; but he was calculatedly studying Emma and Anthony.

'Probably too much exposure to paint fumes,' Thomas suggested mischievously. He did not fancy hearing the tale of the newly discovered Sylvester cousinhood for a third time this evening, and took charge of the conversation's direction. 'So, Felix, tell us a bit more about what you do have in mind for Jenna's place.' Thomas's curiosity extended – only mildly, he told himself – beyond Felix's artistic intentions. Felix was more than happy to snub Anthony.

'I'm glad you ask, Thomas. We had an interesting chat about that earlier today. Something with an exotic but subtle feel, with – as Emma has already divined – a touch of ancient Egypt. A colour palette of pale blues and golds, with touches of desert rose.' Sensing mixed motives behind Thomas's question, Felix also could not resist teasing him a little bit. Once one person annoyed him, he found it hard to retract his claws fully before turning to his next interlocutor, however blameless. 'Something that compliments Jenna's cool mystery,' he continued, 'perhaps channelling some of the elegance of Nefertiti, to create a retreat – or when she prefers, a stage – fit for such loveliness. What do you think?'

'It sounds charming.' Thomas's amused smile was aimed at Jenna. She found that she liked his restrained attention; and as for Felix's flattery, who could object to being bracketed with Nefertiti's legendary beauty?

'Thank you,' she said to both of them. 'I've taken the risk of putting myself entirely in Felix's hands, artistically.'

'You're brave,' Emma interrupted, suddenly not wanting Anthony to be drawn into admiring Jenna too. 'I mean, Felix is being very gallant, but what if he's just doing what suits his portfolio? You might get quite the wrong setting. I think the customer should have more say. How do you work with your clients on their building projects, Anthony?'

Emma turned to him inquiringly. In the moment's startled silence that followed the snub she had just dealt to Jenna, Felix, and to some extent Thomas, Felix leapt to his own and Jenna's defence before Anthony could answer.

'Perhaps my own skill lies precisely in gauging what suits and enhances my clients' inner strengths, before they fully know how to voice it themselves,' Felix said gruffly.

'Yes. That's it!' Tiffany exclaimed, partly to defuse things a little. 'Your USP, Felix – your unique selling point. We can definitely use that concept for your murals. Your unerring ability to tune into and release a client's spirit. I've learnt a bit from Anthony about knowing what's wanted better than the client does,' she added mischievously, keeping her facial expression deadpan.

'W-L-A,' murmured Felix. 'My old mantra: watch, learn, act. Emma remembers, don't you, Emma?' he added, having usefully just remembered it himself. 'I observe my client well, and then I act.' He gave her a triumphant look.

'In that case, I can probably risk Felix's choice of setting,' Jenna intervened quickly, before any fur and feathers could begin to fly, outwardly addressing her reply to Emma. 'Perhaps I'll grow into its challenge.' She was smiling, but skilfully directing the focus back to her own domestic project before Anthony – her own client, after all – reacted poorly to Tiffany's unkind jibe. 'I'll be a test case. I can always paint it out,' Jenna added.

Felix narrowed his eyes at that idea but accepted that Jenna was, for now, in tactical control. 'So be it,' he said, and folded his arms.

Thomas also quietly admired Jenna's skill at steering the conversation into more manageable waters.

Ozzy was enjoying it all enormously.

'See how ruthless you all are, in your own ways,' he commented. 'Be careful Jenna, maybe Felix will sue if you paint out the originals of his early work – or you might risk losing a future fortune if you obliterate them and then he turns out to be a latter-day da Vinci, or a Rafael. Murals are a feature. They are not intended to be as ephemeral as my stage sets.' Felix liked this, and relaxed his shoulders a little.

Jenna graciously conceded the point.

'I promise to consult Thomas on any such legalities, then, before doing anything so drastic,' she replied lightly, 'and your set designs are not ephemera, Ozzy. We all know that they're always being reproduced in glossy books, and kept safely in storage to be wheeled out again for future revivals of marvellous productions. I suspect you of false modesty.'

Anthony laughed at that, almost ruining Jenna's emollience, and earning a sharp look from Ozzy that he failed to understand.

'Quite the contrary; Ozzy is just shameless,' Emma chimed in brightly. 'Look at that yarn he spun us this evening – casting outrageous doubt on my grandparents' conduct. Now the calumny is out there, it probably won't ever go away completely.' She pretended to frown at her non-uncle uncle.

'Dear Emma, it was first put "out there" – and then buried – by others, several decades ago,' Ozzy pointed out to her. 'It could go underground again. You've missed a revelatory evening, Anthony, which no doubt Tiffany will bring you up to speed on later. Are you back for long, this time?'

Anthony looked slightly uncomfortable, and answered the second point. 'No, not very long. I need to brief my team here about the political situation in Cairo, and how we stand financially, and to discuss a few technical details – and then it's probably politic to put in an appearance back there, to keep in touch with all the players on the ground. You know the sort of thing. But I hope to keep any trips to just brief visits while things are so volatile.' He glanced at Tiffany, still half-expecting her to protest again about his intended absences. He wished they would all go home now, so that he could explain things to her alone.

'Only brief trips?' she said levelly. He took this calm response as concerned relief.

'Yes, I think that's best at present. Please don't worry. I wasn't expecting to get back so soon this time, as you know.'

'I do remember,' Tiffany said acidly. 'Never mind. Let's hope that everyone's projects will work out well.' She raised her glass only slightly in his direction, and then took in the whole group with her gesture, but her smile was directed at Felix, who grinned – like the Cheshire cat, Anthony thought – and toasted Tiffany's wish with his glass of iced water.

Anthony, confused and irritated by their obvious complicity, said coldly: 'I suppose you have images of pyramids against the sunset for your next murals, Felix? Vast temples where priestesses worship cats because they think they can control the moon – the sort of thing Ozzy might work into his theatrical sets? Of course it's all very different in real life. Today the pyramids are slap-bang up against the noisy sprawling city; and the sphinx has grown decidedly moth-eaten as, of course, are the local cats nowadays. No-one worships them anymore. Modern Egyptians have their eyes focused on the future more than on the past – although, as I said, the tourist dollars help to fund progress when the region is not in turmoil. Any priestesses left are more likely to be found in modern temples of Mammon.' He took a swig of brandy.

'Businesses whose "temples" you design and build,' Tiffany observed tartly.

'Do many women work in finance, over there?' Emma asked at the same moment. Felix, delighted to have provoked Anthony, let them direct the conversation; but Jenna was still monitoring the situation carefully. What is wrong with them all, she thought, at each other's throats tonight?

'Anthony, are you up to your old tricks of just pretending to be a philistine?' she teased, to offer her client another easy way out, but Anthony took her question too seriously.

'I'm a realist, Jenna, a problem-solver, and a lover of clean lines. Not unlike some of Ozzy's beloved ancient Egyptians – the temple of Hatshepsut for instance could have been designed today. That's what makes me a good architect; and, by the way, I am concerned about what might happen to the archaeology, if political turmoil damages it. The pyramids alone are buildings with a lot to teach us.' He put his brandy glass down decisively on the table, as if dismissing them all.

'Very true,' Ozzy said approvingly.

Glancing across at the open door to the garden, Tiffany could see the moon hanging huge, and close. She had read in a news report that it was at its nearest point to earth now than for many years, due to some rare yet predictable variation its orbit. Maybe it's a bit too close, unsettling us all tonight, she thought, although Anthony seems rather good at disturbing the atmosphere unaided.

She thought back to the first time the pair had met, on that return flight, but could no longer recapture the frisson that she had felt as their first conversation had deepened. 'I'm sure it was there,' she murmured, his remarks just now about the archaeology briefly stirring something. But it slipped away.

'What are you muttering to yourself about, Tiffany?' asked Emma. She was tired now, after all the revelations and tensions of the evening, and probably should go home. Tiffany looks ready to get rid of us all now too, she thought.

'Oh, just something I'd forgotten about,' Tiffany replied. 'Nothing very important.' She suddenly felt lighter. 'Emma, your glass is empty. Fancy a refill?'

'Maybe not. I have to stay sober enough to find my way home.'

'You're not driving tonight are you, Emma?' asked Ozzy, sounding avuncular after all.

'No, no, I came by bus. It'll be easy to get back, there are usually loads of cabs passing the end of the road at this time of night.' She smiled reassuringly at him. There was no point in offering to share one, as Ozzy's place was in the opposite direction to hers, and in any case she was still annoyed with him for besmirching her grandmother's reputation to the whole gathering. She might have to ask her formidable mother for the full facts now which, despite all her new resolve, made her feel edgy. Iris could be very dismissive if an idea seemed ridiculous to her, so Emma generally preferred to approach tricky topics indirectly, if she wanted to glimpse where a deeper truth might really lie.

'No need for a cab.' Anthony's voice cut through her thoughts. He was again regretting his impetuous decision to drive straight here from the airport, where his car had been valet-parked and waiting for him. 'I'm bushed, and need to get home. I just wanted to say hello to Tiffany first.' (Although she doesn't seem all that pleased to see me, he thought). 'But I need my bed; so I can give you a lift home if you want, Emma.' Tiffany's bed might not be available tonight given how icy she is being, he reasoned, or at least not before a tiring row and reconciliation, for which he simply did not have the energy now, whereas Emma's company in the car could be soothing; and leaving with a passenger in tow would transform his retreat into a nobler exit.

'Thank you.' Emma, agreeably surprised by this offer, responded within her new, more calculating persona. 'I'll take you up on that; and so maybe on a tiny refill, too, Tiffany – just a couple of sips, though, as I don't want to keep Anthony from his bed for too long.'

I bet you don't, thought Felix, delighted. You have had your eye on him ever since he walked in here – don't think I didn't notice, sweet Emma, with eyes that have gained the glitter of gold-speckled lapis lazuli. So our chat in the café has paid off. I can't think of a better way to offload Anthony. Well, I can, but this one will do for now.

Without realising it, he licked his lips.

Anthony realised that, in accepting his offer of a lift but prefacing it with a valedictory drink, Emma had charmingly conspired to provide the dignity he had sought to reclaim. He was, once again, almost grateful. I never realised how astute and resourceful Emma is, he thought, as he watched her sip from her modestly refreshed wineglass. There's real strength and structure there, and in a more elegant form than I remembered. He continued to consider her.

'Excellent,' said Felix, happily observing all this. 'And I should gather the rest of my paints up, and prepare for the morning's work on Jenna's place.'

Alleluia, thought Jenna, at last we can get out of here.

After Emma's and Anthony's exit, Ozzy made the rest of his goodbyes beneficently. In the general round of farewells, Jenna nipped up to the bathroom to give Ozzy and, she hoped, Thomas, time to leave before her own exit with Felix in tow.

'You weren't tempted to take the opportunity of a lift with Anthony and Emma?' Felix asked Ozzy, on the way to the front door.

'No room for any more in his sporty little car, dear boy, now that Emma has climbed aboard; and besides I live in a different direction, as you now know. Good night again – and thank you for a fascinating time, Tiffany.' With a final wave, he left the building and strolled away in search of a taxi, perhaps the very one that would otherwise have carried Emma home.

'I never quite know what Ozzy is up to,' Tiffany said to Thomas as Felix returned to the flat's own hallway. 'He certainly knows how to make an evening more interesting, but I often feel he's really just experimenting on us.'

'I suspect we're not alone there,' Thomas suggested. 'He's probably trying out ideas, and testing reactions – no doubt all linked with the plot of something he means to design a set for at some point. Ozzy likes to keep a few steps ahead of everything.' Although he disapproved of Ozzy's games tonight, Thomas was growing better at seeing a little further ahead himself.

'Maybe.' Tiffany was thoughtful, and tired. 'One for the road, Thomas?'

That's me dismissed, thought Thomas, and smiled at her. 'No thanks, Tiffany. It's been quite an evening, and I too must get back to my bed. I have a mountain of work to think through before Monday. I've already said goodnight to Jenna, so I hope she won't consider me rude if I slip off before she comes back downstairs.' He kissed Tiffany's cheek, and shook hands with Felix. 'Good to meet you too. Let me know if you do need any legal advice, and I'll recommend someone suitable.'

'Good man,' said Felix, as Thomas stepped into the urban summer night. Once he was out of earshot, Felix turned to Tiffany and added 'And he's nobody's fool, Tiff. Pity that you still don't fancy him.'

'No, Felix, do drop that refrain,' Tiffany led him into her sitting room, dropped on to the sofa, and kicked off her shoes. 'He's too much like an extra older brother to inspire the requisite lust, I'm afraid – and I don't really think his loins stir for me, either.'

'The gods and pharaohs of Egypt,' Felix persisted, 'according to Ozzy, almost always married their sisters, so a cousin is hardly a relative at all – as Jeb and Nattie obviously thought.'

'Thomas is not a pharaoh,' Tiffany pointed out, yawning, 'nor as far as I know, a god.' She paused to wonder which god might suit him.

'Thoth,' said Felix, reading her thoughts. 'God of mediation, judgment, and wisdom – perfect for a lawyer with his personality.' He waited for her to ask which ancient deity she might channel, but she was tired and, for now, did not follow the trail he had laid.

'Very good,' she said, 'if a bit obscure for me. I think we've all done enough creative thinking for this evening. I did wonder if Thomas would offer to drop Jenna off on his way home, but—' Felix shook his head. Jenna was his prey, not Thomas's, and he was beginning to find Tiffany's persistent refusal to distract Thomas herself rather irritating.

'A small change of plan,' he told her. 'We had a quick chat and decided that it's simpler if I just go there with Jenna tonight – and get started first thing on the mural project. Just in case Anthony comes back here in the morning,' he added, disingenuously.

'Thanks for the moral support,' said Tiffany sarcastically, 'or do I mean immoral?'

'What's immoral?' asked Jenna, entering the room, with subtly touched up make-up and the glow of someone whose evening was just beginning, not ending.

'The speed with which Felix is moving into your place,' said Tiffany, only half joking, 'though of course he is only being mindful of how Anthony might feel about him living here; right, Felix?'

'Exactly,' he said sleekly. 'It's not in my interests as an ambitious muralist to upset an architect who may actually have some interesting contracts. I might want him to factor my work in to one of his projects one day. Nor do I want to rattle the cage of your own client, of course, Jenna,' he lied. 'He is one of your PR clients, isn't he?'

'Yes,' Jenna said cautiously, not wanting him to let the cat out of the bag tonight about the phone call from Anthony (information still unshared with Tiffany) that she had admitted to earlier. 'And avoiding upsetting him unnecessarily is probably wise policy on the work front.'

Tiffany nodded. 'I'm sure you're both right. Are you taking all your stuff now, Felix, or do you want to pop back for some of it in a day or two?'

'Most of my few possessions are already installed. I'll keep you posted on progress though. Maybe you and Jenna will plan another little party, perhaps at her place when the work's done, for any more prospective clients you can think of.' It sounded more like a demand than a suggestion. Cheeky brute, Tiffany thought.

'I'll be in touch about managing your affairs, don't worry,' she said, only partly in character again for the close of the evening's charade. She went with them into the hall, setting her glass down to give Felix a light hug and to whisper 'Good luck.' Releasing him, she added more audibly: 'Goodnight, Jenna. I'll call you soon.'

The two young women brushed cheekbones as usual. When she was sure they had left the building, Tiffany took her glass up from the shelf again and drank the last drops of brandy pooling in its curve. Tidying up could wait for the morning, she had already decided. I am going to sleep like an innocent for hours, and hours. An almost-innocent, she corrected herself, glancing up at the four statuettes, silent and watching from the shelf where Felix had set them the morning after his transmogrification. She nodded absently at them and, as she left the room, smiled at the painted jay in the hallway.

Above the garden, a huge full moon hung closer than usual to the earth, and guarded what remained of the brief summer night.

Chapter 12

Felix stood in a band of late afternoon sunlight that splashed across Jenna's neat, high-ceilinged drawing room, thinking about the warm and slightly unnerving shower he had just enjoyed with her. He still had reservations about deliberately standing under falling water and so had kept, outwardly generously, to the periphery. As a result, flecks of pale blue and rose-gold paint were still in his hair, and freckled his cheekbones. Now he wore Tiffany's cotton robe, which he had kept. A quick check in the mirror above the white mantelpiece confirmed that he still looked magnificent.

He held Tiffany's matte black round tray pierced with a pattern of stars, removed from her flat with his few new possessions, and now loaded with a glass jug, a wine glass and two tumblers. Felix decided to place it on the low glass table in the window bay and was already pouring himself a tumbler of cold water as Jenna came through the doorway holding a newly-opened bottle of chilled white wine by its slender neck. She set it on the tray next to the jug of iced water. She was wrapped in her favourite light-turquoise silk robe, whose colour ought not to have suited her skin, yet did, as she had been amused and delighted to discover when she first held it up before the mirrors of her favoured clothes shop.

'So, you gorgeous creature,' she said, pouring herself some of the pale gold wine. 'Won't you even have a sip of this with me, to celebrate completing your glorious murals, and this beautiful sunny afternoon? Iced water still seems rather puritanical for one so louche in other ways.' She touched a curve of her full glass against the lip of his, and drank without lowering her teasing gaze. Felix shook his head and pointed to the empty tumbler still on the tray.

'This one's for you, if I can tempt you to join me. Besides, I'm still in thrall to the mint tea you served while

I painted – and by you, delicious Jenna. I do feel at the peak of my creative powers.' He expanded his chest as he spoke.

'I can't argue with that,' she said, and sat down on the pale green armchair in the curve of the bay window. She loved the way that the imperfections in the panes of cheap wartime glass, installed decades ago as repairs, dimpled the sunshine, and how any breeze swaying the leaves of the plane trees outside set the light dancing and rippling through the room.

'You look like a beautiful siren there, lurking just below the surface of a clear sea,' said Felix, reminded again of illustrations seen in old book plates on some of his past explorations. He had turned her small bathroom into a corner of a lost underwater city where two sleek Egyptian granite statues, caressed by strands of seaweed, now stood and dreamt of a glorious past, and the pale, slightly ribbed tiles of her bathroom floor echoed and extended the sandy ocean bed.

Jenna laughed. The moving sunlight dancing across the drawing room also set off the glints of copper and gold in her russet hair, now gradually finding its neat shape again after being lightly towelled dry.

'Whereas you resemble one of those sea people that you told me about, in that robe, with a seasoning of sand and broken shells,' she answered him, looking at the fine paint spatter on his hair and skin. Felix has told her about the mysterious and fearsome raiders of the ancient Mediterranean coast, catching her imagination – although ultimately in the fullness of time these marauders had also come to grief. 'Are you going to sweep me away completely, or do I carry you off on a breaking wave?'

Felix looked at her calmly. 'The sea is not really my true element. Don't you want me to escape in one piece, Jenna, before it's too late either way?' He strolled over to her, and touched his forehead tenderly against hers for a moment.

'Not quite yet. Perhaps not at all,' she teased. He straightened up, leaving behind a flake of gold on her brow, as she added, 'I'll have to find more and more rooms for you to transform. Maybe I'll put in a bid for the flat upstairs, and the one below, and the one across the landing, just to keep you painting close by and in need of mint tea, and showers.' She sipped her wine again.

'Could you afford it?' he wondered, uneasily, retreating to the coffee table as casually as possible.

'No, sadly; although if I could sell on each flat with murals by the hottest new artist in town – or interior decorator, whatever we present you as – I'd probably make a decent return. So would you, of course, and win lots of new commissions. I am a rather good PR director after all, or so they tell me, so I should be able to market your talents all over Europe, if you want me to. Think about it.' Jenna was thinking fast herself now. 'You know, Felix, it's not a bad idea. Don't be alarmed, I don't literally mean I could buy up all these flats, but I probably can make you and your murals the new must-haves of the next year or so, here at least. Tiffany can still run the business admin side of things for you, of course. Would you like that?'

Cotton reels, he thought, she's trailing cotton reels across the floor in front of me, just like Tiffany used to do in the old days.

'To have my pick of wealthy and glamorous clients?' he asked. 'Could be irresistible. Go to it, Jenna – do with my talents whatever you will.' He opened his arms wide to the world.

'And share all of them with every taker?' She was still teasing, but there was a trace of rue in her voice. Felix shrugged.

'Not necessarily. It could compromise too many projects. Why spread myself too thinly? But a little gentle flirtation helps the spheres turn, just as you lay on the charm a bit for the Anthonys of this world. A few tantalising strokes can be sufficient.'

Jenna wondered if that was what had been going on there, all this month.

'Yet look what happened to Tantalus,' she said, and set her glass down on the windowsill. The warning made him shiver. Felix felt she was too clever sometimes. He glanced out of the window for something to replace the sudden image of an eternally thirsty Tantalus, standing forever in the water that swirled and eddied away every time he cupped his hands to drink some, and fruitlessly reaching to pluck something juicy from the branches that hung so close, but not close enough, above him on the riverbank.

'You think I should rein in the charm a little?' he wondered.

'Maybe save the best of it for the truly special clients.' She wanted to wrap him in her arms, and hold on to this day forever, sensing that with the murals finished the best of their time together was already eddying away from her. Felix looked across at her and felt, rather than saw, a shadow flicker across her features as the sunlight danced on the walls. He went to her again, knelt down and kissed her more fiercely than the sensual, slow seduction they had enjoyed together. Then, his arms still around her, he focused on her timeless beauty.

'Dear Jenna,' he said. 'Come who and what may, you have always been special. Let's make a deal. After tonight, you market me in whatever image you choose; and I'll deliver you someone who will truly value you. To show you that I mean it, I'll seal this bargain with a sip of that wine you're so keen to get me to drink; and you must seal it with my chosen drink, a glass of pure water. Maybe with a sprig of mint.' He rose, and went to pour iced water from the jug into the lonely tumbler still on the tray. Jenna watched him with mixed feelings. This was getting a bit theatrical for her taste, she felt, but so what?

What am I doing? she thought. Screwing the decorator – as Anthony would undoubtedly put it – and almost making a fool of myself just because he is s-o-o sexy, and then striking professionally insane bargains, and toasting them with iced tap water and a few leaves. I must be out of my mind, or already tipsy, or both. Surely I'm nowhere near old enough yet for a mid-life crisis? She smiled helplessly at Felix as he turned towards her again, filled tumbler in hand. How does he mesmerise us all like this? Time to get back to my senses. She held her breath for a moment and then exhaled softly before answering brightly.

'Right. I'll drink to that unorthodox proposal.' She passed her wine glass to him, and stood up to accept the tumbler of iced water in exchange. 'We'll do it like this,' she said, showing him how to link arms and hold their glasses as couples do at weddings, to drink from a twinned-loving cup. 'Starting tomorrow: a career launch for you, Felix, in exchange for the best replacement of yourself, by way of compensation, that you can find for me. Should I need one, of course. I reserve the right to say thanks, but no thanks.'

'Really? Very well. Come what may.' Jenna was not really expecting him to deliver his half of the bargain, but it could be entertaining to see who, if anyone, he unearthed. So they clinked glasses and drank. The iced water was much colder than she had expected, making her catch her breath and close her eyes for a moment. Then Felix released their link. Still holding the wineglass, he turned to look out of the window, and finally sneezed.

'*Shu!*' He shook his head. 'Curious. Did you hear thunder? It's getting cooler now. See how the sun is moving round, away from the room. I need to create one more thing for you that will always keep a sense of warmth and light in here with you. Something special.' He fell silent and seemed to be looking far away, as if contemplating strange and half-formed things.

'Thank you.' Jenna spoke more bravely than she felt. 'I didn't hear anything. Shall we eat out this evening? To slip away from the smell of paint for a bit.' She meant, to get away from the sense of loss already pervading the room. He remained motionless, staring out of the window, absent from her. 'I'm going to get properly dressed now,' she told him, putting her tumbler back on the tray. She looked in his unseeing direction for a moment.

Only after she had left the room, did it strike her that Felix had drunk the unaccustomed wine without comment, unless she counted the sneeze. Perhaps the shock of sampling alcohol had generated his somewhat catatonic state. She smiled affectionately as she reached her bedroom with its new, softly golden temple views under pale blue skies, stretching across the wall opposite her bed and magnifying the whole chamber. She thought that she did, after all, hear a faint murmur of thunder. She hoped it would keep its distance for the evening.

Still by the drawing room window, Felix shook himself as if waking, and studied the wineglass before setting it down.

'Very interesting,' he murmured, running his tongue over his lips, and sneezed again, '*Shu*!'

He took a sip of cold water to clear his palate, and blew softly against the window pane. *Hehh.* His breath condensed against the glass. Contemplating first the evening sky, and then turning back to the quiet, restrained room, he whispered: 'Thank you, Jenna; lovely Jenna.' Leaving the drawing room, he called in the direction of her bedroom: 'Yes, let's eat somewhere fun, to celebrate my murals. I'll get moving.'

Ambling across the hall towards the guest room which, though rarely slept in during his stay, was where most of his belongings lay, he did not hear how or whether she answered. Outside, the breeze ruffled the plane tree leaves, and softly rattled the dimpled window panes. With the evening sun now fully moved round, to fall on other places, the lovely room and all its possibilities quietly awaited events.

Chapter 13

As day broke Emma was dreaming, restlessly, about her visit to her father – a visit that had now become even more surreal. He sat in the conservatory and laughed at a joke she could not quite catch, however often he repeated it for her benefit, slapping his knee with his hand and saying, 'now, that's what I call funny!' followed by fresh mirth. Waking up with relief, she struggled for a moment to recall the details of the actual day, as if they might yield a clue to what was so hugely entertaining to him in the imagined one.

***

She had driven down on a fine sunny morning, feeling edgy, and unsure how much this was due to trepidation about what news or demands her father might spring on her, or exacerbated by the unsettling news bulletins on her car radio. It spoke of wave after wave of refugees still fleeing upheaval in the Middle East and, in leaky overcrowded boats, either being lost at sea or reaching northern Mediterranean shores, Sicily in particular, facing an uncertain future. She thought of the paintings in the café, and of the bracing extra cup of coffee she had drunk that morning before setting out for her father's house. She had maintained her new caffeine habit, as if abandoning it might also dissolve her new direction. Her resolve to make radical changes in her own life sharpened her concern for the still-distant migrants that morning, and then she felt ashamed of linking their desperate plight with her own infinitely more comfortable circumstances. She jabbed at the car radio to find a music station instead, and tried to focus on the road ahead of her.

Arriving at the rambling house in which she had grown up, Emma observed that her absent mother's lusciously colourful front garden was just as bright, but more regimented than before. He's been busy out here, she thought. Getting it ready to sell, I suppose. She still had a door key, but preferred to ring the bell. It confirmed that this was no longer her home, that she had another life to live elsewhere and on her own terms. She squared her shoulders. Her father threw open the front door.

'There you are!' he declared. 'Bang on time. You've never managed that before. Come on in.'

'Hello Father,' she said, keeping her voice steady, ignoring his dig. Though she still thought of him as 'dad', she now preferred the distance of the more adult-sounding 'father' aloud in public. Determined not to be undermined, this time, by his habit of adding a final cutting edge to any apparent compliment, she entered the house almost jauntily.

'Good journey?' he asked her routinely, amused by her briskness, and ushered her towards the kitchen where a tray on the table was already loaded with a cafetière of freshly-made coffee, a stack of cups and saucers, milk, small spoons and a bowl of brown sugar. 'Of course – you would probably prefer tea. Brought any of your funny sachets? There's English breakfast or Lapsang Souchong in the cupboard. Is that a new haircut? Suits you.'

'Coffee will be fine this time, thanks. Lapsang? That's unusual for you. Not much traffic today, so it was an easy run, thank you.' She responded in kind, allowing a lull before whatever shocks might lie ahead. There were three cups on the tray, she noticed, puzzled. 'Who's coming?'

Her father smiled. 'You'll see. Let's take this into the conservatory.' Picking up the tray, he led the way. Emma, wondering if perhaps her father's solicitor was to be present at this meeting, or if her mother were going to appear too – unlikely, she hoped – followed him with fresh unease. The conservatory was airy and bright. Its glass panes were clean, the door to the garden stood open, and sunshine bounced cheerfully off the shiny leaves of the plants inside as well as on those outside. She glanced quickly around. There was no-one already hovering in here. She decided to grasp the nettle.

'What are you up to, Father? You're being very mysterious.'

He beamed delightedly. 'Am I? Good, good; that's good. I told you, I've been making some plans that I want to fill you in about, face-to-face, rather than on the phone.' He put the large wooden tray down on a small white table next to a couple of rattan chairs, arranged the cups on their saucers and poured three coffees. 'Take a seat.' She obeyed. 'You remember your mother?'

'Of course I remember Mother,' she retorted, startled.

'Ran into her old friend, Lucinda, recently,' her father said, adding milk to one cup and passing it to her.

'Lucinda-the-lawyer?' Here we go, she thought. 'How is Lucinda?' she asked, determined not to be tripped up again.

'In splendid form. Your mother was over, visiting her too, lately.'

'Mother was over here? She didn't call me.' Emma had been wrong-footed after all.

'No?' said her father. 'But she did drop in on me. We had a very long chat.' He paused for effect. 'As a result of which, I am planning to sell this place now and give your errant mother her fair share of the proceeds.'

Emma, on high alert for what was coming next, kept her counsel, waiting. Had he found one of those sheltered housing developments for older people? That would be great news. Please don't suggest buying a little place for me with an aged-parent flat attached. She braced herself to be firm.

Her father was mildly impressed, as well as amused, by her composure so far. Someone's already been thinking ahead, he judged; good for her. Let's see how far she's got. He teased her with a calculated pause while he added sugar, stirred and briefly sipped his own coffee before delivering the main burden of his news.

'And then I am moving in with Lucinda.'

Emma opened her mouth in astonishment, and then quickly shut it again. Her spirits did cartwheels out on the lawn, before getting to grips with the practicalities. 'As – as a lodger?'

Her father was enjoying himself hugely.

'Certainly not! What a preposterous idea. No, you goose, as her "intended", her other half, of course. I shall have to make a new will on re-marrying, and may need to do a bit of inheritance tax planning. I intend to give you kids some of your expectations now, out of my chunk of the house-sale. Might give you a chance to have a bit of fun, Emma, for a change, without having to keep waiting for me to drop off my perch first. Nothing's so spine-chilling as the sight of an ageing brood beadily inquiring about their parents' "health", meaning their likely longevity. You could leave that nice little job your mother fixed you up with and travel for a bit, or something. Or get some better furniture, and some decent clothes – although you seem to have made a start there, already. Do whatever you want. Once I've written the cheque, I shan't interfere with how you use it.'

Emma was speechless and for several seconds could only stare at him as she steadily understood that not only was she reprieved from the sentence of doting, single, daughter-in-residence that she had so dreaded, but was actually being pensioned off herself as surplus (after all) to requirements. Thank you, Lucinda, her heart was almost singing.

'Thank you, Father,' she finally managed to say aloud, as good manners surely required. Then she ventured, carefully: 'But won't you need it – for the future?'

'For my dotage, you mean? Yes, I expect I shall need some of it, which is why I am not going to be giving all my funds away yet. Provided I last another seven years, you won't have to pay a penny of inheritance tax on what I do give you now, which frankly is far more satisfying than me just looking after it for the taxman's potential benefit. I have every intention of lasting considerably longer than seven years – which you will now, I trust, be glad to hear.'

Emma felt perfectly happy to hear it. She did not even wonder, yet, just how much money he intended to give her. For now she was simply hugely relieved that the task of entertaining her father for the foreseeable future was passing to Lucinda – who presumably saw it as an altogether more attractive prospect than his youngest daughter could. The promised financial handout was a secondary benefit, although also a welcome one.

'I am thrilled to hear it,' she replied with the enthusiasm of truth. 'All of it. I mean, that you have found a whole new life, and that you and Mother have stopped warring over things – and, of course, for Lucinda.' I hope, she added silently. Her father chuckled at her happy expression.

'Yes, indeed – Lucinda. Well, I must say, you are taking it in a calmer and nobler spirit than your siblings, whom I dealt with by telephone early this morning. They were torn between accepting my largesse now, and wondering how much of the remainder Lucinda, being a decade younger, might snaffle someday as my widow.'

Emma had not thought of that, but was still so relieved to be off the hook of caring single-handedly for an eventually ageing parent (a hook from which her siblings, having always reserved it for her, could have had no such gratifying sense of escape) that she really did not care how much of the remainder might be consumed by Lucinda. A price well worth paying, and even more so if it also annoyed Emma's self-serving siblings.

Dropping her guard – and, unawares, sounding more like each of her parents than she had ever done before – she said: 'Well, I should think if she's prepared to take you on, Father, she probably deserves every penny of whatever's left.'

Her father roared with laughter. 'Good for you. You always were the sharpest of the bunch, despite that slightly fey, butter-wouldn't-melt act that you used to put on. Glad you haven't really lost your "edge" after all. Of course, I'm not saying that we're getting married overnight – I haven't divorced your mother properly yet – but that will come. LUCINDA!' He shouted towards the open conservatory door into the garden. 'Your turn.'

Lucinda, tall and slim and no-nonsense, in cream slacks and a striped cream and navy cardigan over her crisp white shirt, strode in carrying some newly-cut roses and a pair of secateurs. 'We really ought to try to move some of your roses with us, George, or at least take some cuttings, before you leave here,' she said. 'Hello, Emma. Everything alright?'

'Marvellous,' said Emma, rising to kiss Lucinda on the cheek. 'It's great news, really great. I had no idea, but I'm delighted.' Lucinda, who could guess why George's only unmarried daughter would be more enthusiastic than her siblings about her father's plan, was content with the support of at least one of her future step-children. Emma herself did not care whether her father and Lucinda would eventually marry or not. She was in her sunniest mood for weeks, months even – perhaps years – and almost giddy with the sudden sense of approval and warm goodwill.

'So what about this coffee, then?' interrupted her father, handing Lucinda a cup from the tray.

'The coffee? It's very good too, thanks. But if I'd known, I'd have brought you some champagne,' Emma answered.

'There's some in the fridge, but I'm not opening it before noon.'

Emma laughed. 'Are you sure you can put up with this stickler for conventions?' she asked Lucinda, briefly forgetting the neat weekend garb and trim deck shoes.

'Indeed I am,' Lucinda replied. 'And your mother seems to think we are admirably suited, whatever that may mean.'

'I wish now she'd come to see me, when she was over here,' Emma said. Despite her own mixed feelings about Iris as a parent, it was dispiriting to have a mother who failed completely to let her daughter know when she was back from overseas, while still finding the time to look up old friends, and even an estranged husband.

'She'll be back,' her father said briskly, 'to take away anything she still likes of the furniture, and so on. She'll want to see you then. Her last visit was strictly about planning this move.'

Emma nodded. She would decide later if it was funny, tactless, or another form of liberation to be bundled in for consideration as part of the furniture that her mother might still want to retain. 'Tell her I'm looking forward to a bit of time together.' Now that she, too, was off the hook of running her father's home, she meant it. Besides, she might find a way to clarify her mother's provenance, so recently muddied by Ozzy's dinner party gossip, and find out something useful about the Tod-person.

'You should go and visit her in Egypt,' suggested Lucinda. 'I've been out there. She's very settled now.' Emma looked startled.

'You went out there? Recently? No-one tells me anything! Well, until now.' She considered. 'I might go there. I'll certainly spend some of my windfall on an adventure of some sort.' Emma smiled at her father.

'Make Iris pay for half of it,' he half-growled, but with a smile. 'She'll be able to afford it, believe me.' Lucinda glanced at her watch.

'It's noon now. Go and get the champagne, George. Emma deserves a glass.'

'She does, she does,' George agreed, getting out of his chair. 'Make those plans, Emma. Time you surprised us.

'I will,' his daughter replied. 'It's my turn; and I intend to.'

***

Remembering all this in her half-waking state, Emma slipped back into sleep and began to dream again. Now she was back there, sipping coffee and watching her father and

Lucinda, who had started waltzing round the conservatory, when her mother entered from the garden in a billow of colourful flowing robes. Brandishing a small watering can, Iris was announcing: 'I really can't understand why we didn't reorganise things properly years ago.' Unsure whether her mother meant the garden, the conservatory, or her marriage, Emma was about to greet her when the "clunk" of a heavy cup and saucer being set down beside her abruptly woke her up.

The scent of coffee followed her from the dream into full wakefulness, as a man's voice said: 'I have to go soon – and so, I imagine, do you.' Emma sat up among the pillows and the overflowing duvet. Anthony stood, fully dressed, in dark green flannel trousers and a well-pressed but casual cream shirt, by the bed. He smiled. 'Coffee to help you wake up. It's seven o'clock.' She was in his territory, again, a huge, quiet loft above the city streets.

'Thank you.' She smiled a little sleepily in return, and savoured the steam rising from the coffee before taking a first sip. 'I'll grab a shower in a minute.'

'I'll be in the galley,' Anthony replied. He was already striding back through the bedroom's open sliding door. Soon Emma, refreshed and dressed, stood beside him in the long galley kitchen, coffee cup in hand, contemplating the early morning light over the roofs and railway lines that stretched away into the distance beyond the apartment's dramatic floor-to-ceiling windows. Every external wall of the wide loft was window, with pane after pane of glass wrapping the converted building.

'How do you ever get any work done?' she asked. 'I would spend all day just watching the outside world and the sky changing around me.'

'You get used to it,' he said, refilling the lower section of a moka pot with water, to a precise point just below the valve, and then tamping freshly ground coffee into its metal basket. 'You soon shut it out when you concentrate on the drawings in front of you, and tap back into it when you need a moment to break off and think things over.' He twisted the top section of the pot firmly onto the lower one, and put the whole thing on the heat to brew while he talked. 'The blinds drop down if you really need to shut the outside world out for a bit. I don't work that much up here, though. The office one floor down has a more focused atmosphere. I bought both floors so that I could use one loft as the workplace and this top one, with the best views, to live in. They interconnect, of course – no need to go into the main lifts to get between the two; at least not for me.' He smiled. 'None of the team has a key to the internal lift to get up here without me, of course. This is strictly private space.'

'Good to know,' said Emma calmly, watching the world below. 'That was very good coffee, Anthony. Does the office get the same?'

The refilled moka pot was beginning to burble as steam forced the now-boiling water up through the ground coffee and into the top chamber.

'Oh yes. Well, via a state of the art coffee machine. Got to keep the troops properly fired up and productive. Coffee and breakfast are essential perks.'

'Breakfast? You provide breakfast downstairs?'

'Fresh croissants brought in early, and fruit, that sort of thing. It's a good way to keep staff,' he said with a shrug. 'They'll work all night on a big project, or come in early, knowing the best caffeine, pastries and fruit in town are "on tap" to make them feel human again.' He passed her a warm croissant from the head-height oven as he spoke. 'You should get your lot to provide it.' Emma eyed the croissant, thinking this one had better not be an employees' perk.

'My lot, as you put it, may work late but rarely all night,' she said. 'Coffee comes in your own recycled cup from the corner café, or in a chipped mug from a scruffy cupboard of a kitchen which seems constantly messy with spilt granules, small puddles of milk, and a sprinkling of assorted kinds of sugar – which is probably why I went off coffee for a few years. They do manage to be imaginative about the choices of sugar, but that's as far as it goes – in the coffee stakes, anyway. Fortunately the productions we all work towards are considerably more inventive.'

She had worked in the fundraising department of the small theatre for the last two years now. It was poorly paid, but she liked the changing shows, the briefings with their directors, and evenings spent schmoozing the more generous donors at patrons' events, as well as watching some dress and technical rehearsals, rising to the daily challenge of preparing funding applications – and of course the buzz and approbation whenever a grant or cheque arrived. Her childhood and adolescent years keeping the peace between her fractious family members had given Emma many of the skills required. Now, with the theatre about to go 'dark' for a bout of major refurbishment – towards the costs of which her fundraising skills had contributed in part – and with her father's unexpected largesse heading towards her own bank account, she anticipated bowing out gracefully, and then making some waves of her own.

The tone of the bubbling moka pot changed, growing more urgent. Anthony took it off the heat.

'You'd better have a top-up then, before you float off to coffee hell.' He refilled her cup, and Emma added frothy milk from a smaller steel jug already standing on the black granite kitchen counter. She made a decision.

'So shall we "float out" together in public sometime – or is this all a secret?' she said. It was not her first night in the loft since Tiffany's dinner party. Looking at him steadily across the top of her replenished coffee cup, she was briefly veiled in its aromatic steam. Anthony watched.

'I don't set all the rules, Emma. What's your preference?'

Emma still looked steadily back at him, composed. 'Well, I suppose a graduated "coming out" would work,' she suggested. 'Gives us time to change our minds without embarrassment – and time for you to decide what to say to Tiffany.'

'Ah. I think she has pretty much written me off already.' Anthony looked uncomfortable for a moment. 'That decorator chap seemed to have taken over at lightning speed while I was away.'

'Felix,' she said helpfully. Anthony paused.

'In any case the spark just wasn't there any more for me,' he said gruffly. 'You must know by now, Emma, that I am happier with someone more in tune with my world view. I just needed to work out how to let Tiffany down gently.' Emma opened her eyes a little wider at this deft edit of his intentions that evening at Tiffany's, but did not let it trouble her.

'As it turned out, she'd already solved that for you,' she said pointedly. 'But now I rather think Felix has already moved on too, or perhaps outlived his usefulness? He's been staying at Jenna's while he works his magic on her boudoir, no doubt in all senses. So Tiffany still hasn't been in touch with you since that evening?'

Anthony grunted, not quite sure how to take her remark about Felix's usefulness.

'No.' He paused, and then added, 'I haven't told her that I've been on another quick trip to Cairo since then, and she hasn't tried to find out, as far as I know. But I should call her, to say hello and put things on a civil footing, and so on, soon.'

Emma was satisfied.

'I sent a note to thank her for the evening, but I haven't spoken directly with her yet either,' she said. 'My head's been too full of other things, including some remarks Ozzy made about my family that night – and weighing up you, of course.' Anthony found that he liked her unsentimental approach.

'I wanted to see you again, as soon as possible, after I got back,' he admitted, 'to find out whether that week was just one of those unexpected opportune moments, or rather more than that. I'm glad you came over last night at such short notice – and could stay.' He suddenly looked almost bashful after saying this, surprised to feel slightly nervous about how she might reply.

'More than just an "opportune moment" for me, or for you?' Emma asked, probing his tactlessness. She was enjoying translating her earlier sensibility to other people's little ways and tactfully managing those situations, into a dry humour that robustly served her own new sense of purpose. With some of my father's humour, and my mother's ruthlessness, she thought lightly, I am my parents' daughter without a doubt, whatever Iris's own pedigree may be.

'Both,' Anthony said hastily. 'I mean for both of us.' She reprieved him with her smile.

'Good. At least we've established a level playing field.'

'God, Emma, that's a bit brutal, isn't it?' He was relieved, and slightly scandalised. It felt enlivening. 'You always seemed so demure before – that is, before I got to know you a bit better – but I like the steel beneath the charm, and all that.' He appraised her for a moment, feeling a definite desire again, and then spoke fast. 'Look, don't worry about Tiffany. I'll give her a call today, arrange to meet for a coffee or lunch or something, and propose an amicable change of direction in our relationship or whatever she wants to call it. It'll be fine, trust me. She would have tracked me down by now, if she wanted to know what I was up to. I just don't want to leave any loose ends.'

He meant that he did not want any anger Tiffany might be nursing to damage his professional relationship with her friend Jenna, nor his social standing with a useful connection such as Ozzy – although, of course, in Emma he now had an even better link to Ozzy and his contacts.

Emma knew exactly what he was thinking and said: 'I think you're right. You were fish-and-chip paper once Felix was around.'

'Fish and chip paper?' Anthony repeated blankly

'Yesterday's news,' she explained gently. 'Surely you know how they used to wrap fish and chips, to take home, in the previous day's newspaper to keep them warm and soak up the cooking oil. Once the food was consumed, the paper went in the bin.' Anthony blinked. This description, applied to him, felt a little harsh.

'Tiffany is like that, you know. Or perhaps you didn't.' Emma added consolingly, 'And I agree with you, that her silence means she has moved on. I've seen her do this before: a period of non-communication, then all bright and breezy and friendly as if there had never been a love affair to get over. Most men are quite relieved that there hasn't been a scene, if it was their idea to break it off, and she usually makes them think it was.'

Anthony looked at Emma with renewed curiosity, wondering if Tiffany had really manipulated him that cleverly; and whether Emma now thought she held more of the strings in their new affair than he. It was like an exciting challenge, provided it did not get too far out of hand.

He said, 'Even if you're right, she never really understood the creative processes and the pressures I handle – whereas you deal with people every day who work in a creative environment and feel intensely about what they do.'

'True.' *Am I reeling him in, or is he reeling me in now?* She was not quite sure, but felt this distinction might not matter too much. 'And I can also see when it's time to stand back and look at the bigger picture for a moment.' She glanced at her watch. 'I really must go. I sometimes pop into the wine bar across the road from the theatre after office hours, for a break or change of scene. Why don't you pop in too one evening for a drink, probably around seven, and see if I'm also in the mood for a spot of dinner? Maybe on Thursday. I'm a bit busy for the next couple of evenings.'

It was for work events, but she deliberately left out this detail. She had said enough to convey that she was not always available at short notice. If he wanted to see more of her, he might have to start committing ahead, and keeping dates. She put down her empty coffee cup, leant softly against him and kissed him fully on the mouth, her hand briefly straying down his torso. It was a fleeting touch, if not particularly subtle, that should leave him wanting more from her.

'Have a good day,' she said lightly, picking up the neat, dark grey leather laptop bag that had replaced her old, rather capacious bright blue leather shoulder bag, and began to walk towards the loft's front door where she turned to look back at him. 'Hop into that interconnecting lift of yours, and get down to some creative tension. You can update me on progress when you next catch up with me. Bye.'

'Bye.' Anthony watched her leave. Emma definitely had developed some style. A touch of Lauren Bacall in her heyday came to his mind. He waited for the heavy click that meant the loft door had securely closed. Then he picked up his cup and drained it. Setting it down, he said aloud: 'Sly little tease. Two can play at creative tension. I can wait till Thursday.' He looked for a moment out of the windows and stretched, before striding to the internal lift that would whisk him to his architectural practice in the loft below. 'Thursday,' he repeated, already looking forward to it, as he walked into the office. There was something else of importance that he needed to get to grips with; and this felt like a very good day to begin.

Chapter 14

'So where's Felix got to now?' Tiffany asked Jenna, kicking off her shoes as they sat in Tiffany's garden, soaking up a few rays of evening sunshine.

'Schmoozing Ozzy again, I think.' Jenna spoke quietly. 'He's practically taken up residence in his studio. He went back over there this afternoon to plan ways to be launched into the right circles.'

'I thought you were going to organise a creative launch for him?'

'Yes, I'll help with a little deft publicity.' Jenna had suggested getting a couple of articles about his murals into the right kind of newspaper and glossy magazines. 'We'll need some good photos of the rooms he has transformed, that sort of thing. Trouble is, we also need more than just my home and yours to persuade the sort of people Felix is after that he's the most exciting choice in town just now, when it comes to revamping their decor. News of, or a feature about, one really high-profile client's place would be a useful jumping-off spot, and that,' Jenna concluded, 'is also where Ozzy and his address book can help a great deal.'

'So.' Tiffany sipped her drink, a Campari and orange juice tonight, whose glorious blood-orange colour glowed richly in the evening sun. 'The social campaign is already taking shape.' She felt a thrill of anticipation.

'Exactly.' Jenna tasted her own drink, paused, and then set the glass down. 'You know, I don't really feel like drinking this after all. Can I be a bore and just have some mineral water? Preferably still?'

'Good Lord, Felix's habits are rubbing off on you! He hasn't got you onto a clean-living regime, as far as drink is concerned, has he?' Tiffany wondered. Jenna, unusually, looked a little embarrassed.

'Not exactly,' she answered. 'No. It's just that I've been feeling like cutting down a bit lately – it doesn't have the same appeal as before.' She hesitated. 'The truth is, Tiff, I hope you aren't going to be cross with me, but the truth is in the last few days I've starting to wonder if I might be – pregnant.'

Tiffany stared at Jenna in astonishment. The tall highball glass almost sipped through her fingers. Putting it down clumsily, she stammered: 'Might be what? Are you sure?'

'Well no, or I would have said so,' Jenna replied. 'I just think that I could be, and I'm going to give it a couple of weeks or so and then try one of those tests from the chemists.'

'And you think it could be Felix's?' Tiffany asked incredulously, wondering how complete Felix's human genome could be – a question that had not previously crossed her mind all this time.

'No other candidate, thank you.' Jenna sounded amused.

'Goodness, that would be fast work,' Tiffany continued tactlessly. 'What will, I mean would, you do?'

'Actually, and I've surprised myself, I think I'd go ahead with it,' Jenna said calmly.

'What?' Tiffany was stunned. 'But you can't, Jenna.' Horrified at the thought of what Felix's progeny might prove to be, she forgot all tact and sensitivity. 'What about your career, and your lifestyle – your figure – all the things you enjoy?' Beginning to panic, she threw in every obstacle to Jenna having a child that she could think of. 'It would change everything so much, Jenna. I really don't think you know what you'd be taking on.'

'Tiffany!' Jenna was shocked, and hurt. Confiding in Tiffany this early was clearly a mistake. 'I didn't realise quite how much Felix means to you, or I wouldn't have said anything yet. I could be mistaken anyway.' She wondered why, if so in love with Felix herself, Tiffany had encouraged – or at least, not sought to hamper – Jenna's own liaison with Felix; and looked questioningly, and not entirely kindly, at her old friend.

'No, no, it's not that,' Tiffany said hastily, feeling queasy now. 'I'm not in love with Felix, for heaven's sake, it's just that – well, I know a bit more than you do about what he used to be like, and I just don't think—' How to put this, when she couldn't tell Jenna the real reason for her alarm? Tiffany leaned forward in her chair, and spoke intensely. 'He wouldn't make a good father, Jenna. He's so unreliable, he's probably not going to stick around much, and goodness knows what his offspring would be like.'

Jenna stared at her.

'Is there some sort of genetic illness in the family that I ought to know about? You might have warned me to be more careful.' Her tone was chilly.

'No, not exactly, it's just that he's – they're – very unconventional, you know. There's something a bit mercurial about him. It's a very unusual family.' Tiffany knew she was floundering, and only making her overreaction seem worse. Jenna stood up, and smoothed her skirt.

'You don't say. He's *your* cousin, after all,' she observed, unkindly. 'You're being very peculiar about this, Tiffany. Or are you holding something else back from me?' She considered Tiffany's guilty expression. 'Is he married, or something? If you had wanted him for yourself, you should have said so and hung on in there, instead of passing him on to me so lightly. I'm quite happy with the idea of being pregnant, don't you understand? I don't expect Felix to stick around, but that's OK. I know he's not a stayer. Unexpectedly, I find that I've started to like the concept of being a mother; and frankly I can probably afford to go ahead on my own. I thought that, of all people, you'd understand that, and I'd have your support, Tiff – but apparently I'm treading on some very sensitive ground, so let's just stop the conversation right here before we really quarrel. I'm going now, OK?'

She began to walk down the garden towards the door back into the kitchen, where she paused and added: 'If there is some lurking genetic or heritable condition that I should know about, Tiffany, I'd appreciate being fully informed about that as soon as you get your thoughts together, and the sooner the better. Alright? I'll see myself out.' She was gone. Tiffany remained seated at the garden table in shock.

How could this happen? she kept thinking. It shouldn't be genetically possible. It's all my fault for accepting his crazy story, and then helping him cosy-up to Jenna. What might happen to Jenna, if she really is pregnant? This has all the makings of disaster.

She got up and began to pace the garden. Maybe Felix did make the whole transmogrification thing up, and I was just stupid enough to fall for it.

She knew she was grasping at straws.

Or maybe his offspring would be normal people – could that be possible? Her whole body radiated alarm.

Even the birds fell silent.

***

'Don't blame yourself, Tiff, nobody would have believed you if you had told the truth about me,' said Felix half an hour later, watching her carefully from the sofa. He had popped round on a whim to say hello, and now understood why he had felt a need to do so. Something had flickered on his personal radar, like cat's whiskers, picking up her alarm call. 'What else could you have said to her, this evening, anyway?' He leaned against the cushions, feeling a pleasing glow of paternal pride.

'Warned her that you are genetically unsuited to parenthood,' Tiffany snapped back, curled tightly in the high-backed arm chair by the window. 'Said that you do have some inherited condition, some dodgy gene or something that makes avoiding pregnancy vital. I still ought to tell her that much, at least. It never occurred to me that Jenna would take any risk of getting pregnant. She has never, ever, hinted at the slightest tingle of broodiness, for goodness sake.'

'Exactly,' interrupted Felix, still lounging comfortably. 'You had no way of knowing what was lurking in her mind when she welcomed me so charmingly into her home and her bed, and various other furnishings as I recall. Nor, perhaps, had she. I certainly didn't inquire, though I must admit that being cast in the role of suitable sperm donor appeals to my vanity.' He tucked a scatter cushion behind his head, and smiled.

'Hideous tomcat! You can't be more unsuitable.' She threw a scarab-green cushion directly at him. 'If she had talked to me about what she thought was missing from her life, I could at least have steered her towards making a better choice.'

'Calm down!' Felix had caught the cushion, and balanced it on his knee. 'You shouldn't throw things around in here,' he cautioned, glancing up at the figurines on the shelf in the alcove where he had set them, carefully, rescued from their tumbled state in the fireplace on the morning after his transformation. Their expressions were remote, sphinx-like. 'It's not up to you to micromanage your friends' affairs, Tiff,' he continued, 'and there's no need to be so rude to me. If I were "hideous" none of this would have happened. I seem to function rather well as a full-blooded male person, so there's no reason why my progeny wouldn't be as perfectly-formed as me. I don't really see what there is to fuss about.'

Tiffany was exasperated. 'You know perfectly well that none of this should have been possible in the first place, unless of course you have sold me a pack of lies all along. And I am really worried now about what might happen to Jenna, although that doesn't seem to be bothering you in the least.'

'Nothing is going to happen to Jenna, except perhaps motherhood,' Felix answered smugly. 'And from what you've said, she's taking a very relaxed attitude about my future role, or lack of it. A positively feline approach, I'd say. She seems to understand me rather better than you do. I'm rather proud of the way things are going.' He stretched out fully on the sofa now, put his hands behind his head and looked extremely pleased with himself. His default expression, Tiffany thought crossly.

'Felix, can you really see Jenna changing nappies? She is always so poised, and svelte. I can't see her carting a baby round in a sling or a backpack, let alone pushing a pram.' She rubbed her forehead. 'Now if it were Emma who suddenly wanted children, I would find that a bit easier to picture, somehow – although she seems to have changed a bit lately, too.'

Felix yawned. 'Jenna can afford a marvellous nanny to do all the dirty work. Who knows, if my projects go well I might be able to help too, though I don't really want to set a precedent there, just in case.' He smiled wickedly. 'Perhaps there'll be others.'

'Heaven forbid,' Tiffany said with a shiver. 'You'd better sit on your tail until you see what happens with Jenna. She still might take you to court for paternity money.' She still sounded annoyed but as usual her imagination and her spirits were rallying.

'Tricky, as I'm not in the system.' Felix again sounded a bit too smug. 'Officially, I don't exist.' Before Tiffany could reply unkindly, he hurried on: 'As for Emma, she's far too ambitious to be broody. A calculating miss. I'd say any children she conceives will be meticulously planned, not accidental.'

Tiffany was still irritated with him. 'What makes you think you know all my friends so well?'

'I've observed them for years, in my previous guise.' He gave up trying to relax on the sofa, and stood up. 'I should go to congratulate Jenna on her excellent taste in a mate. Funny that you didn't get pregnant, Tiff.'

'I had no intention of doing so, and certainly not with you.'

'I think you would be a delicious mother, surrounded by charming little minxes just like yourself.' He crossed the room to kiss her un-proffered cheek. 'Mind if I head out to offer a suitably protective arm to Jenna now?'

Bit late for "protection" isn't it? She kept the unkind retort to herself.

'Felix, don't let on that you already know that she may be "expecting". I'm sure she was telling me in confidence, and would prefer to announce it to you herself when she's certain. I was so astonished by the news, and that she thought I was jealous, that we didn't really finish our conversation properly.' Felix began to stroll towards the door.

'Relax. She can reveal it on her own terms, and now I can respond admirably. I'll even gloss over your reaction, if she mentions it. I can suggest that the news was a double whammy, given how hurt you already are at the speed with which Anthony's dropped you for Emma—' he said, over his shoulder.

'What?' Tiffany was outraged but had no cushion left in reach to hurl at his back.

'You didn't realise? Surely you guessed, after the two of them left your dinner party together?'

'You really are being beastly today, Felix. Anthony's already admitted to me that he's attracted to Emma. He and I had a coffee together the other day, and parted on amicable terms with no strings. I don't miss him at all. So don't you dare go around suggesting that I'm heartbroken.' Felix paused to consider this development.

'So Anthony let you think that he hadn't yet acted on his interest in Emma, and was just securing your blessing in advance? Impressive. The duplicitous rat. Now Jenna really will feel sympathetic, and forgive you.'

He blew her a kiss, and reached the door as she answered sharply: 'Felix, I refuse to be painted as a victim of anything. Just tell her, if you have to say anything at all today, that I'd had a foul day at work, temping for a real pain of a boss, and had an imminent headache, all of which is now true. I'll call her tomorrow to make my peace with her. Now go away.'

'Certainly. You can use whatever you like as your excuse, dearest Tiff, but I'd play the Anthony card if I were you,' he said, as he left the room.

'Get out! I've had enough of your stories!' she shouted at the empty doorframe. 'Damn!' she said, more quietly, as the entrance door of the flat clicked definitively behind him. 'Now I've fallen out with Felix too. At this rate I'll have no friends left.' She looked up at her four statuettes, lofty in their new location on the shelf in the alcove between the chimney breast and the window ever since Felix had restored their physical dignity.

'Sorry about throwing the phone into you,' she said suddenly. 'I've replaced it, by the way. Thank goodness you weren't damaged. It wasn't meant to hit you.' She paused and reflected. 'I don't suppose you know anything about what happened to Felix that evening, do you?' She stared hard at them. She had often chatted like this to them when she was small. They had remained impassive, of course, then as now, though it had not seemed to matter then. Perhaps another comforting bath would settle her thoughts. She retreated upstairs to run the water, with liberal doses of her favourite oils. Lying in the silky, steamy water she was cocooned from the world again, safe and warm. Like being back in the womb, she thought – but, oh no, unfortunate analogy. She gazed absently at the mural of cats now leaping across the bathroom walls.

I was too *laissez-faire,* she thought, ignoring the entire issue of her very active complicity in Felix's recent fortunes – and now the consequences are racing beyond our control. She sighed, sat up in the water, climbed out of the bath and wrapped herself in a large towel. Maybe it'll be alright, she hoped. Jenna will have a perfect child and be a marvellous single mother, or else she's just mistaken and it will all come to nothing. No other options bear thinking about. She left the space to the machinations of the leaping cats and startled birds, and went upstairs.

Chapter 15

'And you are serious about this?' Thomas asked Jenna. 'You'd be giving up a lot.' They were sitting in a quiet corner of the wine bar talking earnestly, over a glass of red wine in Thomas's case, and a slim glass of sparkling water for Jenna.

'Yes,' she said. 'I really want to work out if I could build my own business, starting with representing Felix, instead of working in a big agency. I thought you would be a good person to talk the idea through with, to tease out all the options. There's a possible extra complication, though. There's a chance that – and there's no way of putting this obliquely – that I might also have a child to think about.' She watched for his reaction.

'You're planning to adopt – as a single parent?' Thomas asked. He couldn't picture Felix as an adoptive father. Jenna was amused by this apparent obtuseness.

'No, I mean I might have a child of my own,' she said. 'Possibly – no, probably – as a single parent.' She sipped her water, watching him over the rim of the glass.

'With?' Thomas asked cautiously, wondering for a moment where on earth this was heading and not quite sure whether to be more alarmed or interested.

'Well, Felix is the obvious candidate at present,' she said, her eyes dancing with a little mischief now. Of course, Thomas thought, unsure now if he was relieved or should be slightly disappointed. He took a drink of wine to give himself a second to steady his thoughts.

'And you've discussed it together?' he hazarded.

'Not yet,' she admitted. Thomas was really puzzled now. He set down his wine glass.

'Let me get this straight. You're trying to work out whether you can combine starting your own business with starting a family, possibly with Felix involved in both ventures, even though you could probably manage both – I mean, manage Felix's career and have a child in your well-paid present job – with all the benefits of maternity leave?' Something does not add up, he thought, and Jenna does not seem the reckless type.

'Well, the business idea came first, but then the other question arose,' she said slightly defensively. 'I just want to get my head round the options.'

The penny dropped.

'You think you're already pregnant,' Thomas said, 'by Felix.' She didn't look that pregnant to him. His fecund sister always started to glow practically from the moment she conceived. Jenna, however, looked a bit peaky today. Lovely, as always, but pale. 'So how are you feeling?' he inquired more gently.

'Apart from surprised? Serene,' she said with a soft smile. Thomas was unconvinced. He drank some more of his wine, mulling over what he had heard so far, and why.

'So Felix doesn't know yet,' he stated. Jenna shook her head.

'I haven't told him yet, though he is suddenly being very attentive for a man who has just moved out. He's finished my murals and is staying with Ozzy now, working on things there,' she explained quickly. Thomas wondered how Felix was going to react; perhaps the artist would be less inclined to have his career co-managed by a pregnant ex-girlfriend than Jenna anticipated.

'And you haven't you told him yet because…?'

She was going to have to admit it.

'Because I haven't done a pregnancy test yet. I want to wait a bit longer, to be sure, and to give myself time to think it all through. To research how I would want to organise my life.'

Thomas scrutinised her carefully.

'You mean time to consider whether you'd go ahead with it, or not, if the test is positive?' he wondered. Jenna looked uncomfortable for a moment, and then recovered her poise.

'I haven't felt that I'd need a way out,' she explained. 'Though to be honest, that's the reaction that I always thought I might have, if I got unexpectedly pregnant – but it just isn't the case. Tiffany's the one who's reacted really badly to the news. It was very clear that *she*'d prefer me not to have Felix's baby. It was a bit upsetting,' she confided, forgetting for a moment that Thomas was Tiffany's friend, and cousin.

'You told Tiffany, but not Felix, and she took it badly?' Thomas repeated, astonished. Had his freewheeling cousin hoped for more herself from this Felix than a business venture, after all? He shook his head, puzzled. 'Now I really need a drink to work this one out.' He poured some more wine from the bottle on the table into his glass and looked at Jenna to see if she wanted any now too.

'She swears she's not in love with Felix,' Jenna said hastily, waving away the proffered bottle. 'In fact she implied that there's something dodgy in his background that could be an issue, but she won't say what – which isn't entirely helpful,' she added.

'Well, she hasn't confided in me, if that's what you wanted to know,' Thomas said, feeling that he ought to protect Tiffany's back, and find out more himself before commenting on her reported reaction. 'Your doctor will ask you about medical histories, and there are tests for various issues.' Perhaps Tiffany just thinks you are mistaken, he thought and then wondered if it was something mysterious about Jenna, not Felix, that had made Tiffany react oddly. He would find a way to ask his cousin discreetly. For now, he shifted the subject back to the safer subject of Jenna's career options.

'As for your work options, I can run through a few thoughts if you like, but you'd do much better to have a chat with a colleague of mine who's an employment expert. I'm more of a copyright man, intellectual property and all that. I can put you in touch with her for an exploratory chat, if you like, and you can both decide if you need formal advice.'

'OK. That sounds perfect, thank you.' Jenna felt she had achieved her immediate goal. Thomas too was ready to move their meeting on a bit, and in the process perhaps begin to understand Jenna a little better.

'Should we eat? I'm starving, and you could probably do with some fuel,' he suggested.

'Of course,' she said. 'I pretty much know the menu here by heart.' They ordered, each with their own degree of relief, and then she turned lightly to another topic.

'What did you make of all that stuff about Emma's family, at that dinner party, by the way?' she asked.

'I felt far more sympathy for Tod, the perhaps-cheated first husband, than for anyone else.' Thomas replied, and suddenly wondered if Jenna's measured approach to her own possible pregnancy also reflected her evident distaste, that evening, for the ugly hoo-ha that Iris's conception had allegedly once generated. He looked at her with renewed curiosity.

'You too? I thought the rest of them sounded utterly self-indulgent,' Jenna said. 'So have you ever been married, Thomas?' She remembered something being said about why he had been renting a room off Tiffany last year.

'For a little while,' he admitted.

'Tell me?' she asked. 'You know my secret now, after all, and I promise Felix will today.' They were meeting after lunch.

Thomas gave in.

'Mine's hardly a secret. We met as students, and got married just after graduating. It seemed a natural progression, before we started applying for jobs – carefully avoiding any that might land us in different locations. As it turned out, that was an unnecessary precaution,' he said, dryly. 'We were reasonably happily married, or so I thought, but then it seemed we'd really been developing in different directions after all – or so she eventually told me.' (And now I've just told Jenna that my ex-wife found me boring, he realised.)

'Were you upset?'

Thomas looked sharply at her. It sounded an odd question and yet she had a point.

'Upset? I was a bit fed up of course,' he replied slowly. 'Disillusioned, disgruntled – and definitely out of pocket – but ultimately relieved, I suppose.' He drank some more of the red wine that was also helping to mellow his thoughts. Jenna was certainly perceptive, he accepted.

'We'd made a mistake, carried away on a youthful wave of lust and forward planning. Mary was a great planner,' he added, 'though neither of us imagined that graduating and chasing down our first jobs were still just way-stations on the road to growing up. I don't blame her now for finding her own pace; and I think she's stopped being angry with me for turning out to be unsatisfactory.'

You don't seem unsatisfactory to me, thought Jenna. Reserved perhaps, but in a good way. It was rather relaxing. 'Do you ever see her now?' she probed.

'Not often. We still have some friends in common, so there's the occasional party where she, her new husband and I overlap.'

'Oh.' It was almost a question.

'It's fine,' he answered. 'I think she had him earmarked for the role before giving me the boot – she's quite a planner, as I said.' This wine is making me say too much, he thought, setting the glass down again. Why is the food taking so long to arrive?

Jenna, pleased to be almost confided in, felt momentarily awkward about having sounded too much of a ruthless forward-planner herself this afternoon – although of course it was an uncharacteristic lack of planning that had caused her own present re-calibrations, she reminded herself. Thomas, if he had any of the same thoughts, did not show it.

'Now I enjoy knowing that I'm making my own decisions,' he heard himself say, 'and deliberately ignoring each other when we do overlap would feel,' he paused, 'like a denial of that time as students and the fun we had then, and of course the mutual friends; and what would be the point of airbrushing all that out? I don't want to pretend that my student years never happened.' He could see a waiter moving slowly towards them with a loaded tray of plates.

'Well,' said Jenna, 'I admire your philosophy. No new soulmate, yet? You weren't tempted to make a play for Tiffany when you were living there, or since, for that matter? I think there's a vacancy now.'

Thomas had to laugh a little at that. 'Tiffany is a minx, whose feckless antics I grew up alongside, and I'm very fond of her, but no, she's not in my sights, nor indeed was I ever in hers. Her friends, however, are perhaps another story. Whom would you recommend?' he teased back. Jenna appeared to ponder. She liked this easy banter.

'Hmm. I think Emma now has her claws into the rejected Anthony – and of course she is yet another cousin, so that probably lessens her mystery for you,' she said, forgetting the example of Jeb and Nattie. 'I am *hors de combat*, so that leaves you with the second division – some of whom I am sure we can introduce to you at one of Felix's launch parties, if you really want us to.'

At this moment, the diversion of the food arrived. As the waiter unloaded the tray, she eyed her steak frites and salad. 'Pregnant women need red meat, especially if they can't have red wine,' she had said lightly when ordering it. Now she reconsidered.

'Since I am trying to keep up my red blood count by eating this stuff, Thomas, do you think I could risk boosting it further via a very small glass of your red wine?'

'Only if you also eat all your salad,' Thomas suggested.

'Until recently, I ate almost nothing else!' she protested.

'Men apart?' said Thomas drily. He turned to the waiter. 'One more wine glass, please, for my friend – and some more water.'

The way he said "friend" sounded warm to Jenna. She liked it, and touched her half-drunk tumbler of iced water against the lip of his wineglass.

'To friendship and the future,' she suggested, 'whatever they deliver.' They drank to that, but then the chilly glass in her hand made her shiver. 'Oh,' she said. 'Is it me, or is summer cooling off already?'

'You're just hungry,' he answered, and recognised that she was still apprehensive behind her apparent calm. He felt glad now that she has sought him out for practical advice. Whatever the pretext, Jenna might need some dependable friends in the days ahead and no-one could claim that either Tiffany or Felix were entirely reliable.

A watching brief, he realised, that's what Jenna's offered me, and found that he liked the idea. I'll take that, he thought, and smiled at her.

Chapter 16

When Anthony walked into the wine bar that evening, to meet Emma, his first thought was that he was pleasantly surprised by the bright, clear quality of the light. Given its location in the sub-basement space of an old town house, whose upper floors were now home to a clutch of small businesses, opposite the Victorian theatre where Emma worked and sandwiched between restaurants, an art deco cinema and the scatter of quirky shops that characterised this area of town, he had half-expected exposed brick and dark wooden floors with a scattering of sawdust. The exterior gave little hint of the aggressively white walls, minimalist furnishings and daylight-imitating strategically-placed lights that greeted him.

Of course, he reflected, the planners round here would never have let them alter the front of the building. He stood in the doorway refocusing his eyes after the comparative dimness of the natural early evening light outside, as he checked out the various tables.

'Can I help you?' asked a waiter in a white shirt, jeans, and a black apron.

'Thank you – I've just spotted who I'm looking for at that table in the centre. Will you bring me a wine list; or has she already got one?'

'The lady has one. I'll be with you presently.'

'Thank you,' said Anthony again. "Presently" indeed, he thought. I hope he does mean promptly. He walked over to Emma. 'This place suits you,' he commented as he sat down opposite her.

'Meaning?'

'Dazzlingly bright, steely, bold and crisp behind the original eighteenth century façade.' Anthony picked up the wine list from the table. 'Curiously, the waiter used Elizabethan English. Perhaps the cellars are sixteenth century.' Emma fixed him with an appropriately steely gaze of her own.

'Should I be I flattered by the dazzling bit, or offended by the eighteenth century facade?' she inquired, mockingly and choosing not to dwell on the sixteenth century cellars. So, he had turned up, and on time, but this was hardly a romantic opening.

'It was a fascinating century, with some exciting developments in the architecture of the day,' Anthony hedged awkwardly. He had not meant to insult her appearance. Far from it. 'I simply liked the contrast. Walking from that time, into here, is like stepping into an exciting new future – with hidden depths.'

And with the new me in it; excellent, Emma thought. 'If you insist,' she replied. He picked up the wine list, partly as a way to re-calibrate the conversation.

'I see you've already got a glass – what about a refill? I like this one.' He tapped an entry in the red wines section. 'It's a wonderful Lebanese wine, you don't often find it over here but it's excellent. If you fancy a change of colour, I'll get a bottle rather than a glass.'

'This was just the house white,' she said, tipping her own glass slightly sideways as if to examine its contents better.

'So how about keeping me company now?' He waved discreetly at the waiter, who actually began to cross the floor towards them.

'Now that expression does sound rather eighteenth century. Is it what I am doing, "keeping you company"?' Emma inquired.

Anthony considered. 'I suppose it is – and I'll admit to hoping that you'll continue. Do you think you can stand my faux pas?' He felt oddly liberated by admitting to gauche moments.

'Who says you're tactless, apart from me? Tiffany, I suppose.' Emma wanted to hear how that chat with Tiffany had gone, if it had taken place.

'That, and a few other things, in the past,' he conceded. 'But when we met the other day she was rather more gracious than I expected.' He turned to the now-hovering waiter. 'A bottle of this please, and two glasses.' Then he noticed the question in Emma's eyes. 'We had a quick coffee on Tuesday. It seemed sensible. Now you and I don't have to be discreet.'

'I'm glad,' she said. Progress was going a little faster than she had anticipated.

'Me too.' Anthony felt too busy to want a complicated love life. His arguments with Tiffany had taught him that if nothing else. Someone as unflinching and purposeful as Emma was proving to be a relief. No, a joy, he corrected himself. He nodded his approval at the label on the bottle that the waiter was already presenting to him. It was swiftly uncorked and a little of the wine poured for him to taste. 'Yes, that's fine; thank you.' When the glasses had been properly filled, he turned to Emma. 'May it only get better,' he said.

'Us, or the wine?' she asked.

'Well, the wine is already perfect.'

She laughed. A joy, he repeated to himself. What a relief.

'Dinner afterwards?' he suggested. 'I could take you to my favourite restaurant.'

'No,' said Emma. 'You probably took Tiffany there. You can take me to my favourite restaurant this evening.'

'Alright,' he conceded. 'I will do that, after we have given this wine our proper attention.' She is looking very good tonight, he thought. He pictured her at his side at dinner with clients. She would be entertaining but reliable – she would draw them out nicely, but not pick a fight for fun, or over a point of principle. He pushed away memories of Tiffany teasing one of his clients and nearly causing a row. ('I enjoy a good debate,' she had protested when Antony remonstrated with her about it. 'And I don't enjoy annoying a good client unnecessarily,' he had snapped back.)

The restaurant was a short taxi-ride away but Emma preferred to walk tonight. She did, however, phone ahead to see if they needed to book a table. Anthony enjoyed letting her take control. It was a fine evening and their walk took them away from the theatre quarter, past more offices squeezed into old townhouses, above the coffee bars, sandwich shops and fast-photo businesses on the ground floors. There was a florist at one corner, with bright buckets of flowers and foliage still out on the pavement, catching the evening sunshine and recommending themselves as impulse buys to the early evening passers-by.

'I like it round here,' Emma revealed. 'It's a shame the theatre has to close for a bit, although the refurbishments are vital. The planners insisted on keeping that rather temple-like facade, but inside it'll be a state-of-the-art playhouse. I'll miss coming to this street every day while the building is "dark".' She had not yet mentioned her windfall from her father and her thoughts of quitting the job and, in reply to the unspoken question about the theatre on Anthony's face, she elaborated. 'The shows will still go on of course. The company will just be peripatetic for a while, staging things in other theatres and venues. It's a place of fluctuations round here, and pop-up events. Things change all the time. The restaurant's just through that arch'. They stepped through the archway into a courtyard that opened out behind the shops and office fronts. 'I suppose this was a mews once, but it's all been re-developed in recent years too.'

Anthony had not felt this relaxed in years.

'Much as your choice of wine bar has been. Take me to your restaurant, and then home to bed? You're in charge tonight.'

'Uh-huh.' Emma felt she was still reeling him in satisfactorily.

The restaurant was as bright as the wine bar had been, but in this case vibrating with blocks of near-primary colours.

'Like eating inside a Mondrian artwork,' Anthony commented, looking around, just as a clear voice reverberated in the shiny space.

'Emma, Anthony, you sly little foxes – come and join us.' It was unmistakably Ozzy, and with him was Felix.

Emma's heart sank a little. Not now, she thought. Although she had not forgotten that she was first brought here by her uncle – or whatever he was – she had not expected him to be present midweek. At the sight of Felix, Anthony suddenly looked thunderous.

'What a delight to see you both,' Ozzy called, waving imperiously in their direction from a small table in the middle of the restaurant. They approached reluctantly. 'You can confirm how wonderful Felix's work is,' he added. 'He's trying to persuade my friend the *patron* here to hire him to transform this motley patchwork into something glorious and altogether more seductive.'

'Ozzy, hello. And Felix, what a surprise. But isn't it colourful enough in here already?' Emma responded, regretting her insistence on Anthony bringing her here tonight.

'Yes, and far too colourful for the purpose, in my opinion,' said Ozzy. 'It was fun at first, but these places can't stand still. Not around here. How are you my dear?' he continued, as a waiter busily began to pull another small table against Ozzy's, and then went to fetch two more chairs. 'Looking wonderful, quite the new woman, and Anthony – in the pink, I see? You know Felix already, of course.'

Anthony produced a curt smile and said 'good evening' in the same efficient tones he had used on the waiter in the wine bar. Felix arranged his face into an innocent expression.

'Anthony, Emma, what a bit of luck. I didn't expect to run into you here. You must put in a good word for me with the proprietor. Of course, you both only glimpsed a tiny bit of what I did at Tiffany's and I don't suppose, Anthony, that you've had a chance to look over Jenna's flat, but she thinks I should offer my talents to a wider public; and now Ozzy is kindly lending his moral support, and some introductions, to get things rolling.'

The waiter indicated the two extra chairs now making a cosy foursome at the enlarged table arrangements. They were trapped. It would be rude not to sit down briefly. Emma glanced at Anthony as she accepted a proffered seat with passable grace. She knew of course that, in remaining standing, he was not simply politely waiting for her to be seated first.

Enjoying Anthony's stony expression, Felix swept on: 'Of course, you may not like my style. If it's not your thing, I won't embarrass you by asking for your endorsement too – although every little helps.' Emma intervened before Anthony could react to this sideswipe at the value of his, admittedly-unlikely, patronage. Her old skills at seeing off awkward moments clicked into play and she spoke brightly, answering Ozzy as if Felix had not said a word.

'Yes. The food is good here; but perhaps the decor could do with a change now.' The smile she directed at Anthony said "take a seat too, it's not for long". If there was to be no easy way of escaping Ozzy and Felix this evening, she could perhaps make it into a manageable or may be even useful encounter. 'We just stopped in for a starter and a coffee,' she improvised, impressing Anthony.

'Ah you poor underpaid child, surely your beau can do better than that,' said Ozzy. Emma met him head on.

'It's all I want. We're planning an early night.'

Anthony was delighted to hear it. He had no desire to have supper with Ozzy and Felix. If they could get away with just a starter, he could still take Emma to his preferred restaurant. He was actually quite hungry.

'How's your father?' asked Ozzy. For a moment Emma thought he was making an old-fashioned smutty joke but then realised he was only asking after George. She immediately suspected that this meant Iris has already been in contact with Ozzy. Will the wretched woman never ring me? she wondered, irritated. Feeling ambivalent about her forceful mother still did not make her happy to be treated as an afterthought.

Felix, deciding to escape this family update, waved at the restaurant owner and went to speak further with him about his own ideas for murals.

'Father is fine,' Emma told Ozzy. 'Very well in fact. I suppose you know that he's planning to marry again?'

'Word did come my way,' he replied, adding to her annoyance. 'And has your mother been in touch with you, yet?' She did her best to sound relaxed about Iris's elusiveness, or perhaps evasiveness.

'Not yet; but I gather that she's dealing with the practical things first, and then we'll have some proper time together,' she improvised again, as the waiter started to put a selection of *amuse-bouche* on the table. 'How lovely, at this rate we won't need any starters after all, and can leave you and Felix in peace to sort out the practical details of his new venture.' Anthony was pleased to hear it, and accepted a titbit from the plate.

'I've never met your parents,' he commented to Emma, beginning to enjoy the skill with which she was paring this encounter down to the minimum necessary for politeness.

'Well, soon there'll be three of them to meet – my father, Lucinda, his bride-to-be, and my exotic mother to contend with,' she joked. 'but as Mother lives abroad, there won't be many summonses to Sunday lunches with her.'

'Where does she live?' Anthony asked. A long weekend somewhere interesting might be agreeable if it fitted with his schedules.

'It varies. She flits about a bit,' Emma said cautiously, 'doing academic research in various spots, or so she says. She seems to have acquired visiting lectureships all over the place. I can't keep up.' (Mostly because she doesn't bother to keep me up to date, she thought.)

'Last destination was Luxor, with a brief stop in Cairo,' Ozzy revealed, startling Anthony. 'She took some useful photographs for me at various ancient and modern Egyptian locations. Background research for my next opera sets,' he elaborated. 'I needed some up-to-date images. And no doubt in Cairo, despite these turbulent times, she will have topped up her supply of perfumes and unguents. Iris tells me that nothing beats what they still create there.'

'Really.' Anthony fell silent. He had not realised that Emma's family had current links with Egypt, having assumed Ozzy's interest to be purely academic, for his operatic designs.

'She's been going through a long phase of exploring the world, courtesy of her new-ish career as an academic,' Emma told him. 'A sort of mid, or later life crisis.' Which might be explained, she suddenly thought, by Iris finding out from Ozzy that her father wasn't Jeb but the disillusioned Tod-person who went off to the desert after divorcing her mother, Nattie. Maybe Iris went looking for him, or traces of him, and that's what she meant when she walked out on my father saying that she had things to do, places to go. As she considered this possibility Emma began to feel a bit more sympathy for her mother, who had perhaps felt the ground crumble beneath her feet and a desire to establish some reliable facts.

'I'll tell you more later,' she said to Anthony. 'There's a perfectly good reason.'

Felix was strolling back towards them now, looking pleased. 'I think I have the client in the bag,' he announced as he sat down at the table. 'He's ready to embrace something new.'

'Congratulations,' Ozzy said approvingly. 'Should we have a toast to success here?' He beckoned the waiter back, and ordered a bottle of champagne with four glasses. Anthony resigned himself to a few more minutes in this company. Perhaps he should make a bit more effort to cultivate Ozzy, he reasoned. The man was, after all, very successful and well connected. If he were prepared to introduce a newcomer like Felix to possible clients, then it would be sensible for a more-established man like Anthony to be friends with him too, particularly now they have a family link through Emma. Antony's intentions towards Emma were rapidly leaping ahead.

'Yes, congratulations,' he therefore said civilly to Ozzy's current protégé, Felix. 'Well done.'

Felix acknowledged this with an unfathomable, glittering look.

'You are a fan of Felix's work, then?' Ozzy tested Anthony. 'Perhaps some of your own clients might like to meet him.'

'It's not quite in my style,' said Anthony hastily, recalling the painted jay in Tiffany's hallway, 'but it's certainly well-executed of its type, and works on its own terms, particularly in certain domestic settings. Maybe not so much in offices,' he added carefully. 'But of course if the right client and the right opportunity arise…' This was not quite how he had meant any networking to go, but if he wanted Ozzy to champion his own work, he could hardly be churlish in front of him about the incumbent protégé.

Well-executed? One of these days that could be your epitaph, Felix thought, his eyes still glittering at Anthony with renewed mischief. He bestowed his pointed smile on his victim, while the waiter busily opened the champagne and began to fill the glasses.

'"Well-executed" will do nicely as a testimonial from an architect renowned for his precision,' Felix said. 'I'll tuck it away for later use, if I may. You're right, dining is still a fairly domestic activity, and a good restaurant can feel like a better home-from-home. I do agree with you, Anthony, that my work could lend itself well to creating that sense. Clinical enjoyment of food in stark surroundings seems to me to leave out so much of the experience. I prefer to take people further, to drop their guard and embrace the unexpected.'

Boxed-in for now by this interpretation of his remarks, Anthony avoided replying by accepting one of the primed champagne glasses for the proposed toast. He glanced at

Ozzy who, as the host he supposed, would want to say the magic words. Ozzy obligingly passed a glass to Emma and then looked inquiringly at Felix.

'I know you usually prefer water, for some peculiar reason, but perhaps on this occasion…?' He had after all, seen Felix drink prosecco at Emma's party, and this was vintage champagne. Felix realised that he, too, had been cornered and accepted a glass. After the effort of charming the restaurant owner and staying civil, more or less, to Anthony, he was starting to feel restive.

'So you are going to paint murals here?' Emma asked him. He nodded.

'Here's to Felix, and his creative juices,' suggested Ozzy.

Emma wrinkled her nose after sipping her champagne, puzzled by Ozzy's toast. 'What sort of mural does that mean?' she pressed.

Felix, who had also wrinkled his nose slightly due to the champagne bubbles, could already feeling them popping in his system. He liked the instant indiscretion they released.

'Actually, he means that I may have inseminated the lovely Jenna,' he announced. 'I have distributed my seed, and my progeny may stalk the earth.'

Emma, briefly speechless, stared at him.

'That's what I could describe as the Old Testament version,' Ozzy commented. 'I'm afraid spending time with me discussing ancient Egypt is affecting Felix's diction.'

'Jenna's pregnant?' Emma was wide-eyed. Anthony's immediate reaction was relief that it was not Tiffany. That would have been humiliating so soon after their break-up, and would have cast a very different light on her fairly gracious acceptance of his new allegiance to Emma. Perhaps he had misjudged Felix, whose interest all along it now seemed had been in Jenna. He was not at all sure that he approved of this either, but he was not going to pass comment on his own PR adviser's personal life in front of Ozzy or Felix.

'Congratulations again,' he said a little stiffly, 'you would appear to be on a roll.'

'Jenna.' Emily repeated. 'Goodness. So what happens next?' She was wondering if there were to be a wedding, yet could not picture Felix as a groom.

Nor could Felix, who backtracked a little.

'It's not official yet,' he said. 'Various tests ahead, and so forth. But I'd love to have dozens of little ones.' The bubbles have made him boast prematurely, he knew, but Jenna could explain her own version of things to people in due course.

'Roll on all our futures, then,' said Ozzy. 'Here's to the wheel of fortune.'

'Ozzy,' cautioned Emma, 'that does sound a bit like tempting fate.'

'Does it? It's my usual incantation at the start of a technical rehearsal, as a *deus ex machina,* professionally-speaking. Nothing happens on set if the wheels of a scene-change fail to turn.'

Felix set down his glass. If wheels were to start turning, perhaps water would be safer for the moment. More food arrived, and Emma and Anthony gave in to Ozzy's encouragements to eat there. Felix, however, bolted his meal, and then huddled at the next table with the restaurant's proprietor, discussing sheaves of drawings and then pacing round studying corners of the restaurant with him.

Coffee was ordered, and Anthony and Ozzy headed for the men's room. Anthony was again looking forward to escaping soon from this enforced socialising, and just going straight home with Emma. He was tired, and had other things on his mind too, as Ozzy quietly surmised, studying his companion's slightly sullen expression.

'You look worried, Anthony. Not about my niece, I hope; no little surprises like Jenna's in the offing, I trust?'

'Good Lord, no, nothing of the sort – not yet, anyway.' It was Anthony's turn to improvise a little to show that his intentions towards Emma were serious. In the washroom he accepted that the wearisome evening presented a good opportunity to establish a familial friendship with her successful uncle, and on emerging he hovered by the restaurant's bar for a moment, looking absently at a whisky label. As Ozzy reappeared he said casually:

'Actually, your talk about wheels of change set me thinking about my grandfather.' Ozzy looked interested, and suddenly Anthony did want to talk about the old man. 'He brought me up. My mother had died producing me, and when my father also died – of malaria – I was very small. Grandfather brought me up, so when the old boy pegged out just after I graduated, that was the end of my family unit.'

'Where was this?' Ozzy leaned against the bar and listened.

'In the Middle East,' Anthony said. 'He had a stroke out of the blue, although looking back later there was some sort of business deal that backfired, and I think the extra stress took its toll. He was a bit of a fixer for overseas firms, and that world was becoming more frowned-upon.' Anthony hesitated.

'He was working out there for a long time, then?' Ozzy speculated.

'Decades. He was a local agent for a variety of firms, helping engineering clients win contracts, that sort of thing. "Oiling the wheels of commerce" he used to call it. Like you moving your scenery around, he was quite proud of his role in reeling projects in, and sorting out any local hiccoughs. He liked to say he'd done more to bring some places into the twentieth century – which was his era, of course – than all the politicians put together. Maybe it was true. He had a lot of anecdotes about various deals he'd facilitated, and some that had gone a bit awry.' Ozzy remained silent, looking attentive. Anthony fell into the trap, and said into the silence, 'I suppose in his stories he was trying to teach me a few things about the pros and cons of business there – or anywhere, for that matter.' He had not quite meant to say the last five words. Ozzy tucked them away for later consideration.

'So he stayed on, then?' he prompted.

'Oh yes. He sent me back here to study when I decided that I wanted to be an architect, but sadly he never saw much of my work. He had his stroke just after I got my final qualification.' Anthony turned to move back towards their table, but Ozzy put a gently sympathetic, or perhaps restraining, hand on his arm.

'In what way, business "anywhere"?' he asked. 'Have you perhaps run into some local difficulties on any projects, or agency difficulties, of the sort he described to you?'

Anthony looked awkward. 'Overseas agents have to be more at arm's lengths these days,' he said, dodging the question. Ozzy released his hold.

'So what else set you thinking about your grandfather this evening?' he probed, as they strolled towards their seats. Emma, left temporarily alone there and not wishing to appear neglected, had briefly joined Felix in chatting to the proprietor about his plans but now, seeing Anthony and her uncle returning, also began to make her way back to their table. Anthony watched her, ahead of them. She increasingly seemed a prize worth putting his house in order for.

'Emma's remark to you about tempting fate,' he replied to her uncle. 'You're a creator, but sometimes you still have to engage with the money men too, don't you Ozzy? You see how the world turns. Look how you're helping Felix a little, with introductions and so forth. Wheels still need oiling in the world around us here, as well as in your theatrical contraptions, you could say, but how and where do you draw the line, or put on the brakes?'

If Anthony were hoping for guidance from Ozzy, or a masterclass in modern business pragmatism, he was not going to get it that easily.

'I take it then that you have already started to feel some motion-sickness,' Ozzy said bluntly.

Anthony felt a chill in his tone, and back-pedalled. 'Some of my colleagues – my local contacts – may have got a bit over-enthusiastic, nothing more.'

Ozzy allowed himself to look sceptical.

'And the shade of your grandfather is tapping a warning on your shoulder perhaps?'

'No, but some clients might, if rules continue to change. Rich men these days get more twitchy about rumours of hidden fees and little kickbacks, and so does the taxman.' Anthony felt that he was still unburdening himself more than he had intended, and added, keeping his voice low: 'Nothing major to worry about, as I said, just a little updating – regularising – to show that the right amount of tax does get paid, in the right place, at the right time.' As they reached the table, and Emma's earshot, he said more loudly, 'And all I really want to spend my time on is designing buildings, you know, and see them built.'

Ozzy noticed Emma's approval of this detail as Anthony sat down and drained his small, waiting cup of now-lukewarm coffee, as a precursor to leaving at last.

So that's it, Ozzy thought, Anthony has indeed been paying kickbacks somewhere, probably to keep his schemes afloat in these trying times, and has now realised it may come to light and look bad. Of course he wants to protect his growing reputation, and now suddenly wonders if Emma's *éminence grise* of an uncle can offer advice, or even shelter.

Ozzy considered. Did Anthony merit his interest, or would Emma be wiser to set her sights elsewhere? He decided to weigh Anthony and his history further, and waved at Felix ambling back across the restaurant towards them.

'Interesting acoustic in the corners here,' Felix said pleasantly, as he sat down. 'You'll have to explain the workings of it to me, Anthony, or perhaps Ozzy can.' Anthony, tired, did not understand the remark. Once he and Emma had made their farewells, and finally their escape, Felix bestowed his pointy smile on Ozzy.

'Another revelatory evening,' he said, and waited.
'Indeed.'

Ozzy had replied without elaboration, and no further inquiry as to Felix's own meaning about the acoustics.

Felix grinned, sure now that he has stolen a useful march over them all.

Chapter 17

Jenna's mobile phone was ringing imperiously on her desk as she came back from the executive washroom feeling uneasy. She sat down on the ergonomic swivel chair and looked at the caller name on the screen. She decided to answer on loudspeaker.

'Yes.' Her tone was distant.

'Jenna? It's Tiffany.'

'Yes?' Jenna was not going to help her to close the gap.

'Jenna, I'm really sorry about the other day.' Tiffany spoke carefully, sitting upright on a park bench in weak sunshine, a half-eaten lunchtime sandwich on her lap. This was not a call she had wanted to make at her desk in the office. A bevy of city pigeons, eyeing the sandwich, began to gather near her feet in hopes of crumbs. 'I've been feeling awful. I didn't mean to sound hostile when you told me your news, I was just so surprised. I value our friendship and I'd like to redeem myself, if that's possible?' Tiffany had thought hard about how best to phrase this. Jenna sighed, and picked up the handset, switching it back to private conversation mode.

'I don't know what to say, Tiffany. I was upset, of course, but Felix has assured me that your reaction was nothing to do with how you feel about him. So I suppose I'm sorry too, if I got that bit wrong. He says your unexpected split with Anthony had set you thinking about what you want now, and that's why my own news jolted you so much.'

Tiffany rolled her eyes, unable for a moment to reply reasonably to this calumny. I will strangle that cat when I see him, she thought.

Taking her silence for agreement, Jenna continued, 'I would like us to stay friends, Tiffany, but please don't judge my choices against your own life-targets, or regrets.' There, she thought, I've said it now.

Regrets? I don't do regret, Tiffany was thinking, astonished again at the spin being put upon on her reaction. Unable to tell Jenna the truth, she remained speechless.

Jenna preferred not to spell out that Felix had also intimated that Tiffany, of all people, had got rather broody lately and so was quite jealous of Jenna's possible pregnancy news. He had implied that Tiffany might need to work this through on her own, for a bit. Confused by Felix's unexpected degree of insight, but accepting that it sounded plausible, Jenna had found it surprisingly easy to wait for Tiffany to feel ready to make contact (and of course to apologise), while gaining time for her own annoyance to subside.

'Jenna—' Tiffany wanted to protest but knew that Felix's false trail did provide her with a useful, if galling, explanation. If she could grit her teeth and accept this calumny for now, she could perhaps patch things up enough with Jenna to be available as a shoulder to cry on later, should Felix's origins deliver complications down the line. Perhaps I could even be a godmother if I grovel enough first, she considered, which would be a good alibi for hovering over the child with a watchful eye in future. So she temporised.

'Jenna, if you can forgive me, I'd rather not go into the reasons for being so graceless that day but just apologise wholeheartedly, and ask if we can start over.'

Fortunately, Jenna could not see the contorted expression on Tiffany's face.

'I'd like that,' she replied, carefully, glad to sidestep any further analysis of the whys and wherefores of Tiffany's behaviour. Although Jenna never felt fully committed to the clock-ticking, usually thirty-something conversations that punctuated so many of her peers' careers, typically after the fourth glass of wine or well into the third high-octane cocktail, she had heard enough to understand that even the most unlikely person could find someone else's sudden, unsought pregnancy quite irritating at best, and distressing at worst. It helped her to show more understanding towards Tiffany, now, without dwelling on too much detail.

'Good, great. Thank you, Jenna,' said Tiffany, also highly relieved to skirt the truth and allow any further lies to rest at Felix's door – where of course the blame also mostly belongs, she thought, flicking sandwich crumbs onto the pathway now for the jostling pigeons and a couple of quick sparrows – not that he even has a door of his own yet. Some parent he'd be! She did not associate tomcats, even metamorphosed ones, with good parenting skills.

'Why don't you come and meet me at the office next Friday, around six?' Jenna suggested. She preferred her own ground as the starting point for their rapprochement. 'Then if you want, you could come on to the little restaurant where Felix's been trying out some new murals. It's the size of a postage stamp, and he's whizzing through it making his usual magic at breakneck speed. Ozzy and I have invited a few people to a sort of unofficial preview that evening in hopes that some of them may like what they see, enough to commission other work. If it's a fine evening we can spill out into the courtyard outside, and it could be fun. Some interesting people should be coming, mostly drummed up by Ozzy.'

'You mean good gossip-column fodder with a few bob under their belts?' Tiffany already sounded back on form. She tore some more crust from the remains of her sandwich and crumbled it for the plump but eager pigeons.

'Absolutely.' Jenna relaxed a bit more. 'People with the cash to indulge in a whim, and famous enough for others to fancy being able to boast about hiring the same muralist, too. As it's an unofficial preview party, the diary editors are delighted to come, or send along a minion, in hopes of some juicy snippets. If we get the right sort of mentions of Felix's work, and I intend to see that we do, then we can go for a grander event next.'

'You have been busy. What have you three got in mind for that?' Tiffany was happy to let the conversation flow again.

Jenna leaned back in her ergonomic chair.

'Oh, a show of murals of course, but this time on large panels that we can move around, or sell on the spot, and install in any building that a client wants them moved to. That sort of thing. Not on canvas, they still won't be paintings in that sense, but on lightly-skimmed panels. The show has to be bait for new commissions of permanent murals too, so there'll be some gorgeous photos of what he's done in my place, and of the restaurant, and,' she paused for a moment, 'and I had been wondering if we could photograph the murals at your place too, especially that amazing one all round the box-room walls? Would that be OK? We might even make up a nice little portfolio of photos taken in all three places to give to people at the restaurant unveiling next Friday, if we move fast enough.'

So that's why I'm being forgiven so briskly, Tiffany surmised: Felix needs to lay a PR trail with enough artistic temptations in it.

'Of course,' she said aloud. 'Let me know when you need access to the flat. Who's paying for all this promotional stuff, by the way – not you, I hope?' She knew too well how happy Felix was to live at others' expense. Jenna frowned slightly at the question and, down the phone, Tiffany thought she divined a defensiveness in her response.

'No. Some of my time is in part-payment – in kind as it were – for the murals at my place,' Jenna admitted, 'while the cost of canapés, cocktails and some photography for Friday's little soirée are covered by the agency and the restaurant between them. The restaurateur's delighted to get the publicity and potential extra custom, and for now Felix is a client of the agency on a sort of trial arrangement. We'll be taking our fee out of his first commissions, rest assured. I'm not daft,' she concluded crisply.

'Thank goodness.' Tiffany decided to risk teasing her a little. 'I'd be really worried if your brain was going soggy so soon – and of course I'd love to be there on Friday. I'm deeply impressed with how fast Felix is moving forward.' Deeply alarmed is growing nearer to the truth, she thought, but ever since his arrival the truth and I have had a distorted relationship; and at least while Jenna's influence and Ozzy's patronage last, he'll be able to afford this life.

'Yes. Well, he needs to make the most of the moment,' Jenna said levelly. 'The world he wants to court is fickle, so he may only be the "must have" artist for a season or two, or a couple of years at best. Then he'll either have to reinvent himself with a new style, or go back to the provinces and do it all over again there.'

If only you knew, thought Tiffany.

'Quite right,' she said. Looking around the little park during this conversation, she had glimpsed a slightly battle-torn gingerish cat crouched under a shrub in one of the borders, watching the birds feeding on the pathway. They ignored any crumbs that fell too close to his patch. Maybe you need a home, she wondered, observing him, but although I miss having a real cat, I am done with taking in strays. She pulled her jacket a little tighter around her body. It was growing cooler sitting out here than she had expected. She would need to head back to work soon anyway. Tucking the phone under her chin, she threw a bit more bread from her neglected sandwich for the birds, further away from the cat's hideout while she carried on speaking to Jenna.

'I'm sure he'll respond magnificently to all challenges. Where's he living now, by the way? Is he still encamped at your place? I haven't spoken to him recently.' She did not bother to say why and Jenna, who thought she knew why, did not ask.

'No, not at the moment,' she replied instead, looking absently at the gathering clouds visible through the windows opposite her desk. 'I believe he's living above the shop, as ever, in a little flat on top of the restaurant.

The proprietor's family home is further afield and he either lets the flat to staff or uses it as an office for his paperwork. Now Felix has the run of it, he can paint downstairs all hours of the day and night, as the spirit moves him. As to where he goes next, I'm not sure. There's still a room for him with me for a while if needed, of course, but I think he's limbering up to move into Ozzy's studio next, with a view to learning everything he usefully can there.' Jenna spoke without rancour or nostalgia.

'Is that wise?' Tiffany wondered, flicking a few more crumbs from her lap and preparing to leave the now cooling park. Felix would think he was calling the shots, but the idea of Ozzy trying to gain closer control of Felix worried her. 'Has Ozzy agreed to let Felix take lessons in set design from him or has he ulterior motives, such as going into the portable murals business himself?' Jenna laughed at that idea. Tiffany sounded back on form.

'Unlikely, don't you think? He prefers to be the guru, not the acolyte, though I think perhaps the same is true of Felix. Who knows what Ozzy's motives are for anything? The man's an enigma on purpose. I suspect that, having seen what Felix can do, the last thing he wants is a charismatic young rival stalking the stage set business, so it's much better to keep tabs on him and promote him as a muralist for your home or swanky office – the man to set your personal stage, as it were – but as you know with Ozzy, his agenda and patronage changes. I have no qualms about harnessing his professional interest in Felix while it lasts.'

'Good for you.' Jenna clearly still had her own ruthless streak. Tiffany turned and threw the last bit of her salmon sandwich straight at the startled ginger cat which jumped up, revealing faint, tabby-like bars on its legs and tail, and then inspected the scattered contents.

'Enlightened self-interest, as I'm sure you are thinking,' Jenna retorted. 'I'm glad you can come on

Friday, though. Meet me here at six and we'll go together, as a united front.'

'Good.'

Watching the odd cat polish off the traces of salmon, Tiffany began to look forward to seeing what Felix had done with the restaurant.

'See you then,' they chorused. As she put her phone back in her bag, Tiffany lent against the back of the bench for another moment, to let the tension flow out of her frame. That was easier than I feared, she reflected. Even so, she had doubts, wondering if a high media profile was right for Felix. He would bask in the limelight of course but that could become problematic if he grew careless or indiscreet. Jenna would have to be encouraged to have a PR strategy in place to cover his unpredictability, without ever knowing the underlying causes.

The ginger cat had vanished from sight but a small 't-t-t' sound from the bushes told her it was still there, its mouth twitching open and shut as it observed the comings and goings of the sparrows and pigeons on the grass. She stood up to shake the last few crumbs from her skirt. Falling right next to the bench, they would draw the birds a little further away from the cat.

When I get home I'll tidy up the flat, she decided, ready for Jenna's photographer; and by the time she was back in the office, a message had already popped up on her phone that he could arrive the next morning, 'if that worked for her'.

Chapter 18

Jenna's photographer arrived promptly at eight-thirty in the morning, mindful of the speed with which his client wanted her publicity photos. Tiffany opened her door to a tall, rather bony man with a thin but handsome nose and a relaxed smile. His clothes seemed to hang off him and, although a little crumpled, were expensive and fairly new, she noticed. He looked both creative and attuned to making his clients, and no doubt his subjects, feel at ease. You would not mind being snapped by him at an event, she felt.

'Tiffany? I'm Mike. Jenna's office sent me.' Tiffany smiled back and held the door wider open.

'Yes. Come in.' She led him into the flat itself. 'I've tidied up a bit. Do you want me to show you all the murals first, or would you rather just look around on your own and decide what you want to photograph? I'm just making a pot of coffee so if you'd like a cup, you're more than welcome.' Mike nodded.

'Coffee would be very welcome. If you point out the rooms with the murals, I'll just walk around for a minute or two and think about what shots I want to take.' He was businesslike, but at ease, and pleasant. Tiffany liked him already.

'How do you take your coffee?' she asked.

'Black, two sugars, brown if you've got it.'

'I'll check. The pièce de resistance is the little room just round there.' She indicated the closed door to her former box-room. She had shut it so that he would experience the full impact of the mural on opening it and entering the space. 'And the bathroom just up the stairs there, off the landing, is great. There are a few things dotted around this hallway, too.' She glanced up at the acquistive jay above the lintel of the door to the sitting room. 'Come into the kitchen when you're ready.' She pointed down the corridor.

'Will do.'

Her kitchen was bright with early morning sunshine. After putting the kettle on, and spooning some of her stock of ground coffee into the cafetière, Tiffany unlocked the door to the garden, letting fresh air and the sound of birds drift indoors. She took two large mugs down from a cupboard, and a half-empty bottle of milk from the fridge for her own coffee. She knew there was still some brown sugar lurking somewhere and after a brief search unearthed a battered packet, held shut with a blue plastic clip, from the middle of her herbs and tins cupboard. She could hear Mike saying something from beyond the kitchen, and the click of the camera. Talking to me, or to himself? she wondered, pouring the hot water into the cafetière, and waited for a couple of minutes before pressing the plunger down. She liked the way it travelled smoothly under the lightest pressure when it was ready. Now she could pour the aromatic coffee into the mugs. Finally, she stirred sugar into one, and added milk to her own.

'Smells good,' his voice said, close behind her. She jumped.

'I thought you were still pottering amongst the murals,' she said. 'You startled me.'

'Sorry.' Mike smiled. 'I've taken a few polaroids to get a feel for what I plan to take, and the smell of coffee was irresistible.'

'Polaroids?'

'They've been back for a while,' he smiled. 'Technology gone full circle.'

He spread several small squares of photographic paper on the table and, waiting for the last of the pictures to emerge, picked up the mug she had been stirring.

'It's pretty hot still,' Tiffany warned. Mike cradled the mug.

'That's how I like it.'

Tiffany warmed further to him.

'So what do you think?' she asked, standing in the sunshine. 'Do you like Felix's artworks?'

Mike nodded. 'He's good. I can see why Jenna thinks his work's worth promoting. He's a friend of yours, this artist? Hadn't heard of him before, myself, but if Jenna's on the case I guess everyone will do pretty soon.'

Tiffany agreed.

'The question will be how long she can keep him basking in the limelight of publicity,' she said, 'though knowing Felix he'll make that bit pretty straightforward. Maybe too much so, though.'

'Bit wild is he?' Mike tried his coffee. Tiffany considered how best to reply.

'Not in the traditional carousing-but-talented artist mode, if that's what you mean,' she said. 'He rarely drinks alcohol, for starters. He's perfectly at home in drawing rooms but equally likely to go off on the prowl on occasion.'

'Sounds guaranteed to sweep all the socialites off their feet overnight.' Mike drank some more of his coffee and set down the mug. He moved some of the developed polaroid pictures around on the table.

'That's what I'm afraid of,' Tiffany said without thinking.

'Boyfriend then, is he?'

'No! Not mine, anyway. He's an old family friend, whose launch into the art world is being – well, was – largely laid at my door, when people like Jenna started to fall in love with his work. So I feel vaguely responsible for how well it goes next. I hope he's going to be more than just flavour of the month.' Liar, she thought, I'm actually beginning to wish he'd just disappear before anything else weird happens. She smiled brightly at Mike while wondering if he knew about Jenna's possible situation yet. Probably not.

'Really?' he responded, to her spoken words. 'Well, it's time for my share of any responsibility for his progress.' He held up the polaroids one by one and considered them again, pocketed a few and left the rest on the table. 'Have a look through those. I'll take the real photographs now.' He left the kitchen.

Tiffany leaned against the table, sipping her coffee. That's a really nice man, she thought, sadly not my type, but so pleasant to be around. She finished her coffee slowly, waiting for Mike to do his work, and enjoying the quiet calm of a weekday morning at home. I shan't rush into work when he's gone. I'll take my time slowly today. She breathed in, savouring the luxury, lost in idle thought. When the photographer came back into the kitchen to thank her for the coffee and say that he was off to discuss which ones Jenna would select, and would let himself out, she had almost forgotten Mike was there.

'OK,' she said. 'Bye. Might see you at the opening.'

He nodded. 'Probably. I'll be on duty to take publicity shots on the night. Look glamorous and I'll snap you too.'

Tiffany laughed. 'Well, I'll try, but no promises!'

'Good on you.' He was thinking, interesting woman, not really my type – if I were free – but I know who might be intrigued. 'See you next Friday then,' he said, and headed into the hall to pick up his camera bag. 'Keep the polaroids.'

'Bye,' Tiffany repeated as the flat door clicked shut. Another coffee, I think, in the garden just for half an hour. She looked again at the polaroids. Well, Felix, you're on your way. I just wish I knew where. She poured what remained in the cafetière into her mug.

Mike, strolling onto the street, paused to consider his direction. I wonder if Ash is about, he thought, pity not to drop in while I'm so near. He swung left from Tiffany's door, and walked purposefully past a dozen more redbrick Victorian houses, now mostly converted into two or three flats if the block of doorbells on each one was a guide, before turning a corner and stopping beside a gently rusting MGB Roadster in racing green parked on the road. Looks a bit cleaner than it did – he must have been working on it again, Mike thought. Let's see if the man's in. He walked a few yards down this street, before pushing open a small wrought-iron gate, strode up a short steep flight of steps to a front door with faded, slightly peeling blue paint, and pressed the bell for the ground floor flat. After a few moments, a disembodied voice answered through the battered intercom.

'Yes?'

'Ash, it's Mike. Let me in, you old bastard. I've come to drink some of your famously disgusting coffee.' A laugh crackled, followed by a harsh buzzing sound and a click that told him the front door's catch had been released. Mike pushed it open and strode into the hallway just as the ground floor flat's own door swung wide, revealing a tall, slightly tousled, lightly tanned man drying his hands on a tea towel. His light brown hair had been streaked blond in strands by the sun, and his greenish eyes danced with greetings.

'Mike, you recluse, where have you been? Good to see you anyway. Coffee's coming up. Come through to the kitchen. What are you doing here? Hardly your neck of the woods.' Mike set his camera bag down on the wooden floor.

'It's called working, mate. Just been taking some publicity shots up the road, and thought I'd drop by.'

'Publicity shots in this little backwater? Someone must have a sense of humour,' his friend replied, listening carefully to the slightly dented espresso pot burbling on the hob.

'Some artist has been painting murals in a flat up the road, and my client is unleashing his genius upon the world – so pictures of his recent efforts are required. Actually, his work's not bad. You should come along on Friday, to a little restaurant he's working on now – there's an opening bash to show his latest work. I have to take some shots of whoever turns up to admire the new murals over their champagne and canapés. You could get away from tinkering with that old banger for a few hours, and mingle with polite society. You know how they love you.'

'I like tinkering with my cars,' said Ash, turning off the gas and lifting the espresso pot. 'Just as I like being on the road. What's so great about this opening? Is the wine going to be decent?'

Mike grinned. 'Can't say, as yet, but there's going to be someone there who might appeal. An early client of the artist, in fact, a rather attractive young woman.'

'You reckon? Leave it out, Mike. I can find my own girlfriends you know,' Ash mocked his old friend.

'Only too well,' said Mike. 'Keeping them's another matter. Not many seem to have liked competing with rusting MGs, or long disappearances on expeditions.'

'Short disappearances. Supposedly makes the heart grow fonder, although you may have a point. How is being settled down?'

'Works for me.' Mike said happily, accepting the small ceramic cup of fragrant espresso that Ash held out to him. 'Although I'm "spoken for" now, take it from me, in the bad old days photographers always got another chance, whereas rust-stained single explorers who start behaving like hermits the moment they return, apparently don't.'

Ash gave a mock frown.

'You're not wrong,' he said, thinking of the rather pretty young woman in a hurry who had snapped at him a few weeks ago for cluttering the pavement with spanners and car parts – to his amusement more than his chagrin, although he had apologised to her departing back – and wondering if, or when, she would give him a second glance sometime. He had noticed her in the area since but had not, so far, been recognised or acknowledged himself. 'But maybe I'll come along for the excursion anyway – to prove I'm no hermit, though I don't promise to pursue whoever it is you think you've lined up. Will Angie be there to rescue me?'

Mike chuckled.

'Absolutely, mate, we'll both be there on duty. She'll give you her considered opinion right enough, but the woman I met today is quite interesting, even if she doesn't set your pulse racing. A friend of the artist – his local discoverer, I believe.'

'I've been discovered,' Ash pointed out, 'with my name in lights any time I want. I just prefer to be left alone to plan my next project in peace.'

'I don't think she impresses easily,' Mike suggested. 'You might have to make an effort if you did want to register on her radar. She has different coloured eyes, by the way. One blue, one brown. Unusual.'

Ash drained his espresso.

'What the hell,' he said. 'Come and check out the Roadster.'

'Been working on improving things in here too?' Mike observed, as he glanced through the open living room door on their way from the kitchen to the flat's exit. Ash nodded.

'It was all overdue a coat of paint. I'm thinking of finding a lodger to keep an eye on the place next time I'm travelling, and I couldn't really expect anyone to put up with the state I'm prepared to live in. Except that my plans still haven't quite gelled, and I don't want someone here until I'm more or less ready to ship out. So nothing much has happened and I'm getting the benefit of my own clean-up. Trouble is, I'm also having to be careful not to trash the place myself before I attract a lodger.'

Mike had an idea.

'Maybe you could get our muralist client to liven it up a bit before he gets too fashionable and expensive, which is what I'm sure Jenna is building him up towards. You should see what he's done in the place up the road – an extraordinary mural in the bathroom of cats all over the place, very feral; and a remarkable wall-to-wall, dusk-to-dusk panorama in an otherwise tiny box-room. I'm quite curious to see what he's done in this little restaurant. Should get some interesting pictures, if the guests let their hair down a bit, with his stuff as an exotic backdrop.'

Ash grimaced as they entered the communal hallway.

'Cats? I had enough of cats when I was repainting this place. Some wretched tabby kept coming in and padding about amongst my paint pots and leaving hairs and paw-prints all over the place. He wouldn't be chased off for long: kept sneaking back in through the window that I had to leave open to get rid of the paint fumes – you'd have thought those would have deterred him, but alas not. I drew a line at resorting to violence, so in the end I had to bribe him with scraps to keep him in one place while I painted; and he still kept sitting on my manuscripts and notes. Haven't seen hide nor hair of him since the painting stopped, and the need for bribery ran out with it. I reckon he checks out every house with some trick to get extra rations.' He patted the back pocket of his jeans to check that his house key was still there before letting the front door swing shut behind them.

'Sounds like you on some of your early travels,' Mike remarked, as the two men strolled down the front steps and headed for the rusting MG just up the road. 'Perhaps the cat should come back and sit on the car – that way you might be driven to get it back into working order sooner.'

'It works fine,' Ash told him. 'I've spent hours this spring getting this baby back on the road since I unearthed it, unloved, in someone's old nettle-infested 1960s carport. All that's left is to get the exterior looking as good as the engine now does.'

'Still sounds like a labour of love to me,' said Mike.

'It is, and if I don't complete it before my next trip the council will probably try to tow it away as a wreck, licensed or not. So I either need to finish it or find somewhere safe to keep it, or both, come to think of it.'

'You need a proper girlfriend with an empty garage,' said Mike. 'Free parking and a warm welcome. You can always re-house the car if she realises that it's your true love, once you get back. Where is the next trip to, anyway?'

Ash paused by the Roadster.

'I'm not that calculating. The next trip? My publisher thinks Kazakhstan is ripe for my kind of travel writing – or rather, that our readers are ripe for my kind of travel writing about it. There's a British-owned steam railway out there, did you know that? and all sorts of businessmen have been venturing out there, not to mention the potential for lots of wannabe space tourists keen to know about blasting off from Kazakh launch pads. Meanwhile, unless someone can put me in space too, apparently ambling around Kazakhstan itself and writing about it in my allegedly inimitable style will do nicely. I have to pick the best time of year to go, which for maximum reader impact probably means starting with the worst time and persisting until the kindest one, so that the book moves upliftingly from beleaguered traveller in an antique land, to enchanted would-be spaceman, you understand – so I may have to bend my mind towards starting with a Kazakh winter. On the sunny side, though, I might fortify myself first with visits to some of the old vineyards that are now doing well again in the former Soviet states, if I can arrange to do all that in time.' Ash lent against the car before continuing.

'Did you know that parts of Mother Russia are home to some of the most ancient viticulture in the world? The archaeological evidence – of wine residue and various artefacts – suggest that over millennia wine-making spread gradually from there to the rest of the world, via Egypt and the Middle East long before it got up to Italy and France. I fancy a detour around the old evidence, and of course the new products, in the first cradle of winemaking. It could make a nice little travelogue. *Travels with an Amphora, through Russia Past and Present,* if you like. Maybe you could catch up, to take some photos for it.'

He crossed his arms and looked inquiringly at Mike to see what he thought of the idea in general. Mike absently patted the flank of Ash's car. He knew that Ash's publisher would be in touch if the casual suggestion developed into a serious proposition.

'Maybe. You're not a bad photographer yourself Ash, when you put your own mind to it. I'd forgotten that the history of wine used to be one of your "things", though. You definitely need to get to a party or two again here, in that case.' Mike grinned. 'So why not amble your way round to ours next Friday around four-thirty, and then I'll take you into this little bash. Don't be late, as I won't wait for you. I really am there to work, at least to start with, and intend to arrive on schedule, which means ahead of the guests. Maybe you can find an opportunity there to work the room a little to see if your new book idea would fly, even if its working title's a bit pedestrian.'

Ash shrugged off the friendly insult, and opened up the bonnet of the old MGB Roadster.

'Wine still is one of my things. As is this. Look at that engine. Beautiful, no?'

Mike had to admit that indeed it was.

Chapter 19

Tiffany quashed a sudden flutter of nerves as she entered the crisp steel and glass building housing Jenna's office. Inside, an elegant youth beamed soothingly from behind the smooth undulating line of a long wooden reception desk. We may look steely, but we are also warm and understanding, the interior seemed to say. Good veneer, she thought, realising simultaneously that the description matched both desk and receptionist.

'I've come to meet Jenna Fenix. She's expecting me: Tiffany Jay.'

The young man glanced down at the list in front of him.

'Ah yes, Miss Jay. Welcome. Please take the lift to the second floor, and her secretary will meet you there.' He indicated the sliding doors to Tiffany's right, smiled again, and lifted the phone. 'Miss Jay on the way up for Miss Fenix.'

Tiffany pressed the lift call button. The doors rolled open at once, smooth and whispering. She stepped in, avoiding her multiple reflections in its mirrored walls at first, and looked for the panel of buttons to punch in her second-floor destination. Then she stood back and surveyed herself. Slim at the moment (reflecting perhaps a few days of worrying about Felix and Jenna, on-and-off, she considered), and now lightly tanned enough to replace her natural paleness with a sun-kissed early summer glow; well-bobbed dark hair, with hints of auburn; and a flattering just-to-the-knee summer cocktail dress teamed with strappy high-heeled sandals that looked elegant while – amazingly – also being just comfortable enough to stand around in all evening. Yes, she looked just fine. She straightened her back a little, raised her chin a fraction, and walked confidently out of the lift.

'Miss Jay, how are you? This way.' Jenna's secretary was tall and efficient, with a hint of mindful reticence that made you want to confide in her.

'Fine, Angie, thanks. I wish you'd just call me Tiffany. How are you?'

Angie smiled serenely. 'Very well. Jenna's all set.' Tiffany followed her towards Jenna's office door.

'How is she?' she asked cautiously. Angie glanced at her.

'Very busy.' She tapped at the closed door.

'Hello, come in!' Jenna's voice was upbeat. As Tiffany crossed the threshold, Jenna rose from the chair to step round the desk and offer an almost contact-free hug, her hands barely brushing Tiffany's back. Tiffany knew this restrained embrace was close to Jenna's equivalent of a bear-hug of forgiveness from someone like Thomas, for example.

'Great to see you,' she responded as Jenna stepped back again. 'You look wonderful, Jenna. I'm so looking forward to this evening.'

'You look pretty cool yourself in that kit,' Jenna replied, surveying her outfit. 'Ready to roll? It's such a nice evening that I thought we might just go straight to the restaurant, and perhaps have a little drink in the courtyard ahead of the crowd. We could walk round there – it's probably quicker at this time of day, and quite close if you know the shortcuts.' She paused, contemplating Tiffany's shoes.

'I can stroll around the streets okay in these. Better than on lawns, actually. Walking over there will be fine, as long as we're not in a tearing hurry.' She glanced in turn at Jenna's own high-heeled footwear. Jenna nodded.

'Yes, ditto, and we've plenty of time to get there. Let's go.' She lifted a pale olive linen jacket and tiny handbag from the cream sofa that also graced her office, and led the way out. Tiffany discreetly assessed Jenna's appearance while following her to the lift. Still slender, perhaps a little curvier than before – I'm not sure, she thought.

'Have a nice evening,' Angie said from the open door of her own office.

'Aren't you coming?' asked Tiffany, surprised. Angie nodded.

'Later on. I'm hanging on here a bit longer to field any last-minute calls from lost guests. Bye for now,' she added, as the lift doors slid open.

'Thanks, Angie,' Jenna said. 'See you soon,' she and Tiffany added in chorus, as the doors closed and the lift carried them down to the waiting world.

On their stroll towards the restaurant they stuck to bland topics. Jenna mentioned that the theatre was shortly going dark for refurbishments. Tiffany idly wondered what that meant for Emma. They admired the vibrant flowers outside the florist's door. When they arrived at the courtyard that housed the restaurant, Felix was leaning against the flat pilaster that flanked the left side of the establishment's open double doors. Tiffany saw him as soon as she and Jenna came through the arch and began to cross the York stone courtyard. He looked magnificent, vital, energised. Oh dear, she thought, all ready to pounce, again. He glanced across and waited, watching them walking towards him.

'Jenna, Tiffany, my favourite muses. How gorgeous you both looked coming across the courtyard. Isn't it a glorious evening?' He touched Jenna's arm lightly at the elbow as he kissed her cheek, and then lent across to brush Tiffany's cheekbone with his own warm skin, making hers tingle.

'Felix, you're electrifying, as ever,' she said. 'Pre-launch nerves obviously suit you.'

He agreed. 'I can't let Jenna down after her sterling work on my behalf. I have to be on top form. Are you ready for a quick preview?' He indicated the open doors. Jenna smiled fondly at him.

'I've already seen it in the finished state. I came down earlier for a quick check on the party arrangements. You've turned a small place into a panorama to feast the eye and spirit, as well as the appetite,' she said encouragingly.

'Exactly what I was trying to do. Don't you think that description should be in our publicity material somewhere?'

'It is. You really should read what I give you, Felix. Now take Tiffany in and wow her with the art. As people start arriving, I want the artist indoors with his creations, while I field the guests out here and usher them in to experience the wonder of your work. You could hold court in there until it gets too full, or too warm, and then come out here to mingle,' she instructed, though she made it sound like a suggestion. 'The crowd will go where you do. Food and drink will follow wherever they go. The waiting staff are briefed to top you up with iced water, and plenty of canapés to keep you fuelled and able to captivate everyone. Ozzy should be here soon – and, as we owe the introduction for this commission to him, Felix, make a decent fuss of him. Lots of the guest list are his clients and contacts and, as we'd like him to introduce you to more in future, we're still casting him in the role of your benign discoverer tonight.'

'But Tiffany found me first,' he said, paying his dues. He still needed her support.

'Yes; and Ozzy was quick to realise the full extent of your talent, and generously chooses to reveal it to his own carefully selected public tonight,' Jenna said briskly. 'Keep to the brief. It's perfect. Ozzy is, after all, used to staging shows and illusions.' Felix felt a curious sting in her remark, and wondered if she was making fun of him, but also saw Tiffany's warning glance at him. Don't argue, it said. He gave Jenna a mock bow of acceptance.

'You know how to pull his strings,' he suggested.

'For tonight's purposes, I do – and in everyone's mutual interest,' Jenna reminded him. 'But Ozzy will still have his own underlying agenda, you can be sure of that.' Felix nodded. Jenna was right.

'To the task in hand, then. Tiffany, come and view the terrain. I truly want your approval, you know,' he added, as he led her inside the restaurant.

Tiffany gasped. Every wall, ceiling, nook and cranny had been translated. The patchwork blocks of colour had been overgrown by gardens that in turn yielded vistas of rolling sunlit parkland, lakes and, beyond these, distant fields, woodland and hills. Spaces that had been intimate alcoves of block colour, tucked inside the restaurant, were now the quiet, secret corners of a maze colonised by jasmine, and opened up by breaches in the hedges, offering tantalising glimpses of the infinite views and skies that stretched beyond, and emerged above, their leafy embrace.

Life was everywhere, from untrammelled plants and tumbling sprays of flowers to small birds perched in the foliage. A few mice scuttled about in corners – that's a hostage to fortune for a restaurant, thought Tiffany – and watchful cats lurked or stretched in the grass and the shadows (of course, she reflected). Looking around, on one wall she saw a small fox slipping along the edge of one field, glancing back as it went. Following the line of its alert gaze led Tiffany's eyes to the foreground where a sleek tabby gazed directly into the restaurant. It was the only creature aware of the external world, and clearly a self-portrait drawn from Felix's former incarnation. Tiffany followed the line of the cat's stare across the room; and there, perching on the lintel of the double doors through which she had entered the restaurant, was a beautiful jay. Its head turned as if to examine a painted crack in the wall within which the trompe l'oeil edges of bricks and something tucked between them, a secret *billet-doux* perhaps, gleamed softly.

'Felix,' Tiffany whispered, 'you have really made magic here. No-one will ever want to leave.'

He swelled with pride. 'Thank you, my dearest Tiff,' he said. He bent towards her and looked into her splendid blue, and brown, eyes. 'Stay within the spell,' he whispered back to her. Then he turned her around to look towards the kitchen, where a waiter had just emerged through what now seemed an old ivy-covered garden door carrying a large round silvered tray loaded with tall glasses of champagne and a slender frosted flute of iced water. 'A celebration,' Felix said cheerfully, passing her a glass of champagne and taking the flute of water from the tray for himself. 'To Tiffany, without whom none of this could exist.'

'If you insist on putting it that way.' She accepted her glass. 'But not forgetting the artist – long may his talent last.' Felix eyed her thoughtfully, as she drank, and then was distracted by someone coming through the double doors. Pausing just beneath the painted jay was a tall, thin, rather bony man whose linen shirt and cotton trousers almost seemed to be wearing him rather than the other way round. He slid the broad canvas strap of a stippled metal case from his shoulder, and dumped the case on the floor. Straightening up, he looked around, and whistled low.

'It's Mike, the photographer Jenna's hired to cover tonight's party,' Tiffany said. 'He took some promotional pictures of your murals in my flat the other day.'

'I know. He was here earlier in the week, snapping bits and bobs as I worked.' A second man was now strolling towards the open restaurant doors and for a moment Felix looked genuinely startled. Then he narrowed his eyes again, and stepped forward smiling to greet the photographer.

'Mike, good to see you again. Liking the finished effect? You've seen a good deal of the work in progress.' They shook hands.

'Excellent job,' said Mike, nodding at Tiffany and making her wonder if he meant her appearance too. As she smiled back at him another figure appeared, silhouetted against the evening light outside, his features indistinguishable to her as he paused in the doorway. Mike's assistant perhaps. She returned to examining Felix's artworks, and in particular the tabby cat.

'Mind if I start by taking a few shots before the place fills up more?' Mike said to Felix. 'This is Ash Lennard, by the way,' he added, indicating the second man, who had now strolled into the restaurant and stood directly below the painted jay. 'You may know the name. Friend of mine who lives down the road from you, Tiffany,' he added, speaking more loudly to recapture her attention. 'I thought he needed a change of scene this evening.'

Tiffany, turning again to reply, caught her breath. It was the man she had been so horribly rude to in the street only a few weeks ago. His car toolkit and clutter had been all over the pavement when she was trying get home, carrying all her food-shopping for the dinner party for Felix that Anthony had gate-crashed. Running late, she had snapped 'Must you take up the whole pavement?' at the figure crouched over the rusting sportscar's open bonnet, as she stepped over a pile of spanners and lord knows what bits of car, lugging her heavy supermarket bags.

'Sorry – do you want a hand with those?' an attractive male voice had replied as he stood up.

'No thanks,' she had replied curtly, still irritated, and now off her stride. 'I'll manage.' As he had turned towards her, she had seen too late that he was as handsome as his voice, and had a heart-stopping smile. She had stalked off towards her flat still feeling cross, but now mostly with herself for being so graceless. The memory brought a slight flush to her face again tonight.

Ash shook Felix's hand, and glanced at the apparently flustered Tiffany without comment before turning his gaze to the walls while absorbing what had just occurred. So it was her – an amusing coincidence – and Mike was right, her eyes were different colours. As he focused on the murals for a moment, the portrait of the tabby cat staring straight at him suddenly caught his attention. He did a double-take, frowned for a moment, and then laughed. This place was apparently filling up with troublesome, if entertaining, past acquaintances. The evening was already more interesting than he could have hoped.

'Damned cat,' he said to Tiffany, as she was nearest. 'It's the spitting image of the tomcat that put its paws all over my fresh paintwork and then sat on my page proofs. It's clear where some of your inspiration is from,' he added, turning to look at Felix. 'I gather you've already done some murals in our neck of the woods. You must've had a similar problem with the same feline. I'm not surprised you've decided to immortalise him, though – a pretty good specimen, isn't he? Although I think I prefer him immobilised like that.'

Felix, glowing with satisfaction, nodded without elaborating. Ash glanced again at Tiffany who, lips parted, seemed about to agree; but her eyes just grew wider and she took a sip of champagne instead, trying to reel in a sense of panic.

He knows the original Felix, she thought. Stay calm, stay calm, breathe. There's no way he could work it out. Look at Thomas, he knew Felix really well as a cat, and has never suspected a thing. It's going to be OK. She smiled carefully at Ash across the top of her champagne glass, and then introduced herself properly.

'Hello. I'm Tiffany. It was my flat that Felix painted first. We must be neighbours.' Ash shook her proffered hand. She felt warmth and relaxation flow up from his touch, up her arm and across her shoulders, and looked at him with surprise. How does he do that? she wondered.

'Yes,' Ash continued, keeping straight faced. 'I've seen you around the area. I didn't realise it was your flat that Mike was talking about. I'm the one who is always tinkering with cars.'

Tiffany blushed properly this time.

'I realise,' she said. 'I'm so sorry I was rude to you that time, with all the shopping. I was in a bit of rush that evening.'

'I noticed.' He grinned wickedly at her now, rewarding her frankness. It made her heart beat faster. 'Don't worry about it, I'm quite used to getting in people's way. It's a professional hazard, when you travel as much as I do.'

'Oh,' said Tiffany. 'Why do you travel so much?' She was trying hard to place his name now. Ash, Mike had said. Ash Lennard. Where has she heard that before?

'It's what I do,' Ash replied. 'I write travel books, articles – and tinker with my MGB Roadster. That's my life, an open book, on the open road. And you?'

'Oh, I'm a PA,' Tiffany wished she had said something more exciting. 'Of course, I've seen your books.' (How dim can I be?) 'I travel a bit too, between jobs.'

'Between jobs?' queried Ash, noting that she only claimed to have seen, rather than actually read, any of his *oeuvre;* and liking her for not pretending. 'Let me guess – too rude to the boss to stay put for long?'

Tiffany flushed again.

'No, but I guess deserve that comment. I like to work for eighteen months or so, maybe less, and then go on a long trip and then come back and do it all again. I enjoy the variety of working for lots of different people and businesses,' she explained, trying to stop the words from tumbling out too fast.

'So you're good at what you do?' he suggested, thinking, I suppose she must be if it's that easy to snap up another job each time round.

'Very,' said Emma's voice, from behind Ash. 'She was even PA to one of our major sponsors of the local theatre, for a bit. None better.' For a moment Tiffany was grateful but then Emma continued, 'Although sadly she's not a stayer. How are you? This is Anthony – another of Tiffany's "exes".'

Even Anthony shifted awkwardly from foot to foot for a moment.

'This is Ash Lennard,' Tiffany said stiffly.

'I know,' said Emma. 'We've met before.'

'Hello Emma,' said Ash, calmly. 'You look as if life's treating you well.'

'Oh yes,' she replied brightly just as Jenna, still outside, looked in through the double doors and called out to them.

'Emma, Anthony, grab a drink and have a look round before the crush – and don't crowd the doorway!' Anthony, thirsty, moved quickly towards the nearest waiter bearing a tray of glasses; and Emma, her hand tucked into his arm, had to follow or be pulled inelegantly along. Tiffany was glad.

'Sharp cookie,' Ash commented. 'Looks like butter wouldn't melt and then suddenly you're toast. We had a couple of dates a year or so ago,' he explained in answer to Tiffany's surprised expression, 'after meeting at some fundraising event for her theatre. Not entirely my type, though, as it turned out – nor indeed I, hers. We didn't get beyond the drinks stage.' He lifted a glass from the tray that the waiter was now offering to them. Tiffany's was still half-full.

'I think she's found a better match in Anthony,' Tiffany observed tartly, and then realised this sounded like an insult directed at Ash. (What is wrong with me tonight? Damn and double damn). But he seemed to find her reply funny, and laughed.

'You're not too heartbroken about your ex, then? Since we are revealing each other's romantic past, perhaps we should discuss the talented muralist next.' He was teasing, but Tiffany winced inwardly.

'A family friend,' she said, rather too quickly.

'Really?' Ash tried his glass of champagne. Tiffany nodded, and changed the subject

'Why are you known as "Ash"? Is it short for something?' She let the waiter top up her glass a little.

'No. Ash is the Egyptian god of oases and vineyards. My mother was into her myths, and my father was fond of his wines – so the name was inevitable. It also means lion-headed, by the way. Ash is said to be the more benign counterpart, some even say the alter ego, of Seth, the god of storms and deserts – and chaos.'

'Goodness. That's a lot of information to live up to,' Tiffany observed, and drank deeply.

Ash nodded. 'Indeed. I opted to concentrate on the wine and bounty.'

'My great grandfather was an Egyptologist,' she ventured, thinking of her figurines, 'so I know a bit about Seth, though I don't think I've ever heard of Ash – but I realise, now, that I have read some of your travel articles. Sorry that I was being very slow earlier about placing your name, although if you ever need a good PA to organise your trips, or during them, do let me know! My current boss is a dreadful bore,' she added.

Immediately she felt this sounded both tactless, and too like a clumsy pass at him. She took another sip of champagne to hide her incompetence and silently cursed herself for being so off-message tonight. She glanced round for someone to join the conversation before she made an even greater a fool of herself. Rescue seemed to arrive instantly in the tall, efficient form of Angie strolling through the door, who waved, and made a bee-line for Ash, draping an affectionate arm across his shoulders.

'Hello darling,' she said, 'glad you could make it.' Ash grinned happily at her.

'Yup. The art all looks very good, as do you! We should come here again.'

Tiffany was crushed with disappointment. He's Angie's boyfriend, and I have been a complete ass, she divined. She glanced at her once again half-full glass. 'I must find a refill,' she said, 'and I really ought to circulate more. Would you excuse me?' She smiled weakly at Angie, and headed for the nearest waiter. As he carefully topped up her flute glass, she looked around for someone else to gravitate to. It would be doubly embarrassing to be seen wandering about alone after her lame excuse for leaving Angie and Ash's company. Emma and Anthony were within reach, but did not appeal. Felix, surrounded by guests, all elegantly turned-out men and women, looked equally sleek and pleased with himself. She could go outside and see who was in the courtyard, but that meant doubling-back and passing Ash and Angie. Mike was still inside, but busy taking shots of the guests clustering around Felix. Her glass was now full. She thanked the waiter and took a sip.

'I'll take some of that too,' a voice from slightly above her said. She looked up and saw the familiar form of Thomas, now holding out his glass to the waiter for a refill.

'Thomas!' She was delighted. 'How lovely to see you. Have you just got here?' She gave him an enthusiastic hug of welcome that was observed by Ash, glancing just then across the room towards her.

'I was waylaid by Jenna in the courtyard for a moment – I brought someone along that I'd promised to introduce her to. I've left them to it now. How much of this stuff have you had already?' The strength of her hug had surprised him too.

'Not enough yet. Who did you bring?' Tiffany was intrigued.

'Oh, a legal chum, an employment lawyer who Jenna wants to consult about how she might develop her own PR sideline for smaller clients like Felix, without rocking the boat too much with her current lot. Something she can set up now, ready to combine with working from home in due course, that sort of thing. I thought Lucy might as well meet Jenna and see the art, and indeed the artist, before they get down to discussing the practicalities more formally.'

'That's very good of you.' Tiffany hesitated. 'Lucy – you say – a new girlfriend, by any chance?'

'Sadly not,' Thomas was amused. 'Nor my generation, although very attractive. An office friend, and sometime drinking companion; good at parties.' Tiffany decided to change tack.

'So tell me, what do you think of the art?' she asked, looking round the restaurant.

'Splendid.' Thomas meant it. 'I particularly like the hypnotic tabby – surely a portrait of your AWOL moggy? I swear I recognise him.'

'Yes, it is very like him,' she answered, and quickly switched topics. 'By the way, I ought to thank you – for apparently sorting out all my friends' legal questions.'

Thomas smiled at her. 'For passing them on to others to sort out, you mean. Not that Felix seems to be much in need yet. I'm still not quite sure what game plan he had in mind.' He looked questioningly at Tiffany.

'I am. I believe he was considering how to steal some of Ozzy's thunder, but I think the murals business is proving an acceptable diversion for the moment,' she said lightly.

'Ah.' Thomas felt that he now understood why Ozzy was singing Felix's praises so highly, to the rooftops, out in the courtyard and telling his rich friends and acquaintances that the chance to set Felix to work on their own walls was simply not to be missed, before sending them inside to see for themselves.

He sketched the scene to Tiffany, adding: 'I see. So if Ozzy has his way, Felix will now be kept far too busy – and fussed over – to want to challenge Ozzy in his own domain for quite some time.' Tiffany's merry laugh at this caught Ash's attentive ear. He glanced across at her again, wondering again who the tall muscular man entertaining her so successfully might be. He studied them as she talked animatedly to Thomas.

'Good for Ozzy!' she was saying, although Ash could not quite make out the words. 'He doesn't miss a thing, does he? Sometimes I think he is way ahead of us all the time – he seems instinctively to outmanoeuvre everyone. It's hard to keep up.' Thomas looked affectionately at her, although why she would want to keep up with Ozzy's progress was a puzzle. Her laughter had brought her fully into focus. The surroundings suited her too. She suddenly seemed to be glowing from within.

'You look great, Tiff,' he told her, 'in really good form.'

'It's the champagne, and release from a guilty conscience.'

'*You* have a guilty conscience?' mocked Thomas. 'What is the world coming to? So what do you have to feel guilty about now, anyway?' he added, taking her fractionally more seriously.

'How about... having introduced Felix to Jenna, and Jenna of all people apparently getting pregnant, and me reacting badly to the news, and generally being graceless about the whole business?' She confessed in a rush. Thomas looked at her carefully.

'I didn't think Felix was *that* significant to you,' he said, 'or am I very unobservant?'

'Not unobservant at all, quite the reverse, and I love you for it,' said Tiffany. 'You are right, but everyone else thought I was spitting tacks over Felix getting so wrapped up in Jenna, or the other way round. He even had the nerve to tell Jenna that I had gone all broody, and getting bitter and twisted about maybe missing the baby boat myself, but it's just not true. It's Jenna that I'm worried about. I already know Felix too well to expect him to be any real support to her, and besides – well, there's a bit of a family history on his side that makes me wonder if any baby will be, um – okay.'

She was almost whispering now. She hesitated, not wanting to be drawn much further into explaining her anxiety here. Perhaps she has already gone too far. 'Maybe I shouldn't mention that stuff, but I gather that Felix hasn't, and so I'm a bit concerned,' she tailed off feebly. Thomas took her hand gently in his, still watched by Ash, who had made out the shape of the words 'I love you' on Tiffany's lips, and was trying to work out what was afoot.

'Oh Tiffany,' Thomas said. After his meeting over lunch with Jenna, he was relieved to hear this confirmation from Tiffany that the oddness, whatever it was, lay in Felix not in Jenna. 'I'm so sorry you've had to keep all that to yourself, all this time; but you were probably right not to go into details so far – especially if she hasn't even done a proper test yet. Until then it's still up to Felix, not you, to let the cat out of the bag, if there is one. In any case, I'm quite sure that Jenna would have all the checks and things that are on offer these days. The last thing you'd want to do is to make her worry unnecessarily throughout a pregnancy – that can't do her any good.' Tiffany looked at him gratefully despite his one unfortunate turn of phrase, unaware that Thomas had spared her his own remaining and rather different reservations about Jenna's condition.

'Of course, Thomas, thank you. You're right, so level-headed. I just wasn't thinking things through properly. None of my close friends has had a baby.' Ash, who had managed to lipread Thomas's 'I'm so sorry', despite the difficulties posed by other guests and waiters randomly breaking his line of sight, now also made out Tiffany's last sentence about having a baby. Angie, still next to him, was chatting cheerfully to more people arriving and did not notice what was fascinating Ash.

As Thomas reassured Tiffany, he turned slightly as he spoke, and it became harder for Ash to read his next words.

'My sister has produced an entire warren of children so I am well versed in all this stuff,' Thomas was saying. 'Don't worry, Tiff, let things take their course for the moment, and we're all here to support Jenna if needed.' Tiffany nodded. Forgetting for how short a time Thomas has been included in Jenna's circle, she did not query his status as one of the back-up team. Ash nudged Angie, now with her arm draped over Mike's shoulders.

'Who is that Tiffany whatsit, with the mismatched eye colours, talking to so seriously?' he asked. Angie looked across to see.

'His name is Thomas, and he's a lawyer. Jenna had lunch with him recently to pick his brain about something. I believe he's a very old friend of Tiffany's, but exactly what kind of old friend you would have to ask her – or him. Or try Jenna. She will know.' She smiled. 'Go on, bro, get your adventurer's hat on and chat her up for yourself. Mike's done the legwork, getting you here – the least you can do is make him feel it was worth the effort this evening, even if nothing comes of it later. Get out there and good hunting!' Ash shook his head, and grinned.

'Sisters!' he said to Mike. 'You don't know what you're missing.'

'I'm not missing it at all, mate,' Mike said, his arm around Angie's waist. 'I married her, didn't I? She bosses me about all the time.' Ash laughed.

'So you did. OK, I know when I'm no longer required.' He glanced at Tiffany again. 'Here I go – once more into puzzling and, as I recall, sometimes downright hostile territory.' My kind of adventure after all, he thought, as he ambled towards Tiffany and Thomas; but Jenna got there first, whisking through the door from the courtyard and straight past him to descend on the pair with relief.

'Hello again, at last,' she announced. 'I'm no longer needed out there. Ozzy is doing such an astonishing PR job for Felix, praising his talent to the heavens, sending them in to admire the work, and making sure that they get plenty of champagne at all times, that I simply don't need to try any more tonight! He must think it's all going to pay dividends for him in some form, or perhaps he's just enjoying taking the credit, and the limelight. Hello Ash, are you enjoying the evening?' Ash, arriving at the little group, bent to kiss her cheek. Of course they would know each other, Tiffany realised, given that he's her secretary's boyfriend.

'Jenna, you look gorgeous,' Ash said, and Tiffany felt a twinge of envy. He had such a lovely voice. 'Yes, I find it all very intriguing.' He smiled directly at Tiffany, quickening her pulse. Stop that, you're with Angie, she thought, and frowned at him reprovingly. 'How do you do?' he said, turning to Thomas. 'I'm Ash Lennard.' Thomas shook Ash's outstretched hand.

'Thomas Ibbetts. I've read your books; enjoyed them. Does Jenna handle your PR too?' Ash shook his head.

'No, the publishers sort all that out, although having a sister involved with the PR world has its uses if I need a little informal guidance.' Thomas looked confused; Jenna had not mentioned a brother so far. Jenna saw his puzzlement, and rescued him.

'Ash doesn't mean me, at least not in the sister department! He's Angie's brother – my secretary Angie, she's here somewhere. Thomas, you've spoken with her on the phone.'

'Oh,' said Tiffany, just as Thomas said 'of course'; and she suddenly felt quite lightheaded. Then she regretted the reproving frown.

'So what have you done with Lucy?' Thomas asked Jenna.

'Oh, she's busy sizing up Felix with some of Ozzy's crowd – over there, I think.' Tiffany looked across at a tight knot of people around Felix.

'You've done a great job for him tonight, Jenna,' she said, feeling happier but not daring to look at Ash again until she could somehow decommission that unfriendly frown. 'What a launch.'

'Yes, I'm pleased with the way it's going. We should get some good mentions and, after this turn-out, it shouldn't be hard to persuade someone to do a glitzy piece about his murals, and even better if we can say we've a commission from one of Ozzy's celebrity pals.' She looked around for a waiter to find her a glass of water.

'Promising progress then,' Thomas suggested. Ash was still watching Tiffany, trying to gauge her mood, and her relationship with Thomas. She doesn't look pregnant to me, he thought, but what do I know?

Before he could think of a way to get some answers without a direct question, Thomas continued: 'So, how are you feeling? Seen your GP yet?' Tiffany tensed. Ash waited for her reply.

'Next week.' To Ash's surprise it was Jenna who answered, sounding slightly evasive. 'We've been so busy with this show.'

Ah, Ash thought, so it was Jenna that Tiffany was speaking of to Thomas, and perhaps they're all talking in riddles because Jenna's still waiting for the twelve-week all-clear before making it known officially at work. And Felix is the father? That seems – unfortunate.

'Is Felix going with you?' Tiffany was asking.

'No,' Jenna replied; and accepted a slim glass of iced water from the waiter's tray.

'Someone should,' Thomas suggested, glancing at Tiffany, 'or at least meet you afterwards, to share the exciting moment. My sister always dragged me along, if her husband wasn't available, after the first three.'

'Three!' said Jenna. 'How many does she have now?'

'Six,' said Thomas, 'and the last lot were twins. Quite a litter.' Tiffany winced at the word.

'I don't think I could handle twins,' Jenna said. 'Or the thought of ending up with six!'

'Why don't you and Tiff meet up after you've seen the GP?' Thomas persisted.

Tiffany stared at him. Why was he so keen for her to be there? Puzzled, she said: 'Shall I?' to Jenna.

Feeling cornered, Jenna decided that if Tiffany was genuinely keen to make amends, it would seem churlish to say no. She gave in.

'OK. On Tuesday. Why don't we meet in the coffee bar opposite the health centre entrance first, around eleven-thirty, and then I'll rejoin you there afterwards?'

'I'll take the morning off,' said Tiffany. Ash was still observing them with interest. Something was odd about all this, and he was intrigued by whatever was being played out. Why was Thomas being so pushy, and what was he to Tiffany? Or to Jenna, for that matter? Ash shrugged. If he couldn't fathom the Tiffany-Thomas link-up tonight, he could always ask Tiffany outright. She could not be any ruder to him in reply, than she already had been, after all.

That thought entertained him. He wandered off to look at more of Felix's work in the restaurant first. Tiffany's gaze followed him.

He's a neighbour, she thought. I can bump into him, or stroll past when he's outside tinkering with his car and stop to invite him for a drink, to make up for being so offhand before. All was not yet lost. She looked around the party and glimpsed Emma, outside, framed by the double doors to the courtyard, calling to someone.

'Lucinda!' exclaimed Emma. Stepping out of the crowded restaurant for some air, she was astonished to see her stepmother-elect out there, and apparently about to leave the gathering. 'What are you doing here?'

Lucinda smiled warmly.

'Emma,' she said. 'I rather thought you might be here, but I didn't spot you in the crush.' She bent forward and kissed the younger woman on the cheek. 'Tom Ibbetts brought me – we're in the same law practice, you know. I still work there part-time. He invited me to meet a friend who might like a little background advice.'

'Moonlighting?' Lucinda had always seemed so upright.

Lucinda, amused, shook her head.

'No. Just a friendly faintly-exploratory chat. If she needs more, she'll have to become a client like everyone else.'

'I'm glad to hear it, I'm not sure Father would like it if you suddenly started bending the rules too often.' He would probably laugh uproariously these days, she found herself thinking, and gave Lucinda a wry smile.

'Just the rules that we've bent already?' Lucinda teased her gently. 'You still don't mind our liaison, then?' Emma shook her head.

'I told you, I'm delighted, although I would never have expected it. Stupid of me not to guess it was likely to happen, really. You've known each other so long, and always had fun – I seem to remember lots of laughs and jokes whenever you came round when we were small.'

Long childhood summers seemed to float before her eyes. It was true that whenever Lucinda popped round, Emma's siblings had seemed to become more fun and less combative.

'I'm glad you are so at ease about it. Your mother continues to be very gracious too,' Lucinda responded.

She paused, so Emma took up the topic. 'So you both said. I'm actually seeing her soon – she finally rang to pencil in a get-together for when she's finished running about sorting out various things.'

'I was sure she would. Saving the best to last,' Lucinda said kindly, and noticed a tall dark-haired man coming through the double doors, carrying two glasses of champagne. He stopped next to them in the courtyard.

'Lucinda, this is Anthony,' Emma said. 'Anthony, this is Lucinda. I told you about her?' Lucinda looked him over.

'How do you do, Anthony. I'm an old family friend of Emma's.'

'Lucinda will soon be my stepmother,' Emma reminded Anthony, as she relieved him of a glass, freeing him to shake hands.

'Ah yes, of course, many congratulations,' Anthony replied, surprised to meet Lucinda here. Although he was now aware of Emma's parents' changing lives, he had not expected to be introduced to any of the protagonists tonight. 'Let me get you a drink. In fact, take this one. I'll get another.' Lucinda accepted the flute of champagne and, as Anthony moved towards a waiter with a tray of full glasses, she turned to Emma.

'The boyfriend?' she asked.

'It looks as though it's going that way.' Lucinda liked this reply.

'Nice-looking chap. Good luck. Does your mother approve?'

'She will,' Emma said firmly.

Lucinda couldn't help laughing. 'You sound so like her,' she said.

Emma was surprised, but not offended. 'Good, I think,' she answered, adding. 'Here's to Mother.'

Lucinda echoed the toast.

'To Iris – and to you and Anthony,' she replied.

A stepdaughter busy with a new relationship was a better proposition than a single one who might still want to manage her father a little too much. Not that George was inclined to let anyone manage him – quite the reverse. Nevertheless, he would be glad to hear that Emma had found someone on whom to focus her own potentially formidable, transformative talents. George might secretly be a bit of a pussycat at times, but no child of Iris's, however benignly-intentioned, should be taken lightly.

Chapter 20

Jenna was already sitting in the coffee bar on Tuesday morning, flicking through a slim file of newspaper cuttings and some glossy photos but not really concentrating on them, as Tiffany arrived. It was peaceful, well after the early morning queues and rush of coffee addicts on their way to offices and work stations, and she had settled in a leather armchair with a low table in front of it.

'Tiffany,' she said, half rising now to give her friend a kiss on the cheek. 'What'll you have?'

'I'll get it – you keep the comfy seats for us. Anything more for you?'

Jenna shook her head. 'No thanks, I've cut down on caffeine lately.' She indicated a barely-touched glass of mint tea on the table.

Tiffany wanted to ask her if she would prefer a 'decaf' coffee instead of the tea but something in Jenna's manner made her just say 'OK', and join the short queue at the counter. She chose for herself a soothing latte. Returning with a full mug, she took another sip before sitting down, and asked: 'What have you got there?'

Jenna closed the folder before answering.

'Cuttings from a couple of gossip columns about Friday's bash, some notes about the online coverage, and copies of some of Mike's photos – there's a nice one of you and Thomas chatting, if you would like it.' Jenna passed the file over to Tiffany to leaf through. The photos were good and the diary pieces were, as expected, more about Ozzy's coterie than Felix, but at least the party was described as a glittering event unveiling the latest fabulous work of stunning muralist and deliriously handsome Felix Sylvester – 'whose murals are surely the must-have interiors of the moment.'

'That's great,' said Tiffany. 'It all makes Felix sound established and yet the latest hot property, all at the same time. Are you pleased?' To her, Jenna seemed more preoccupied than thrilled. Nerves ahead of seeing the GP, Tiffany supposed. She pushed her own uneasiness away.

'Of course, and Felix is positively drooling with anticipation of plump commissions,' Jenna was replying drily.

'How very inelegant,' Tiffany joked, thinking suddenly of the ginger cat almost gibbering at the pigeons in the park. 'That's got to stop! No dribbling on fashionable clients' upholstery.'

Jenna had to laugh at that. 'Really Tiffany, you're still the only person who can put Felix in his place.'

I wish I could, sometimes, thought Tiffany – ideally back where he came from – but she just smiled back.

'I've known him too long. So, how are you feeling? All set for the GP visit?' She looked at Jenna's barely curving stomach beneath the loose, cowl-neck fine cotton T-shirt and elegant button-through skirt. Bump or no bump? Bit too soon to show, she supposed.

Jenna tucked the cuttings and photos into the folder again and put it back into her neat briefcase. She was not going to admit yet to Tiffany that she felt nervous. Instead she glanced at the time shown on her mobile phone, and said, 'I should probably head over there now, in case there's a queue for the screen thing.'

'Screen at the GP's? I thought they did that bit at the hospital in another few weeks?'

'No, silly, the system that you tap into on your arrival at the GP's, these days, to let them know you've turned up for your appointment.'

'Oh'. Tiffany rarely went to a doctor. She stopped spooning up the remaining froth of her latte. 'Shall I come across too, and wait for you over there?'

Jenna was about to shake her head and ask Tiffany to wait in the café, as originally agreed, when a tall figure hurried through the door

'Thomas – what are you doing here?' Jenna exclaimed, as he bent to kiss her cheek.

'Seeing a client just up the road, and remembered you two were meeting here today. Thought I'd drop in for a coffee and lend some additional moral support.' He glanced at Tiffany and greeted her too.

'Actually I'm just going over to the surgery now,' Jenna said. 'A bit early but I'd rather be there in good time.' She paused and then added, 'So I suppose you'd both better come too. Unless you would rather stay here for that coffee?' She suddenly felt the need for someone other than Tiffany to wait with her, someone with no complicated feelings about Felix. 'To tell you the truth, now the moment has come, I'm having kittens.'

Tiffany froze for a nano-second, temporarily unable to breath. Don't be an ass. Pull yourself together, she thought. As Jenna stood up, Thomas put a friendly arm around her shoulders.

'Come on then,' he said. 'You too, Tiffany?'

Together they left the café, crossed the road and went into the health centre. Once Jenna had checked in – there really was a screen to tap, Tiffany saw – they sat, each in their own thoughtful silence in the bland waiting room as other patients came and went, until Jenna's name and a consulting room number flashed up in red lights on the electronic display that summoned people to their appointments.

'See you shortly,' Thomas said to her, his grey eyes serious. Tiffany gave her a tiny wave, watched her go, and then turned to Thomas.

'What is going on?' she whispered. 'Why are you here?'

'Well, if you must know, she doesn't seem that pregnant to me. No pregnancy glow,' he murmured back. 'I've seen it all with my sister,' he reminded Tiffany before she could ask what made him such an expert all of a sudden. 'So I wondered if there was something else going on, as you'd put it, and I didn't think Felix would be here to be supportive.'

Am I not good enough? Tiffany wondered, but knew she was already too compromised, by her disbelief and then disapproval of this particular pregnancy, to be the most appropriate friend in need if things did go awry. (Or correct themselves, she thought guiltily, not daring to voice aloud what would only sound cruel to anyone unaware of Felix's pedigree.)

Only now did she notice that Thomas had no briefcase or papers with him, and realised that he had not been visiting a client in the area at all but had come to find them specially – and perhaps partly because Tiffany's comments at the party on Friday had alarmed him. Felix is right, she thought affectionately: Thomas is a rather wonderful human being, but too good for my own taste. Besides, I want to find out more about Ash. So she nodded in reply to his explanation, and resumed waiting, watching passers-by through the window, and tried to think of nothing at all.

'Here she comes,' Thomas nudged her elbow discreetly. Jenna was walking slowly across the waiting room, her briefcase dangling, satchel-like on a long strap, from her shoulder. She looked like an automaton, or a sleepwalker. Tiffany experienced a strange and slightly nauseous mix of alarm and nascent relief as she took in the remote, but almost embarrassed, expression on Jenna's face.

'Let's go,' Jenna said quietly to them, ignoring their inquiring scrutiny. 'I need a drink. Preferably gin,' she added flatly. Tiffany understood at once that if Jenna had briefly believed she was pregnant she did not think so now. Thomas showed no surprise, just concern in his handsome grey eyes. They followed Jenna out of the health centre and stood outside on the pavement together in silence for a moment. Thomas gestured to a pub a little further along the street.

'It's open now, and has some of those old-fashioned booths – shall we try there?'

'Fine,' said Jenna, stalking ahead of them. She pulled a light grey pashmina from the side-pocket of her briefcase as she walked, letting the material unfold in ripples, and slung it round her shoulders. Inside the pub, she went straight to the bar, but Tiffany intervened.

'I'll get these,' she said, 'you and Thomas go and find a booth. Gin for you too, Thomas?'

'A beer,' he said. She ordered a decent craft beer for him, and two gins and tonic. 'Doubles,' she told the young and rather good-looking barman, 'and go easy on the tonic. Lots of ice, and slices of lemon, though.' He gave her a tray to carry the glasses to the booth.

'You knew, didn't you,' Jenna was saying quietly to Thomas as Tiffany set the drinks in front of them. 'That's why you came.'

He acknowledged it. 'I wondered,' he said. Tiffany sat down, waiting for the facts.

Jenna took up her gin and cradled the cool glass for a moment, before taking a considerable swig and then saying: 'It was a phantom.'

'A phantom?' Tiffany repeated the word nervously.

'A phantom pregnancy. The test at the GP's was negative. It was all in my imagination, apparently,' Jenna said grimly. 'My brain was tricked into thinking I was pregnant – and so convincingly that I even felt enough early symptoms not to bother with an over-the-counter test, but came direct to my GP. You can't imagine how stupid and embarrassed, and disappointed with myself I feel right now. But I'll get over it. The doctor said I could still go for some scan, to double-check, but frankly the test's left little room for doubt. Thank heavens I hadn't made any misguided over-excited formal announcements already.' She looked rather pointedly at Tiffany, 'And especially at work. You know what the most confusing thing is?' she added. 'Discovering that part of me is capable of dreaming up an imaginary pregnancy. Where did that all come from?'

She stared into her glass, where tonic bubbles clustering briefly around the ice cubes suddenly broke free and joined others racing towards the surface.

I may know, Tiffany thought, and it's not because there's anything wrong with you, Jenna; but she since could not reveal the detail, she said instead: 'We all have our unexpected moments.'

Thomas gave her an odd look, and asked, 'So who's going to tell Felix?'

'I suppose that I should,' Jenna answered quietly.

'Let me,' Tiffany offered. She was planning to alert him first anyway but this time would rather do so properly than secretly. 'Or, I can find him, and ask him to pop round to see you, if that's more helpful,' she added quickly, in case Jenna thought she was in some way revelling in these developments. She did feel a guilty relief, but still wished that Jenna had not suffered this whole charade through Felix's weirdness, and his vanity.

'No, I'll do it,' Jenna said flatly. 'You can fetch him. He'll be at Ozzy's studio. Just tell him I need a word with him about something.' Her tone forbade argument. She drained her glass. 'Thomas, would you come with me, to my place for a bit? I won't be going back into the office for today.' He nodded.

'Of course.'

Jenna knew he would be supportive without fuss or too much comment while she took stock of events, and recalibrated some of her thoughts and feelings. His quiet good sense and wry intelligence were exactly what she needed around her for now.

Chapter 21

Tiffany hesitated on Ozzy's doorstep, and then raised the hawk's head on the brass knocker. She let it fall three times, like a knell. Soon she heard firm footsteps and the door opened, revealing Ozzy clearly in work mode, and with a harassed look in his hooded eyes.

'Tiffany,' he said. 'Looking for Felix I suppose.' He paused and observed her more carefully. 'Is something amiss?' His gaze suddenly seemed a laser, cutting into her thoughts.

'In a sense. Jenna's lost the baby,' she blurted out the news in a rush. 'That is, there wasn't any baby – it was a weird mix-up. I said I'd fetch Felix to see her.' Ozzy's expression softened slightly, as if releasing her from interrogation, and now he looked fascinated.

'Really. Poor Jenna. How curious. Come in, come in.' Tiffany stepped across the threshold and entered the shabby mansion that housed Ozzy's workplace. As he led her towards his drawing room the hallway's peeling wallpaper and the ochre traces of ancient damp further subdued her spirits, but the light airy studio was a sudden delight. As her eyes adjusted to its brightness she saw Felix, across the room, examining something at the vast glass table. Various tall wooden panels, propped up against its far side, faced him, their backs to her. The chinos and the linen shirt that she had first bought for him were clearly now his working clothes, thoroughly paint-spattered, and he also seemed to be wearing a pair of old cowboy boots whose elaborate stitching had unravelled on parts of the scuffed leather.

'Tiffany,' he said, straightening up from his study of a small panel, laid flat on the glass table. 'Greetings. What brings you here?'

He wiped his hands on a paint-stained cloth and propped the picture against his side of the desk, with its back turned to her.

'Developments,' she answered, 'or rather the lack of them.' She felt little need to protect his emotions. 'News from Jenna. Are you ready?' Felix, alarmed by Tiffany's businesslike tones, wondered if she was going to announce that Jenna had abruptly withdrawn her PR patronage – but surely not, it was far too soon.

'What's happening?' He waited, alert, tensed in the light like a still from an old theatrical poster. Puss in bloody boots, Tiffany suddenly thought savagely.

'No baby, is what's happening. Jenna went to the GP this morning and it turns out that it was all a false alarm. One of those phantom pregnancy things. I always said that—'

'Don't speak,' he commanded sharply, wary of what she might blurt out next in front of Ozzy. 'I'll go to her at once.'

Tiffany took this for shock, and perhaps genuine concern for Jenna, on his part. She softened a bit towards him. Perhaps I have just been a bit brutal, she decided.

'I'm sorry, Felix, sincerely,' she said more gently.

He turned and looked out of the window, contemplating the allure of the wild garden for a few moments. 'Where is she right now?'

'Going home to get her head around things.'

'Things?'

'Well, apparently she could still have a scan to confirm what the GP says, if she wants, but Jenna seems sure that his diagnosis is correct.'

'You let her go home alone?' Ozzy inquired now, sounding censorious.

'No, no, Thomas is with her – he happened to be at the health centre building this morning.'

'Handy,' said Felix, not fooled. 'Always thought he was a thoroughly decent man. I should still go to see her, though.'

'Yes,' said Tiffany firmly. 'You should.' She remained standing, to underline the need to leave now.

'Right. I'll finish sorting through this lot later.' Felix glanced at Ozzy, who nodded.

'What is all that?' Tiffany asked, her curiosity unleashed now that she had delivered her message.

'Felix's next show,' said Ozzy from his observation post during these exchanges, by the window. 'He's working on a series of large but lightweight panels, so that his murals can become moveable feasts for the eye – easier to tempt clients with. Not everyone wants to commit a wall to a permanent artwork; this way they can ring the changes without any loss of investment.'

'Ah,' she said, recalling now what Jenna had already told her. 'Clever.'

'And, of course, he can exhibit these works in any large space,' Ozzy continued, 'which is what we have planned for these panels.' He sat down in one of the armchairs.

'Sounds very practical.'

'Always,' Ozzy retorted drily, crossing his legs. Felix, who had been pulling each panel forward to examine, extracted one of the smaller, more easily portable, ones.

'I'll take this one to Jenna now.' He held it up for Tiffany to see. It was a beautiful oil painting of a slender woman standing by a sunlit window and turning to look back at the viewer, in three-quarter profile, glowing with light. Tiffany was enchanted.

'It's wonderful, Felix. It's Jenna, isn't it? And somehow more than Jenna. It's stunning.' She was astonished again, not just by his skill but the speed of its development. Felix was satisfied.

He laid the panel gently on a sheet of bubble wrap, covering and layering it as though he were tucking Jenna herself tenderly into a cocoon. Tiffany watched, suddenly fascinated by his methodical actions. Absorbed in his task, his thoughts seemed to be in another world.

'Aright, let's go,' he said at last to Tiffany, taking the package carefully under one arm. Ozzy rose and patted Felix on the shoulder as they passed him.

'Sorry, old chap,' he said. 'Give my best wishes to Jenna.' There was an odd, and slightly questioning gleam in Felix's glance at Ozzy, as he acknowledged this remark with a wordless nod.

As they stepped out of the house onto the short gravel drive, Tiffany asked: 'Are you alright?'

Felix considered. 'I'm sorry how it's turned out. It would have been interesting to see my progeny. More sorry for Jenna, of course,' he added quickly, before Tiffany could interrupt him. 'You were right. Blame my pride in my potency.'

Perhaps your 'potency' is all in the art, given the energy put into that, Tiffany thought. It seems more durable, anyway. She pulled her linen jacket closer round her and walked silently onto the busy street beyond the dusty laurel bushes. Felix paced beside her, with the wrapped panel under his arm. On the main road, Tiffany saw a taxi approaching with its 'for hire' light on. It seemed heaven-sent and she hailed it. She wanted to drop Felix at Jenna's quickly now, and go home. Depositing him outside Jenna's apartment block, she directed the cab driver towards her own address and then asked him to stop shortly before her street. The brief walk back might help to settle her uneasy mind. Perhaps she should have had that cat neutered young. Too late now, alas.

'Tiffany! Not speaking to me at all, this time?' A man's voice close by broke her train of thought, sending pleasanter chills down her spine. Ash! In the street, still tinkering with his car. She stopped by the open bonnet.

'I didn't see you. I was thinking,' she answered, and then inwardly chided herself for sounding witless again. Ash stood up.

'Thinking? What about?' he asked. 'Not good thoughts, by the look on your face.'

'I am furious with Felix, if you must know.'

'Oh.' Ash was curious. 'Want to tell me about it? I make excellent coffee.' He indicated the steps up to his own front door. 'Or maybe something stronger?'

'I think I could use both.'

'Both it is then,' Ash replied, closing the bonnet of the MG and wiping his hands on a grubby rag. 'Shall we go in?' Tiffany walked up the front steps and stood aside to let him open the door. 'It's on the latch,' he said. 'Just push.'

He was tantalisingly close. Tiffany let herself enjoy the tingling feeling this gave her, pausing next to him for another moment before pushing the door and entering the building. Ash registered the tiny hesitation, but was not quite sure yet of its cause. Inside the tiled narrow hallway, Tiffany turned questioningly towards him.

'Left,' he said, nodding towards the half-open door to his flat, 'and then bear right for the kitchen and I'll put the kettle on and dig out a bottle. What do you feel like?'

Tiffany was about to say gin, but then she thought of Jenna in the pub earlier today, and a frisson of guilt stopped her.

'Cold?' Ash looked at her. 'You need a hot toddy along with that coffee. Trust me, I make a good one. Sit down,' he added, pulling a chair out from the kitchen table, 'and watch an expert at work.'

So Tiffany watched, as he moved easily round the kitchen in the late afternoon sunlight that filtered in through the foliage of the tiny back garden outside his kitchen window. He always seems so calm, she marvelled, perhaps from all that travel and the patience required on long trips. Then Ash put a mug of coffee down in front of her, followed by an open milk bottle, a small pot of brown sugar, and a spoon.

'Help yourself,' he said, and began to mix the hot toddy.

'Thank you,' she murmured, and decided that a little sugar might indeed be a good boost today. She was still slowly stirring the coffee when he put the toddy glass down in front of her too, pulled out a chair and sat down at the oval table about a third of the way round it from her, not too close, but not too remote either. She sipped her coffee, already cooled enough by the milk she had poured into it, and then lent forward to breathe in the steam from the hot toddy.

'Oh that smells good,' she said, savouring its headiness. 'So what's up?'

Tiffany hesitated, and took a tentative taste of her hot toddy, testing its heat, swallowed, and sipped again before setting the glass down with a grateful sigh.

'It's to do with Jenna,' she answered carefully. 'You know how we were talking about her maybe being pregnant, at Felix's opening in the restaurant? Or maybe you don't – and we should have been more discreet, anyway. Today she found out that it wasn't real, that it was a phantom pregnancy. She's mortified, and I feel to blame.'

Ash eyed her curiously. 'Why would you feel to blame?' he asked, thinking, sometimes the unknown can be right on the doorstep. Tiffany chose her words cautiously.

'I've always known there was something odd – I mean, not quite normal – about Felix, but I let him pursue Jenna without warning her,' she said, cradling the toddy glass again.

'Why would Jenna imagining that she was pregnant be due to Felix being the odd one?'

Tiffany sipped the toddy to give herself time to think how best to answer.

'He's quite compelling, and she's very independent – so perhaps he seemed the perfect donor if she did want to have a child, and that's what tipped her into this phantom thingy,' she suggested. 'He's also quite vain, so he might have rather liked the idea. I just feel that I might have saved her this grief, if I'd hinted better in the first place about his whackier side. It might have made a difference.

It was careless of me.' She drank some more hot toddy for comfort.

Ash looked at her, seriously considering his reply. He wanted to tell Tiffany that it was likely to be more complicated than that, and he still could not see how she would be to blame. Jenna and Felix were consenting adults, after all. Perhaps he needed to know a bit more first.

'And is she grieving?' he asked, 'or does she realise it may have been a lucky escape?'

'I'm not quite sure,' Tiffany admitted. 'More embarrassed than grieving, now – I think – and certainly putting a very cool face on things. That's more like the usual Jenna, but now it also worries me. Thomas has been a brick,' she added, 'a real friend in need.'

I'll get round to asking about Thomas, Ash thought, but let's put Felix to bed first, so to speak.

'So explain to me about Felix,' he said. 'What's so odd about him, and how do you know about it?' Tiffany decided to gamble with telling as much of the truth as possible.

'Felix,' she started. 'What can I say?' She drank some coffee. It was cooler, and less heady, than the hot toddy, and she needed to concentrate hard for a moment. 'He comes from right by my childhood home and I've known him since he was tiny. He was always a bit different, a bit wild. Recently he turned up here, in town, and stayed in my flat for a while. I've a slightly careless habit of giving temporary lodging to what Thomas and Felix both call my waifs and strays,' she added with a smile. 'And when he changed – that is, when Felix started painting murals for me and actually seemed to have a talent for it – I invited Jenna and other friends round to see his work and even encouraged Jenna to hire him next, as a live-in interior decorator painting murals for her in exchange for bed and lodging. Then she started to promote his career, and one thing led to another. Or vice versa.' She paused for Ash to respond but, having listened in silence, he still waited to hear more. Tiffany resorted to a swig of hot toddy this time – dutch courage, she thought – and resumed her account.

'Then Felix got his hooks into Ozzy as a potential mentor, and took up artistic residence with him. When I went round to the studio this afternoon, to tell Felix that Jenna needed to speak with him, he and Ozzy were conspiring over a great stack of paintings on panels that they plan to exhibit somewhere or other. It's remarkably soon after the restaurant opening to have so much else ready. I'm not sure if Jenna knew quite how far advanced their plan was – but she will now, as he took a panel round to her this afternoon. It's beautiful piece, a picture of her, absolutely magical. I don't know how Felix manages to work so fast.'

Ash wondered if she meant romantically, or artistically. Tiffany read the query in his look and smiled ruefully.

'Both,' she said again, and won a wry smile back from her host, 'but I meant the pictures. It's as though he's painting against time.' A realisation hit her. 'Perhaps he is,' she said pensively, following its trail. 'Perhaps he thinks this lightning success can't last, and wants to make his mark as fast as possible. I mean, he used to be quite a lazy creature but now it's as if he has to press on full speed ahead, regardless of everything else. I'm not even sure that he finds it fun anymore, and before he would just give up if he got bored with something.' Tiffany thought of her easy-going tabby cat, and wondered why Felix's character was proving a little different. 'Now it's more as if he's racing to get to the next project as soon as the previous one can be wrapped up.' Her expression changed as, with the wide eyes of a revelation dawning, she thought – is Felix in such a rush now because he thinks he will change back soon?

'Maybe he's just really enthused, for a change,' was how Ash answered the question in her eyes, distracted by how much he enjoyed the depth of their two different colours. 'Perhaps he wants to know just how far this newly discovered talent can take him – and it is a prodigious talent.'

'Yes, prodigious,' said Tiffany. 'It certainly is that.' Ash tipped back his chair a little, as he sat quietly and reconsidered what she had told him so far.

'Well, if it's any comfort, and maybe it isn't,' he said reflectively, 'I still don't see how you could be to blame for Jenna's unfortunate mix-up. She and Felix were co-conspirators in their relationship even if they didn't realise how that was going to turn out. I think you should stop beating yourself up. Maybe focus instead on supporting Jenna discreetly. I suspect Felix can look after himself.'

'Yes, too well so far,' she said, still wondering if Felix might revert to cat-hood, and how much it might be a relief. 'You're probably right, Ash, on both those fronts.'

Perhaps teasing her, Ash raised his toddy glass to this answer. Just Thomas's role to flush out next, he supposed, but something tells me he is not at the forefront of her mind just now.

'So what's done is done, and now onwards to a better future?' he suggested to her.

'I guess so,' Tiffany agreed, 'and talking of onwards, I really must get home for a bit.' Ash's last comment had sounded a bit like Felix talking, but voiced more kindly, she decided – and he really is just as annoyingly attractive.

She finished the hot toddy, setting the glass down on the table with its lip just touching Ash's glass, and gave him the full benefit of her beautiful eyes and her loveliest smile.

Chapter 22

Tiffany's mobile rang while she was on her way to the local Italian café with Ash. She had not, after all, gone straight home after finishing her hot toddy, but accepted Ash's easy suggestion of going to get some food en route – a very late lunch by now, or maybe early supper – around the corner. She glanced at the screen. It was Thomas, so she answered.

'How are things with you?' he began.

'Good,' she said brightly. 'Actually, I'm being ably supported at the moment by Ash, who scooped me up on my way home from dropping Felix outside Jenna's place. I assume he did go in,' she added, suddenly fearing Felix might have had cold feet and failed to go into the flat.

'Aha, swift work, coz – give Ash my regards. Yes, Felix appeared, and I left them to chat. All calm, I think. I'll call you back later.' Thomas could not help feeling that Ash would be a great improvement on Anthony.

'Alright, thanks Thomas. Goodnight.'

'Goodnight? Go carefully,' he suggested. Not that she ever did, he knew.

'I will,' she lied cheerfully.

Putting her mobile away she turned to Ash with a sweet smile. 'Thomas sends his regards.'

Ash was amused by the smile. The half of the conversation that he had overheard, and Thomas's message, confirmed his new assessment of where Thomas stood in Tiffany's affections. There was a distinctly brotherly air to that relationship, he decided. Still, there was no need to rush anything. An early supper, suggested on the spur of the moment, was not yet a date.

'Thank you,' he said. 'Come on. I'm hungry.'

Ash's engaging company and his traveller's tales carried Tiffany well into the evening, and finally deposited her at her own front door feeling fed, consoled, and slightly blurry after several glasses of wine during the meal, on top of the hot toddy. He walked to the door with her, kissed her lightly and said: 'I'll see if you're around tomorrow evening, shall I?' before strolling quietly away up the street. Elated, she had the presence of mind to drink a large glass of water before tumbling into bed and sleeping far more soundly than she felt she deserved.

Awaking early in the morning, she lay in the warm bed watching daylight slipping round the gaps at the sides of her white blinds, and gauzy curtains; gradually recalling the previous evening. Definitely an improvement on their first two meetings. Sleep was not returning, so she got up and went to make herself a coffee. She had taken yesterday off but had to be back at work today; and getting there early seemed the best way of securing a timely exit tonight.

Fergal Finch-Smith, Tiffany's present boss, was out for the morning so she decided to tackle a few outstanding routine tasks that needed attention. She plodded away at returning calls and emails about diary dates, finished some filing, and grudgingly started researching flights and fares for his family's next holiday. When Finch-Smith arrived in the office, he plonked a bulging green folder on her desk.

'Help me with this, will you?' he asked. 'I don't have the time to dig out all the answers myself'. He waved a bulky form at her. 'See what you can extrapolate for this thing, from the folder, and then let me know what the gaps are.' He headed off to his own large desk.

The 'thing' was his tax return, with a fat A4 booklet explaining how to fill it in, and the folder was full of a personal papers, bank statements and assorted dividend tax credit details. She sighed. I'm not your accountant, she muttered under her breath, or even *an* accountant, and this is not what the company is paying me to do. It's enough that I book your holidays, go out and get your wife's birthday present, and keep "mum" about the odd elasticity in your expenses. Hope there's a decent Christmas bonus in the wings for me for all this – if I stick around here till then.

She might take another break soon, and go off on one of her jaunts, or maybe even travel somewhere with Ash. With this tantalising dream in mind, she studied the tax form as it lay on the desk before her and began to leaf through the papers in the folder, slowly at first, and then with mounting curiosity.

Later, at home, she poured herself a gin and tonic at about seven and was sipping it in the kitchen, still pondering the day's efforts when Thomas called her back.

'Did you have a good evening yesterday?' he asked. She could hear a smile in his voice.

'Of course,' she said. 'And what is your news?'

'I called in on Jenna. Thought you'd like to know. She's looking much better, and still seems to be taking a very down-to-earth approach to the turn of events. I'm not sure if she's just very good at hiding distress, or impressively able to re-adjust.'

'Sounds to me like Jenna getting back to normal,' Tiffany confirmed with relief. 'She's very pragmatic, you know. Actually, on that front – now that I think about it – you two could be made for each other.' This had never occurred to her while Thomas was lodging at her own flat, and Jenna might have taken longer to notice Thomas's steady qualities if they had met then, but now – given that everything else seemed to be happening in fast-forward since Felix's arrival – why not also spur this new idea on? she reasoned. If it worked out well, it would certainly ease her conscience.

'Gently does it, Tiffany,' Thomas replied, a little gruffly, yet did not contradict her.

'Well, you know what they say – faint heart never won fair lady,' she advised mischievously. 'I see a formidable couple taking shape in my tea leaves.'

'Tea?' He knew her after-work habits.

'In the bubbles of my gin and tonic, then.'

'That sounds more like you. Jenna suggested that you drop in to see her at home tomorrow, on your way back after work, by the way. She's giving herself the rest of this week off, to take stock, as she puts it.'

Tiffany was pleased with this invitation.

'Great, I will do – just for a little while – at about six, give or take? Will I see you both there?'

'Possibly,' he said. Minx, he thought once again.

Tiffany leaned back a little against the kitchen table as she put her phone down on its smooth surface. She felt absolved. Lost in reverie, she jumped when the doorbell rang. She knew it must be Ash, and felt a tingle of excitement at the prospect of repeating, and developing, that light kiss. She moved purposefully to the flat door and buzzed him into the hallway, where she wrapped her arms about his neck and embraced him passionately.

'Well,' Ash said, eventually detaching himself gently, 'I'm delighted to be so welcome.' They steered each other into the flat. Neither needed to talk much, or debate their intentions, discuss the future, make plans to travel together or separately but meet up at pre-arranged destinations, yet – all that could wait for less decisive moments, to luxuriate in together later. For the moment only one thing mattered: to confirm and complete their discovery of each other as a pair. Gin and anticipation – and a new sense of power that the various reassurances and discoveries of the past twenty-four hours had variously delivered – made both Tiffany and Ash determined to secure each other before any other predator cruised into the field and attempted a challenge.

The combination was electric, and enlightening. They embraced greedily and got no further than her sitting room before hands and arms, and legs and thighs, bellies and backs, curves and dips, mouths and touch and lust and tenderness had all been shared.

'This calls for champagne, and I happen to have some in the fridge,' said Tiffany later, reclining on the carpet and smiling contentedly at Ash.

Propping himself up on one arm he said: 'That's very well-planned of you.'

Tiffany grinned. 'Actually, it's been lurking there since my last dinner party, but I see no reason why you shouldn't be allowed to benefit, and share it with me.'

'Sphinx,' he said, rising to his feet. 'Have you got any brandy? I think champagne cocktails are more in order than just some bottle of fizz you happen to have waiting for an excuse to drink, wouldn't you say?'

'Better and better,' said Tiffany. 'You may just have to become a regular feature.'

'I was intending to,' said Ash.

Tiffany sighed with happiness. 'Brandy's in the cupboard to the left of the cooker,' she called after him, as Ash headed towards the kitchen. It was Anthony's duty-free bottle, still lurking. At last a good use for it, she thought, rolled up on to her feet in one smooth movement and went in search of the silky kimono that had replaced the white cotton one appropriated by Felix after his transmogrification. Then she fetched some appropriately elegant glasses to mix their cocktails in. No nonsense from Ash about only drinking still water, and still waters running deep, she thought. This man is everything he appears to be – and that is exactly what I already adore about him.

Later they cooked together, devising a meal out of the hasty shopping Tiffany had done on her way home from work, and whatever else was edible in the fridge. They clinked glasses and kissed again. Outside it was dark now, and very quiet. Inside the flat was softly lit, warm and peaceful.

Everything seemed to have paused to give them this evening in which to bond together strongly enough, and tenderly enough, to keep their links to each other intact when the business of the next day, and future days, swept them forward.

Chapter 23

Tiffany arrived at Jenna's the following evening with a large bunch of exuberant sunflowers, bought on the spur of the moment and at silly expense per stem from a small florist and fruit shop near Jenna's flat. For a moment, she had wondered if flowers were appropriate, but the sunflowers were so bright, so brash and so full of life that she felt they struck the right, positive, forward-looking note.

Turn to the sun, girasole, she thought. Why not? I'll take them to her.

Their loud cheerfulness startled and delighted Jenna. She had not really been looking forward to Tiffany's visit, and the commiserations and questions that she had expected it to bring; but the sunflowers in Tiffany's arms seemed to burst through the drawing door ahead of their purchaser, sweeping away any air of gloomy condolences.

'Tiffany, what wonderful flowers! Wherever did you get them?'

'Just down the road. Aren't they glorious?'

'Fabulous,' agreed Thomas, who had let Tiffany into the apartment and now followed her into Jenna's calm drawing room. He was impressed by her choice, and admired her for finding the right note for her entrance. After that, conversation was easy, and natural.

'I'm feeling so much more focused,' Jenna told Tiffany laying her bouquet of sunflowers carefully on the coffee table by an open bottle of chilled white wine and three glasses, two clearly already in use and a third one waiting to be filled. 'Help yourself, Tiff.' She settled into the sofa again. 'I think my mind and body are springing back to rights at double speed after whatever tipped me into this whole phantom pregnancy thing. I was feeling a bit weird when I wondered if I could be pregnant, and just assumed that's what it's like in the early days of expecting a baby.

Somehow my imagination just made it feel so real, and it seems my whole system just played along. I had no idea that could happen. I'd been working very hard too. Maybe that tipped me into all this.'

She decided not to go into the part about how intoxicating her time with Felix had been, and the role that her twinge of sadness when the murals were finished, about the ephemeral nature of their affair, might have played. She gave Tiffany a half-smile. 'Of course it was a shock on Tuesday; and somehow hugely embarrassing too, but now I feel,' she paused, 'I feel almost liberated, able to make some real plans for the future. Does that sound unnatural, or even callous, to be able to recover so fast?'

'Given all the circumstances, no it doesn't.' Tiffany replied truthfully if not transparently, pouring herself a glass of wine and heading to the armchair in the bay window. There was little 'natural' about what went on around Felix at present, she felt. 'So what plans are these?' she asked, to move the topic onto safer ground, and arranged herself comfortably to listen to the answer.

'Well,' Jenna began, 'I was thinking about going solo and setting up my own venture, but the firm had invited me to become a main board director with some equity – shares – in it; and now I think I'll take them up on that. This way I'd keep all my existing clients, Felix could be a more permanent one if he likes, and I get a stake in the business with a bigger role there. Plus of course the usual perks – and proper maternity leave if I ever do want it,' she added, glancing at Thomas, who was returning with a large jug of water for Jenna to set the sunflowers in. Tiffany, unaware of the details of Jenna's conversation with Thomas a few weeks earlier in the wine bar, was intrigued by this exchange of looks.

'That sounds great, Jenna,' she said as Thomas put the jug down beside the flowers on the coffee table, and then sat by Jenna on the sofa. 'So you haven't been put off by all this, then?' Maybe Jenna really was secretly broody all along, Tiffany thought, in which case Thomas is definitely a much better option than Felix.

Jenna looked at her friend and shook her head.

'I've been doing some serious thinking since Tuesday,' she replied, putting the sunflowers into the jug, stem by stem, 'and maybe some pretty muddled thinking before it. I really don't believe that what happened was because I'd subconsciously wanted a baby – whatever the medics may say – but now, I can't quite forget some of the excitement of thinking I was pregnant.' She paused for a moment, and continued: 'So, having experienced that rollercoaster of emotion, I know that I'm not going to rule real parenthood out. That's all.'

Tiffany's mind flooded with relief. Jenna was coming through not so much unscathed, as recalibrated.

'Well, line me up as a godmother, as and when,' she said, almost adding 'especially if it's ever Thomas's.' Instead, she asked: 'So when are you back in the office?' Jenna put the last sunflower in the jug, and leaned back comfortably onto the sofa cushions.

'Next week. I've just told them I had a touch of flu and ought to take it easy for a couple of days, but I'll go back in on Monday to check my diary – and secure my deal with the board. Thomas here has promised his good offices with the legal bits, or at least the help of one of his colleagues, to avoid any conflict of interest,' she said, smiling.

I think that last bit means she is definitely flirting with him now, thought Tiffany. Miss Fenix is indeed rising from the ashes.

'Great,' she said.

'So, Tiffany, would you like to share with us what you've been up to in the last couple of days?' Thomas asked.

She stuck her tongue out at him. As if he hasn't guessed, she thought.

'Not yet, Thomas, but I can tell you that Ozzy is planning to invite us all to some event that he has up his sleeve, that he's been working on.'

'Working on for Felix?' asked Jenna, looking across to the portrait on panel that he had brought to her on Tuesday afternoon. Propped up on top of the neat desk in the corner of the room, it waited to be found a permanent place. Perhaps I will also lose Felix as a client, she thought, but it won't affect my new deal at work and might be for the best. She could feel the tug of a different, and deeper, attraction now.

'I should think Ozzy still means to pull just enough strings to promote Felix without letting him stray too close to his own carefully protected patch,' Thomas commented. 'It's remarkable how good Felix is at getting everyone to further his cause – me included,' he added, thinking back to their first meeting. Tiffany kept silent about her role in preparing that ground.

'I don't think Felix's talent would ever be a real threat to Ozzy's work,' Jenna said, 'and although Felix could certainly paint brilliant stage sets if chose to, he's not got long enough patience to handle all the other things involved. If Ozzy's willing, he might agree a one-off collaboration on some sets for a state-of-the-art new show, or avant-garde opera, or whatever – with Ozzy as the overall master of illusion. You know Ozzy's style!'

'*Deus ex machina*,' murmured Thomas. 'I remember.'

'Yes, and with plenty of machina-tions,' Tiffany commented. Somewhat hypocritically, she has doubted Ozzy's reliability as a narrator ever since that night of her dinner party, with his curious is-she-isn't-she tales about his sister's pedigree.

'Poor Felix, he might chafe a bit under Ozzy's stern gaze. I almost feel sorry for him,' Jenna said.

'Don't!' said Tiffany without thinking. 'He's got several lives to spare.' Has he? she wondered suddenly; how many might he have had already? The idea of him desperately running out of time began to take clearer shape in her imagination.

'Why am I not surprised by that idea?' asked Thomas. Tiffany shot him a startled look.

'Whatever,' she said. 'Just don't tell Ozzy I said that – he's bound to invent something sinister around it.' She made it seem a joke, but wondered again how Ozzy would deal with Felix if he ever suspected the truth. Why was Ozzy really so keen on helping him, anyway? She pushed all these troublesome thoughts away, for now.

'So have either of you seen or heard from Anthony and Emma lately? I'm not up to date with the gossip there,' she said. Last time Tiffany saw Anthony it was to hear him explain how he now understood that theirs had been a pleasant but short-lived dalliance, and to thank her for re-introducing him to Emma. She had found it hugely amusing, then, to let him off so lightly, before all the spin Felix had wickedly put on this recalibration of affairs.

'Anthony is discreet when it suits him,' answered Jenna, successfully diverted, 'but I gather he and Emma sometimes meet for a drink or two *à deux* in the wine bar across the road from the theatre.' She still did not mention her own lunch there with Thomas, which amused him.

'At what time of day?' he asked, to tease her a little.

'After work, of course,' Jenna answered insouciantly.

'Aha,' declared Tiffany, 'so it must be official now. Anthony would never be seen in public with the same woman more than twice, in the evening, if they hadn't agreed to become a fixture for a bit.'

'Ouch,' said Thomas, amused by her cattiness. 'Does that explain why your own brief liaison was conducted so exclusively? You didn't socialise with the rest of us much then.'

'Bastard,' said Tiffany, not clarifying whether she meant Anthony, or Thomas, or perhaps both. 'Maybe I was the one keeping all options open.'

'But you went public as a couple in the end,' Jenna pointed out.

'In the end is the expression! Going public was the beginning of the end, I'd say. Anyway, it's all water under the bridge now, and I learnt something useful,' Tiffany added.

'Such as?' asked Thomas, sceptical.

'Such as, Anthony is not my type and I still prefer people who are relaxed and upfront and quietly confident, rather than intense and moody and secretive and convoluted and scheming.'

'Well that is damning; and could cover Felix as well, I suspect. I hope Jenna and I count among the first band, not the second,' Thomas retorted, 'for I don't think I, for one, could survive the vitriol.'

Jenna and Tiffany laughed at him.

'Definitely in the first band, Thomas – although I suspect the occasional temptation to scheme a little on your part, too,' Tiffany remarked.

'Me? Only with the best of motives.'

'That probably is true, of you,' Tiffany conceded, before changing the subject again. 'Am I the only person here who is hungry?'

'No,' said Jenna, 'I think I am.'

'Let's have a takeaway here,' Thomas suggested. Jenna pointed towards the hallway.

'There's a pile of takeaway leaflets on the shelf just inside my front door. They probably need sorting out – shall we go through them and choose one?'

Tiffany volunteered to fetch them. She wondered for a moment whether to call Ash to join them, and then decided to keep him to herself for a little longer. She would stick to their existing plan and call him when she leaves here, to say that she is on her way home.

Chapter 24

Emma was glad she had chosen her outfit so carefully before going to the smart boutique hotel favoured by her mother. Iris was already scrutinising her daughter's appearance as Emma walked through the hotel's afternoon tearoom, on the chime of the agreed hour.

'You look different,' Iris pronounced from a tiny, elegant settee in the bay window. The lustrous blue and gold striped upholstery provided a jewel-like setting for her fine figure and fiery dark eyes, 'And if I may say so, a lot better presented than you used to. It suits you.' She accepted a peck on the cheek from her daughter. 'What's changed you? Your father's largesse, I suppose.' Emma smiled – enigmatically, she hoped – at this other provocative parent.

'You haven't changed a bit since last time. Lovely to see you too, Mother.' She sat down on the neat matching armchair set at a right angle to Iris's satiny settee. At least her own well-cut sea-green dress, and her recently highlighted and equally well-cut long blond bob, meant she did not clash with the surroundings. Iris looked almost feline in sandy ochres with details in scarab green, and seemed to glow against the blue and gold settee. Sphinx-like, as usual, Emma caught herself thinking, and is that a touch of henna in her still-dark hair? No sign of any grey being allowed to creep in yet. 'And yes, since you ask, Father's generosity does make a difference. I feel able to make more plans with a useful cash cushion behind me. Don't you?' she added mischievously. With Iris you had to be frank, or suffer. Her mother snorted.

'Huh! Lack of capital never stopped me from making, and executing, plans.'

'No,' observed Emma. Her mother softened, and from the low table between them picked up the small teapot that already stood there, accompanied by two pretty teacups, matching sugar bowl, milk jug, two little plates and a three-tiered stand of carefully-spaced tiny cupcakes and equally small and artfully-piled crustless sandwiches.

'I already ordered the tea. I'll pour. It's pleasant here, isn't it? I don't deny that finally getting my share of the worth of the marital home out of your father is useful. What do you make of his liaison with Lucinda?'

'Don't you mind?' countered Emma, accepting a poured tea cup.

'Mind? I always thought he had a bit of an eye for her, and frankly she suits him better than I do. Or than he suited me, for that matter. We married out of lust you know, carried away on the enthusiasm of the moment, and finally had you lot, a bit late in the day. We understood each other pretty well eventually though – so, no, I don't mind a bit. I bailed out first, after all. Can't blame your father for taking up the chance to have his way with Lucinda after all this time, can I? And it stops me from feeling guilty about deserting him.'

'Do you feel guilty?' Emma asked in surprise. Guilt and Iris had never seemed twinned.

'Rarely. I just wanted to press on with my own life and other interests once you lot were all grown, instead of accommodating everyone else.'

You mean tolerating us, Emma thought. I remember it more as being tolerated, but maybe that's because I was the last one, and any scope Mother had for 'accommodation' was very thinly spread by then. Iris carried on, as if reading her daughter's mind:

'I don't mean to be harsh, dear. I do love you all in my own way but it was my turn, you know, to get a few other things done before I lost the energy.' She took a sip of tea, as if to replenish it. 'So with you three pretty much launched, I beetled off to get on with life before anything else could stop me. I realise now that it seemed a bit sudden to your father at first and perhaps to you, so yes, I might get the occasional twinge of conscience about the apparent speed of it all, but not about doing it – not at all.'

Case dismissed, Emma thought. Actually, I can relate to that, now that I've taken a fresh grip on my own life. She was not giving any hostages to fortune, however, so kept the words to herself and just nodded thoughtfully as she tried her own tea. No point in asking yet if any revelations by Ozzy about the Tod-person had anything to do with it.

'So you will divorce now?' she checked, instead.

Iris smiled at this calm response.

'In the fullness of time, yes. As you know, we've put the wheels in motion and, unusually – your father being a decent enough sort – I've already got most of my cash. Of course he would be civilised, as he's the one who actually wants to be free legally to remarry fairly promptly now. I am not currently planning to bind myself to anyone else.' Iris bit decisively into a small cucumber sandwich.

'So he's buying your easy co-operation in this divorce process. Is there no-one in your life, then?' Emma risked asking. Her mother's obsidian-dark eyes danced.

'Let's just say that I may have some dear friends, but no serious commitments. I like life to be unfettered. What about you? Still living alone in that rather floral little ground-floor flat?'

'You chose it. Yes and no. I, too, have options open.'

Her mother considered this.

'Now what you should do, Emma, is marry for money. You already look better with money, and your father's distribution won't last forever. Get the spoils early, and then you can be as independent as you like for the rest of your life.'

Emma was startled, despite everything she thought she knew about her wayward mother's single-mindedness.

'That's appalling, in this day and age!' she protested as though the retrograde thought had never crossed her mind. 'What's wrong with building my own career? And whatever happened to your praise just now of unfettered independence?'

'You're not listening, child. I am talking about strategy,' Iris said. 'For millennia, men as well as women have married for money and the freedoms they think it brings. Frankly, you haven't built a well-paying career and if you were going to, you'd have got started on it by now. Climbing the corporate ladder is not, so far, your particular strength. Don't get me wrong, a career is a fine thing, but doesn't have to be done solo. What you are good at is enabling others – like your present little job – but on its own that can just leave you high and dry in life, as everyone else moves upwards and on. I'd say that you should start to concentrate on directing and steering those others in ways that will be of far greater value to you. Play to your natural talents, as I do.' She took another sandwich.

Iris's blunt assessment and her choice of words brought the conversation in the café with Felix swirling back to Emma. Iris always knew how to grasp the essence of things. It was if she reached into your heart and squeezed hard. It hurt; but perhaps thanks to Felix, Emma was ready this time.

'You mean manipulating others?' she said acidly.

'No, no; well – yes, if it's for their own and your good. You might do it by managing a financially successful spouse, and regard that as a job to make it a really winning partnership; or if you must go it alone, become a brilliant consultant in something. Have you got another field of expertise to try? Head-hunting, perhaps?' Iris looked challengingly at her daughter.

Emma parried. 'What if I don't want to tie myself to a high-flying husband? You dumped one.'

'Only after he retired and was suddenly around all day. You tie *him* to your reins, dear, not the other way round. Of course you could try being a mistress instead, but long-term that's far from satisfactory: much of the fun, yes, but all of the risk and – so often these days – no reliably bankable rewards.'

Emma could hardly believe what she was hearing. How ruthless my mother is, she thought. I could learn a lot from her.

'What century do you think we're living in, Mother?' she asked. 'Things have moved on a good deal since your youth.'

'Well clearly in this one, at present, and the available options may have increased exponentially, but not everyone has eschewed the age-old ones yet,' Iris observed crisply. 'If you don't want a dynamic husband to direct, then of course you will have no real choice but to develop an exciting career yourself. Good luck. But one can get fired from those too, of course, and, unless you are a clever entrepreneur, the payoff is still likely to be much less. Not to mention that you haven't exactly got started yet.' She sat back on the firm sofa.

'What about Tiffany's way?' Emma ventured, after allowing herself a dignified pause and a sip of tea. 'Or even your new direction? She specialises in being peripatetic in her career, to suit herself, and doesn't seem interested in having a husband.'

'Or not one of her own!' Iris retorted gleefully. 'Tiffany is a collector and connector of interesting people – a catalyst. That's her career, whether she knows it or not. Her failing is that she's still far too quick to hand on her discoveries to the next person. She squanders her imagination, and her expertise at collecting people, just as she only ever earns sufficient money to float off to some fresh corner of the world and back again. Like that vanishing great-grandmother of hers, my great-aunt Kitty. Here for a bit, gone when you blink.' She offered Emma the array of tiny sandwiches as she spoke. Emma accepted one thoughtfully. This could provide the opening to find out about Tod-thingy.

'Kitty? I thought she died of fever on one of Sir Freddie's archaeological trips and was buried out there, leaving him with a convenient fortune,' she said casually, taking a small bite.

'Death overseas is a convenient veil,' Iris replied mysteriously.

'You don't mean he bumped her off for her money? I was always told he was devastated when she died,' Emma persevered.

'Devastated but rich, and that allowed him to continue to fund his excavations and satisfy his ambitions,' Iris pointed out. 'Have some more tea, too, dear. No, I don't suggest that he bumped her off. More likely that she bolted off. She popped up unexpectedly in the first place, visiting one of his excavations and, seeming very well informed archaeologically, won his heart, and supported his ambitions with some of her fortune – heavens knows how she came by it – but then I suspect she got bored with him, and probably just went her own way again. I take her as something of a role model there. Alas, I don't claim a share of her genes – she was only my great-aunt by marriage – but her bloodline may explain Tiffany's tendencies, of course.' Iris might have been scattering conversational crumbs to distract her daughter, but Emma was too determined to learn something about Tod.

'Are you sure Kitty was a bolter?' she asked. 'Tiffany never suggested anything of that sort, and Ozzy said your mother Nattie was the bolter. I had no idea she'd been married before Grandpa Jeb. I always thought he was my real grandfather.' Now she had raised the issue.

Iris looked sharply at her and took back control of the conversation.

'So he may have been, my dear,' she said airily. 'Impossible to check back then, although no doubt modern DNA tests would take all the mystery and speculation out of it now. So dull. But as for Tiffany's apparently indisputable bloodline, she's not a patch, yet, on her great-grandmother, nor her intriguing history. But I'm just speculating wildly about Kitty. I do that,' she said, before adding severely 'and, please note, that I do it now by way of encouraging you to think more imaginatively.'

The sudden change of tone distracted Emma from asking if Iris had ever had the chance to meet Kitty, as her mother swept on, saying: 'For instance, I have put my new academic researches to extra use and reinvented myself as a rather superior tour guide in my current home of Egypt. Part-time, days agreed as suits, for a very superior travel company. There are some marvellous new excavations to visit, as well as the usual ones, and I can still pursue my ongoing research into revealing and repeating the mysteries of ancient Egypt with considerable skill. It's a symbiotic relationship, and I'm very good at it.' She drank some tea and put the delicate cup down rather firmly. Emma feared for its fate before remembering that porcelain may look fragile but can be as tough as nails. Another useful model.

'So you have swapped a husband for a career, after all,' she said pointedly to her mother. 'I can picture you pontificating to well-heeled tourists about the sites – if tourists are still going on those sorts of trips just now?'

Maybe business has dried up during the current uncertainties over there, she thought, which may explain why Iris has turned up here again. If she keeps on the subject of the Middle East, or thereabouts, Emma may be able to flush out the topic of Tod that way, if he were the reason for her mother's interest in the region.

'I bet they daren't argue with you, either,' she commented. 'No doubt you cheerfully convince the more susceptible ones that they've been there before in some previous incarnation while you're at it. I'm surprised Ozzy hasn't come on one of your trips. He's busy working on an Egyptian theme for his latest set design as I expect you know – oh!' Light suddenly dawned on Emma. 'Of course, you've been sending him information. He said he had some research coming in that was useful.'

She felt annoyed that Iris and Ozzy have so evidently remained in regular family contact while she, Iris's daughter, had heard nothing from her absent mother for many months. Why should I take this impossible woman's highly amoral and not particularly maternal advice now? Emma wrenched the conversation spitefully towards a new topic, forgetting her efforts to dig out Tod for a moment. 'Although, Ozzy seems to be getting far more from his new protégé than from any of us. Have you met the fabulous Felix yet?' She bit into a tiny, iced lemon cupcake with delicate ferocity.

'Fabulous Felix?' Iris seemed to savour the thought. 'Tell me about him.' She helped herself to a tiny smoked salmon sandwich.

'A friend of Tiffany's. He paints extraordinarily compelling murals, and now seems to be contributing his skills to Ozzy's set-designing business. Either that, or Ozzy is mentoring him. It seems to be a symbiotic relationship.' Emma couldn't resist a little dig at her mother. 'Tiffany discovered him, of course, when he redecorated her flat with murals. He claimed to be some sort of long-lost cousin – on Kitty's side of the family. Then he moved onto transforming Jenna's place, not to mention rearranging her entire life,' she added without clarification. 'You might find him fun. He's very charming, quite the cool cat.'

'Really?' Iris finished her sandwich thoughtfully. 'How interesting. But you don't like him?'

'Not as much as I did at first,' Emma admitted. 'I thought he was devastatingly gorgeous to begin with, but actually he is quite odd. A bit too clever by half, far too pleased with himself, and rather careless with other people's feelings – not that I've got involved with him in that way,' she hastily added. 'I'm far too caught up in someone quite different.' She had not meant to add that bit or mention Anthony yet, and certainly in not such committed terms, but Iris pounced on her indiscretion with relish.

'Aha,' she said. 'Tell me.' Her tone was imperious.

Emma, trapped, replied stiffly. 'He's an architect. Anthony. Anthony Wright? You may have heard of him as he has a big project in Cairo. He's probably just about successful enough so far to satisfy your criteria, by the way, if I were in the market to marry a high earner. A potentially very high earner,' she added for greater effect.

Iris, far from looking pleased, seemed lost in thought.

'Wright, you say? Yes, I believe I might have heard of his Cairo project. It's run into some delays, hasn't it? Difficult time for that sort of business over there.'

Emma knew that Anthony had returned early from Cairo on the night of the dinner party at Tiffany's, to tidy up some funding and accounting details that still seemed to be not fully resolved. She went on the defensive, but kept her tone calm.

'All these big projects take longer than people think, to dot the i's and cross the t's. He has lots of irons in the fire here too, of course, and Ozzy seems to have taken him under his wing a bit, so perhaps he means to introduce him to a few more, useful, people.'

It was an attempt to indicate to her sceptical mother that Anthony had passed the test in influential Uncle Ozzy's book, at least. She could feel childhood irritations tugging at her well-cut dress, and smoothed its skirt, brushing off invisible cake crumbs.

'Did you know, Emma, that my possible father's surname was Wright?' Iris asked, picking up the threads of their earlier conversation. Emma stared. She means that Tod's surname was Wright? No, no, no she thought, I am not going to play that game, Mother. Glad now to have been forewarned by Ozzy's indiscretions at Tiffany's dinner party, she remained silent.

'I mean my mother's first husband, before she was married to Jeb,' Iris continued after the brief pause in which Emma did not react. 'I was supposedly a honeymoon baby, arriving in an unseemly hurry a month or so before full-term, as I gather from your unruffled silence now that Ozzy has already seen fit to inform you on my behalf. Lots of Wrights around, of course!' She gave her daughter another piercing look.

'Anyway, poor Tod went back to Egypt and stayed on, after the European war, to recover from Nattie's alleged treachery – so maybe he did father me, after all, and I can attribute to him my urge to go there! Still, I doubt it. He would have demanded custody of his own child – which of course in those days, he would have got – on the divorce. But you know all this, don't you? Apparently he also accused silly unreliable Kitty of having encouraged Nattie to stay so chummy with her married first cousin Jeb. Did you know about that bit?' Iris gave her delicate teacup a small shake and then looked into it as if reading tea-leaves.

'The whiff of mischief-making stuck to Kitty for a bit,' she continued slightly dreamily now, 'so perhaps that's why she preferred to accompany her husband on his long expeditions away from home. I was maybe twelve when she apparently met her demise – or bolted – on their last trip together.' Iris lent forward conspiratorially in her seat and lowered her voice to an insistent whisper.

'Wouldn't it be amusing if she'd re-encountered and decided to make it up to the brooding Tod out there, and bolted with him! Kitty was so much closer in age to him, and to Jeb and his late first wife April, Ozzy's mother, than to her own husband Sir Freddie – and Kitty was, by all accounts, a rather fascinating and persuasive creature. A degree of chaos always seemed to follow in her wake, I'm told.'

Emma was distracted by a sudden twinge of sympathy for April, who now seemed to be the only real loser in this tangled history of deceit.

'Poor April,' she said aloud but Iris waved an impatiently dismissive hand.

'April was a piece of work herself, but that's a story for another day, if you really want to know it.' She returned to her own theme. 'However, I expect Kitty really did get the flu in the end. There was another epidemic around then that killed millions.' She appeared to ponder briefly. 'Tod was an unusal first name. Tod Wright,' she repeated as if to drive the surname home again.

Emma was wondering if Iris's odd description of April might indicate the genetic source of some of Ozzy's loftier behaviours. Parents, she was beginning to think, had a lot to answer for. She said, deliberately dismissively, 'I don't think Ozzy ever mentioned this Tod's surname but, as you say, it's hardly an unusual one. Like yours, ten a penny!' To steer Iris away from asking about Anthony – and since her mother seemed to have dispatched any question of the misled Tod-person being Emma's genetic grandfather – Emma swept on, saying: 'Anyway on the subject of Felix, and Ozzy's interest in his work, they're planning an exhibition of Felix's latest efforts quite soon. Will you still be here for that? I'm sure Ozzy would want to invite you.'

Emma took sly pleasure in usurping Ozzy's right to issue the invitation to Iris first, while using the suggestion to hint that she might like her mother to stay long enough to attend. Iris, rather admiring her daughter's determination to change the topic, appeared to consider the idea, and patted one of the small firm satiny scatter cushions perched jauntily at the corners of the unyielding sofa before suddenly smiling at her.

'I think I will stay on for a few weeks,' she said. 'It's been so interesting catching up with you, and I'll look forward to meeting all these new people in your life while your father and I finalise our affairs – financial and marital. Do tell Ozzy, should you see him again before I do, that I'd love to come to this Felix creature's exhibition. He sounds intriguing. Now, I must get on with a few things. I'm sure you're busy too. We'll plan another get-together very soon.'

Dismissed, Emma rose, and pecked her mother on the cheek again. She left the small hotel feeling a mixture of relief and irritation. Being back on her mother's radar was still a mixed blessing but she was glad not to have been entirely forsaken. She had held her own ground pretty well today, too, she felt. Yes, she had an adult's perspective of Iris now; and their attempt at reconciliation – if that is what their afternoon tea had been – could have gone far worse. She would definitely ask Ozzy if he planned to invite Iris to Felix's show. Reaching home feeling more benevolent, she picked up an appeals letter from some charity that was lying on her doormat and, instead of binning it unopened, took it into the sitting room with her, where she sat down to ring Ozzy.

Ozzy sounded receptive to the idea of inviting Iris. 'And how was my half-sister today?' he asked. Emma noted the distinction. Half, not step, sister this time.

'Ruthless, as usual,' she replied, opening the charity's envelope as she talked and leaving the letter it contained on the coffee table to look at later. 'Almost inhuman.'

Ozzy was delighted by the description. 'Glad to hear she's in such good form. I might pop round with that invitation for her myself. They're due back from the printers any day. Is she staying with you, now?'

'Good lord no, she's in a nice little boutique hotel.' Emma suspected that he knew this perfectly well, but gave him its address and reception number anyway.

'I'll swoop round there in the next day or two,' Ozzy said. 'You'll get your invitation shortly too, in the post. I'll see you at the event, my dear, if not before.'

'Of course. Looking forward to it with interest.' Swoop, she thought as she hung up, that's a peculiar word for Ozzy to use about himself, although there is something rather hawkish about him sometimes. It made her shiver a little.

Errand done – and exhausted by the afternoon's business of keeping her mother at arm's length, as if for survival's sake, even while accepting her rapprochement – Emma decided to stretch out on her own familiar sofa to watch the early evening television news. She had missed the headlines, and the programme had moved into a longer report about Sicily calling for international help to cope with the continuing flood of refugees from upheavals in the Middle East – those who had survived harrowing and treacherous sea-crossings – reaching its shores. On her coffee table, the charity's opened letter asked for donations to help these same people. She glanced through it now, and made a mental note to think about sending something, soon.

Then she closed her eyes, and allowed herself a restorative nap.

Chapter 25

Ozzy usually enjoyed catching up with Iris. It delighted him to see his half-sister and childhood companion sparkling with life and crackling with wit.

'I hope you don't mind,' he told her over tea and the neat cucumber sandwiches in the blue and gold drawing room off the lobby of her little hotel that had hosted Iris's encounter with Emma a couple of days earlier, 'but I've invited my protégé Felix to meet us here in a bit, before he and I return to the studio to finalise which of his panel-paintings are ready for his new show. I thought you might be interested to meet him before the big event. Like you and I, he's been taking an interest in things Egyptian lately. You might have some ideas in common.'

Iris looked calculatingly at him.

'Really? I look forward to learning more. And, on the subject of Egyptian projects, first tell me about this Anthony fellow whom Emma seems so interested in. I think I've heard something about his business activities in Cairo, although I haven't met the man himself so far.' She settled attentively on what had become her favourite little sofa there. Ozzy savoured a sandwich, weighing up his views on Anthony.

'Bit of a dark horse,' he suggested, 'not above a dash of bribery and corruption if that oils the wheels on a project – call it being pragmatic, if you like – but not irredeemable, if that's what you're asking. The man has some sort of conscience, I think, and a real talent, which is chiefly what has got him to where he is.'

Iris considered this balance. 'But is he good for Emma?' she wondered.

'Is Emma good for him, is a question one could also ask; and on balance I would say "yes" to both aspects, now that she has come out in her truer colours.'

'Come out as what, in your view?' Iris queried.

'More as her mother's daughter. Your – what did she call it? – "almost inhuman ruthlessness" seem to have emerged in her this summer. Like a butterfly, little Emma has cast off the somewhat dowdy chrysalis she'd cocooned herself in since your departure, no doubt in reaction to feeling abandoned by her mother, and has emerged as an altogether more brilliant creature after all.'

'Butterflies are fragile,' Iris said crisply. 'I don't wish Emma to be in the least fragile.'

Ozzy bit into another tender cucumber sandwich. 'In its rare appearances in ancient Egypt's art, the butterfly always flies off safely,' he said casually, recalling a tomb painting of a hunting cat, bird in mouth, while butterflies skimmed safely away. 'Nothing obviously fragile about Emma at the moment, although perhaps her wings still need to harden a little more. A steel butterfly! Or maybe like those bright tin ones, only less gaudy: a little malleable, but durable, and quite cutting on occasion. As this process began before your return, and seems to be what has attracted Anthony, I can only assume the disturbing influence of Felix may have triggered it.' He finished his sandwich.

'Your mysterious artist – and how is he disturbing? Emma commented that she wasn't too keen on him.' Iris loved gossip, particularly when it unearthed facts she could work with.

'All the young women, and I daresay some young men, are very keen on him to start with,' Ozzy said, with a shrug. 'The fellow can be quite hypnotic, as you will see, with some interesting effects, but he's also not one to hang about for long and the clever ones soon sense that. Tiffany seems to have got his measure particularly quickly and – being Tiffany – in all regards. Emma, possibly after a moment's wishful thinking, also seems to have neatly sidestepped him. We perhaps have Anthony's sudden availability to thank for that. Others have found it more traumatic to discover that this Felix ultimately walks alone.' Iris looked sharply at her half-brother. She sipped her tea, contemplating his turn of phrase, and set the cup delicately on its saucer again.

'You think his influence deliberately disruptive?'

'That could be a bit unfair of me,' Ozzy conceded. 'Mischievous, amoral, and let's say unfortunate for some. Perhaps he is more of a catalyst – for good or for bad – without deliberate intent but, between them, I suspect him and Tiffany of a fair bit of wilful mischief-making.'

'And we have seen such escapades before,' Iris stated, her expression hardening. Ozzy inclined his head in confirmation. Iris leaned against the back of the sofa, a far-off look on her face now. They sat in thoughtful silence for a bit.

'Your return seems to have improved Emma's new sense of purpose,' Ozzy eventually remarked, breaking Iris's concentration, 'and you seem quite back to your old form.'

'Oh yes. Older, wiser and even more manipulative,' she warned him, her expression brightening. 'So, we need to ensure that this Anthony doesn't get too mired in "pragmatic" business dealings, if Emma is determined to make something useful of him here for herself. And what's this Felix fellow's other name? I assume he uses one. Do we know what event led him to Tiffany's door?'

Ozzy was enjoying this debate. He had missed Iris's incisiveness, during her travels.

'He claims to be a Sylvester and, despite a divergent spelling, thus a distant cousin of Tiffany's on her great-grandmother Kitty Silvester's side of the family – hence his arrival at her flat, allegedly.'

Iris sat forward sharply. 'He knows Kitty's history?'

'He knew her name, but perhaps nothing more. I may have volunteered some snippets in passing, at a dinner party he attended.'

Iris digested this information.

'Snippets which Emma also absorbed. I gathered from her remarks that you had been gossiping. And Anthony's surname is Wright! What a very small world it always

240

turns out to be.' Iris narrowed her dark eyes. 'Do we believe this Felix's claim to have links to Kitty?'

Ozzy considered his empty teacup. 'Why not? It's possible,' he said, obliquely.

'Then for the time being we must treat him as part of her legacy,' Iris said decisively, 'and follow his path with watchful interest. I presume this explains why you are so interested in how his career progresses?'

Ozzy put the teacup down and stared out of the window behind where Iris sat.

'I'm always interested in keeping an eye on unusual arrivals in our field,' he said. 'Felix has his uses as well as his talents. He's particularly good at tweaking Anthony's tail, by the way. Should you, for example, wish to jolt Anthony into becoming squeaky-clean businesswise, as a potential consort for your daughter, you could do worse than apply Felix to the task of winding him up sufficiently to take fright and put his house in order. There seems to be a natural antipathy there. One could be forgiven for thinking their mutual dislike goes way back.'

They exchanged a conspiratorial look.

'So he and Felix exhibit traces of personal history?' Iris asked thoughtfully, her mind on how an ancient world's "connective justice" once linked all creatures, gods, underworld and cosmos.

Ozzy nodded. 'Not that they are necessarily aware of why,' he said, 'beyond a short-lived rivalry for Tiffany's unreliable attention. Does that sound familiar? There is something of Kitty's flightiness in her of course. Anthony lost first, by the way.' Ozzy had been keeping an eye on who passed by the bay window, and now added: 'Here Felix comes now, slouching his way towards us.'

Felix did slouch a bit today, as he entered the room and looked around.

'Over here!' Ozzy waved at him. 'You look tired, dear boy. This is Iris, Emma's mother, and my half-sister, as I think you know. Sit down and have some tea with us. Iris has just come for a visit from her present home near

Luxor, where she is something of a self-made expert in all the ancient sites and religions, and keeps abreast of the latest discoveries and current-day goings-on. So if you have any more Egyptian research to do for your projects, she's another invaluable source. Iris, meet Felix.' Felix understood that he was being steered towards something but, indeed feeling tired, decided to take his time responding. He shook Iris carefully by the hand before speaking.

'Thank you for letting me gate-crash your tea party.' He sat down on one of the little armchairs and watched Ozzy pour him a rather milky tea. 'Unless Ozzy wants any help with his latest opera set, I'm generally moving on from things Egyptian now, although I have certainly dabbled. I hope you'll come to my new show during your stay?' He produced his pointy-toothed smile.

'I hope so too,' Iris replied, studying him, 'especially if Ozzy ever produces the promised invitation to the opening.'

'I have it here,' Felix said, producing an envelope from the pocket of his soft linen jacket with a flourish, 'straight from the printers. The rest are being delivered to Ozzy's studio shortly.' He passed the thick card in its handsome envelope to her. Iris set it on the tea table unopened for the moment, watching him lift the delicate tea cup with both hands and sip from it. Felix replaced the cup neatly on its saucer. 'So tell me how is Cairo – or did Ozzy say Luxor – these days?' he asked.

'Volatile, but still very interesting,' Iris replied. 'I think we may all have an acquaintance over there in common.'

'Really?' As Felix wondered who or what she meant, Ozzy leant forward to interrupt.

'Yes, Emma's new beau Anthony,' he said. 'Isn't that a coincidence? It seems Iris knows all about his Cairo project.'

Felix could not resist the bait. 'How interesting. I've never grasped the details of that scheme, just snippets in conversation.' He waited.

'Oh the devil is always in the detail,' misquoted Iris cheerfully. 'Have a sandwich, Felix. I think there are some smoked salmon ones tucked in among the cucumber ones, if they appeal more. You look hungry.' He saw no harm in taking one.

'Do we know any exciting details?' he asked with his mouth half-full.

'I think we do. Do you want to hear them?' Iris tempted him again. Felix paused for a moment, licking his lips carefully, to consider why Iris might be taking the conversation in this direction.

'Will they come in handy?' he asked. He reckoned that in the unlikely event of wanting to commission Felix's art for one of his projects, Anthony would tell Felix so himself – or speak with Ozzy first, perhaps, he thought. This Iris is up to something.

Iris got tired of his thoughtful expression and tried another approach.

'It might be helpful to Emma, if Anthony realises that someone's taking note of aspects of his operations over there,' she suggested. 'If he tightens up his practice, it might save her from embarrassment.' Felix looked quizzically at her. Cotton reels again, he thought, and now like daughter, like mother.

'I don't much care for Anthony myself,' he admitted, 'but does that make him an embarrassment for Emma? She likes saving people from themselves, doesn't she? If you're trying to help her, why not give her these mysterious details yourself.' He watched for Iris's reaction.

'I've hinted, but what child believes their parents' cautionary tales?' Iris sighed. 'Or their uncle's, for that matter?' Ozzy looked absently out of the window again for a moment. 'But,' Iris resumed, 'coming from a friend or even better an acquaintance with an ear to the ground – well, that might make a difference.' Felix hunched a bit on his seat and thought about this.

'So you want me to ruffle Anthony by hinting in Emma's earshot that I may know something about his dodgy business practices, to see how he reacts? Bit convoluted isn't it?'

Iris smiled assent.

'We think subtlety matters here,' Ozzy explained, leaning forward again in his chair. 'Anthony has very good prospects here, provided he updates some of his overseas habits. We just want to inspire him a bit more to sort those out, before they catch up with him over here. Or indeed there, for that matter – as one thing leads to another. It could be a bit awkward if we raise the topic directly, however. You'd be doing us – and Emma – an immense favour.'

Felix felt trapped. He had little desire to do Anthony any favours but still needed Ozzy's goodwill, especially so close to the exhibition's opening; and it would undeniably be fun to tease or even torment Anthony again. He licked his lips.

'You think he's worth the trouble of saving from himself?' he inquired unkindly.

'At this stage, yes,' Iris said, watching him being reeled in. 'A successful architect with potential to go much further remains a good proposition for my daughter, but a somewhat flaky one does not. We would like to see whether he has the good sense and intelligence to resolve matters without the clumsiness of us having to spell it out to him.'

Felix eyed her carefully again. This time she held his gaze silently. She reminded him of a patient predator, not unlike himself but less engaging. Something else felt familiar about her, perhaps a resemblance to her daughter, or a more subliminal similarity to her half-brother. It troubled him. Felix finally blinked. He would enjoy the game better if Anthony failed the test being set for him and, while the outcome might be in the lap of the gods, he might skew the odds to suit his own purposes meanwhile.

'Very well,' he said. 'You'd better tell me what you know – or suspect – and I'll play a little game with Anthony.' He flexed his shoulders in anticipation.

'Excellent,' said Iris.

Ozzy settled back into his chair, satisfied.

'Good. Iris has a particular knack for finding these tactful, arms-length ways to rescue people from the brink,' he said cheerfully, and took another sandwich. Felix looked at Iris again. She was smiling intensely at him now, and he could feel the force of her charm and energy flowing his way.

'Right,' he said, filing all this away for future consideration when he was alone. 'I'll bear that skill in mind. Well, you two had better spill the beans about Anthony to me, or I shan't be able to achieve much.' He chose not to reveal that he overheard Anthony confiding a little in Ozzy in the restaurant earlier in the summer.

Ozzy looked at his watch, and stood up to leave.

'Iris has the inside track,' he announced, 'so I'm going to leave you two to finish your tea, while I head back to the studio to take delivery of the rest of the invitations. I'll see you there, within the hour if possible, Felix – we still have exhibition work to do.' Felix bristled a little at the direct command, but managed a courteous nod, and sat tight. Iris, who had noticed his irritation, was perhaps worth having on his side – a potential counterweight to Ozzy's controlling tendencies.

Leaving the hotel, and walking up the road a short distance, Ozzy was surprised to see Anthony himself standing at the street corner. He was looking brooding. Positively saturnine, Ozzy thought, and hailed him.

'Anthony, what a pleasure. I've just been taking tea with your newly-beloved's mother. You look preoccupied, if I may say so?' He preferred to move Anthony away from this street to minimise the risk of him passing the hotel's bay window and perhaps glimpsing Felix in conference with Iris. 'There's a charming old-fashioned club just along from here that I belong to. It used to be boys only, but that's changed now of course. Come in with me for a little timely fortification, and I'll introduce you to the club secretary.' He gestured in the opposite direction from the hotel and set off briskly while still talking, obliging Anthony to walk with him.

'It's the sort of place you might find useful to join, to make a few more contacts here,' Ozzy informed him. 'No business or professional conversations allowed on the premises, you understand, but there's nothing to stop like-minded folk from meeting up outside the club, if you ever get a steer from one or two that they might be interested in your field. You need to be nominated of course, but I can support your application and find you a second nominator – Iris perhaps, as she's a member too.'

Anthony, feeling in need of a little moral support, allowed himself to be led further away from the crossroads and down a turning on the left, into another and quieter street.

Chapter 26

Inside Ozzy's club it was hushed, a little shadowy, discreet. Ozzy nodded at the doorman in the small lobby just inside, and led Anthony up a short flight of stairs. Crossing a handsome high-ceilinged hall, the two men entered a large wood panelled room, where Ozzy gestured at a pair of comfortable leather armchairs by one set of tall windows. 'Take a seat there. I'll just sign you in,' he said, heading towards a long wooden bar further along the room. Anthony settled into the comforting embrace of one of the armchairs, and looked around him. He could feel himself begin to relax in the cool peace of this visually restful, timelessly undemanding place. When Ozzy returned with a couple of brandies, he felt almost cosseted by the older man. He inhaled the brandy fumes and, after politely wishing Ozzy good health, took a large swig.

'Thanks,' he said. 'I needed that.'

'Problems?' Ozzy inquired, looking solicitous. Anthony cradled his glass absently.

'You could say. I've been weighing up how best to sort out the little anomalies overseas that I – er – mentioned, that evening we bumped into you at the restaurant. I'm beginning to think that there's more to them than – well, than I feel comfortable about.' Was it reckless to confide further in Ozzy like this? 'I can trust you to be discreet, of course,' he added.

Ozzy smiled as consolingly as he could. It amused him to prepare the ground a little more for Felix's upcoming game of cat and mouse with Anthony.

'There's no-one I like more than a reformed sinner putting his house in order,' he said smoothly, startling Anthony, who had not marked Ozzy down as a religious man. 'Perhaps I can be helpful? We aren't supposed to discuss business matters in here, so I will have to speak in parables – or broad general terms.' Ozzy leaned back in his armchair with his elbows on its armrests, and brought his fingers to form a pyramid as he talked. 'I see so much in my own travels, when shows go abroad and they need me to tag along to advise on how to transfer or recreate my sets, in all the various venues. Attitudes and methods are so very different in differing places, are they not? Yet, alas, our own accountants and taxmen don't always understand some of the more pragmatic choices that can crop up away from home.'

Anthony nodded, but took another mouthful of comforting brandy before replying.

'You mean that some firms' overseas arms still need to pay one or two local "fixers" for their services in cash, or kind, off balance sheet,' he said, and shifted in his seat, 'and that as the rules tighten up over here, auditors will ask more searching questions about what resources were applied to those costs.' As Ozzy seemed to give a tiny nod, Anthony continued: 'It boils down to a question of cash flows versus allowable expenses.' He paused. Was he keeping non-specific enough in his language for this club's rules? No-one else was in earshot anyway. Ozzy stretched his long legs and looked earnest, as if weighing Anthony's words before replying.

'Yes, I suppose unreported cash payments made to a local Mr Fixit do have to find their way to him via some suitably obscure design,' he said. Anthony tensed. Ozzy's reference to obscure design shook him, since it was also the name of a small offshore subsidiary of his business. The coincidence, if it were one, made him eye Ozzy more cautiously.

'We don't do that sort of thing nowadays, you understand,' he said, although this was only strictly fully true in the last month or so, 'but it seems the past has to be re-accounted for. It's only awkward if any new arrangements lead to delays while adjustments are put in place.' He rubbed a hand across his forehead as if smoothing away any wrinkles, and drank more brandy.

'Quite so.' Ozzy, enjoying Anthony's evasive use of language, spared him a frank summary of the situation, which clearly boiled down to how to account now for any past bribes and unofficial 'thank-yous' paid in cash or kind to 'oil the wheels', as Anthony had previously put it, of various projects. No doubt these disbursements had been disguised by overstating some other expense, or carefully lost somewhere in a currency translation.

Ozzy wondered, too, if such sweeteners had only been paid overseas, or perhaps some here too? This discreet chat with Anthony was yielding a picture that he might usefully tally later against Iris's knowledge, if she really had anything more than gossip to go on. He liked gaining a slight march on his imperious half-sister and decided to put her scraps of information to use before Felix got to work.

Ozzy stopped warming his glass and inhaled his brandy's fumes before saying sympathetically: 'My sister tells me there are already delays now on some construction projects in Egypt, due to the unprecedented number of new archaeological investigations that have to be done first, these days, and a plethora of recent discoveries in some areas. The costs of seeking advice on all that must soak up a fair bit of a new construction project's budget, before you can even break any ground to start building. Plus of course the cost of the additional delays while the archaeologists do their thing.' Ozzy took a mouthful of the glowing brandy itself now, as Anthony absorbed and processed his words.

'Ye-es. That sort of risk analysis is certainly advisable in many areas nowadays,' Anthony answered slowly, 'even over here.'

Ozzy nodded sagely. 'I expect some people were rather more far-sighted than others in beginning to research the likely costs of any archaeology-related delays,' he suggested, enjoying laying a new trail to see if Anthony would follow it. 'I imagine those sorts of expert consultants don't come cheap.'

'Quite,' Antony answered, sitting a little straighter in his armchair. He swirled the brandy in his glass and took another sip, concentrating hard. Inspiration was beginning to flow through his veins. 'Of course, in the past that's exactly the expertise that used to be provided by local people often thought of as 'fixers', whose advice on the likely concerns of the antiquities people was invaluable,' he added thoughtfully. Trying to push the topic out further from himself, he added, 'As I imagine Tiffany's old Sir Freddie found, back in the day.'

Ozzy continued to smile benignly at him. 'Well, it's a legitimate set of consultancy fees that modern geophysics will oblige more people to cost into any construction project, in an ancient cradle of civilisation,' he suggested.

'Quite so,' Anthony echoed, looking more cheerful. 'Indeed. It's just a question of description. A really proactive firm might want to revisit some overseas projects' accounts retrospectively, to re-assign certain cash flows correctly to archaeological "due diligence" – and of course declare that exercise.' He followed the trail further. 'I suppose there could be a small penalty for late payment of any balancing sums of tax due; or perhaps not, after taking into account the cost of any construction delays also concerned.' He began to enjoy his brandy.

Ozzy nodded encouragingly. Now for the next step.

'For what it's worth, I gather the tax authorities here recently embraced a new approach: and if a business uncovers any past mistakes or any administrative howlers that it is eager to get onto the correct footing, they'll help it to re-do the sums without incurring undue disgrace. The business still has to pay any tax arising of course, and with interest, as you say – but that's cheap at the price for the peace of mind, and the preservation of reputation, don't you think?'

'Absolutely,' Anthony agreed hastily. He would call his accountants first thing tomorrow and start the ball rolling, now that he can see a clearer way ahead. Ozzy suddenly changed the topic.

'By the way, didn't you do a rather good house on the south coast for that high-tech entrepreneur – somebody Fford – the fellow on the new opera board? I really ought to get to know him,' he said casually.

Anthony understood, almost immediately, that an introduction to Fford was the price, or part of the price, of Ozzy's useful counsel. He also very much wanted to preserve his own reputation with Fford who, like so many self-made men, was sharp-eyed about finances. Fford was not only wealthy but architecturally adventurous, which made him an attractive client on both counts, and had recently become a considerable supporter of the arts. Anthony was quite surprised that Ozzy did not already know him personally. It would be awkward if Ozzy dropped any hints to Fford that Anthony had not always been squeaky-clean in some of his projects. Yet these two titans were bound to meet eventually, and so it only took this moment of hesitation – forethought – before Anthony paid his dues and responded to the hint.

'I'd be very happy to introduce you when a good moment arises. I enjoyed doing that house. He has another interesting property in the south of France, and various other things on the go. He likes my work, and I'd be glad to develop the relationship further. He's bound to know of you, of course,' he added. 'This has been a most insightful chat, by the way, Ozzy. You keep very well informed.'

Ozzy smiled thinly. He had noted the brief hesitation, and was not sorry that Felix was to be unloosed on Anthony.

'I've been looking into a few things for my young friend Felix, too, who has also got himself into a bit of a financial corner,' he said rather chillingly, 'due in his case to a peripatetic lifestyle and the apparent general mislaying of vital documents. That Cattermole woman was either scatty or useless,' he added.

Cattermole? Who was she? Anthony was puzzled. An assistant?

'All in hand now,' Ozzy carried on saying, 'but it does show that if people must bring up their offspring all over the place, they ought to keep track of their paperwork or nobody can confirm that they are for real. Not unlike reconstructing a company's financial history when certain significant records have been mislaid.'

Confused by Ozzy's sudden switch to this colder and unkind demeanour, and with no idea of who the unfortunate Cattermole woman could be, Anthony suddenly felt a fleeting sympathy for Felix. Despite sounding supportive, Ozzy apparently has a hold on each of us, he realised; and he then wondered if whatever Ozzy knew about Felix would be worth discovering. It might be useful to keep the pesky artist in his place. Before he could start to puzzle over the curious references to offspring and identity, Ozzy's voice cut across his thoughts again.

'Don't worry, old chap,' he said in tones that sent a chill through Anthony that the brandy in his veins could not overcome, 'both your secrets are safe with me. I'd update Emma by the way if I were you, at some point, about the interesting new archaeological considerations that you're factoring back into things – just in case she gets wind of any concerns, from her mother for example, who evidently knows a good deal about what goes on in Egypt these days and does love to meddle. Quite the mischief maker, at times, I must admit, even though she is my sister.'

So that's what all this quasi-avuncular advice and sudden sternness is all about, Anthony thought. Ozzy wants to protect Emma from her clearly alarming mother's interference; and if he's showing me a way to regularise my problem instead of just warning Emma off me, then he must be happy about our relationship and so, I suppose, Emma herself is the one to thank. He shook his head in amazement. Who would have thought she would become the passport to sorting out his accounting dilemma? I'm going to have to be wary around her mother though, he considered, as she sounds like a monster.

Aloud he said: 'Of course I'll chat to Emma about it, if you think I should.'

'I think you should. She has a very good head for figures, you'll find. And now I must go. I'm expecting a delivery at the studio very shortly. No sign of the club secretary yet, but I'll have a word with him later to put your name forward for membership. It'll take a few months, so that gives you time to get your affairs in order. Nice to have this place as a refuge from the speed of modern life.'

Anthony finished his brandy in one gulp and stood up.

'I must press on too. Thank you, Ozzy, I really am most grateful for your guidance.' The two men left together, shook hands outside the main door, and headed off in their different directions. Ozzy turned briefly to check that Anthony no longer looked likely to pass the hotel window, beyond which Felix and Iris might still be in consultation.

I'll add that Fford man to the exhibition guest list, and if he turns up we'll see how Anthony reacts, Ozzy decided, as he walked on. It'll remind him of his obligation. I wonder how Felix and Iris have got along?

Felix was still sitting attentively on the prim armchair by the tea table. Iris had moved on from plotting ways to discomfort Anthony, to gossiping about the intrigues of his own supposed Silvester relation Kitty and her circle to add to Ozzy's earlier tales, and Felix needed to concentrate and remember it all.

'What an amusing tangle that all would be,' he said now, in response to her suggestion that perhaps Kitty, tiring of Sir Freddie, had subsequently consoled the cuckolded Tod in his desert retreat before her untimely demise – or disappearance. Felix was grinning; or looking like the cat who just got the cream, Iris noted.

'Come and see me again anytime, Felix, if you encounter any difficulties yourself,' she suggested, as she signed the bill for tea. 'My brother is not necessarily your only available mentor, should things in your life ever start to unravel. Now run along. You have another appointment with him to keep, I believe.'

Felix got up a little stiffly. 'Too much painting,' he said in answer to the interested query on Iris's face, 'combined with sitting for so long on this rather small chair.'

'Indeed,' said Iris sympathetically. 'It happens. Let me know if I can help. I am rather good with restorative massage oils,' she added. 'I have a fine collection.'

'Right,' said Felix, a little surprised. 'Thank you. I'll be off, then. See you at the show.'

'Indeed,' she repeated. As she watched him leave she picked up the invitation still propped unopened on the tea table, and put it straight into a copious tapestry bag that had lain, neat and unobserved, at her feet all this time.

Chapter 27

Summer was already beginning to lose its strength. On a disappointingly damp Saturday morning, Tiffany sat in the large armchair in Ozzy's suddenly rather chilly studio, and contemplated the two figures before her. Felix stood staring out of the window, his body taut with irritation, while Ozzy leant pensively against his glass worktable, arms folded, and a concerned frown on his face.

'It's not very good timing, this development,' he said. 'You must have made a mistake with the paints you used.'

'No, no,' Felix insisted, 'it's not the paint. I used the same kind of acrylics in the restaurant as I did on Jenna's walls, and her murals are fine – and nothing's wrong with your ones, is it, Tiffany? I used little pots of house paints for the first of those. ' She shook her head.

'No, so far they're all fine; just as good as day one.'

'It must be the restaurant's walls then,' Felix said firmly. 'Something on the walls, in the plaster or whatever – damp, perhaps? That could explain why it's happened so fast. At Tiffany's and Jenna's I was painting onto plain wallpaper, or lining paper, not plaster.'

'Did you see any evidence of damp when you were working on the murals for the restaurant?' asked Ozzy. Felix started to pace the room restlessly.

'None, but he'd just had most of the blocks of colour that were there before painted over, two or three times, in white, or a whitewash or something, so that I'd have blank walls to work on, and he'd had the odd spot of replastering done too. That could have hidden old defects that are coming through again now.' Felix rubbed a hand over the stubble on his chin and scowled.

'Surely you can point that out, and insist on knowing if there was something he didn't tell you before that could be causing the problem now?' Tiffany suggested. 'I mean, does he have a case for compensation or whatever from you? It's a restaurant after all, and all that cooking and steam and so on must cause condensation, which could be bad for murals – not to mention people breathing! You know, like the caves at Lascaux, or Tutankhamun's tomb or wherever it was, where visitors' breath changed the air so much that the ancient paintings began to go mouldy.'

Ozzy gave a short laugh that sounded more like a screech, or maybe a high-pitched bark, Tiffany thought, startled.

'Not practically overnight!' he snapped. 'No doubt the old rogue will claim that Felix should have thought of the effects of steam, and a heavy-breathing clientèle, and used more waterproof paints or applied a protective undercoat before setting to work. And, Tiffany, the thinking of experts now is that the "mould" marks dotted all over King Tut's wall-paintings were present from day one, thanks to sealing up the tomb before letting the paintings dry fully – a product of undue haste, so perhaps there are some parallels here after all.' He looked at Felix harshly with hooded eyes, and then turned back to Tiffany.

'But you may have a useful point about the steam and ventilation; and Felix you may be right about something perhaps already infecting the walls before they were re-skimmed and painted blank. I can probably undermine most of the proprietor's arguments and stave off huge bills for compensation if any more of the paintings start to peel off – but in the meantime, you had better go and touch up the dodgy bits, to keep him quiet for now.' Seeing Felix stiffen at this order, Ozzy grew more severe.

'You've got a big show coming up, Felix, and you don't need any bad publicity just before it. No-one's going to buy your heftily priced panels if they think your work's liable to go into some kind of paint meltdown within weeks of completion.'

Felix had stopped pacing and stood by the windows again, his arms crossed defiantly.

'My panels are painted in oils, onto wood primed with gesso or onto canvas – they're all in a completely different medium to the murals,' he growled, 'and we can spell that out to any doubters. They are not going to peel or melt, or anything else for that matter.' He was bristling with annoyance.

'Which bits at the restaurant are peeling most, Ozzy?' Tiffany asked quietly.

'Mostly the large cat in the middle, which makes it rather obvious,' he replied sternly. She bit her lip, thinking. Those walls were painted when Felix himself was starting to look a bit off colour. Maybe he somehow transferred that into his self-portrait instead? She looked at him carefully. If he had been channelling some kind of riff on that old *Picture of Dorian Gray* story, either it's not working properly, she thought, or he needs to smarten up a bit anyway, and maybe shave more often. The electric razor I bought for him soon after his metamorphosis was pretty easy to use, after all, even though he said its buzz gave him the shivers sometimes.

Ozzy was still thinking hard, plotting how to turn this setback into an advantage or, at the very least, to justify it. He was beginning to enjoy rising to the drama of the occasion.

'If it were just some bit of paint in a corner somewhere,' he speculated aloud, 'you could almost pass it off as deliberate: the artist allowing decay in the real world to break through his illusion, and bring us back to our own earthly clay – all frightfully clever.' His voice gathered pace as he extemporised. 'A reminder of the frailty of things and the decomposition to come, delivered in the midst of diners stuffing their faces with food and drink. We could make a terribly clever claim that the whole thing was programmed from the start, and perhaps we still can and turn a potential embarrassment into a positive virtue, an ongoing study of life – but I'm not at all sure that it starting with the cat is the best place.'

He made a decision.

'What you must do, Felix is pop round there to tart up the old tomcat a bit now, and paint a bit of fake decay in around the edges of the murals here and there, so that if the rest of the damn thing starts to fail you can claim it was all planned: a modern version of those plates of fruit and still-lifes that, in the past, artists liked to make studies of as the items decomposed, and intended as a comment on our times. Mine host at the restaurant may not be too keen, but we can say we're planning some brilliant publicity about the project for immediately after, or even at, your new show – announcing that the work at the restaurant is effectively an installation for diners to visit regularly to see how it's changing. It could mean a few more regular customers for him to fleece.' Ozzy clapped his hands decisively, as if making this illusion into reality.

'Even better,' he added, 'we'll get that photographer – Mike – to set up some time-lapse cameras to create a record of the process for a future show. Let's say that it'll immortalise the restaurant, blah blah, and then the walls can be whitewashed over again, in all senses, at the right moment. We may have to offer to pay for the whitewashing. It won't be crippling.'

Felix had recovered from his sulk and brightened up during this speech, although the idea of whitewashing out all his work made him bristle a little again.

'I might be able to persuade him that he's still got the latest thing on his hands,' he grumbled, 'although he may not be as easily convinced as you that signs of decay and a dash of *memento mori* on the walls are ideal for a restaurant.'

'It's no worse than some of his food and wines,' Ozzy answered crisply. 'Talk to him about well-hung game, blue cheeses, sweet wines and noble rot. Suggest that he develops some menus that pick up the theme and develop a whole narrative of food around it. Make it all part of the plan: an artist's commentary on the nature of decay and new cycles, paralleled and complemented by a restaurateur's ability to conjure great gastronomic experiences out of the same. It'll be the talk of the autumn. Jenna and I can see to that. In fact, the more the murals decay, the better – but get that cat looking less moth-eaten first. It's not edible, and far too prominent at the moment.'

Tiffany applauded now, delighted by the speed of Ozzy's reinvention of the situation. 'Bravo! Bravissimo!' she said, and Felix curled his lip into something that might have been a conspiratorial smile, or perhaps a snarl, she thought.

'Perfect,' he said, with a trace of sarcasm. 'I'll go over there this afternoon, armed with your concept, except that I'll say it was mine, although endorsed by the great set designer and gourmand himself – you, Ozzy – and we'll see what a bit of touching-up, charm and some cod art history will do. Want to come with me, Tiffany?'

She scrambled out of the armchair.

'Of course, if you'd like some moral support, or an audience. It should be entertaining. Tell me quickly about the new show first that it's now meant to be the hors d'oeuvre for, though. When and where is that served up?'

'Soon,' said Ozzy, flipping the lid off a cardboard box on his table and pulling out one of the invitations. 'Here,' he said, passing it to her. 'At one of the more fashionable fringe theatres that I sometimes slum it with, and design sets for – keeping my name burnished among the more avant-garde. It's going dark soon for major renovations. Just before they rip everything up and out of it, Felix is invited to display his latest works for a weekend in its exposed innards – before too much has gone, and it gets too dangerous to let the punters pick their way amongst the ruins, but after a tiny bit of creative damage has been done.' Tiffany looked at the address on the invitation.

'You mean that old theatre where Emma works,' she said, crushingly.

Ozzy brushed this truth aside. 'It's perfect. New art amongst the entrails of the old theatre. Our solution to the unfortunate development at the restaurant ties in nicely now as part of the overall concept. A moveable feast from theatre to restaurant, with the fruits of summer gently disintegrating over the autumn,' he declaimed, impressing

Tiffany again with the speed of his imagination. 'Felix, you'd better include some panels for the show that reference the murals at the restaurant as they were when new,' Ozzy instructed, 'to prepare the ground, set the scene, and provide the continuity.' Felix considered this, reluctant to do yet more work yet liking the cunning and duplicitous solution.

'Maybe,' he said, stroking his chin again, his eyes growing bright and mischievous as Ozzy, satisfied, resumed updating Tiffany.

'A modest percentage of the price tag of each panel sold will go towards the theatre's restoration fund,' he told her, 'thereby ensuring that the great and the good, who love to be known as patrons of the arts, should find it harder to resist this combined opportunity to confirm their status and their social credentials. We'll have a big party for them on the first night, and it'll be just a weekend's show before the demolition men really get going. Almost ephemeral, although the artworks, Felix, must not be. The party's by personal invitation only to a priority entry hour or two, and then the box office opens for others to buy entry tickets – perhaps in hopes also for a chance to rub shoulders with the glitterati inside, should any linger. That way those who just come to see and be seen, but don't buy any art, still cough up something towards the theatre fund via the ticket price, and of course to our admin expenses.' He walked round his desk and sat down in his metal chair. The imperial seat, thought Tiffany.

'It sounds marvellous,' she said. 'Can I come to the glitterati party, or is this one just for me to inspect?' Tiffany fanned herself gently with the invitation Ozzy had passed to her.

'Of course you must come to that bit,' said Felix, reaching for it to write her name on the top. 'It wouldn't be a proper party without my first benefactor there.' Tiffany smiled warmly at him and pocketed the invitation.

At his desk, Ozzy pulled forward a sheet of paper with a long list of names, with more sheets stapled beneath it. He tapped the top one.

'A favoured few, dear Tiffany, including yourself and your inner circle, will of course be invited to join the celebrity opening. The great and the good invited are mainly chosen for their chequebooks, and track record of supporting the arts, with a few thrown in that might be led by the general glamour of the occasion to buy too. There's a condition however: the favoured friends and family are also expected to turn up the afternoon beforehand, and help to hang the show.'

'How exciting,' Tiffany replied. 'Count me in. So when do these invites go out?'

'This week. The party's barely forty-eight hours after the theatre's final performance, in its current manifestation, so we'll only have that amount of time to prepare the space and set up the artworks. The whole point is to make it feel immediate, a stunning pop-up show, a one-chance-to-buy event. We want to give people just enough time to reschedule their diaries to be able to join in the excitement and celebration of a last-minute, almost last-night, party.'

'What is the final show at the theatre?' Tiffany asked, trying to remember whether Emma had mentioned it at all.

'*The Tempest*,' Ozzy replied. 'In a short but dramatic run, with some surprises. Previews started last week. Haven't you noticed the advance publicity for it? What or who is distracting you from the world so effectively, I wonder? You should go to see it. It's going to be remembered.' Tiffany recalled some posters that she had barely registered on her journeys to and from work.

'Have you done the set for it? I thought you were busy designing for *Akhnaten*.'

'I am. My role regarding *The Tempest* is advisory only this time. They can't really afford me but I like to provide some goodwill input occasionally, if convenient for all concerned. Unexpectedly, their demolition contractor couldn't start on the interior on the day originally intended – some sort of over-run on its part – so it was decided to extend the show's own run by a few days, and my timely suggestion of the fundraising possibilities of hosting Felix's exhibition on the premises over the remaining weekend was leapt on. Serendipity, one of my favourite approaches.'

'I thought serendipity involved chance?' said Tiffany, to tease him, wondering if Emma had been roped into this little ruse to find a venue at short notice for Felix's exhibition. Perhaps not, given that Felix is not one of Anthony's favourite people, she supposed. As Felix, who was still rootling about gathering paints and brushes together, seemed in no hurry to set off to the restaurant yet, she returned to the comfy armchair.

'You have to see the potential for such happy accidents on the horizon,' Ozzy explained nonchalantly, 'and be ready to help them along a little. Anthony knows a thing or two about that and, in fact, I believe he also knows the demolition company. I think he has a relationship with one of their overseas subsidiaries though some offshore interest of his own – something called Obscure Design, for some no doubt nefarious reason.' He had wondered what she knew about it, but Tiffany looked up at him, clearly startled.

'Really? Why would Anthony need an offshore company anyway? Oh, to squirrel away his overseas profits I suppose. Typical.'

'Some overseas projects need extra inputs kept handy for contingencies, before final funds are repatriated,' Ozzy suggested. 'It's a pragmatic thing.'

'As I said, typical,' Tiffany responded. She supposed that Ozzy has used this information as some kind of leverage to make Anthony persuade the demolition company to hold off for a week, creating the ideal opportunity to stage Felix's pop-up show in the empty theatre. She found it amusing that Anthony may have had his arm twisted into inadvertently helping Felix. Felix was looking rather pleased, too.

'Clever idea,' he commented, meaning the offshore company. 'Interesting.'

'Not for you, Felix,' Ozzy countered. 'Your sales will be very much onshore, at least for now. You don't need to squirrel any money overseas. We'll put your proceeds through the small local company that I've already set up for the purpose, and pay you regularly in cash net of the tax that my accountants will deduct to forward to the tax collectors on your behalf, until your mislaid ID has been found, or re-issued. Then you can open a bank account to receive monthly inputs.'

Felix, thinking that some money stashed away overseas could be just what he would like, opened and then shut his mouth. There was no need to alert Ozzy to the new idea forming in his thoughts.

'Goodness,' Tiffany was saying, 'you have been busy, Ozzy. You could do my job in your sleep. What's all this about missing ID then?' (As if I didn't know why Felix has none.) 'Are you helping Felix to track down his passport?' she asked, disingenuously, knowing this would need to be produced to satisfy any bank.

'He's got me some horrendous forms to fill in,' Felix said hastily. 'We're getting it sorted out.' He gave Tiffany a look that banned further mischievous questions in front of Ozzy.

'Great,' she said. 'Well, are we off to schmooze the restaurateur with our cunning new narrative, or what?'

'Yes. Let's get it over with. I'll take my paints there right now.' Felix picked up the large canvas bag into which he had bundled his selection of paints and brushes by its broad strap and slung it from his shoulder. 'Catch you later, Ozzy.' Ozzy waved a hand lazily towards the studio door as Tiffany rose to follow Felix from the room.

'Make sure he keeps our plan sounding plausible,' he cautioned. She shot him a curious look from the doorway. Could Ozzy suspect just how implausible Felix even being here is? she wondered – surely not, yet look at how he extracted all that offshore information from Anthony.

Aloud she said: 'Of course, and I'll make sure he fixes that moulting cat straight away, too.' But as she hastened after Felix, Tiffany wished she had left out the comment about the tabby. Ozzy looked thoughtfully after her, his eyes hooded and dark again.

Chapter 28

Felix did his best to mollify Shay, the restaurateur, with his new explanations and offer of prompt temporary restoration 'so that we get the timing right for the link to the exhibition,' as he explained.

The bag of paints and brushes spoke greater volumes. Told that the immediate revisions would resolve the apparent damage, and ready the murals for an up-to-the moment link to a headline-grabbing new art show, Shay relaxed a little. He intimated that if Felix could let it be widely known that a trip to the restaurant was effectively an extension of the new exhibition, he was satisfied; and there would be no further question of dispute between them. Tiffany picked this moment to speculate aloud whether, if the restaurant offered the exhibition's invitees and ticket-holders a modest discount on production of their used ticket – for a limited period – quite a lot of additional customers might be attracted to its doors to try the new autumn menu. Shay eyed her shrewdly.

'Perhaps I could see my way to a ten per cent discount, or a free bottle of house wine for them,' he said. 'I will work something out, but that's not enough to tempt your rich and famous admirers here, Felix my friend. They will come for the pictures and the menu itself, so why not have a little private dinner here after the show, and bring some of them along? I can prepare a tasting menu.'

Felix grunted. He was inspecting the flaking tabby cat with a worried frown. It looked distinctly mangey, and even a bit ginger in some places. He pulled a cloth out of his pocket and rubbed off a few flakes, and then began to open his bag of paints and brushes.

'A private dinner after the show, Felix?' Tiffany prompted him. He looked up.

'Maybe. I'm not sure that we could commit to a specific time on the night,' he said, 'but it's an interesting thought. Let me discuss it with my business partner, Ozzy, and get back to you. It would have to be a late dinner, I think.'

'So much the better!' Shay rubbed his hands with anticipation, menu thoughts already forming. 'My regular customers can come as usual, and when that rush is over, you and your friends will have our complete attention. I can keep the kitchen open longer that night.' He pulled a small pad from his pocket and began to make some menu notes.

'Excellent plan,' Felix said absently, beginning to apply deft strokes of paint to the stricken cat. 'Give me a moment to sort this out. I'll come back tomorrow to work on the rest – I mean the next phase of the concept.'

Tiffany silently marvelled at the speed with which he was restoring the cat, but secretly wondered how long these repairs would last. The cat's appearance had certainly been deteriorating more than Felix's own – so far – she noted. First his supposed baby turns out to be imaginary, then his painted alter ego goes flaky. She decided not to dwell on whether this was coincidence or significant. It was more likely that Felix's lightning progress was marred by a certain slapdash carelessness on his part. Ozzy is pushing him too hard, she thought. No-one can keep up this fevered rate of creativity without errors creeping into their work. Perhaps she should point this out soon, or Felix could be heading for burn-out.

'We'll give your dinner party idea some serious thought by then, too,' Felix added, as he worked. He stepped back a few times to check, and when he was satisfied, put his paints and brushes away. 'I'll just take a quick walk around the restaurant, to identify – I mean confirm – the best areas for phase two,' he said, 'and then we'll be off for today.'

He shook Shay warmly by the hand as they finally left. 'We'll talk more about your splendid idea tomorrow,' Felix told him. As he and Tiffany left the courtyard and were definitely out of earshot as they walked back up the street, she asked him why he had painted his former likeness so prominently in the restaurant in the first place.

'A stupid joke,' he answered, 'because the owner's name was Shay.'

'I don't understand,' she said. Felix looked uncomfortable.

'I did it because Ozzy had told me that Shay was also the name of an Egyptian god who presides over your destiny,' he said gruffly. 'I thought it would be amusing to park my previous form for safe-keeping in this Shay's restaurant. A harmless prank, I thought. A little in-joke between me and the cosmos.'

'Tempting fate,' said Tiffany. Felix grunted.

'If you say so. That was a neat way you drew him into the rescue plan, Tiff. He was practically eating out of your hand back there.' She agreed, though the thought of the stout restaurateur presiding over anyone's destiny unnerved her a little.

'That's probably because there was something in it for everyone, Felix. Scratch his back nicely, and he'll scratch yours,' she suggested.

'You think? Scratch my back and I'll sheath my claws,' he replied. 'You people always did have the wrong version, in my opinion.'

'Our version works for us. We don't have claws,' she said.

'You think?' he repeated. 'In your case, I'd say they were just well hidden and perhaps a little stiff from irregular use. Unlike some others we know.' He hoisted his canvas bag a bit higher onto his shoulder as they walked.

'Who?' Tiffany considered. 'Surely you don't mean Anthony? He's just tactless. I'd say that Emma, and Ozzy of course, have proved to have sharper moments.' She glanced at him. 'What did you make of Ozzy's remarks about Anthony today, by the way?'

'Implying sharp practice on Anthony's part of course,' Felix said bluntly. Since the information tallied with what he had overheard previously, and with Iris's 'snippets', Felix privately assumed it was mentioned in his hearing as ammunition for use when baiting Anthony, in furtherance of Ozzy and Iris's scheme for him.

'Mmm,' Tiffany murmured. 'I was never quite sure about some of his business methods. There often seemed to be some local agent or Mr Fixit on the phone in the evenings about handling some difficult early stage of Anthony's projects, if you know what I mean.' She paused by the little flower shop, enjoying the vibrant colours.

'You mean he pays bribes,' said Felix. 'Of course he does. It's probably the only way he can get certain projects to run smoothly. Don't look so shocked at hearing it spelt out. You do the same.'

'I do not! What on earth do I have to pay bribes for – or with, for that matter?' she protested.

Felix laughed so much at this, that several passers-by glanced back to see what could be amusing this striking man so greatly. Tiffany changed her mind about the flowers and began to walk on, rather frostily.

'Tiffany,' he said, quickly catching up with her, 'what about all those cotton reels tied on string that you used to tweak across the floor to entice me to play with, when I was a youngster? And the titbits, as rewards for being adorable? You were softening me up, so that I would remain a charming house guest rather than a wild beast.'

'Yes and look what I got,' she retorted. 'A house guest who became a bit too charming, if you ask me, and is still a beast. So much for bribery, if that's how you define it. It backfires – sometimes big time. As my current boss may find out, if he's not careful,' she added. Felix was instantly curious.

'What do you mean?'

'Got you again! Still can't resist a cotton reel rolled in front of you, can you? He's been getting me to fill in his wretched tax return, and given me a wodge of his paperwork to dig out the relevant details from. Only he didn't sift through it first. From what I've gone through so far, and bank statements, I'd say he's got some very interesting undeclared income building up somewhere. When I asked him about incomings and outgoings that I couldn't reconcile with his salary and expenses and investment income, and so forth, he just laughed and said he'd got lucky and come into a couple of inheritances, and not to worry because there was no tax to pay on those.'

'Naturally you don't believe him?' Felix paused, contemplating the wares in a butcher's shop window. Duck, rabbit, even pigeon.

'No I do not; not least because inheritances are not usually transfers in cash by, guess what, the Obscure Design Company.' Felix stopped examining a handsome pheasant hanging near the counter inside the shop, and turned to look at her instead. 'What do you make of that startling coincidence?' Tiffany asked him.

'Remarkable,' he murmured, delighted with this detail. 'Why would Anthony's curiously named subsidiary be paying kickbacks here, to your boss, I wonder?'

'They may not be kickbacks, but reimbursements, and after Ozzy's comments today I certainly have more doubts about them. Are you going into that shop or just going to drool on the pavement? Let's walk on, then. Normally I'd assume it's because Finch-whats-it owns a consultancy with clients in Egypt amongst other places, and presumably one of those clients is Anthony. I did get the job with him, or at least the job interview, because Anthony introduced me to the man at some party and said that I was a top-class PA looking for work after returning from a spell overseas. Which was true – you know how I like to go off and explore for a few months, until the money runs out again.' Felix nodded.

'I do, and it was also after one of those early jaunts that you decided to scoop me up and take me away from my home in a barn, and turn me into an altogether more urban creature.' He glanced at her.

'Yes. Perhaps I should just have got a goldfish instead of a kitten.' They walked on in silence for a bit.

Then Felix said casually: 'I might have a bit of fun with Anthony about these "obscure designs" if the right moment arises.'

'Must you?' Tiffany looked sideways at him. 'Even he can be ruthless at times, and you're in a rather vulnerable situation until you get a passport sorted, courtesy of Ozzy – who seems to be taking over your life, by the way, though I suppose you are benefitting. If Ozzy's being this indiscreet to us, about Anthony, what might he be saying about you? He so likes to gossip and spin a yarn. Look at that dodgy story he told us ages ago about his own family, for instance. So tread warily, Felix. I mean, strictly speaking, you don't exist! Not as a fully-authenticated human being, that is.'

A young woman walking past them, on her way to a rehearsal, overheard the last comment and looked sympathetically at Felix. Poor guy, she's giving him a hard time – I wonder what he's done to deserve it, she thought. I wouldn't be so rough on a bloke who looks that good. Felix intercepted her glance and smiled ruefully back. Tiffany elbowed him in the ribs.

'Stop it, you old tomcat,' she hissed. 'Pay attention! I'm serious. Anthony could still shop you, far more than you can shop him.'

'Not any more,' Felix said, returning his gaze to Tiffany, and linked arms with her to show there were no hard feelings, 'or at least, not that easily. You see, I really am about to exist in your sense of the word.' He waited for her reaction so Tiffany stopped walking and looked sternly at him.

'Is this good news or bad news? Details, please.'

Felix yawned, his teeth looking a bit yellower and pointier than usual, she thought. I suppose we ought to find him a dentist sometime.

'News that Ozzy, that master of invention, has dug up my salvation, as he pretty much revealed earlier today at the studio. Perhaps you had better not ask any further.'

'But of course I ask further. You're my responsibility – sort of.' Felix almost yowled with amusement.

'You, Tiff, accepting responsibility for anything? There's a transformation. I thought you offloaded me very deftly onto Jenna, and then onwards to Ozzy. But a cat can walk alone, you know, and so can this person.' He indicated himself with a sweep of his free hand. Tiffany calmly released his other arm.

'So walk,' she said. 'I did end up feeling responsible for introducing you to Jenna, and not warning her about your highly suspect origins. I don't fancy any more mishaps among my friends. So what else are you and Ozzy cooking up, apart from restaurant menus founded on destiny and decay?' Felix knew she would want to know eventually and was rather looking forward to telling her how cleverly he had played Ozzy along.

'Ozzy had sneakily searched for my birth record,' he told her, 'but of course couldn't find a birth certificate of the right sort of era for a Felix Sylvester. When he mentioned this curious fact – he was fishing, of course – I told him that Sylvester was actually my mother's maiden name which we both took to using after we returned to her home village, so of course there was no record of me under it. I added that I was actually born in Egypt, and would have been registered under her married name. Her first husband, born here, ran off with someone else not long after my birth, and when she brought me back as a very young child I was listed on her passport, which was still in her married name. Apparently children still didn't get their own passports at that time, rather conveniently for me now, but travelled on a parent's one. And of course, I've been over here ever since, so I've never needed to apply for my own one in adulthood, till now.'

'And he believed you?' Tiffany was astonished by this complicated tissue of invention.

'Listen on.' Felix actually capered in a tight circle, for a moment. 'I then explained that my mother, being a bit unconventional, not only ditched her faithless ex-husband's surname but decided to home-school me in the village we'd settled in, and where you first met me if you remember our broadly accurate story about that. Naturally she took to being very self-sufficient in other ways, didn't believe in doctors and dentists, and generally lived "off the grid" – as you are well aware, given her actual circumstances. Hence young Felix was pretty much off the official radar growing up, and when she remarried and went away I was old enough to stay on to complete my education with my equally scatty Sylvester cousins – and thus I have no idea what happened to any paperwork from my childhood.' He bowed to her.

Tiffany shook her head at this account. 'An excellent performance, Felix, with neat manipulation of some facts, but you've added far too many layers to our story – though it kind of works,' she admitted.

Felix agreed. 'It's fun, isn't it?'

'And Ozzy's accepted it?' she pressed again.

'Why not? He loves to think he knows people's secrets, and of course I told him all sorts of stuff about my boho upbringing with the complete ring of truth. Now get this – a handy acquaintance of his in Egypt has dug up what appears to be a record of "my" birth near Cairo, in the right sort of year – so we sent off for a replacement birth certificate. I'm waiting for it to arrive shortly. Next stop, my own passport, and then I can open a bank account, and I will have nothing to fear from Anthony or anyone else.'

'Except the highly likely risk of indiscretion on Ozzy's part,' Tiffany pointed out.

'So what? He thinks he's working with the truth. I am both the artist known as Felix Sylvester, of this country – and Christopher F. Cattermole, born in Egypt!'

'Who?'

'You don't recall young Chris? His mama, daffy Mrs Cattermole – now née Sylvester in my version – was rather pretty, and claimed to be a divorcée when they arrived in your village, genuinely so as it turns out. She claimed to be an artist too, also rather conveniently for me now, although

272

she scratched more of a living from doing a bit of housekeeping and duly found herself a nice older husband through that, who carried her and her son off to some other corner of the world. Your mother was reminiscing about her for some reason on the day you collected me and shoved me into that wretched cat-carrier to bring me back to town. Probably because that was a highly stressful experience, I remembered the conversation, and the interesting name. Cats and moles! Ozzy seemed rather touched by my reminiscences of a secluded childhood in the English countryside, laced with trace memories of the sounds and scents of Egypt.'

To his disappointment, Tiffany, worried now about how many new loose ends Felix might have created that could trip them up, frowned.

'Come on, Tiff, don't be dreary – it all fits. I just elaborated on things that you and Anthony said about Egypt, and some useful pictures seen in someone else's books when I was exploring your neighbourhood – and suddenly it felt so real, like some long-lost memory actually flooding back.' He paused. 'Has that ever happened to you?'

'Déja vu,' she said absently, wondering if the books had been Ash's, now that she knew about her cat's past visits to his flat. She was curious too about how this Cattermole person's records have been so conveniently found and appropriated. 'Déja vu,' she repeated as they neared the entrance to her favourite small park. 'It means you feel you've already seen it, by somehow living it before. Though in your case, false memory syndrome is more likely.'

He ignored the dig.

'Déja vu, exactly! The history draws me in, given the ancient Egyptians' exceptional respect for the true essence of the feline. Did you know that Mau, the divine cat, was present at the dawn of creation, and older than many of their gods? Apparently he holds the secrets of eternal life and divine knowledge, and protects the Trees of Life. Shall we go through the park?'

Tiffany could not decide whether to laugh or scold him so just nodded, and they swung in step through the open gates. They would close at dusk, but that was still an hour or so away and late afternoon sunshine had replaced the morning's greyness.

'I persuaded Ozzy to talk me through a lot of Egyptian mythology and history while picking his brains about his designs for that opera set there,' Felix explained, 'and gradually it began to sound familiar. We even talked briefly about your figurines,' he added.

'You did?'

'Well, the powers they represent. I particularly liked the sound of Nephthys and her powers of magical resurrection,' he told her. 'That bit reminds me of you, but then moving on from your statuettes so does the cat goddess Bastet, who likes her creature comforts – and, actually, I think of you as channelling more of Hathor, a goddess of love and rebirth, as she's also very fond of a drink. In fact, she's at her best then.' Tiffany was about to agree that a drink soon would be a fine idea, when he added 'But she often has the head of a cow.'

'Well that's just great,' Tiffany said, 'thank you for that image, Felix. Any other charming suggestions?'

'Relax. She's the Lady of the Sycamore-Fig tree and its fruits' milky juices, that took over from the first Tree of Life. The Greeks considered her a dead ringer for their own Aphrodite,' Felix retorted. 'You should be flattered, not offended.' His expression grew dreamier and his pace along the path slowed. 'It took me a while to figure out who Jenna might usefully model herself on, but now I've plumped for Maat, goddess of truth and cosmic order. Jenna does much prefer order, doesn't she?' he said. 'And, rather agreeably as it turns out, apparently Maat was married to Thoth, the god of wisdom, judgement, mediation, integrity and truth. Who does that put you in mind of?'

'Thomas! As we discussed before, I think,' Tiffany answered, warming to this game now.

'Thomas, through and through,' agreed Felix. 'A perfect match, if not quite what I had initially imagined for her.' He looked up at the trees, sparkling with the rain that had fallen earlier, their leaves just beginning to show signs of turning to autumn colour.

'What about Anthony?' Tiffany suggested with mischief. Felix pulled a face.

'Tricky one. Of course Ptah is the god of architects, but I refuse to elevate Anthony, who can remain a slavish acolyte as far as I'm concerned.'

'Done,' said Tiffany, 'but where does that put Emma?'

'Still working on that one. Maybe she's the one channelling a bit of Bastet these days. Or possibly warlike Neith. A work in progress.'

Tiffany considered.

'And you?'

'Some free spirit or other,' he said airily.

'Or channelling Seth perhaps,' she suggested darkly, 'the god of chaos – very appropriate, in your case, although maybe you could sidestep all the war, pestilence et cetera that he generally unleashes.'

'Ptah is the god who covers the arts and crafts,' said Felix, loftily now, 'and I am an artist.'

'So you are, and crafty with it, but you're not getting the top slot of creator god either,' she teased him.

'I'll throw in my lot with ancient Mau, then, and pre-date and sort out the lot of you,' he suggested, curious to see her reaction.

'The original cat?' Tiffany said. 'Sounds right up your alley.'

'Ha ha,' he said. 'You seem to forget this was all your doing.' Was it, though? she wondered. And either way, what does it reveal about me? – other than that Felix reckons I'm a cow.

'So what about Ozzy?' she said to change the subject. Felix hunched his shoulders as he walked, resisting the thought of Osiris, god of the underworld, and his powerful half-sister Isis, who heals the sick amongst many other things. He looked across the grass, scuffed by the summer and yellowing in patches.

'Ozymandias, king of kings, surveying the empty desert, about to be bereft of his former power, riding for a fall,' he suggested, sounding cruel now.

Tiffany bit her lip. Perhaps this game was a bit too silly.

'That's rather harsh, Felix, considering how much he has been trying to help you, even if he is too controlling at times,' she said.

'True. You know, he expressed shock at how remiss you were, in not helping me to sort out my passport yourself – but I defended you. I said that you had no idea I was without these things, as I'd painted your murals in exchange for bed and board and a little cash, as I did for Jenna; and around the village I'd always worked for easy handouts and payment in kind.' He was tired now, after all that remedial painting and the stress of the morning's debate about how to rescue his artwork. A nap would be nice.

'Very funny, and thanks again Felix,' Tiffany said sarcastically, 'as usual you've painted me as a very thoughtless and self-centred creature.'

He looked sideways at her, but only said: 'Well, you suit me well enough. Let's sit down for a moment. There's a spot over there that I like. Anyway I told Ozzy that I was to blame for putting off a lot of tiresome effort to sort the passport thing out – and, naturally, he undertook to fix me up with someone who could check out a few details about the Cattermoles in Cairo.'

'I bet he did,' she said, hoping the fixer had not been Iris. We don't need her taking a close interest in Felix too, she thought.

'I just provided the Cattermole boy's name and age, and that was it. Task done. Splendid in here, isn't it?' he added, thinking of contented days patrolling the park and ruling the neighbourhood gardens. 'Here's my favourite bench. Yours too, I think.' He had spotted her there sometimes, on some of his old expeditions. 'Let's sit.'

Tiffany still felt uneasy about these secretive developments afoot, while she had been happily distracted by her developing relationship with Ash.

'Congratulations, I think,' she said, 'but what happens if this man you're impersonating comes back here, or his mother, for that matter?'

Felix shrugged – his default response to tricky questions, pending further footwork, she knew.

'I have no idea,' he confirmed, yawning as he settled more deeply on the bench, 'but he probably has a busy life wherever he is – assuming he is still alive, of course. Naturally I couldn't ask anyone to check for my new name in the register of deaths. He may have changed his surname to match his step-father's, for all I know. People do things like that, I gather. His mother probably asked him to adopt his stepfather's surname. Worst case I'd just be his accidental namesake. Lots of people have the same name, even unusual ones.'

Tiffany nodded, watching a bevy of pigeons pecking at breadcrumbs on the other side of the path, probably the birds she had shared her sandwich crusts with last time she sat here. At school she had known two unrelated girls with unusual and identical first and surnames, and only an academic year apart. She noticed some larger crumbs closer to the bench that the pigeons seemed to be avoiding today. The birds eyed Tiffany and Felix beadily, as if waiting for them to leave.

You city pigeons are usually bolder than that, she thought. Maybe Felix doesn't fool you yet, in the way that he's fooled Ozzy and the rest. She considered the pigeons, while Felix resumed talking. To Tiffany it sounded as if he were persuading himself, more than her, that his elaborate new identity would be readily accepted. She felt that his story sounded too complex to ring true to others, and yet life was often more complicated than fiction. Perhaps people would bear that in mind when he started using this new name. She brightened up at the thought that he probably didn't need to make it generally public, as his persona here as an artist would always be just 'Felix' after all this promotion of his work and name so far. Christopher Cattermole could be for admin purposes only, or, if Felix's art did all turn to dust, perhaps even a heaven-sent alias.

'My name has changed several times already anyway,' Felix was now saying, interrupting her thoughts. 'Twice by you, if you recall: first I was KitCat, because it was cute for a bit before I grew up properly, and became Felix. I prefer Felix.'

'So stick with it for the art. It's a lot more stylish. And what about that branch of the Sylvester family tree we so carefully created for you?' Tiffany said. 'How do we explain that away now that you're a Cattermole?'

'We don't.' He stretched his legs in front of him. The pigeons withdrew a little further. 'My mother's still a Sylvester by birth, and that's what'll be in the family tree I've drawn, when I get round to completing it.'

'Enough of your inventions,' Tiffany said, who despite the late afternoon sunshine was starting to feel cold sitting still on the bench. 'You're as bad as Ozzy when it comes to spinning yarns. I'm getting a headache trying to keep track. I need to go home – and you'd better head back to the studio. You've got some additional panels to finish now, remember?'

They rose, scattering the pigeons who flew off in alarm as Felix, eyes glittering, finally glanced in their direction.

Chapter 29

Another fortnight passed calmly for everyone except Felix, who was in a frenzy of creativity. The day before his show opened was bright and clear. A hint of autumn chill was in the air, crisp and clean, giving a cutting edge to the blue sky and the golds and reds of the leaves. Every breath Tiffany drew as she stepped out of her home early that morning felt invigorating. She revelled in it, almost dancing along the pavement.

'Going my way?' inquired Ash, leaning over his dilapidated front gate as she approached.

'You bet. I've come back for some of your famous coffee, and to ask a favour. I agreed to turn up at the theatre this afternoon to help with any finishing touches to hanging Felix's show, and generally provide moral support in case he gets cold feet. It would be great if you came too.'

'Bit late for "cold feet",' Ash said. He swung the gate open. 'By the way, you left your bracelet here in your haste to get home at the crack of dawn to make yourself presentable for work.' Tiffany waltzed up the path, and led the way up the front steps.

'I knew there was a reason to come back here again first.'

'And I thought it was for my coffee and company,' he said, following her. Over the coffee and toast they agreed to rendezvous at the theatre around four that afternoon. Tiffany was confident that her erring boss would not – could not – object to a charming request by her to head off a little early today. Knowing now all about Finch-Smith's susceptibility to bribery, she planned to present the rogue with a ticket for the opening if necessary, and had one ready.

It worked. Finch-Smith, frowning when she first broached leaving early, waived his instinctive objections as she hurried on to say that she realised it was a bit of a liberty to change her plans at such short notice but, as a thank-you she'd managed to blag him a prior-entry, complimentary, VIP ticket, in case he was interested in seeing Felix's work?

'And what might this VIP ticket involve?' he asked, on cue.

'Well, a sight of the art before the general rush, mingling with the starry cast of *The Tempest* and the great and the good generally. My cousin's uncle, who arranged the venue, has an amazing address book. People don't turn his invitations down! Plus the drinks and canapés. You won't have to buy any of the work, just enjoy schmoozing with the glitterati.' He looked quite keen now, she noted with satisfaction. Maybe I'll ask Felix to paint his jowly face quickly into the edge of a populated panel. He won't be able to resist buying it. I'll take a photo from the company blurb for Felix to work from.

'After the VIPs' free exclusive access to the show, people can buy timed-entry tickets at the box office, but numbers will still be limited to how many the old theatre space can hold at any one time, so there may be queues.'

Word had spread like magic about this show, she explained: it seemed that the combined appeal of the venue – whose electrifying version of *The Tempest* had included pools dug into the floor before it went 'dark' for a major refurbishment – and an exciting new artist staging this 'definitely amazing' exhibition for just the weekend, was proving compelling.

'Are you going to Felix Sylvester's pop-up show ?' had become the question to be able to say 'yes' to; and 'let's meet in the queue, I hear there'll be cocktail waiters and entertainment for the line,' was highly acceptable too – but 'see you in the VIP golden hour' was the most desirable mantra *du jour*. Ozzy had been up to his best tricks and gold dust would surely settle on those enjoying the brief magic of Felix's art.

Tiffany's boss gladly accepted the ticket, and even wished her luck with the setting-up.

When she reached the theatre, a large van was parked outside the classical facade of its main entrance. She found Felix and Ozzy in the old auditorium, surveying the first panels carried in. The lower tiers of seats that previously filled a half-hexagon in front of and partially around the stage area had all gone. In the process, a few chunks had been gouged out of parts of the surrounding bare brick walls, and in places these had been enhanced for best cosmetic effect. The final production's pools of water, seeming hacked deep enough into the old stage floor for the mariners and Ariel to plunge into, had now been boarded over to spare any of Felix's illustrious guests an unscheduled tumble, but clever use of stage lights created moving patterns and reflections that recalled the water and, when someone moved across them, broke and dappled as if all present were now under the sea.

The walkways and gantries that the play's sailors had staggered about as their ship foundered were still there, and some of Felix's larger panels were now being hoisted up onto them for maximum visibility, and effect. Other panels were being screwed to the auditorium's encircling walls. A handful designed as triptychs and screens waited to be lifted on to blocks, of varying heights, salvaged from the stage set and now scattered 'randomly' around parts of the exhibition space.

Tiffany stood just inside the old stalls entrance, and watched quietly for a minute or two. Higher up, where the circle seats had been, the small balcony still remained but its tiered benches had been removed, leaving a series of broad curving steps like terraces climbing a bare hillside. A spiral staircase, stored from an earlier production, had been wheeled out again and fastened securely to provide internal access to and from this balcony from the seatless stalls, as well as via the original steep steps to the circle's external street exit. Ozzy stood at the top of the spiral stair, directing the men hoisting a particularly large panel to one of the mariners' former walkways, while Felix watched from the centre of the old stage. He seemed thinner to her, rangier, and sported several days' worth of stubble.

Glancing towards the pool of daylight suddenly streaming from the door that Tiffany had left open, he saw her, and beckoned.

'Tiff, come over here and tell me what you think. I know it still looks chaotic but we are actually nearly done.' He gestured expansively, arms wide, eyes glittering. She moved slowly towards him.

'It's going to look fantastic,' she said – thinking, which is more than you do. 'I like the tricks with the lighting, too.' He glanced around.

'Ah yes, the lighting. That's Ozzy's idea. People need to be able to see the pictures, of course, but as the evening goes on, he says we'll turn down the spotlights a bit and do more with the moving patterns, and generally deepen the mystery. He reckons the combination of alcohol and romantic and mysterious lighting will encourage any laggards who hesitate to sign up for a panel earlier, to splash out before midnight tolls. Then the 'house' goes dark and all our revellers must head for home in their respective pumpkins, though a select few can come to the restaurant to dine with us.'

'That late?' asked Tiffany.

Felix waved towards a clock-face made of light that had appeared on part of the curved brick wall. 'This illusion, as impermanent as time itself, can show whatever hour we want, and will appear only when we want it, too. Midnight in this house could be ten o'clock in the outside world, or two in the morning, or centuries ago, or deep in the future. Time will be particularly permeable here tonight. Ozzy and I will gauge the mood, and choose the moment, the witching hour.' As he spoke the clock faded and disappeared.

Tiffany clapped softly. 'Very clever.'

'All part of the evening's magic,' Felix said, a little wearily, 'but never mind the artifice – what do you think of my own rough art?'

'You actually read the play?' she teased, picking up the textual reference although really she thought, disloyally, that Felix was more like a curious blend of Caliban and Ariel than a Prospero – and one that Ozzy would seem to be having some success in civilising, so far. She surveyed the panels still awaiting hanging, or being manoeuvred into place. 'Not rough, Felix. This art is magnificent, especially against this backdrop.'

'Saw it,' Felix said, 'I saw the play. I watched the final performances. Very instructive.'

His paintings' subjects had been carefully picked to show his range. Several of the larger panels evidently drew on Mike's portfolio of photographs from the opening night at the restaurant. From those and from memory, Felix had created versions of a glittering gathering against the backdrop of his own murals: depictions that included clear portraits of people who had attended the restaurant show – and, tucked more into the middle ground, of some who had not. Presumably this device increased the odds of one or another among them investing in a purchase.

'That reminds me,' Tiffany said, digging a small brochure out of her bag, 'do you have time to put this guy's face into one of those social group panels? It's my boss, Fergal Finch-Smith,' she added. 'I'd love to bounce him into buying a panel out of sheer vanity.'

Felix stroked his unshaven chin. Scruffy and gaunt, he had been too busy lately to pay attention to personal grooming, but would have to smarten himself up for tomorrow night. He could feel the dust of the old building settling into his skin.

'OK, I'm doing a few last-minute touches. I'll try to squeeze a likeness of him in to one of the minor groups over there,' he said. Taking it, he carefully tore out the photo and put it into his jacket pocket before handing her back the gutted brochure. Tiffany squirreled it away, and looked around at the walls again. Several panels – some tall, some horizontal – were of landscapes, capturing the spirit of his first murals, particularly the one in Tiffany's tiny box-room.

Dusk, night, and dawn glowed again in these from the depths of grasses and flowers painted in astonishing detail, and then slowly merged into softer treatment of the terrain beyond before giving way to a sky in one of its nocturnal phases. Some depicted the gloaming, others moonlight, and a few showed the first indications of morning's approach. Each painting explored a different, mysterious blurring of earth and sky, light into dark, dark into light, spaces where the horizon couldn't be focused on and all life's possibilities seemed either trembling into decision, or about to melt into another dimension and be gone.

Felix had captured that immanence when individuals feel closest to merger with the cosmos, the very moment in old tales when someone chooses to step into the mist between worlds and disappear, perhaps forever, from human eyes. Tiffany was transfixed, feeling almost transported herself.

Below this magical field within each picture, the world of grasses, wildflowers, and small creatures grew, in increasing detail, until the bottom of the panel was reached. Here the night still seemed shadowy yet became precise, in the glimmers of light on gossamer cobwebs and grass stalks, or in a few petals gently emerging from the dusk. In one panel the fur of a field mouse gleamed so sleekly that it took Tiffany a moment to realise that its form was too limp to be living, and a smudge of blood clogged the nap of its cheek. In another, the shine in the bright eye of a shrew bustling through some fallen leaves showed it was very much alive, but the dark shape of a feline paw, with its curved claws just edging into part of the foreground, suggested a very un-mystical transition from forager to fodder was also imminent for the tiny creature. Tiffany shivered, but then decided that in the painted moment, suspended and preserved within time itself, the shrew clearly lived on forever. Nevertheless, she challenged Felix.

'You're sure someone will want dead mice on their walls?' she inquired. Felix looked surprised.

'Why not? People have bought plenty of *nature mortes* in previous centuries. Besides my dead mouse is only a small part of the larger picture. Some collectors still like a little shock with their culture, and it amuses them to see how other people react to it. I don't paint anything that isn't true. What's the difference, for instance, between this shrew about to be pounced upon, and the lively girl in that panel over there, being chatted up in the restaurant? Both of them may escape their observer's clutches.' Tiffany looked at the panel he had pointed to, and wrinkled her nose.

'Yes, perhaps,' she agreed, 'but the shrew would prefer to escape and will be terrified when the pounce comes, whereas the girl may not be in the least scared, or may even be planning a pounce of her own – there's your difference.'

'Your difference, Tiffany, my predatory friend,' Felix said. 'And if you look more closely you will see that the bright-eyed shrew is about to snap up a shiny little beetle. It's all a question of perspective. The beetle may scuttle safely away, the shrew may manage to bite the cat and leave it with a wound that festers, the girl may be trying to get her claws into the man. The new owners of the painting can make their own minds up about what happens next – or if nothing much does.'

'Oh come on, Felix, you know your pictures don't leave open the option of nothing happening next – they are full of possibilities,' she remonstrated.

Too full, he thought. It was becoming tiring to paint so much suspended time. 'Like my own life, Tiff, refulgent with inexhaustible possibilities; and talking of which,' he was looking past her, 'I see one stalking your way, right now.' Tiff turned, and saw Ash had arrived. She waved, and as he strolled towards them, she glanced wickedly back at Felix.

'So do I,' she said.

'Ash, good of you to come.' Felix shook hands with his former neighbour. 'We could use your extra muscle to get these screens onto those blocks.'

Ash squeezed Tiffany's waist and nodded at Felix. 'That's what I'm here for. Looks as if you might be getting a bit more help in a moment, I saw Thomas climbing out of a cab outside.'

Felix registered the squeeze, and nodded approvingly.

'Now that I have a better idea of the standpoint from which you are interpreting my work', he said to Tiffany, 'I'd say that prey and predator prove surprisingly well-matched, on this occasion.' As Ash looked at Tiffany for illumination, she just smiled sweetly back and gestured in the direction of the images they had been dissecting.

'What do you think of these? Look carefully.'

Felix was already moving towards the door to intercept Thomas, greeting him warmly.

'Thomas, this is extraordinarily good of you. Is Jenna coming along tomorrow?'

'I know it is,' Thomas responded. 'And yes, Jenna will come to the launch party, and hopefully for the dinner afterwards too.' They looked at each other calmly.

'That's splendid,' said Felix, 'And now to work.' He indicated a folded triptych. 'This one needs to go up on its blocks next.' He glanced back at Ash and Tiffany. 'Ash! Ready for you.' The trio soon had the piece up and unfolded, and Tiffany was consulted on the fine detail of its position on the blocks carrying it.

It was one of the works that re-interpreted the earlier gathering at the restaurant. In the foreground of the main panel were some famous faces; and in one of the wings Tiffany and Ash were captured, chatting, turning three-quarters away and drawing the viewer's eye deeper into the recreated restaurant where, in the mural on its back wall, a splendid tabby cat at its centre again looked out, this time directly into the new venue. How many versions of himself has Felix tucked away in paint for future resurrection? she wondered.

It gave Tiffany a frisson to see him there, still waiting and watching.

The other wing of the triptych offered a glimpse of Jenna and Thomas conversing, and turning towards the viewer. Around and behind their images, a blur of other people drank and gossiped against the recreated mural's rolling sunlit landscape, interrupted only by the tray of drinks and canapés being borne into the picture through the crush. In the background, Anthony could also be seen, extending a glass towards Emma. His gesture also directed the viewer's gaze towards the main panel, into which she already seemed to be staring intently.

'What a penetrating look you've given Emma!' said Thomas, stepping back to look at the picture properly.

'Weighing up the future,' replied Felix.

'Is she considering or rejecting Anthony's offering?' Tiffany wondered.

'We may soon discover. I've invited them both to dinner after the opening tomorrow,' Felix revealed. Tiffany gave him an amused but warning look.

'How noble. Don't play cat and mouse with them too much, Felix. You might want Anthony to include commission of your panels in his next architectural project.'

'Now there's a thought,' said Felix, as if neither idea had ever crossed his mind. 'But it might be more trouble being nice to Anthony than it's worth. On the other hand, it might be very handy. I'll have to weigh up these rival possibilities rather carefully. Perhaps Emma will persuade Anthony to invest in this panel for her.'

'So you don't expect her scary mother to snap it up? I gather Iris has turned up and is coming to the show,' Tiffany warned, but Felix, having invited Iris himself, was unperturbed.

'No need for her to feel obliged, I have already prepared a little sketch in oils of the beloved Emma that Iris or Ozzy could have, if wanted – and I have something to present to you, dear Tiff, as a more personal token.'

Observing them from his eyrie in the old circle above the auditorium, Ozzy interrupted their chatter.

'No slacking down there, plenty of screens still to put up and caterers to deal with. Tiffany, greetings and to the makeshift kitchens with you, if you would be so kind, to check that all that the equipment needed for tomorrow is in hand. Thomas, Ash, welcome and please gird your loins again, to help Felix lift those three pictures onto their plinths too. We still have much to do.'

'He's in his element,' Felix said to the others, 'setting the scene. Best to let him work his own brand of sorcery here. Can you manage to lift these? I have a few minor touches to a panel over there to make.' He felt in his pocket for Finch-Smith's slightly crumpled photo.

The following night's opening was a huge success. Ozzy and Felix had been right: the glamour of the fringe theatre, the allure of passing an evening in the company of its directors and their cast before the building's refurbishment, and confirmation by a leading gossip-blogger that Felix was the hottest new artist in town, all proved a potent draw. The glitterati came in pleasing force, to their prior-entry hour; and the ticket queue was heavily populated by the rest of the *jeunesse dorée* who loved the cocktail-order-takers and servers, and jugglers that Jenna had arranged outside for their amusement and diversion.

As Felix had hoped, sales went well. His images of some of the attendees and their close companions at play against the flattering backdrops of his earlier murals proved irresistible when coupled with the information that in buying their own images – or indeed any of the pictures – the art lovers were supporting the theatre's renovation fund, and could be specially recorded as such by name on an elegant board to be hung prominently inside the new foyer. A handful of guests who considered themselves more cerebral, and some who wanted to show that it was not simple vanity that drove their choices, also signed up for one or other of the various dusk-to-dawn panels. Felix, surveying the party with Ozzy from the circle for a few moments before giving the nod for the light-clock to mimic midnight, felt that he had indeed made a killing that night. His other prey, Anthony, had been successfully toyed with too, if perhaps more than strictly needed to meet Ozzy and Iris's objective.

***

Felix had stalked Anthony slowly, waiting for him to begin to relax after a couple of glasses of champagne. Iris was introduced to Anthony at last by Emma, and chatted pleasantly with him about Egyptian antiquities, while professing to be still very much the 'expat' in Cairo, and not yet in the local political loop. 'Unaware of business gossip' was the reassuring impression she now gave him. In the middle of their conversation, a rather squat man emerged from the crowd, clearly about to greet him. Anthony looked startled, and spoke first.

'David!' He introduced Iris and Emma to the short quiet man, in a well-cut, expensive suit, as a friend and client. Anthony had designed his house on the south coast, it transpired, and might do more work for him in due course. Iris assumed Anthony's surprise at seeing 'David' at the show was because the rather intense guest seemed an unlikely glitterati party-goer. Then Anthony also mentioned that his client was now a trustee of the new opera house board, and a great patron of the arts, and it all made sense.

'So I suppose you must know our other host, Ozzy,' Iris immediately said to David.

'I know his work – seen some of his terrific opera sets in action – and, of course, by his stellar reputation. So when I received this invitation, which I assumed was his way of introducing himself to me, I thought I should take it up,' David replied. He spoke softly, but clearly.

'Ah,' she said, 'and what to you make of the art he has brought us here to see, tonight? Do you like it?' David Fford looked round.

'My taste is a little plainer, more linear, but I can see the artist has great talent. To be honest, I'm more curious about what they're doing with the building.' Seeing Felix moving lithely through the crowd towards them, Iris turned to ask Anthony for his response to the artworks.

'I too generally prefer abstract art to realism,' Anthony began. Felix had almost passed them, as if in pursuit of a potential client deeper in the mêlée but, hearing this, paused to listen.

'Is that so?' he remarked, before turning to smile at Emma and greet her mother. 'Welcome, Iris!' Turning to David, he extended a hand. 'We haven't met. I am Felix. I know who you are, of course. Thank you for coming to my exhibition.' Then he fixed his gaze on Anthony, forcing an answer.

'Normally, yes,' Anthony hastily responded, 'but I must admit that the extremely realistic treatment of your subjects is changed into something quite disturbing by the unusual perspectives from which you paint, and the ambience you deliver.' This was true. 'It gives a kind of emotional abstraction and somehow the mood you create in the lower section of the pictures makes one thinks of Richard Dadd too – there could be malevolent sprites in that foliage – and also of magical realism…'

Anthony had not meant to mention underlying malevolence, nor mad, murderous and incarcerated Victorian artist Richard Dadd, but felt it was all in the work and getting at him somehow. He also feared that he risked sounding pretentious in front of David, which was not at all the impression he wished to make. He stopped speaking.

'Surprisingly perceptive of you. I do quite like to disturb people,' Felix answered, with one of his pointy grins. 'It's very interesting how sensing the underlying tensions in a picture, as you do, affects each viewer differently. But then you never know what demons, tucked away in their own back story, people suddenly see peering out at them, do you? I call it "the obscure design effect".'

Anthony was astonished. Felix sounded innocent to an un-informed listener, but his choice of his words and the look on his face left Anthony in little doubt of his reference. What might Felix know about his misguided offshore subsidiary? With such an important client as David Fford standing right next to him – a man who Anthony still regarded as vital to his own career, and therefore wished to keep well away from any discussion of overseas kickbacks – he was left momentarily speechless.

Felix nodded at Anthony, and carried on smoothly.

'Well, enjoy the evening. Look after Emma properly, won't you? I expect to see you all at supper later on. Do join us, David, if you have time.' Bestowing a warmer smile on Emma and her mother, which also encompassed the bemused David, Felix noted with pleasure that Anthony now looked unhealthily pale. Satisfied, he moved off towards a clutch of minor celebrities now gathered in front of one of his triptychs. They were drinking and talking and studying the crowd more than the picture, but he would soon woo them into admiring it properly.

Anthony took a sip of champagne to hide his consternation and, having swallowed it, managed to smile at Emma and Iris and, vitally, David Fford.

'Talented chap, Felix, but I don't always get his point,' he said, to cover any concern showing on his face.

Emma was looking wonderful, he realised, and despite all the rumours her mother seemed very pleasant. David appeared completely unaware of any significance to Felix's remark beyond matters to do with art. Anthony breathed deeply. He suddenly felt that it was alright after all, and put an arm round Emma's shoulders.

'You do look absolutely gorgeous,' he murmured. She smiled up at him, and Iris actually beamed approvingly at him. This was a bit strange, but comfortingly reassuring.

His instinct was not entirely wrong; Iris had of course registered that David could be a key to Anthony developing his success, and so his presence tonight was also handy for the little ruse she and Felix had plotted together. If Emma was truly keen on bagging this architect Iris chose to be content, for now, not to jeopardise Anthony's hopes at home – provided he put his own house in order. If the sudden pallor brought on by Felix's remarks was an indicator, he was now primed to do so.

David usefully cemented her resolve by turning to Anthony and saying: 'You must bring Emma and Iris with you next time you come down to the coast, and show them the house.' Iris gave David her dazzling smile, one of many types in her armoury.

'We'd be delighted to come,' she said instantly. 'How very sweet of you to suggest it.' David was not accustomed to being regarded as sweet, and found it engaging in this company. He was enjoying himself more he had expected.

When the light-clock made its appearance, claiming that midnight was close, Felix's satisfied guests and victims were charmed into acting out the fiction that it was indeed pumpkin time, and took their leave, many of them with lighter bank accounts than on arriving. They headed off in supportive groups to bars, and restaurants, and homes, mulling over and mythologizing the triumphs and delights of the evening. Iris lightly touched David's arm.

'Why don't you join us for supper, as Felix suggested?' she said. 'We're sneaking off to a little restaurant that he decorated earlier in the summer. The one featured in some of these panels, in fact. Its new menu is quite interesting too, I hear.' Stout David looked as if he could be a foodie.

'Why not?' he answered after hardly a moment's hesitation, and allowed himself to be steered out of the theatre by her. Eager not to lose the mood, Ozzy was already ushering Felix's supper guests quickly towards a line of waiting taxis.

'Carry them to the source of all this!' he declared to the already briefed drivers, chiefly for dramatic effect. 'We shall follow directly. Iris, will you do me the honour of accompanying me and Felix? And who is this with you? Room for you too, good sir. I am Ozzy, Iris's brother. And you are David, are you not? We meet at last. The rest of you, pile in however you like, and lead on.'

Chapter 30

Once in the cab that he had climbed into with Emma, avoiding inviting any of the others to share it with them, Anthony bent forward to confirm the name of the restaurant with the driver.

Emma leant back against the seat as it sped away. She would have liked to kick off her shoes, after standing for so long at the exhibition, but refrained.

'I am so glad to sit down,' she declared. 'I thought the whole show was terrific, a real *tour de force*, and all those people! Felix seemed to be everywhere and the panels were selling like hot cakes. Do you realise whose wall we are going to end up on?'

'Yes,' replied Anthony drily, whose mind was on the alarming memory of seeing David Fford follow Iris into a cab, and clearly coming to the restaurant too. 'That irritating columnist who thinks he's the greatest influencer in town.'

'Anthony, don't be quite so dismissive,' Emma advised. 'Have you actually read any of his articles? And do you know the size of the advance he just got for his next book? He can afford a state-of-the-art new house, or several *pieds-à-terre*, with that kind of earning power. If he keeps buying huge triptychs and panels he'll certainly need a bigger place to put them all in. You should consider that.'

Anthony admitted that he had attempted to read only one work by the man, with no current plans to repeat the experience.

'Well, you can't judge his whole oeuvre on that one,' Emma suggested. 'It was a very experimental piece, designed to shock, and it got him noticed. He's developed hugely since then. You really ought to try another one.'

Anthony resisted a temptation to roll his eyes. Much as he admired Emma's ability to know what was going on in that world, he was not in the mood for a literary chat. He was anxious about what else Felix might say in front of David in the course of supper. What, and how, could Felix possibly know about Anthony's own business dealings?

He ran silently through the options. Had Ozzy been indiscreet? He thought not, on balance; and in any case he was sure that Ozzy would have no reason to give Felix the name of Anthony's offshore vehicle for handling inducements and kickbacks. Tiffany? But what could she know about it? Jenna? He could not think straight with Emma still talking about other partygoers.

'You choose one of his shorter books for me, then, Emma, and I'll do my best,' he said. She was satisfied.

'I will, and I shall hold you to that promise to read it all the way through. If you do ever pitch to design him a house, you'll need to be able to say something that shows you've read at least one of his works. Do you think Felix enjoyed himself this evening? I thought he looked a bit tired.' She made 'tired' sound as if Felix were an old piece of furniture in need of re-upholstery, or an outmoded garment ready for one of the better charity shops that she had, until recently, patronised herself on occasion.

'If he's really sold as much work as he thinks he has, I should think he enjoyed himself hugely,' Anthony answered acidly, as the taxi bounced over a pothole, giving him reflux.

'You still don't like him much, do you?' Emma said.

'Not really. He always has a manner about him that suggests he knows things that I don't, which I find irritating. Besides, I think the fellow might be a fraud.' He said this more in hope than on any firm information about Felix himself, other than odd remarks that Ozzy had made.

'You don't think he paints the pictures?' Emma exclaimed, shocked and intrigued.

'No, no, not that – I daresay he does paint the pictures. No, I mean that I don't think he's who he says he is.'

'Really?' Emma's lapis eyes grew bright and hard as she considered this possibility. 'Tiffany seems pretty convinced he's her old buddy, Felix Sylvester. I've never heard him called anything else.'

'Something Cattermole,' said Anthony, suddenly making some sense out of Ozzy's throwaway comment in that club. The light of a streetlamp splashed across the interior of the cab as the vehicle turned left, briefly illuminating their faces. 'That's a name he uses too.'

'Goodness.' Emma was impressed with his inside knowledge. 'Is it like a pen name? Some writers have more than one alias for different genres. Perhaps experimental artists do too? Does Ozzy know about his protégé's other identity?'

'It was Ozzy who let the name slip. Apparently he's been helping "Felix" sort out his paperwork after mislaying it all abroad, or some such tale.'

Emma was fascinated. 'Where? And which is he – Felix Sylvester or Felix Cattermole?'

'I overheard him claiming to have spent part of his childhood in Egypt, though I'm not sure quite how that ties in with him knowing Tiffany as a child in this country.'

Emma weighed this information.

'Well, her great-grandfather Sir Freddie was an Egyptologist, and met Kitty out there, so there could still be some distant Sylvester links with both countries I suppose, although I've not heard of any friends or relations called Cattermole.'

She decided against suggesting that they consult her family on this matter, not least to avoid any repetitions of her unreliable mother's own penchant for mischief-making and idle speculation. The less gossip Anthony heard about the murkier side of her own extended family's history the better. He had just missed Ozzy's unsettling dinner party revelations at the end of the spring; and there was no present need to dredge any of that up.

'Odd that Tiffany never mentioned Felix before this summer,' Anthony commented, still on the hunt for ways to entrap him.

'Well she wouldn't, not to you at that point if he'd been an old teenage flame of hers,' Emma pointed out, content to cast her cousin's veracity into question. 'She might have preferred to draw a veil over some aspects of his past.' Anthony considered this for a moment. Would that count as discretion, on Tiffany's part, or evasiveness?

'Is that what how you would have handled it, Emma?' he asked. Emma's blush was unseen in the dark cab, but she held her ground.

'I still might,' she said boldly. 'No point in rocking the boat at the outset.'

He managed to smile at that. 'Huh, Emma, ever the pragmatist. I can't deny that for me it's become part of your charm,' he admitted.

'I hope I've more to offer than pragmatism,' she replied lightly, 'but while on that topic, please don't have a dig at Felix about any of this stuff in front of everyone tonight, will you? David Fford might find that sort of chat off-putting, and I'm sure he's the sort who values discretion in his contacts, especially in public.' She seemed to have some measure of his valuable client already, Anthony noted with approval.

'I'm all for client discretion,' he responded.

Emma was thinking that it was a pity that Fford was so short and stout, or she might have been tempted to charm him further. Her mother however seemed to be making the running there for now; and in terms of developing a partner to suit Emma's own tastes, and enabling him to build on a promising career – rather than one with most of his success already in the bag, which might become a little dull – Anthony was definitely still the more attractive choice, as well as considerably better looking.

'Good,' she said. Their conversation about Felix however was not quite shelved yet, she felt, and returned to the subject.

'So if Felix used this Cattermole name in Egypt, and Sylvester over here, I wonder why?' Emma mused.

'Perhaps it's double-barrelled, or maybe one is a middle name.'

'Whatever he's up to, he seems to be getting Ozzy to help sort something out,' Anthony said gruffly but omitting his own debt to the set designer.

'He probably needs to prove his ID to get properly established here,' Emma decided. 'Nowadays you have to produce a passport or something to open a bank account, which he will want to do if his sales at tonight's show are anything to go by. Although I suppose Ozzy could just bank it through his company, for now, and pass on the net proceeds in cash to Felix.' She frowned, disliking the idea that her illustrious uncle might inadvertently be laundering funds for Felix, however briefly. 'No wonder he's trying to help him get sorted out as soon as possible,' she concluded.

Anthony, still disinclined to let on that he once knew a few ways to disburse large sums without many traces, saw a chance to counter Felix.

'I wonder when our friends at the tax office will get their fair share of Felix's profits?' he said aloud.

Within the cab a sudden frostiness seemed to nip the night air.

'Uncle Ozzy would not risk his name and career on bending those sorts of rules for Felix. I'm sure *he* would keep proper records of everything,' Emma said icily.

'Of course,' Anthony hastily backtracked. Besmirching Ozzy was not his intention. But besmirching Felix, behind the scenes, could be effective, with his own practice tidied up and beyond reproach.

'Are you "anti" Felix because Tiffany discovered him and set him on the path to success? You're not still a bit jealous are you, maybe still carrying a candle for her?' Emma suggested. It was sensible to be clear about this.

Anthony grimaced.

'No. I feel well out of that entanglement, thank you, Emma – and besides, if it hadn't been for meeting Tiffany, I would never have got to know you.' His voice softened.

'Believe it or not, I am grateful for that bit, and tonight more than ever.' He had been surprised but delighted, for instance, by David's invitation to Emma and her mother to visit the coast house, whose privacy was normally jealously guarded.

Emma is so clearly an asset, whereas Tiffany had proved a liability.

'Good to know,' she said, mollified, and leaned a little more against him. Anthony put an arm round her shoulders, and kissed her lightly on the forehead. As the cab neared the restaurant, he gazed through the window at the night-time street. Emma is right, as usual, he reflected. I must keep a lid on my dislike of Felix in public, and cook his goose in private. He turned to smile appreciatively at her as the taxi pulled up.

In the restaurant, the atmosphere was upbeat, electric. Felix held court, although looking rather tired, as Emma had noted, as he toasted them all with his customary iced water.

'Does the fellow never drink like the rest of us?' Anthony muttered in her ear, despite his recent resolution.

'Rarely,' she murmured back. 'He says he needs to keep his senses clear and his vision pure, or something along those lines.'

Anthony meant to keep his thoughts to himself this time but gave an involuntary sneer in Felix's direction. Felix sensed the look, and glanced across at Anthony, registering his air of defiant confidence. Has the wretched man not got the message, after all? I think I'll take this little game to the next level. He padded over to where the duo were taking their seats at the long shared table set up for the celebratory supper party, and surprised Emma with a light, welcoming hug. She felt the disorienting tingle that proximity to Felix could still generate.

'Well, Emma, are congratulations in order yet?' he purred. 'Word is that with you on his arm, Anthony can no longer put a foot wrong in life.' Emma, however, was bemused by the sudden intensity of this compliment.

'Why, Felix, I didn't know you were such a fan!' she responded instinctively.

'Oh but Emma, I'm full of admiration for the "you" that has blossomed ever since our first encounters this summer,' he said, immodestly. 'Surely you know that.'

She stared. It was only a few weeks really since their catalysing conversation in the café, yet somehow also a world away, and she was not going to give Felix the satisfaction of all the credit for her fast-evolving new persona. Nor was she going to fall into his busy arms, and disliked the impression that she may already have done so that his words gave.

'Funny – Anthony says much the same thing about his effect on me, only with more reason to,' she riposted. Felix stepped back and glanced at Anthony.

'Really? I had no idea you were so catalytic,' he said. 'It seems you have stolen my thunder.' He looked at Emma in a way that made her both tingle and feel uneasy. There was something of the night about Felix, she felt, and not in a good way. Without thinking, she put her hand on Anthony's as he sat beside her.

Wondering suddenly if Felix's antipathy to him has always been due to jealousy of his burgeoning relationship with Emma, more than his past one with Tiffany, Anthony had an epiphany. There was no way this charlatan was going to divest him of Emma too, and she seemed to be seeking his reassurance.

'Emma is full of surprises, all of them charming,' he said firmly. Turning her hand in his, he said: 'I didn't realise Felix had taken such a shine to you.' He kept his tone light and affectionate, just loud enough for all at the table to hear. 'Should I be the jealous one here?' Anthony felt sure now that he knew her reply.

Emma felt almost as disoriented as she had on first meeting Felix at her party, although not because he finally seemed to be flirting with her, but because Anthony was openly challenging him for her.

'I don't think you really need to be,' she replied, still managing to sound more amused than confused by the turn of the conversation, and delivering a putdown to Felix at the same time. What on earth is Felix up to? she wondered.

Her reply was perhaps less emphatic than Anthony would have liked, but spurred him into a decision. He embraced the wild idea that had been forming, allowing him to take back control of things and further his own rise. By upping the ante and the speed of events, it would also neutralise all Felix's snide remarks, on any subject, by publicly assigning them to mere jealousy, bruised vanity, and defeat in love.

'In that case, I should seize the day and make sure of you for myself,' Anthony said boldly. 'Emma, will you marry me?'

It was not the most gallant of proposals, but it was a proposal and a very public one. In the astonished silence that suddenly enveloped them all, Emma gasped for a moment and then rapidly seized the day herself.

'I should love to marry you,' she said. 'Yes, Anthony, I will.'

Surprise held the company suspended in silence for a heart-beat, until Thomas broke into generous applause and the rest of the company followed suit, clapping and whooping.

'This definitely calls for a toast,' declared Ozzy as the first excitement settled. 'More champagne all round. Iris, are you going to give them your blessing?' Emma's mother was not displeased by the apparent speed with which Anthony had acted.

So the fellow's no fool, she thought. He knows how to get the message. I daresay he will do for Emma after all – with me keeping a distant eye on things, if necessary. We do perhaps owe his family this favour, this connective justice, of tidying up loose ends.

She said: 'Why not? Children, you have my permission.'

'Give her a kiss, man,' Mike called across the table, just as Anthony suddenly remembered his manners and embraced his new fiancée appropriately.

'Congratulations,' said David from his seat next to Iris. 'An admirable choice.' Did he mean of Emma, as a wife, or of Anthony as her husband-to-be? Either way, the listening architect's heart swelled with satisfaction; and Felix's celebratory dinner had become Anthony's night.

Emma, flushed and laughing, whispered to him: 'Are you quite sure?'

'Absolutely,' he replied. 'Totally. Couldn't be a happier man tonight.'

'We'll make a great team,' Emma replied, with conviction. Or was it determination?

Felix, watching, favoured the latter likelihood. Rather than feeling outplayed, he was delighted by the outcome of his games. My victim is just where we wanted him. Emma will straighten him out in no time, and even if she doesn't, I can still have a little fun jangling his nerves when the mood takes me.

He glanced around the table, feeling smug, counting his tally so far. Emma has caught Anthony, and she will be the powerhouse; Iris and Ozzy should be satisfied. Tiffany has discovered Ash – provider of oases and my friend in art, although he doesn't know that – and all this is my handiwork. Jenna, over there looking palely wonderful, got away in the end but is secured again, with Thomas in poll position now beside her; and I may have a splendid new ally in Iris. I am generating enough money to be my own man in this world – as soon as I wrest control of it from Ozzy – and won't need any of them. A fine list. No wonder I feel so exhausted.

Ozzy, observant as always, seemed to intercept his self-congratulations.

'Stop looking quite so pleased with yourself, Felix, and schmooze our theatrical friends a little more before the evening's over.' He was leaning across the table, speaking quietly. 'You've done everyone proud tonight, one way and another, but they still like having their own egos stroked now and again. There might be a few more commissions in it for you, or the chance to work with me on some significant sets soon.'

Felix stretched his legs under the table. How much longer do I want this imperious man to think he is directing my career? Still, it's good cover, and my new birth certificate hasn't landed on the mat yet. So he smiled lazily at his self-appointed mentor.

'Delighted,' he murmured back, and swapped seats further along the table to ask Kate, the pretty up-and-coming actress, who had played Miranda in *The Tempest* to some acclaim, a few more searching questions about her plans for the future. He had enjoyed her performances, and their chats afterwards in the theatre bar about the play, he told her. It would be nice to keep in touch. Meanwhile, Kate was convinced that he was the man she overheard being needlessly insulted by a girlfriend in the street a few weeks ago. Ex-girlfriend now, if the way the same young woman, Tiffany something, was hanging on to every word being said to her this evening by that quite attractive chap sat next to her was anything to go by.

Felix is up to his tricks again, Tiffany thought, glancing over and then watching him have his usual hypnotic effect on someone receiving his full attention. He should pace himself a little more though. He's looking too thin, and a tad moth-eaten tonight, although I suppose after all this creative effort he would feel a bit run down. The restored portrait of the tabby on the restaurant wall was definitely in better shape just now than its creator.

She turned her attention back to Ash, at her side. His sister Angie, and her husband, Mike, sat with them too; and just down the table Jenna was looking pale but luminous, with Thomas opposite her. So Emma made her choice! I can probably put up with Anthony as a cousin-in-law. All my friends are here, she thought. It's been a good night and now there's an amusing wedding ahead to brighten up the diary.

'It's getting late. Don't you think it's grown a bit cold in here?' Felix asked the sparky actress, Kate. 'I may have to make my farewells to the party and slope off to bed for a well-earned sleep, if I'm to recharge my creative drive.' He paused. 'I don't suppose you'd like to stroll partway with me, to continue our fascinating conversation for as long as possible? I can hail you a cab home at any time you like.'

'I live just round the corner,' Kate said. 'It's tiny, but we could put the fire on and chat cosily there if you like. There's a sofabed,' she added, 'if you drift off.'

A useful hideaway, thought Felix. 'Bliss,' he answered. 'Take me home, Kate, my tender little shrew. You should play that role next, you know. You'd be brilliant.'

Chapter 31

Not wanting a church affair, Anthony and Emma pressed ahead with their wedding plans remarkably fast. Emma swiftly arranged for the bans to be posted at the local registry office, a large Victorian building with a neoclassical facade and imposing rooms. The official proceedings could be witnessed there by a small group, followed by a celebratory lunch – perhaps back at Shay's restaurant, as that had been the venue of the proposal – swelled by a slightly larger list of guests.

The inner circle at the ceremony itself included the handful of mutual friends who had been present at the moment of the proposal. David Fford was also invited. Anthony could hardly leave him off the guest-list, as he too had witnessed the sudden betrothal and neither Emma nor Anthony wished to overlook this influential client. David's accidental presence at the restaurant that night was a coup, and should children ever result from this union Emma had his name already mentally pencilled onto a 'useful godparent' list. As for the wedding, Emma's parents would both come, while Lucinda – although invited – had tactfully indicated that she had a prior commitment on the intended day, that she might not be able to wriggle out of gracefully. Not that she needed to be absent. Indeed Emma felt her presence could be calming, and therefore rather desirable, but Lucinda's proposed absence allowed Emma's brother Jon – still thought to be discomfited by Lucinda's new role in his father's life, though beginning to see its potential benefits – an excuse to set aside some of his huffiness and agree to attend his younger sister's wedding, to which he had no clear reason to object.

Their sister, Janet, was busy in Australia with her brood of children and either could not really afford the time, or was unwilling to find the airfare, at such short notice.

Tiffany's parents had already extended their travels – 'We're having a middle-aged gap year,' her mother had said – and were now in New Zealand.

'We could fly out there and see them all soon afterwards,' Anthony suggested deciding that an Antipodean honeymoon was as good an option as any, and might allow him to network a little towards possible future commissions over there (perhaps making some of the travel into a business expense, his accountant cheerfully suggested).

Hearing of this potential trip, David Fford had already suggested that they visit a property he had recently bought down in the region, and was thinking of substantially remodelling. Anthony was delighted to accept the fairly modest detour involved. He knew they would be well looked after; and that Emma endorsed this interruption. She knew her sister would be impressed by the Fford connection, too – not that Anthony needed Janet's approval, but a degree of familial harmony was, on balance, a good thing at the outset. All in all, both Emma and Anthony felt that their imminent marriage was already yielding dividends.

Felix's challenge disturbed Anthony less when all these other factors seemed so favourable. In sudden moments of uncertainty about the reach of Felix's baleful influence, he reminded himself of the need to stay alert. If a chancer like Felix could stumble across enough clues to make a few sly digs at Anthony's expense in front of a vital client, who else might be in a position to stir things up? He was more aware now that his own brusque manner and sometimes dismissive air could at best lose him friends, and at worst alienate any underestimated – but one day perhaps useful – people. It was time to follow his imminent stepmother-in-law Lucinda's example, and apply some tact: something he knew Emma could help him to develop.

Nevertheless, before a full charm offensive could be mounted, there had to be some preparatory fieldwork. On the Monday after Felix's pivotal show – and the engagement – Anthony had therefore checked with Green, his accountant, that all his business records had been satisfactorily updated, and whether it was time to contact the local tax office to clarify, and agree, any adjustments that might have come up in relation to the changing archaeological requirements affecting any of his Egyptian projects. That was the script he was working to.

'Quite right, best to cough the lot now and get it all done and dusted,' Green had advised with his usual good cheer. 'Leave the initial contact to me.' Anthony disliked the terminology, but had not protested. A reply came back surprisingly soon from the tax office to the effect that it was never too late for customers to initiate contact with the tax authorities to raise and discuss any complex situations arising. Anthony bit his lip at this wording, too, but chose to take it at face value.

'We are all "customers" of the revenue office now,' the accountant commented brightly when they met again, this time to discuss how to follow up the tax regime's response successfully. Apparently the revenue office had recently been re-branded as a service provider, and an enabler of good business practice, 'Which is excellent timing for us – and naturally, Anthony, we don't want you to be mistaken for one of their trickier customers.' Anthony forced himself to smile thinly at Green's brand of humour.

'No, indeed,' he answered, tapping his fingers on the arm of the chair he sat in. 'In fact, my fiancée has been encouraging me to consider the merits of practising a little philanthropy if I have any spare means. There are tax breaks, I believe, but that's not why,' he added hastily. Emma had indicated that building a reputation as a regular, if modest, charitable donor could steadily enhance his public image. She had suggested that they – meaning he – might start by helping some of the newer charities, to whom a relatively small but regular amount would make him a valued major donor, listed in their literature. The beneficial ripple effects of such goodwill towards him could build up nicely and provide a track record that he could develop further in future.

'What about this one, that's trying to help some of the people fleeing the upsets in the Middle East?' she had asked during this conversation, passing him a letter that she had received in the summer. 'Or, if that's a bit complicated, given your professional stake in that part of the world, a local hospital here is looking for support for its intensive care unit. That could be a good start. Do you ever design hospitals?' she had added.

'I prefer to work in the private sector,' he had told her, 'designing offices, as you know, and clients' private houses, but you're right. Supporting a local facility's charity appeal could be good.'

Now Green, the accountant, agreed. 'A bit of careful philanthropy certainly won't do you any harm,' he said. 'I'll make a note of that. The intensive care unit's appeal did you just say? That should be well-received.'

After a brief pause, Anthony asked: 'Should I also drop a word in Finch-Smith's ear about the benefits we've discussed of the tax people's new approach?' Green closed the folder marked Anthony Tod Wright.

'Send him to me by all means, if he unearths a few curious anomalies in his own records,' he replied, once again sounding irritatingly happy to Anthony. 'We should be able to facilitate the regularising of any confusions. As I recently said to you, it's always best to cough the lot, while the new iron is hot.'

Anthony grimaced at the mixed metaphors, but said he would indeed pass the gist of the message to Finch-Smith, before adding: 'I've one more question, about whether – or indeed when – we should bring something else that I've become aware of lately, to the tax people's attention?'

'Something more that you want to resolve?' Now the accountant looked concerned and lost some of his bonhomie. 'I thought we had gone through it all.'

'No, no, there's no link to my own business,' Anthony assured him quickly, 'but I've recently come across this artist fellow Cattermole – you may know of him as "Felix", or Felix Sylvester – who's making a bit of a splash here at the moment. I could suggest his murals and panels to some of my clients, for interiors, but I'm confused by his use of two different names, in two different countries.' Anthony paused, to pick his words as carefully as possible. 'After working so hard to update and regularise, as you put it, my own affairs, I can't commission someone who may be avoiding their own responsibilities, if you follow my drift, even though his work is remarkable.' Anthony almost believed this version of his motives himself now. 'He seems to be bringing a sort of magical realism almost single-handedly back into the art world here, and so far it's being rather well-received.'

Green looked thoughtful, tapping his lip with a pencil while he considered the question.

'Artists in my long experience are notoriously innocent of the practicalities of cash management and tax obligations,' he said. 'It can make them seem a little careless, I grant you. I handle things for several; most start using my services after they've spent all the money from the good days and are struggling with unsolicited back-tax demands, sending them rushing to see an accountant just when there's little left in the kitty to pay one with. I've got my batch into better habits now. It won't help your professional relations with this fellow much, however, if you start off by embarrassing him with the taxman. You'd do far better to suggest to him that he just comes to see me, and sooner rather than later.'

This was not quite what Anthony had intended for Felix, and after a pause, Green took his silence for professional discretion. 'But, if you would prefer to keep your business at arm's length from him, for now, there is another route: the tax people look out for news of successful people popping up suddenly, especially if they've not yet sent back a convincing completed tax return. Has this Felix attracted much publicity here?'

Anthony nodded. 'Two recent exhibitions this year with lots of media coverage, mostly in the gossip columns, and the last one seemed to generate significant sales,' he said.

'Ah. Too soon to be declaring it all of course, as the present tax year has some way to go yet. But, who knows, they may already be keeping a quiet watch on his trail. Leave it with me,' said Green, sounding perky again.

***

Recalling this satisfactory conversation later, seated at his own desk, Anthony relaxed in his ergonomic chair and actually smirked. No-one could accuse him of twisting Felix's tail, as the fellow had already attracted too many column inches of lively reviews in the arts pages, not to mention the gossip columns, since squiring the erstwhile 'Miranda' – what was that actress's name? Kate something or other – around town, to hope to go unnoticed by a curious taxman or woman. That actress changes boyfriends just often enough to provide excellent diary fodder, he thought. Let's generate some more. So Anthony had picked up his pen, and put a firm tick beside 'Kate?', deleting the question mark against the line saying 'Felix and Kate?' on the list of wedding guests that Emma had given him to read through, and discuss, before she sent out the invitations.

In the event, however, the stiff card inviting them to the registry office ceremony, sent care of Ozzy's address, sat in its envelope on his mantlepiece unopened. Felix seemed to have disappeared, presumably immersed in his pursuits with Kate.

'I haven't seen the wretched fellow for at least ten days,' Ozzy grumbled to Tiffany when she rang him from work in a lunch break to ask if he knew how Felix was, two weekends after the success of the exhibition in the theatre. She had not heard a peep from Felix since, either.

'Well, I suppose he's entitled to a bit of time off, after all the frenetic work preparing for his show,' she decided. 'I daresay he'll pop up again when he's ready.'

'Well I certainly hope so.' Ozzy was tetchy. 'No doubt after he's spent all the cash I passed on to him as an advance on some of his exhibition sales while the bigger buyers pay up. I've another project or two to put to him, if he feels so minded. There's some post for him here, including something that arrived today and looks suspiciously like a tax return pack, which seems a little eager on the part of the authorities. I don't suppose you know anything about that?'

Tiffany was surprised, and a bit offended.

'Why would I? Your studio is his place of business at the moment, so far as I know,' she pointed out. 'I'm impressed that you've got him well-enough organised to have even contacted the taxman.' Unsure if Ozzy was aware of how much Felix had told her about his role in establishing the maverick artist with a credible identity, she decided not to ask what name was on the address panel of the envelope.

'I hadn't, yet,' Ozzy responded, 'hence my surprise. I merely put him on the path to tracking down a replacement copy of his allegedly absent birth certificate.'

'Oh. Has that come too, then?' she asked as casually as she could.

'Yes. He got it ten days ago, and I haven't seen him since I showed him what to put into the passport application forms, next, and how to get himself at least a temporary National Insurance number. I suppose that's where the connection with the tax people has come from. Surprisingly quick off the mark, aren't they?'

Tiffany thought about her boss Finch-Smith, and his sudden desire to do everything properly. She had just had to rush all his paperwork, and another pile of records, off to a new accountant. Perhaps there was a crackdown going on.

'Maybe all the media coverage about his show has put him on the tax people's radar?' she suggested, picturing a cotton reel rolling silently across Ozzy's glass desk.

'Indeed. You're right, my dear. Our hero is thoroughly out in the open now, so he'll need the right toys.' Tiffany felt a shock at his words, sounding as if he had read her thoughts, and was glad that Ozzy could not see her startled expression. Was he probing for a reaction? she wondered. Could Felix have been foolish enough to have told him what happened, even as a joke? Highly unlikely, but not impossible, she decided, so it's best to play dumb.

Aloud, she simply said: 'Sorry?' She heard Ozzy's unsettling dry chuckle down the phone, a sound suddenly reminiscent of the rustle of a snake across coarse sand. It made her more uneasy.

'Oh, I see what you mean now,' she blagged, trying to sound natural. 'Of course Felix should get himself properly organised, especially after the success of the last show. I thought you two were forming some sort of partnership, or was that conversation just in my imagination?'

'Your imagination is a most useful commodity, Tiffany,' Ozzy replied, in a rasp that again made her skin prickle, 'but I had indeed just set up a little company through which to take delivery of his sale proceeds for him.'

'Well, that all sounds like progress,' she offered, knowing already that Felix disliked being so beholden to Ozzy, or indeed anyone, which might be why he had gone AWOL for a few days' peace. 'Ask him to call me when he surfaces, will you? I'll see you at the wedding, if not before.'

'You will indeed. Goodbye for now, my dear.' There was a click and Ozzy had gone.

Tiffany put down her phone, with a faint exhalation of concern. She thought back uneasily to their concocted tales about Sylvester family history, and then tried to concentrate instead on the task of sending a few more papers across to Green, her boss's new accountant. When Finch-Smith had relieved her of the onerous task of doing his tax return, admitting that he needed 'more of an overhaul' of his accounting procedures than he'd thought – having 'let things get a bit complicated, with so many different accounts for different parts of the business' – he had still wanted copies of all sorts of documents for the past five or six years pulled out and put together for this new accountant to go through, 'To clarify and simplify things,' as he put it.

'I have a nasty feeling I may owe the taxman a few more bob as a result of being bit disorganised in the past – before your time here, of course,' he told her. 'Past assistants weren't all as efficient as you.' (Rat, she had thought, you're the one who sat on the info).

'Anthony kindly mentioned to me that there's a bit of an amnesty now for people who realise they'd got a bit of past muddle to sort out,' he had added. 'No hard feelings, apparently, if you come forward and ask them to help you work out what's owed.'

Tiffany thought she understood now. Felix's digs at Anthony had obviously found their mark, and he has been busy covering his back – and perhaps paying Felix back in kind, too, while he was about it. No wonder Ozzy was surprised by the tax return's arrival. He does not know how much Felix's been toying with Anthony, she assumed, and now the prey has bitten back. She thought of her discussion with Felix in the theatre on the afternoon before his show opened, about that painting of the shrew, and of the dead field mouse, and shivered. Her nerves jangled as the phone rang again. Ozzy, relentless, was back on the line.

'Ah, Tiffany, I thought you might like to know that I've just been called by Felix's little inamorata Kate. She's very worried about him. Apparently he's been laid low with the flu and not at all himself, and now he's sloped off somewhere. She thought he might have come round here to recuperate, but of course he hasn't. I wonder if he might yet wash up at your place? Let me know if he does, won't you, as the poor girl is most concerned. She says he's been feeling rough ever since exhausting himself preparing for his show, and then went down with this nasty flu bug a couple of days ago.'

Tiffany was alarmed, but kept her reaction in check.

'Poor Felix,' she said. 'If he doesn't turn up at my flat, I'll check with Jenna in case he's over there. Perhaps he's just in need of a break? From Kate, I mean. You know what he's like with women. Unreliable.'

Ozzy did his dry rasping chuckle again.

'Yes, and yet one of his past flings can still be called upon to provide respite and refuge from the current one, in your opinion? Well, you know him best. I'll count on you for intelligence as to his whereabouts.' He hung up. Tiffany leaned back in her chair and frowned. Is Felix genuinely ill, or has he gone to ground for a bit of peace and quiet after all the excitement? she pondered. Or just skipped out on us all? That really would annoy Ozzy now. Part of her hoped that Felix had indeed decided to make himself scarce, even without a goodbye.

As soon as she got home that evening, however, she called softly, 'Anybody there?' and looked round the sitting room door first, on her way down the corridor. Ash was due to call round a little later, but the sofa was already softly indented as if someone had briefly sat down, and there were what looked like ginger cat hairs on the cushion. She frowned. Perhaps a local feline had been taking advantage of the cat door, now that there was no resident animal. The ginger stray from the park? Felix had advised her to lock the redundant cat flap, but she had still not got round to it.

'In the kitchen,' came his voice suddenly. He sounded dispirited.

'Coming through,' she replied, and hurried to find him. Felix sat slumped at the table, his head in his hands.

'Are you ill? How did you get in?' She flicked the kettle on and sat down next to him.

'Still capable of sneaking over walls and through windows,' he replied tetchily, 'though it's harder work than it used to be. Got a bit of a headache now. I've had a touch of flu – more than a touch, in fact, I've been really quite ill. Couldn't get out of Kate's flat at all for two days. Nasty virus, dodgy effects. I used to have injections against that sort of thing, if you recall.' He crossed his arms on the table and rested his head on them.

'There's a human flu injection these days, perhaps you should get those in future,' Tiffany said. She studied him. He looked very weary. 'I thought you seemed a bit tired after your show. Maybe you were brewing it then.' Relieved to see him, she added mischievously, 'Have you been properly looked after?'

'Too well, thank you,' he said in muffled tones. 'Kate kept insisting on serving me dairy-free and meat-free meals. Me! No wonder I got so ill. So I thought I'd come back here for a bit to rebuild my strength. You don't mind, do you, Tiff?'

'Not a bit. By the way,' she added, 'there seem to be ginger cat hairs on the sofa cushions.'

'Really?' He sat up properly. 'You forgot to lock the old cat door,' he said accusingly. 'Cats will take advantage of that and drop in wherever they find evidence of congenial company, you know.'

'So I've heard.' The kettle had boiled now. 'Tea? Or would you prefer some warm milk?' Felix managed a lopsided smile.

'Warm milk, slightly diluted, bless you Tiffany.' He watched her prepare it. When she set the mug down in front of him he lifted it, two-handed as before, but slowly. He drank a little and then set it down.

'I do feel a bit shaky again. Do you mind if I take this, and go and lie down in my old box-room? I need a quiet place to try to sleep this thing off.'

'Be my guest,' she said, 'and when you feel a bit better, we could make plans for Anthony and Emma's wedding. I think your invite is at Ozzy's, by the way, along with what he suspects is a tax return form for you to fill in. I'm impressed with your speed and efficiency in getting legitimised, so to speak.'

'Tax form?' He shook his head slowly. 'Not my doing.'

'Not Ozzy's either, if he's to be believed.' Felix frowned.

'Odd.' He immediately suspected Anthony, but had not the energy to discuss it. 'Maybe the birth certificate and that National Insurance process that Ozzy insisted on, have triggered it. Coming up with stories is fun, but I hate all this paperwork stuff to prove it. Maybe I'll be able to crawl over to Ozzy's tomorrow. I need to check something else there anyway.' Felix paused. 'Did you know that your great-grandmother Kitty went AWOL in Egypt, by the way? No evidence that she died despite the family tradition that the flu got her. Just disappeared, much as she had just turned up out of nowhere in the guise of a bright-eyed, amateur antiquities enthusiast in the first place.

'She'd popped up at one of old Silvester-Jones's archaeological digs, apparently, and charmed the socks off the old boy. Gossips suggested that her money really came from discreet black-market dealing in ancient artefacts in the first place, selling to well-heeled collectors and early tourists. Odd that no-one ever mentioned that to you before, did they? Anyway, there she was, a mysterious young glamourpuss, well-versed in things Egyptian, and apparently with money to spare! No wonder the old digger couldn't resist marrying her and carrying her back home, with the rest of his collection.' Felix seemed quite animated again for a moment. He drank some more of his milk while Tiffany digested this account.

'Disappeared?' She looked puzzled. 'You already know a lot more than me, then. I was always told that she got influenza and died out there during one of their expeditions. Their children were all at home here with a nanny. Freddie was inconsolable, and buried her out there. Came back alone, and broken-hearted.'

'I'm sure that last bit is true,' Felix said rather smugly, 'but I don't like the influenza version very much, at the moment.'

'Sorry. Where does all this suddenly come from anyway? More of Ozzy's variations?'

He shook his head. 'Iris seems to know all sorts of things that Ozzy either doesn't, or has failed to mention in his tales.' He sneezed.

'Iris? What concern is it of hers?' Tiffany objected. 'I thought we were the ones crafting extra bits onto the Sylvester meets Silvester story. This is my direct family history and now it seems there are all sorts of new hints and secrets being dropped by the interfering older generation, and all of them Joneses, so it's not even their business. It's irritating.'

Felix sneezed several more times.

'I would have liked Kitty,' he said. 'She sounds pretty much my kind of girl.' He added slyly, 'I mean, if I were a female, a Felicity, not a Felix.'

Tiffany drew breath sharply and then looked very hard at him. 'Felix please do not tell me that you think she was – like you. Are you suggesting that?' she asked suspiciously. 'You know what I mean.'

Felix gazed unblinkingly back at her.

'If it can happen once, why not more than once?' he said.

'But Kitty and Freddie had children, and you and Jenna couldn't. I mean, it was a phantom pregnancy. Not real.'

Felix considered this point.

'Maybe it works better the other way round,' he suggested. 'Maybe the mother has to be the one that metamorphosed. Is transmogrified, as you liked to joke to me. Perhaps a "she" version as a bit of both species, can host a mixed-species foetus – whereas Jenna, being only human, couldn't manage that last bit, even with the best-prepared mind.' He thought back to the bargain made in Jenna's sitting room, and shrugged. 'Or maybe they just found some children and pretended they were theirs; or

Freddie had some brats of his own from some affair or other, and Kitty agreed to mother them respectably for him. Why would I know now what went on out there between them?' He sounded irritated. 'Maybe you should just ask Ozzy properly for his version, to compare with Iris's gossip.'

'Best not,' Tiffany cautioned, her own thoughts now all over the place. 'I don't want to set Ozzy going. He scares me these days, you know. There's something really intense and hawkish about him, and he's getting more and more manipulative and controlling. All this business about paying your earnings into a company and just giving you some sort of salary in cash to spend, like pocket money. Is he using you as some sort of cash-cow? You don't want to become his hostage, his plaything. Maybe that inquisitive taxman is doing you a huge favour.'

'Cow?' Felix frowned. He was feeling feverish again. 'Cows were good things to be in old Egypt. I told you about Hathor. She often wears cow horns, helps women in childbirth, and welcomes the dead into the next life in the west. She's all about joy and motherhood. Music, too, and foreign lands. The goddess,' he added, in case Tiffany was not following. He could not remember now who had told him all this or even if it was correct. He felt too tired to care, at the moment. His shoulders sagged a little, and he yawned.

'Drink a bit more milk, Felix. Perhaps you should ask this Hathor for help in foreign lands,' Tiffany suggested, as he took another mouthful from the heavy mug.

'She has a dark side,' Felix said, remembering more and perking up briefly as the sip of warm milk got to work. 'A warlike version, which destroys unstoppably – unless she gets very drunk, whereupon she turns back into lovely Hathor.'

'Good for her,' Tiffany said. 'Sadly, getting drunk often works exactly the other way round with humans.'

Felix managed another lopsided grin at that. 'I have never been a cow as far as I know,' he said, 'but I assume from what you said just now about Ozzy, that a cash cow gets milked a lot.'

'Exactly so, with little or no additional input from the one doing it,' Tiffany said, 'so the owner is soon quids-in.'

'No-one owns me,' Felix reminded her gruffly. 'And certainly not Ozzy.' He had bristled at the idea, but the effect just made him look more moth-eaten. Tiffany sighed.

'I know that, there's no need to get huffy with me. You do look awful. Finish that milk and go and lie down. I won't let anyone know you're here.' He drained the mug, stood up rather stiffly, and then slouched to the door.

'Yes, I do need to rest this one out. See you in the morning,' he said, as he headed for the familiar comfort of the box-room. Tiffany watched him go. He looks terrible, really drawn and scruffy. Perhaps I should find him a doctor? I suppose he has no immunity to human bugs. We ought at least to get him a proper course of vaccinations, before he gets carried off by a bout of measles. She wished she could talk this through completely truthfully with someone, but the only candidates likely to listen to her with even a cat's whisker of belief were Ozzy, and perhaps Iris, neither of whom she trusted.

Ash took Felix's presence in the box-room calmly, when Tiffany let him in on at least that part of her secrets.

'Poor fellow,' he said. He was content to accept that Ozzy's ministrations would be too melodramatic and insistent, and Kate's too persistent, for comfort – whereas a return to Tiffany's box-room offered a quiet and untroubled refuge for the influenza patient. Their own evening passed peacefully. Felix did not emerge and they left him alone to sleep off, they hoped, his malaise.

In the morning, when Tiffany went sleepy-eyed to the kitchen to make coffee, and opened the kitchen window blind, she glimpsed a blur of fur hastening across the top of the garden wall. She blinked and looked again but whatever it was had fled, and was out of sight. Was it the invader cat who had sat on her cushions? Most likely one of the urban squirrels that raced up and down the neighbourhood trees. She switched the kettle on and then, turning back towards the table, noticed the small wooden panel propped against one of the chair-legs. She bent down to turn it around. It was a painting, of figs; figs spilling from a bowl set on the ground beneath their tree, whose lower trunk, distinctive leaves and branches filled the background. The fruit looked so real that she crouched down and touched the most luscious one with a fingertip, fully expecting to feel the velvety bloom of its skin.

It was however, definitely paint. Marvelling at the skill, she stood up again and put the panel on the seat of chair, propped up carefully against its back, and went to check the garden.

'Felix?' she called. 'Are you out here?' He was standing in the far side of the small patch of lawn, and turned quickly towards her. She was genuinely relieved to see him.

'Tiffany, good morning! I feel so much better, thanks to your unfussy hospitality,' he answered, moving lightly across to her. He did indeed look much better, bright-eyed and lithe again; but his hands were muddy, his hair was wild and unbrushed, and his shirt was loose and mostly undone. It hung to his thighs. No wonder the squirrel, or whatever she had glimpsed, had fled.

'Button your shirt up before you frighten the neighbours,' she instructed. 'You'd better come in and get dressed. What on earth are you doing out here half-naked anyway? It's chilly out here in the mornings now.'

'Ah, early autumn, I love it,' he replied, looking slightly flushed. 'The falling leaves, the rustlings and scuttlings. I was too hot, and wanted fresh air. But it is a bit cold now with just this bit of cloth on, you're right.' He came indoors with her.

'So tell me about this?' she asked, pointing to the picture.

He smiled fondly at her.

'A memento of our first evening, so that you can never forget me.'

'I've a whole flat of your work,' she said 'I can hardly forget you. But it's wonderful, I love it. Thank you.' She remembered taking the fig from the fruit bowl.

Felix went in search of the rest of his clothes. By the time Ash appeared in the kitchen, drawn by the scent of fresh coffee, Felix was back, fully dressed and in a buoyant, if feverish, mood.

'Morning. Marvellous painting,' Ash said. 'One of your best, surely?'

'Thank you.' Felix was leaning against the kitchen counter, slowly drinking a large glass of cool milk now. 'I'd better be off. It's time I collected my mail from Ozzy's. By the way Tiffany, on the passport form that Ozzy so kindly provided me with, I put this place as my address. Actually I cheated – he'd got a spare set of the forms in case we made any mistakes filling in the first one, so at Kate's I just copied everything onto that one except the address he'd filled in, and put yours in instead. Threw out the old one and posted the replacement version. Cunning, don't you think? I'd prefer to get my own hands on it first, you see, Ash, and not depend on Ozzy deciding to let me know if it's arrived.' Felix was speaking very fast again, the sentences concertinaing into each other. 'I've no idea how long they will take to send it out, and my new birth certificate should be returned with it; so will you keep them both here for me, Tiff, until I come round to pick them both up?'

'Of course.'

'Thank you. Ozzy's help is getting a little claustrophobic,' he explained again, to Ash, who had poured himself a large mug of coffee during this speech, and was now extracting two slices of bread from the toaster. 'I spent so much time there working on my panels for the show that I needed a break to re-assert my independence, but I'm not ungrateful.'

Ash nodded and put two new slices of bread in the toaster before returning to the table with his coffee mug and first batch of toast. He picked the painting up from the chair and set it carefully against the breadbin on the kitchen top, before settling down to drink his coffee.

'I'd open a bank account of your own, Felix, as soon as you can,' he suggested, 'and stop letting Ozzy put all your sales proceeds through this company Tiffany tells me he's set up.' Ash took another contented swig of coffee. Felix nodded.

'Exactly my thinking, and I started the process last week, at an entirely different bank from the one he uses. I went to your branch, actually Tiff, and arranged to return with my passport to verify my identity as soon as it arrives.'

'Did you? So why did that tax return thing go to Ozzy's address?' Tiffany asked.

'I don't know. I told the bank I had a temporary workshop in that area, but am looking for a better one, and that I live here. My office is at home. We're flatmates, Tiff, for the moment, as far as the bank's concerned. They suggested having a savings account to build up some reserves in, and I asked if you could be a co-signatory. They could send us each the necessary paperwork here.'

Tiffany was impressed by this rush of organisational skill and planning from Felix, of all creatures. Perhaps he had help and guidance from Kate?

'Can you do that? You certainly sound on top of things all of a sudden. Maybe Kate's dietary regime did you some good after all,' she teased, testing his reaction.

Felix hissed slightly, and then gave an airy wave of his hand.

'All will become clear. I plan a little research trip soon, Tiff, so I'll need that passport and someone I trust here who can access my funds for me. I've still got some of the cash Ozzy handed over, so that's keeping me going just now. I really must try to get my other post from him now,' he added, looking unenthusiastic about going over there.

'I'll try to update you later.' He put down the empty milk glass, and paused at the kitchen door. 'Goodbye, both' he said softly, and left so fast that Tiffany was still staring at the empty doorway as the front door of the building clicked shut.

'A research trip, where to?' she asked aloud. Ash shrugged.

'Felix is evidently still a law unto himself. Don't worry, he seems to have everything worked out. Come and eat the toast I have made so lovingly for you.' He gestured towards the toaster just as a thin plume of smoke began to curl up from it. 'Damn, it's burnt the stuff,' he said, and jumped up to cross the small kitchen and press the eject button. The toast shot out, glowing red hot and on the verge of flames. He tried to catch it, but yelped and dropped it on the kitchen top, scattering carbonised crumbs. Tiffany burst out laughing and turned on the cold tap.

'Shove your hand under this,' she commanded, steering him towards the stream of cold water. 'I'll clean up the mess.' Ash obeyed and watched her affectionately.

'Domesticity is not my best suit,' he conceded, 'but I do make good coffee and mix excellent cocktails, in almost every circumstance.'

'That's good enough for me,' she answered, sweeping up the crumbs and forgetting Felix's activities for the moment.

Felix slipped over the wall into Ozzy's wild garden and walked noiselessly to the little door that led directly into the studio. It was rarely locked, he had noticed. A pause to listen told him that the studio was empty, so he gingerly turned the door handle and silently let himself in. He stood for a moment and looked around, checking the surface of the desk, and then saw the envelopes on the mantlepiece. He loped softly across to it, teased open the flap of one, very carefully, and eased out the contents which he studied for a moment and then slipped them into the back pocket of his chinos. He checked himself in the large antique mirror fixed to the wall above the mantelpiece, and nodded to his slightly hazy reflection. Back in reasonable shape, he decided. He licked the edges of the flap, to reseal the empty envelope, and put it back where he had found it, beside an envelope addressed to "Felix & Kate" that presumably contained the wedding invitation, and a brown manila envelope holding what must be the tax form Tiffany had mentioned.

Glancing round Ozzy's quiet studio one more time, he murmured: 'So long, old man. It's been fun but now you're getting boring, and I have to move on.' He let himself out soundlessly again through the door to the garden. 'Delightful,' he breathed as he stepped through the tangled grasses, and saw that some of the neglected rosebushes still had a few late flowers. Regaining the wall that separated the garden from the public park beyond it, he climbed lightly over it, only wheezing a little this time, he noted with relief – and was gone.

Indoors, Ozzy was still one floor up, drinking aromatic tea, in his dressing gown and planning the future. Something made him glance once towards the window and he thought he glimpsed movement in the park, just beyond the wall. He watched, scanning the scene. Nothing untoward there after all. Only the squirrels chasing each other up a sycamore tree, and in the distance, a dogwalker trying to keep pace with a black and white spaniel that tugged urgently on its lead, probably eager to flush out more squirrels. Then he spread out his hands and looked at them.

What next, he debated with himself. How to rein in Felix, what tricks have I left up my sleeve? Which shall I deploy, and what part might Iris play?

Chapter 32

'So where on earth was Felix?' asked Thomas, as he, Jenna, Ash and Ozzy followed Tiffany out of the town hall to climb into the taxi waiting to carry them once again to Shay's restaurant, booked for Emma and Anthony's post-wedding lunch party.

'I don't know,' Tiffany replied. She had kept an eye on the door throughout the brief registry office proceedings, expecting him to appear, and then supposed he might just go direct to the restaurant, strolling in with typical insouciance. 'He's been quite erratic lately, and he's always been a bit spiky about Anthony, so perhaps he's decided to continue to make himself scarce.'

'Anthony actually seemed a bit disappointed that he didn't turn up,' observed Jenna, sharing the broad rear seat of the taxicab with Ash and Tiffany. Ozzy and Thomas had taken the two tip-seats with their backs to the engine. 'Perhaps he's hoping for one of Felix's famous panels as a wedding present.'

'I doubt it,' Ozzy said sharply from his perch, opposite Ash. 'Felix has been lying low all autumn, probably since realising that his hasty repairs to the restaurant murals had started to peel and crumble again. If any of the panels he painted in oils go the same way, the theatre's restoration fund is going to be embroiled in angry demands for refunds and, as the organiser of the wretched event, no doubt so am I. No wonder the damn fellow has taken a prolonged walk.'

'Haven't you seen him at all?' asked Ash.

'Are any of the panels deteriorating now?' Tiffany was alarmed. Hers of the figs was fine, as were all the murals at her flat.

'Not the one he gave me,' said Jenna. 'It's just as wonderful as before, as are my murals. Painted in his prime, I suppose,' she joked, giving Tiffany fresh food for thought.

'I haven't seen hide nor hair of him since he went down with the flu and then ran out on Kate,' Ozzy was answering Ash. 'The recent panels are fine, so far,' he admitted, tetchily, 'probably because he used different and better materials for them, but if word spreads about the restaurant murals, some people are bound to worry.'

'But Ozzy, I thought we had all that covered with Shay – naturally degradable art as a metaphor for life's instability and the transitory nature of existence, noble rot, autumnal menus and all that,' Tiffany reminded him as the taxi rattled its way through the rain-streaked streets.

'It's not proving quite as convincing as I had hoped,' he huffed, 'and rot pretty much sums it up, as you well know.'

'You'll be able to schmooze them, Ozzy,' Tiffany said quickly, 'with talk of the kind of materials deliberately used for the restaurant project, and the oil panels being quite different, and so on. Think of it as your penance for having promoted Felix to them so shamelessly. Besides, if anyone does want to sell a panel or two back to you, you've still got access to most of his proceeds, haven't you?'

She made the comment sound innocent, but it was pointed, and effective. She did not mention the envelope from her bank, addressed to Christopher Felix Cattermole, that now sat in a cubby hole of the little desk which had allegedly once belonged to Kitty, nor the co-signatory forms that she had so promptly completed and kept, awaiting further word from Felix. Ozzy looked at her beadily, as he so often did these days.

'Some, Tiffany, but not all of it. Felix has not walked away empty-handed. How cruelly you attribute my actions and motives.' His tone made her feel cold.

'He'll resurface,' Thomas intervened calmly, 'and it is his money, isn't it, Ozzy? Net of the expenses that you incurred on his behalf on art materials and staging the exhibition, and any contingencies arising?'

'Indeed, my legal friend,' Ozzy nodded. 'The contingencies, as you put it, can be met, but I won't tolerate any ripple effects of his bad publicity affecting my own standing, given that I launched him on several of my unsuspecting clients and connections.' The taxi bumped through the rain-filled potholes, splashing passers-by on the pavement.

'Your lot usually look after themselves pretty well,' said Ash. 'Caveat emptor, wouldn't you say, Thomas? Most of them will have insured their panels and will pop them into storage within a few months anyway, to make space for the next hot thing. You can blame the storage conditions for any damage discovered later, or perhaps just arrange to burn the whole facility down, Ozzy,' he teased. 'A good bolt of lightning should do it.' Tiffany's surprised gasp at that suggestion was hidden by Jenna's burst of laughter. Merriment suited her.

'What a bold new champion Felix has found in you, now!' she teased Ash.

'Well, he never tweaked my tail, so I have no problems enjoying his antics,' Ash replied, enjoying her laughter. Fearing this sounded tactless, after what had happened to Jenna that summer, Tiffany squeezed his hand in warning, and then smiled at him; partly to thank him on Felix's behalf and partly to distract him from any further references, however innocent, to lightning – and also to remind him whose partner he now was, at least for the present.

Jenna seemed unruffled by Ash's light-hearted reply. Thomas was opposite her. He knew she was happy in his easy company; and he saw how Tiffany was steadily becoming more deeply invested in her relationship with Ash. Things were settling.

'I thought Iris looked very well this morning, positively fizzing with energy,' he said. 'She seems pretty happy about the wedding, don't you think?'

Ozzy spread his creative hands. 'And why not? Emma will conjure great things out of it all.' The taxi at last pulled over to disgorge them all, outside the courtyard that sheltered Shay's restaurant.

The wedding lunch passed off without incident. Iris was at her most charming, even to her deserted and soon to be ex-husband. George himself was more than happy, in the face of Iris's determined brightness, to look forward to a quiet evening at home later on with Lucinda who had, after all, been persuaded that her presence at the wedding was perfectly welcome. David Fford, meanwhile, enjoyed Iris's conversation and attention, and was impressed by her ability both to radiate, and apparently receive, goodwill towards her erstwhile spouse and his new fiancée without any evident complications.

Ozzy assumed his favoured role of benevolent uncle to one and all, regardless of bloodties, and Emma's brother Jon, though not very conversational, seemed pleased to have attended. With his father shortly to become Lucinda's long-term responsibility, and the family assets already distributed to a reasonable extent, Jon had less reason to regret his little sister's change of status from that of single, unpaid potential carer, to other responsibilities: particularly as her new husband was both parentless himself and likely to do well enough to contribute to Emma's own father's upkeep, were that ever necessary. No-one ever seemed to worry about Iris's future; her boundless energy, evident good health, and the charm she was currently expending on self-made man David Fford all suggested there was no need.

Anthony, as the groom, was being very gracious and Emma almost matched her mother in charm and satisfaction with the day. The food was delicious too. Shay had done them proud, their repeat custom perhaps making up for some of the doubts he harboured about the artwork. He planned a simple refurbishment if needed, on the pretext of keeping abreast of changing fashions in interiors. Perhaps this architect friend of Felix's, Anthony, would oblige – and cut him a deal too, in the circumstances. Shay felt Anthony's elegant and understated designs could prove more durable.

Felix still did not appear, however; and Kate, having never seen the invitation with her name upon it, was also absent. No-one commented during lunch on either absentee, which struck Tiffany as a little odd. She wondered if Iris knew Felix's whereabouts. She might engineer a chat with her sometime soon, but not at this event.

Afterwards, as they finally waved off the bride and groom, Tiffany turned to her friends.

'Shall we carry on with a drink or two at my place?' she asked. If Felix did turn up there it would be alright: for she guessed, correctly, that Ozzy would decline her invitation.

'Not me,' Ozzy confirmed. 'I must get back to my own realm. I still have a big project to resolve, and time is closing in on me.' Iris had already accepted the suggestion from David that she, her son, Jon, and his wife join him for a further drink in a nearby boutique hotel's cosy bar. Other guests were drifting off to their next commitments.

Tiffany relaxed as Ash hailed another taxi and they, with Thomas and Jenna, climbed in. As it coursed through the streets to her flat, the autumn afternoon's fading sunshine gilded the recently rain-slicked pavements and made any lingering droplets sparkle on the windows of the house fronts. She looked forward to kicking off her shoes, to sink onto her sofa, glass in hand, for easy conversation and laughter as evening drew in.

'Sit down,' she said as they entered the flat, gesturing towards the sitting room. 'Ash and I will raid the wine rack.'

'I'll go,' said Ash. 'I brought some supplies of my own earlier on, for which I think the time has come.' He ambled down the corridor.

'Lucky girl,' commented Jenna, glancing after him as Tiffany led the way into the room, 'and a genuinely local boy, too.' Tiffany eyed Jenna cautiously, wondering how loaded her use of 'genuinely' was meant to be – although, as she knew all too well, Felix had never told Jenna the truth about his origins. Nor has he ever told me the full truth, she considered now, just the most recent bit, and a few other improbable snippets. I've been so busy playing along, and ambulance-chasing, that I've barely stopped to wonder where the truth lies. Distracted by the amusing idea that the truth, lies, she suddenly realised that Jenna was still expecting a response to her quip about Ash.

'Yes, local, but well-travelled, as you know,' Tiffany answered her. Jenna laughed, thinking the slow reply and thoughtful expression on her friend's face was a romantic glow caused by Ash.

'Angie approves, by the way,' she said, settling in the armchair. 'She thinks you're good for her brother.'

'Really? Then I shall have to be. I'm too much in awe of Angie to risk annoying her,' Tiffany responded. Thomas picked up a scatter cushion from the sofa to put it on the floor at Jenna's feet, planning to sit there and lean against the armchair.

'Cat hairs?' he said. 'Has that handsome tabby of yours come back at last from wherever he's been tom-catting around?'

Tiffany hesitated

'I'm not sure,' she said. 'I haven't actually seen a cat in here, just the cat hairs. They're a bit ginger to be my mog, don't you think? Felix thinks –' She paused. 'Felix noticed that I'd left the cat flap unlocked, all this time, and warned me that some other opportunistic feline was bound to take advantage eventually.' She glanced over at the window as she spoke and thought for a moment that she saw a blur of movement on the flagstones outside but as her eyes focused, in the dimming light outside there was nothing there but the strip of stone path and the little band of grass, lapping at its edges. The grass soon gave way to bare earth where a handful of shrubs – a mock orange, a rather scruffy oleander, and a couple of things she did not know the names of – nestled in the sheltered crook where the brick wall turned on its L-shaped way, past the kitchen, to encompass the rest of her small garden's periphery, tucking it away from her present field of vision. She turned her gaze back to her guests.

'Plenty of glasses in the kitchen,' she called out for Ash to hear as he selected the wine.

'I'll carry those,' Thomas said, putting the cushion ready, and then heading to the corridor. 'I can't be outdone on the buttling – it used to be my job here.'

'Just as well that I know all about you lot,' said Ash, from the kitchen, 'or I would start to wonder.' (Continue to wonder, he corrected himself privately, remembering.)

You still don't know the half of it, Tiffany thought, but I wish you could. Jenna settled deeper into the armchair near the window, and sighed softly.

'This is cosy,' she said. When the two men returned and the wine was poured, she proposed a toast.

'To the happy couple today,' she said, 'and all happy couples.'

'And absent friends,' suggested Thomas, adding, 'which my smallest niece once mis-repeated as "handsome friends".'

'I like that very much. To handsome friends, then,' Tiffany echoed, 'wherever they may be.' In the garden a light breeze rustled the leaves, and the fading light gave way to night.

Later, after Thomas and Jenna had gone, she eyed the cushion again.

'You go on up,' she said to Ash, who was yawning by the door. 'I just want to tidy up a tiny bit.' She picked up the cushion to return it to the sofa. He smiled.

'Don't be long.'

'I won't,' she replied. 'You don't think I'm going to leave you to fall asleep alone in that gorgeous bath you're about to run for us, do you?' He laughed, and left the room. She waited until she heard water beginning to fill the tub before she went to Great-Granny Kitty's little antique desk in the corner and opened the lid. The envelopes were still there. She took out the opened package from the bank, and the sealed envelope that had come from the passport office, which she now investigated. In it were a passport for a Christopher Felix Cattermole, and a birth certificate. She considered them again for a moment and then put both envelopes back into their pigeon hole. As she did so, the landline rang in the kitchen. Leaving the desk lid open, she went to answer it, hoping it might be Felix but, to her surprise and some alarm, it was Ozzy.

'Ah, so you are back at home,' he said. 'I've just found a message on my mobile. I'd switched it off during the wedding, and forgot to turn it back on till just now. It's from Felix. I thought you'd like to know what he's up to.'

'And?' asked Tiffany, holding her breath and keeping her counsel about Felix's own eschewal of mobiles.

'He claims he's planning to go back to Egypt to research his early past and prepare for his next artistic incarnation,' Ozzy drawled. 'With more than a little help from Iris, I suspect. Not that he'll be able to get there until his passport arrives here, assuming the application has all gone well.'

'Really? Iris and Felix!' Tiffany wondered if all the charm Iris had been expending on David at the wedding had been a front. Poor David – not that he seemed a particularly vulnerable human being.

'Why not? She's a fascinating woman, and very compelling in her own way, even if she is my sister. Why should only you younger people expect to corner all the fun? Curious that she should know something of Felix's youth, don't you think?'

'Really?' said Tiffany again as normally as she could. It seemed to have become her best fall-back word for all occasions, a verbal version of Felix's evasive shrug.

'Apparently she'd heard something about his mother – and thereby, something of a young Master Cattermole's Egyptian days. At first I thought Felix's story was an odd yarn, so I asked Iris if it rang any bells among her older Cairo acquaintances. Naturally her formidable memory, discoveries and good offices sped up the process of getting his birth documents sorted.'

'Goodness,' Tiffany said, still feigning ignorance, and her earlier suspicions about whether Iris knew where Felix had gone to ground gathered substance. 'I can't keep up.'

'Few can,' Ozzy's voice rasped. 'I thought he might be planning a flit, after I realised he'd nipped in and collected some of our little company's bank statements from my place without so much as a hello, or more to the point perhaps, a goodbye. He rather duplicitously re-sealed and left the empty envelope on my mantelpiece, and it wasn't until a slight draught sent it fluttering to the grate when I walked into the studio this afternoon that I noticed.'

Ozzy paused, waiting. As Tiffany remained silent, he added: 'It seems a strange way to behave, rather graceless, after all the opportunities I've put his way. I hope you aren't going to find yourself in any difficulties after all your input into helping our erratic arriviste, Tiffany? But you're resourceful, with such a usefully vivid imagination. I'm sure you'll think of something.'

She knew Ozzy was speaking in riddles in order to get her to say too much, and determinedly held her silence. If Felix had taken the latest company bank statements, then he knew how much was really owed him, in this newly-forged Sylvester fortune, compared to the pocket money amounts drizzled his way so far. Not that Ozzy would cheat him of funds; she felt sure this was all about a desire for control not monetary greed, but maybe Felix reckoned that the bank statements' evidence could embarrass Ozzy, perhaps making them into useful leverage over him now. Cat and mouse games, again, she concluded, and then spoke.

'What exactly are you telling me, Ozzy?' she asked. 'Is there anything else about Felix – or Iris for that matter – that you want to share with me?'

Ozzy laughed. Over the phone rather than face-to-face, it was still a surprisingly disagreeable sound.

'You didn't really believe that he is the Cattermole boy, did you? I assume you do know all about that, after your enthusiasm about his Sylvester connections, now supposedly through his mother? Or perhaps all that was also just a tall story?' He was pushing her now.

'Catter-who? I've known him as Felix ever since he was tiny,' Tiffany reminded him crisply, still trying to give nothing away. 'Lots of people use a mixture of their parents' names in adulthood,' she added, unintentionally weakening her stand. 'So who do you imagine he is?'

Ozzy had been waiting for this small crack in her charade.

'I have the glimmer of an idea, notably since he began to take an interest in learning more about Kitty and the family story of her tragic end. I think developing the flu himself unsettled his nerves considerably. I'm sure you spotted that his mental state seemed equally febrile, and was deteriorating.'

Not just his mental state, Tiffany thought, he looked physically awful, so maybe Jenna was right when she joked about the first murals being fine because they were painted in his prime – and it was not just poor materials, or damp on the walls of the restaurant, that he had to worry about.

'He was very tired after working so hard for the show, certainly,' she blocked Ozzy, but then could not resist adding: 'Maybe you pushed him too hard.'

'Hmm. You know, Tiffany, I doubt if Iris believes, or cares, if he's actually that Cattermole boy. She certainly knows how to reinvent herself, and restore others, so perhaps she's just being too indulgent. Did you know that she's done something similar for Anthony, by the way?' Tiffany, trying and failing to picture Iris as over-indulgent, seized this opportunity to steer the conversation away again from Felix, and his troublesome art.

'For Anthony?' she said. 'But he hates—' She stopped herself just in time from adding 'cats'.

'Hates what? He doesn't much care for Felix, or his work – that was evident from the start.'

'Hates being told what to do,' she said quickly. 'So what has Iris done for Anthony? We all noticed that she seemed to approve of him for Emma.' Ozzy's sigh sounded more like exasperation to her.

'She hasn't told you, has she?' he replied. 'It's ironic. A few degrees of separation, yet each generation goes round in circles. She knows all about Anthony's past.'

'What about it?' Tiffany supposed he meant financial matters.

'His grandfather. First name Tod. Ring a bell?' She stared across the room. The dinner party that she and Felix had given round this very table to spin their yarns about him, when Ozzy took over the conversation, at length, with his own family stories, came spinning back.

'Your stepmother's first husband?' she asked cautiously.

'The very same. Apparently he ended up in Cairo, built up some sort of consultancy business, married or at least had a child, out there – endured various ups and downs, political crisis, flu – and ended up raising his orphaned grandson, whom he put through architecture studies back here: one Anthony Wright.'

'Our Anthony? Are you sure? Wouldn't that make him Iris's nephew?'

'If Tod were indeed her father; but not a blood relation at all if Tod Wright wasn't. You recall there was an element of doubt, in Tod's mind certainly, about Iris's parentage given the closeness of my father Jeb to Iris's mother Nattie, during their respective first marriages.' Tiffany's mind raced through what she could remember of Ozzy's stories that night.

'Yes, yes,' she said impatiently, 'so if Tod were wrong about that doubt, and Iris really was his daughter, then

Anthony could be Emma's' – she paused to work it out – 'second cousin?'

'Possibly. Nothing wrong with that in my book. Although, alas, if Tod were Iris's father that would demote me to mere step-brother again (and second cousin), instead of the half-brother that I so instinctively feel myself to be. Iris may feel she's either conveniently righting a wrong done to Tod, or simply closing a circle by welcoming Anthony back into the fold now. Damage limitation, keeping it all in the family, bringing things under control again, is something of a tradition amongst us.' Ozzy waited for her to understand what else this might imply but Tiffany missed his meaning or warning, lost in amazement at the craziness of it all.

'Does Emma know any of this?'

She could almost hear a shrug, through his tone of voice, as he answered: 'Possibly. She's clearly taken advantage of her mother's acceptance of Anthony, whatever the reason for it; but I doubt very much that Iris would want to flag this connection up to Anthony himself without a very carefully prepared back story.'

Tiffany leant back in her chair at the kitchen table.

'How do you know any of this stuff, Ozzy? Isn't it all just wild speculation?'

'Anthony told me a bit about his background. After that it wasn't hard to work it out, and when I asked Iris to do a little supplementary looking-into Felix's peculiar Cattermole story, I arranged a little digging of my own into some of Anthony's personal history too, though perhaps not enough. It may have been a mistake to harness someone from Iris's network for that bit. Knowledge is power, as you may know. Power that one can use to help, or hinder, others.'

Tiffany weighed this up. I have knowledge too, knowledge that you don't have, or can't pin down, she thought. Outside, dusk had long since fallen, and the kitchen windows were dark against the invisible garden beyond them. Upstairs, Ash had heard the phone ring and assumed she could be some time chatting to the caller. He had settled into the bath, and relaxed into its warmth.

'Why hinder?' she asked Ozzy carefully, feeling more confident now.

'Sometimes complications need to be contained,' he answered. 'Neutralised, even. Rendered harmless.'

'You wouldn't hurt Anthony's prospects?' She was shocked.

'On the contrary, Tiffany,' Ozzy replied impatiently. 'He has just married the young woman that I still consider to be my niece. So long as she wishes to stay married to him, any improvement in his prospects will benefit her.' She could hear papers being rustled on his great glass desk as he spoke.

'So you approve of Iris wanting to ensure things work out for him, then, for the moment?' Tiffany finally began to understand why Iris had been courting David, Anthony's significant client, so assiduously. It was all done for Emma. What a ruthless and terrifying family I have.

'Up to a point. We may be correcting a wrong, but Anthony might yet take offence on his grandfather's behalf if he ever learns what family he has just married into. For Emma's sake however Iris might be wise to reconsider any plans to whisk the troublesome Felix overseas for her own purposes. Such injudicious action might jeopardise my own discretion, goodwill, and intended patronage of Anthony.'

'But why do you want to twist her arm like that?' Tiffany almost shouted it. 'Why shouldn't she befriend Felix? You did, but you don't own him, none of us do.' She almost kicked the kitchen table leg in her annoyance.

'You ask me why it matters?' Ozzy hissed. 'Apart from the fact that he's abused my hospitality and my goodwill, painted careless artworks that are already falling apart and put my own reputation here at risk, that he spreads chaos and upsets as casually and mischievously as he chooses, disturbs the natural connective order of things, and has never once told the truth about what he's playing at? You think he shouldn't be safely contained before everything disintegrates?' Ozzy's voice rose throughout this speech to a rolling thunder.

'Well, maybe Iris can succeed where the rest of us have failed,' a shaken Tiffany blurted, and instantly regretted her indiscretion. It sounded too like a confession. Ozzy knows, she thought, Ozzy and Iris between them, both know more than I do. Heaven knows how, but I am not going to help them to 'contain' Felix. If he was anyone's at all, he is mine – and mine to save from their nefarious schemes for him.

'I've no idea where he is,' she continued more levelly, 'and there's no sign that he's been here.' To strengthen the lie, she added a truth: 'Thomas and Jenna said they haven't seen him, either.' (I hope that stops Ozzy from asking them, and now I don't want to risk Thomas mentioning the cat hairs on the cushion here.) 'If Kate has lost track of him, and Iris hasn't been able to whisk him away, then he could be anywhere in the country.'

There was a silence. Then Ozzy sighed.

'Very well,' he said. 'So be it. Keep in touch. Give my regards to Ash, won't you? He seems a very pleasant sort. Not one to appreciate our enjoyment of dark secrets and incestuous family ties, though, I suspect.' His voice fizzed and crackled with menace, yet the veiled threat only enraged her. Don't even think of meddling with me and Ash, she thought. DO. NOT. PRESUME. She felt as if the words were etching themselves on the buried granite of her innermost being.

Aloud, she replied in tones that cut the outer air into shards of ice: 'So I suppose that, for Emma's sake just now, you'd also like me not to alert Anthony to the trick you have all pulled on him with your stupid games of closing circles, by manipulating him into marrying back into the family that you admit did so much damage to his own grandfather? I think I can manage that for a while, subject to no harm coming to Felix of course. Goodnight, Ozzy. Try to get some sleep.'

Tiffany clicked the phone handset off. Now she had two things to fight for: firmly securing her relationship with Ash; and ensuring that whatever else happened to Felix, he would at least get away both from Ozzy and the evidently equally predatory Iris. Only now did she realise that Ozzy's warning had perhaps also carried another implication; that Iris might help Felix go abroad with her purely in order to 'neutralise' him, possibly by engineering his permanent disappearance. Might some similar attempt have even been behind whatever had really happened to Kitty? Then Felix couldn't harm anyone, and Ozzy might continue to look benignly upon Anthony, and Emma.

She was horrified. Is my imagination running riot, am I mad, or are they both monsters? I need to think this through very carefully.

Perhaps Ozzy's aim of keeping Felix under some sort of surveillance and control here was better. Yet he would hate it. What or who is it that they think, or fear, he was? If she can work that out, she might be able to decide what to do. Seeking inspiration, she took two glasses, put them onto a tray with a small jug of water, and carried that into the sitting room to find her bottle of malt whisky. She poured a generous shot into each glass, adding a splash of water to release the flavours. Standing, she took a deep swig from one glass, and surveyed the room. The desk lid was still open and, she suddenly realised, one of the packets she had been looking at when the phone rang had gone.

Surely Ash would not have come downstairs and taken it? She set down her glass and looked around the room again. Better check the box-room. She glanced up at the sitting room shelf where her Egyptian figurines had stood since Felix had gathered them up from their undignified tumble into the grate on the evening she had lost her temper with Anthony, the evening that Felix had manifested, naked and only very slightly furry, in her bedroom.

She stared at them. What else had her mother said about the statuettes again? She ran through her memories. They'd either belonged to, or arrived with, Great-granny Kitty and later had been left to Tiffany by old Sir Freddie because she'd played with them as a child. Kitty, whose uncertain blood presumably still ran – albeit diluted – in her own veins. Kitty, who may or may not have appeared and disappeared mysteriously in Egypt; and may, or may not have also had a liaison there with disillusioned Tod. I hope that doesn't mean *she* was Anthony's grandmother, Tiffany thought grimly, as technically that would make him my own mother's first cousin, or half-cousin, although barely a decade older than me. Is that partly what Ozzy meant by 'incestuous family'?

Kitty, she now felt almost sure, could have been an earlier manifestation of whatever it was that had recently used Tiffany's tabby cat to become the ruthless artist Felix. If Kitty's anomalous genes somehow flow in my maternal line, perhaps that's how it gets through, she speculated. It needs some kind of link to the last time, as a catalyst, but the gender in which this freeloader next manifests is immaterial. Given Felix's serial but so far infertile affairs, were his reproductions of himself in art intended as templates for a future link; a sort of emergency back-up ? Puss-in-ReBoots, she could not help thinking, and the acid pun cheered her up. Maybe her great-grandmother had really started out as just Kitty, a charismatic young woman of means who was entranced by Egypt, and possibly later died of flu there, but about whom meddling in-laws had later spun extraordinary stories to amuse themselves. Telling tall tales definitely runs in this family, she thought. She took another swig of her whisky and made a decision. Standing in front of them, she addressed the four figurines firmly.

'I don't know if any of this mess has anything to do with any of you, but if it has, I think it's time for us all to stop playing games, and to help Felix find safety,' she said aloud, 'or Kitty, or whoever, and whatever he – it – is. Please,' she included, for good measure. They stared back silently, as always. 'I'm sorry about triggering all this, and being complicit,' she added. 'I really am. Now we need to fix this.' As nothing else happened, she took another swig of whisky, and went to check the box-room.

Nothing there, not even an empty envelope. Tiffany glanced towards the kitchen but its three-quarters-closed door was just as she had left it; and when she went into the room, the back door was still locked from inside. Felix must have slipped in and out by the front door or perhaps, and more likely, entered through the sitting room window, quietly sliding it open while she was on the phone in the kitchen. She returned to the sitting room to check and close it, and to collect her whisky tray. She was glad he had the passport at last, but hoped that he would not be sharing the news with Iris. With no way now of warning him, she hoped too that he had overheard enough of her phone call from Ozzy to work out that a hunter's net was being fashioned to cast around him. 'Run, cat, run,' she whispered, and took a sip of whisky. *Hehh.* 'Tell no-one where you've gone.' She took another sip, concentrating hard on projecting her thoughts, and sneezed. *Shu!*

Felix. Pick up. That carefully created new identity could now become a fatal flaw, a way to track you down. You'll have to start all over again and, above all, don't rely on Iris. I hope you've already worked that out.

Glancing up at her figurines one more time, she picked up the tray and carried it upstairs to see if Ash was still luxuriating in the bath, or already fast asleep in her bed.

Outside in the dark, a scrawny shape crawled groggily underneath the mock orange bush that grew against the garden wall. Crouching, it seemed to be an emaciated person, who tucked a small package into a tatty plastic bag and then with fumbling hands pulled a loose brick from where the sheltering plant pressed closest to the garden wall. The figure smoothed and folded the bag, wrapping the package within it tightly and, hands still shaking, pushed it as far as possible into the back of cavity. The brick was crumbly and he or she broke some pieces of it away and shoved the remaining half-brick into the gap, to mask the small void behind it. Next, the branches temporarily displaced during this operation were carefully pulled back across the hiding place. Finally, the broken pieces of brick were pushed under the soil, so that no outward evidence remained. The figure remained crouched on the ground for a moment, resting. Then it moved to the oleander, using its taller, slender branches as help to scramble rather stiffly up and over the garden wall, sliding heavily down the other side.

On the pavement, anyone watching would have seen a scraggy-looking man leaning against the wall, checking the night street. It was still empty, and silent. Clouds, banking and gathering, obscured the moon and the street lights seemed very dim tonight too; but his eyes were still able to read the dark city. He moved slowly and quietly away, towards the little gardens of the familiar nearby park. He was very tired again now, recognising the returning weight of time, the warp of ages, thinning his blood and bone. He needed more sleep. The air smelled of rain.

A few miles away, Ozzy looked out of his windows as drizzle began to tap at the panes, and frowned. Nothing but the gradually thickening rain stirred in his darkened garden. Tiffany's retaliatory threat had surprised, and even wrong-footed him. How could he have overlooked, albeit only for a nano-second, that as a direct descendant of Kitty she might always carry the latent potential to influence events, consciously or not, and however misguided; and her gaining awareness of this would magnify it. His own earlier failure to ask Anthony anything about his grandmother, instead of just weighing up the question of Tod, also meant he was not yet sure if a genetic link to Kitty, if link there were beyond Iris's mischievous speculation, could ever become viable through Anthony. Ozzy therefore would not yet risk disregarding Tiffany's standoff. He saw that in underestimating her, he had briefly dropped an important thread and with it might have lost his whole design. Iris's scheme was still in play, however. It was time to step back and wait patiently, perhaps for next time.

As day broke, a handsome woman of indeterminate age came through the little park, not far from where Tiffany slept contentedly at home in Ash's arms, oblivious to the steady rain outside.

Carrying a large tapestry bag, the woman sat down on a bench and waited, her hood pulled up against the slowly-improving weather, but no-one came. Eventually she hunched her shoulders against the chill seeping up from the wet earth, and drew part of small loaf of bread from her bag. She threw a few crumbs onto the damp path near the shrubbery, watching to see if the early pigeons, now that day was coming and the rain had eased, could be tempted yet; but, although curious, most of them ignored her offering. Unperturbed, she threw a few heavier pieces of bread further away, onto the grass, which more of the bolder pigeons accepted. Then she threw some bread close to the shelter of the nearest bushes just on the other side of the path. They eyed this, but not one chased after it. She threw some more onto another patch of grass, which this time they hastened to and quickly ate. The woman smiled at them, rose, and still holding her tapestry bag, bent down to examine the bushes closest to the path, lifting their sodden branches to peer beneath them. Crouched deep under one of the shrubs, hidden well away from easy sight, was a weak and ancient, faintly striped, gingerish cat. Ears ragged, and bones angular under the thinning scruffy fur, teeth broken and tartared, its yellow eyes were huge in the narrow skull, their dull gleam still baleful, dangerous. As the autumn drizzle resumed, slowly seeping through the dark leaves, the creature glowered at her, watching and waiting, biding its time.

'Poor old thing, poor bedraggled kitty,' the woman said. 'No fight left in you now. Come here, you ancient

Mau, maker of Felis Chaus. Time has run out for you, the old Tree of Life has grown sallow and lost its leaves. As Persea gave way to Sycamore, others rule now, and Seth rocks the land, but I may still have enough power to cure. Meanwhile, let's get you safely back to mummy.' Having said her spell, she scooped up the almost weightless, weakened creature and put it straight into her copious tapestry bag. Returning to the bench for a moment, she hastily removed the rest of the loaf, and closed the bag more securely. 'You'll be back where you belong soon,' she said, briskly tearing up the remaining bread and throwing it all to the pigeons by way of reward, unaware in her moment of success that she was being watched.

An unshaven young man, a rough sleeper exhausted by the final haul of his long and often dangerous journey by wild seas and roads to this cold wet land where, despite his illegal arrival, he hoped to find refugee status and a future, had risen from his overnight sleeping place on a nearby building's sheltered front steps and was entering the park for a discreet pee before too many people were around to object. His name was Joyful, and he and some fellow travellers, his chance companions, had been released at the dead of night on a quiet country road from their hiding place in a large lorry, hugely relieved to be alive and breathing the fresh air of this new country, even though it was chilly and a slow drizzling rain had started.

He walked several miles, heading for the city before choosing a place to shelter and rest before he worked out how to reach the address of some distant cousins, written neatly on a paper still folded in his wallet, and hoping that they either still lived there or someone would know where to find them. Thunder rumbled softly in the distance as he saw the well-dressed woman on the park bench, surprised by her early morning presence there in the light rain now falling; and then he realised that she was tearing up and throwing good bread at the fat pigeons, while he was cold, wet, and hungry.

An uncharacteristic fury rose up in him like a sudden storm. Throughout the long and challenging journey to this place he had never once resorted to theft; but now he raced the short distance from park gate to bench like a man possessed, and in a flash seized the bag – which surely held more bread in it, that others could share – and ran like the lightning out of the park, down the wet street, and away. The woman yelled, the pigeons all flew up, but it was too late: the young man and the bag were gone. As Iris rose, shaking with anger, to her feet and began to consider how to track him down, Joyful was already regaining the shelter of the entrance to the empty theatre under renovation, beneath whose portico he had rested, to grab his sleeping mat and flee further into the foreign city.

Hurrying up its steps, which were slick with the thickening rain, he had just tugged open the carpet bag to glimpse its contents and find a space to thrust his own few possessions inside, when there was an explosion of hissing and spitting fur, a crack of lightening directly overhead, and an immediate crash of thunder. The triple shock sent him hurtling backwards with a loud cry, tumbling down the broad wet steps in the hail of small glass vials that poured from the bag and smashed around him, splashing him with their contents, which then mingled and pooled iridescently in the puddles that soaked him as he lay on the pavement, motionless, a small piece of gingerish fur in his torn and broken hand. Blood oozed too from a large gash to his head, into the spilt and heavily-perfumed essential oils and rainwater.

From the early morning coffee shop opposite the theatre, housed on the ground floor above its sister business – a wine bar in the basement – apron-clad staff ran out to see what the loud commotion had meant. They rushed to lift the prone figure, but he was already unconscious. Someone used their mobile phone to ring for an ambulance which, with a major teaching hospital nearby, came almost immediately. As the first responders stabilised the young man, and put him aboard, one of the bystanders picked up his soggy carpet bag and shoved the few personal items left at the top of the broad steps, into it. The oils from the broken vials had stained it in places, and a needle-like shard of glass had pulled a small thread in the weave of the tapestry.

'This is all his stuff.' The ambulance team took the proffered bag with them. It might hold some ID that would help the hospital work out who he was; and then the ambulance was on its way, siren blaring. As the patient had a nasty head injury, the driver was directed to a sister hospital with a neurological wing, just a little further away. It meant he would be in the most relevant expert hands as fast as humanly possible.

The bystanders stopped milling around and headed back to the coffee bar, to steady their nerves with caffeine and escape the rain, still falling hard. Iris, who had heard the siren but not yet connected it with her assailant, had methodically made her way up and down various local streets, and now passed the familiar, closed theatre. She stared up at it. The force of the rain, turned now into a furious monsoon, had already pummelled all the slippery iridescent oils down a loudly gurgling drain, diluting their mingled perfumes so much that they were no longer distinguishable, even to Iris's acute senses, over the smells of wet pavement, soaking leaves, twigs, and bits of city garbage swept down the road in a torrent that now capped the already-overburdened drain with rubbish.

She walked on, frowning, thinking. All her healing, and embalming, oils gone with the fugitive. She needed to get back to her little hotel, to get dry and warm, and return to Egypt to restock as soon as possible. Had she stopped at the café for a warming coffee, she might have chatted with people there and heard immediate news of the morning's early excitement, an account of the injured man and perhaps even a mention of his unusual tapestry bag; but she was too wet through, cold and uncomfortable, and annoyed. She hastened past, hotel-bound, her hood pulled up, and her head down against the rain.

Joyful lay unconscious in the intensive care unit. They had found his recent Libyan residency papers in a wallet in a pocket of his soaking and faintly perfumed jacket, along with what seemed to be the tip of a catspaw.

'Eeugh – presumably it's for luck, let's hope it works now for him', said the nurse who first unearthed it. The jacket, a few other items of clothing stuffed inside his otherwise empty, rain-sodden carpet bag, and the bag itself, were all being cleaned and dried out to be kept safely for him. His status in this country would have to be resolved at some point, and the people whose address was found in his wallet contacted. He might yet have to be sent home – wherever that turned out to be – but none of that could be considered until he woke, if indeed he did.

For now, under a cotton sheet and tender blankets, he waited and rested on a gently undulating, air-powered blue mattress to stop his limbs from getting bed sores or blood clots, intubated, his life signs monitored, cocooned in the limbo of the world-between-worlds of this quiet unit – an unfamiliar bourne, where time seemed suspended to all its occupants, and those who returned from its regenerative care rarely did so unaltered.

Iris, back in her hotel room, was soon warm and dry. She booked herself a flight out for that afternoon, and began to pack her remaining bags. She told no-one of her plans.

Ozzy, seated on his throne-like chair before his glass table, frowned at there being so much rain and then resumed his sketching, writing, pondering and planning the future.

Tiffany, stirring in her bed and warm beside Ash, also heard the rain as it began to ease off a little. Remembering that it was Sunday, the clocks had gone backwards an hour, and that Felix had gone too, she snuggled contentedly back under the covers in anticipation of a blissful future with Ash.

If tomorrow she did encounter the paragraph already being written for the local paper, about a mystery youth thought to have travelled here circuitously and perhaps via

Libya, who fell down the empty theatre's front steps during Sunday's early morning storm and was rushed comatose to intensive care, Tiffany might have quietly considered the refugee to be in very good hands for now, nodded thoughtfully at her statuettes and silently turned the page.

In the restaurant, the repainted tabby cat was no longer obviously peeling and flaking but had developed a faded look, Shay thought as he contemplated when to whitewash the walls again; as if the creature's archetypal magnificence was quietly evaporating and drifting away, molecule by molecule into limbo, hidden behind time itself until some felicitous catalyst hurtled them into new form and place.

In between Mau's long sleeps, other gods came and went; and on this late October Sunday morning in Tiffany's city, beyond Shay's restaurant, a cleansing rain fell peacefully all day.

*

Ingram Content Group UK Ltd.
Milton Keynes UK
UKHW012312210623
423738UK00004B/39

9 781803 698298